Praise for beloved romance author Betty Neels

"Neels is especially good at painting her scenes with choice words, and this adds to the charm of the story."
—USATODAY.com's *Happy Ever After* blog on *Tulips for Augusta*

"Betty Neels surpasses herself with an excellent storyline, a hearty conflict and pleasing characters."
—*RT Book Reviews* on *The Right Kind of Girl*

"Once again Betty Neels delights readers with a sweet tale in which love conquers all."
—*RT Book Reviews* on *Fate Takes a Hand*

"One of the first Harlequin authors I remember reading. I was completely enthralled by the exotic locales… Her books will always be some of my favorites to re-read."
—Goodreads on *A Valentine for Daisy*

"I just love Betty Neels!… If you like a good old-fashioned romance…you can't go wrong with this author."
—Goodreads on *Caroline's Waterloo*

Romance readers around the world were sad to note the passing of **Betty Neels** in June 2001. Her career spanned thirty years, and she continued to write into her ninetieth year. To her millions of fans, Betty epitomized the romance writer, and yet she began writing almost by accident. She had retired from nursing, but her inquiring mind still sought stimulation. Her new career was born when she heard a lady in her local library bemoaning the lack of good romance novels. Betty's first book, *Sister Peters in Amsterdam*, was published in 1969, and she eventually completed 134 books. Her novels offer a reassuring warmth that was very much a part of her own personality. She was a wonderful writer, and she is greatly missed. Her spirit and genuine talent live on in all her stories.

BETTY NEELS

The Daughter of the Manor
& A Gentle Awakening

H HARLEQUIN SPECIAL RELEASE

H HARLEQUIN® SPECIAL RELEASE

Recycling programs for this product may not exist in your area.

ISBN-13: 978-1-335-00822-0

The Daughter of the Manor & A Gentle Awakening

Copyright © 2020 by Harlequin Books S.A.

The Daughter of the Manor
First published in 1997. This edition published in 2020.
Copyright © 1997 by Betty Neels

A Gentle Awakening
First published in 1987. This edition published in 2020.
Copyright © 1987 by Betty Neels

All rights reserved. No part of this book may be used or reproduced in any manner whatsoever without written permission except in the case of brief quotations embodied in critical articles and reviews.

This is a work of fiction. Names, characters, places and incidents are either the product of the author's imagination or are used fictitiously. Any resemblance to actual persons, living or dead, businesses, companies, events or locales is entirely coincidental.

This edition published by arrangement with Harlequin Books S.A.

For questions and comments about the quality of this book, please contact us at CustomerService@Harlequin.com.

Harlequin Enterprises ULC
22 Adelaide St. West, 40th Floor
Toronto, Ontario M5H 4E3, Canada
www.Harlequin.com

Printed in U.S.A.

CONTENTS

THE DAUGHTER
OF THE MANOR

Chapter 1

The village of Pont Magna, tucked into a fold of the Mendip Hills, was having its share of February weather. Sleet, icy rain, a biting wind and a sharp frost had culminated in lanes and roads like skating rinks, so that the girl making her way to the village trod with care.

She was a tall girl with a pretty face, quantities of dark hair bundled into a woolly cap, her splendid proportions hidden under an elderly tweed coat, and she was wearing stout wellies—suitable wear for the weather but hardly glamorous.

The lane curved ahead of her and she looked up sharply as a car rounded it, so that she didn't see the ridge of frozen earth underfoot, stumbled, lost her footing and sat down with undignified suddenness.

The car slowed, came to a halt and the driver got out,

heaved her onto her feet without effort and remarked mildly, 'You should look where you're going.'

'Of course I was looking where I was going.' The girl pulled her cap straight. 'You had no business coming round that corner so quietly...'

She tugged at her coat, frowning as various painful areas about her person made themselves felt.

'Can I give you a lift?'

She sensed his amusement and pointed out coldly, 'You're going the opposite way.' She added, 'You're a stranger here?'

'Er-yes.'

Although she waited he had no more to say; he only stood there looking down at her, so she said matter-of-factly, 'Well, thank you for stopping. Goodbye.'

When he didn't answer she looked at him and found him smiling. He was good-looking—more than that, handsome—with a splendid nose, a firm mouth and very blue eyes. She found their gaze disconcerting.

'I'm sorry if I was rude. I was taken by surprise.'

'Just as I have been,' he replied.

An apt remark, she reflected as she walked away from him, but somehow it sounded as though he had meant something quite different. When she reached the bend in the lane she looked back. He was still standing there, watching her.

Pont Magna wasn't a large village; it had a green, a church much too big for it, a main street wherein was the Village Stores and post office, pleasant cottages facing each other, a by-lane or two leading to other cottages and half a dozen larger houses—the vicarage, old Captain Morris's house at the far end of the street, and several comfortable dwellings belonging to retired couples. A quiet place in quiet countryside, with Wells to the south and Frome to the east and Bath to the north.

Its rural surroundings were dotted by farms and wide fields. Since the village was off a main road tourists seldom found their way there, and at this time of the year the village might just as well have been a hundred miles from anywhere. It had a cheerful life of its own; people were sociable, titbits of gossip were shared, and, since it was the only place to meet, they were shared in Mrs Pike's shop.

There were several ladies there now, standing with their baskets over their arms, listening to that lady—a stout, cheerful body with a great deal of frizzy grey hair and small, shrewd eyes.

'Took bad, sudden, like!' she exclaimed. 'Well, we all knew he was going to retire, didn't we, and there'd be a new doctor? All arranged, wasn't it? I seen 'im when 'e came to look the place over. 'Andsome too.' She gave a chuckle. 'There'll be a lot of lady patients for 'im, wanting to take a look. Lovely motor car too.'

She beamed round her audience. 'Would never 'ave seen 'im myself if I 'adn't been coming back from Wells and stopped off to get me pills at Dr Fleming's. There 'e was, a great chap. I reckon 'e'll be taking over smartish, like, now Dr Fleming's took bad and gone to 'ospital.'

This interesting bit of news was mulled over while various purchases were made, but finally the last customer went, leaving Mrs Pike to stack tins of baked beans and rearrange packets of biscuits. She turned from this boring job as the door opened.

'Miss Leonora—walked, 'ave you? And it's real nasty underfoot. You could 'ave phoned and Jim could 'ave fetched whatever you wanted up to the house later.'

The girl pulled off her cap and allowed a tangle of curly hair to escape. 'Morning, Mrs Pike. I felt like a walk even though it's beastly weather. Mother wants one or two things—an excuse to get out...'

I'm not surprised, thought Mrs Pike; poor young lady stuck up there in that great gloomy house with her mum and dad, and that young man of hers hardly ever there. She ought to be out dancing.

She said out loud, 'Let me have your list, miss, and I'll put it together. Try one of them apples while you're waiting. Let's hope this weather gives over so's we can get out and about. That Mr Beamish of yours coming for the weekend, is 'e?'

'Well, I shouldn't think so unless the roads get better.' The girl twiddled the solitaire diamond on her finger and just for a moment looked unhappy. But only for a moment. 'I dare say we shall have a glorious spring...'

Mrs Pike, weighing cheese, glanced up. 'Getting wed then?' she wanted to know.

Leonora smiled. Mrs Pike was the village gossip but she wasn't malicious, and although she passed on any titbits she might have gleaned she never embellished them. She was a nice old thing and Leonora had known her for almost all of her life.

'We haven't decided, Mrs Pike.'

'I like a nice Easter wedding meself,' said Mrs Pike. 'Married on Easter Monday, we were—lovely day it was too.' She gave a chuckle. 'Poor as church mice we were too. Not that that matters.'

It would matter to Tony, reflected Leonora; he was something in the City, making money and intent on making still more. To Leonora, who had been brought up surrounded by valuable but shabby things in an old house rapidly falling into disrepair, and who was in the habit of counting every penny twice, this seemed both clever and rather daunting, for it seemed to take up so much of Tony's life. Even on his rare visits to her home he brought a briefcase with him and was constantly interrupted by his phone.

She had protested mildly from time to time and he had told her not to fuss, that he needed to keep in touch with the markets. 'I'll be a millionaire—a multimillionare,' he told her. 'You should be grateful, darling—think of all the lovely clothes you'll be able to buy.'

Looking down at her tweed skirt and wellies, she supposed that her lack of pretty clothes sometimes irked him and she wondered what he saw in her to love enough to want to marry her. The family name, perhaps—they had no hereditary title but the name was old and respected—and there was still the house and the land around it. Her father would never part with either.

It was a thought which scared her but which she quickly dismissed as nonsense. Tony loved her, she wore his ring, they would marry and set up house together. It was a bit vague at present but she hoped they wouldn't have to live in London; he had a flat there which she had never seen but which he assured her he would give up when they married. And he had told her that when they were married he would put her home back on its original footing.

When she had protested that her father might not allow that, he had explained patiently that he would be one of the family and surely her father would permit him to see to it that the house and land were kept as their home should be. 'After all,' he had pointed out to her, 'it will eventually be the home of our son—your parents' grandson...'

She had never mentioned that to either her mother or her father. How like Tony, she thought lovingly—so generous and caring, ready to spend his money on restoring her home...

Mrs Pike's voice interrupted her thoughts. 'Pink salmon or the red, Miss Leonora?'

'Oh, the pink, Mrs Pike—fishcakes, you know.'

Mrs Pike nodded. 'Very tasty they are too.' Like the rest of the village she knew how hard up the Crosby family were. There never had been much money and Sir William had lost almost all of what had been left in some City financial disaster. A crying shame, but what a good thing that Miss Leonora's young man had plenty of money.

She put the groceries into a carrier bag and watched Leonora make her way down the icy street. She had pushed her hair back under her cap and really, from the back, she looked like a tramp. Only when you could see her face, thought Mrs Pike, did you know she wasn't anything of the sort.

Leonora went into the house through one of the side doors. There were several of these; the house, its oldest part very old indeed, had been added to in more prosperous times and, although from the front it presented a solid Georgian façade with imposing doors and large windows, round the back, where succeeding generations had added a room here, a passage there, a flight of unnecessary stairs, windows of all shapes and sizes, there were additional doors through which these various places could be reached.

The door Leonora entered led through to a gloomy, rather damp passage to the kitchen—a vast room housing a dresser of gigantic proportions, a scrubbed table capable of seating a dozen persons, an assortment of cupboards, and rows of shelves carrying pots and pans. There was a dog snoozing before the Aga stove but he got up, shook himself and came to meet her as she put her bag on the table.

She bent to fondle him, assuring him that no doubt the butcher's van would be round and there would be a bone for him. 'And as soon as it's a bit warmer we'll go for a real walk,' she promised him. He was an old dog, a Labrador, and a quick walk in the small park at the back of the house was all that he could manage in bad weather.

The door on the other side of the kitchen opened and a short, stout woman came in, followed by a tabby cat, and Leonora turned to smile at her.

'It's beastly out, Nanny. I'll take Wilkins into the garden for a quick run.' She glanced at the clock. 'I'll see to lunch when I get back.'

Nanny nodded. She had a nice cosy face, pink-cheeked and wrinkled, and grey hair in a tidy bun. 'I'll finish upstairs. I've taken in the coffee—it's hot on the Aga when you get in.'

Wilkins didn't much care for the weather but he trotted obediently down one of the paths to where a door in the brick wall opened onto the park—quite a modest park with a small stream running along its boundary and clumps of trees here and there. They went as far as the stream and then turned thankfully for home.

The house was a hotchpotch of uneven roofs and unmatched windows at the back but it had a certain charm, even in winter months. Of course many of its rooms were shut up now, but Leonora conceded that if you didn't look too closely at peeled paint and cracks it was quite imposing. She loved it, every crack and broken tile, every damp wall and creaking floorboard.

Back in the kitchen once more, Wilkins, paws wiped and his elderly person towelled warm, subsided before the Aga again, and Leonora hung her coat on a hook near the door, exchanged her wellies for a pair of scuffed slippers and set about getting lunch—soup, already simmering on the stove, a cheese soufflé and cheese and biscuits.

Carrying a tray of china and silver to the dining room, she shivered as she went along the passage from the kitchen. It would be sensible to have their meals in the kitchen, but her mother and father wouldn't hear of it even though the dining room was as cold as the passage, if not colder.

'Mustn't lower our standards,' her father had said when she had suggested it. So presently they sat down to lunch at an elegantly laid table, supping soup which had already been cooling by the time it got to the dining room. As for the soufflé, Leonora ran from the oven to the table, remembering to slow down at the dining-room door, and set it gently on the table for her mother to serve, thankful that it hadn't sunk in its dish.

'Delicious,' pronounced Lady Crosby. 'You are such a good cook, darling.' She sighed faintly, remembering the days when there had been a cook in the kitchen and a manservant to wait at table. What a blessing it was that Leonora was so splendid at organising the household and keeping things running smoothly.

Lady Crosby, a charming and sweet-tempered woman who managed to avoid doing anything as long as there was someone else to do it, reflected comfortably that her daughter would make a good wife for Tony—such a good man, who had already hinted that once they were married he would see to it that there would be someone to take Leonora's place in the house. She was a lucky girl.

She glanced at her daughter and frowned; it was unfortunate, but Leonora was looking shabby.

'Haven't you got anything else to wear other than that skirt and sweater, dear?' she asked.

'Well, Mother, it's awful outside—no weather to dress up. Besides, I promised Nanny I'd help her with the kitchen cupboards this afternoon.'

Her father looked up. 'Why can't that woman who comes up from the village see to them?'

Leonora forbore from telling him that Mrs Pinch hadn't been coming for a month or more. Her wages had been a constant if small drain on the household purse, and when her husband had broken an arm at work she had decided to give up her charring and Leonora had seen the chance to save a pound or two by working a bit harder herself.

She said now, 'Well, Father, I like to go through the stores myself once in a while.' A remark which dispelled any faint doubts her parents might have had.

'Do wear gloves, dear,' observed her mother. 'Remember it's the Willoughbys' dinner party this evening—your hands, you know!'

The Willoughbys lived just outside the village in a small Georgian house in beautiful grounds, and since they had plenty of money it was beautifully maintained. They were elderly, good-natured and hospitable and Leonora enjoyed going there.

The cupboards dealt with, she got tea with Nanny and carried the tray through to the drawing room. Even on a cold winter's day it looked beautiful, with its tall windows, plaster ceiling and vast fireplace in which burned a log fire that was quite inadequate to warm the room. The furniture was beautiful too, polished lovingly, the shabby upholstery brushed and repaired.

Her mother was playing patience and her father was sitting at a table by the window, writing. She set the tray down on a small table near her mother's chair and went to put more logs on the fire.

'I thought we might give a small dinner party quite soon,' observed Lady Crosby. 'We owe several, don't we? You might start planning a menu, darling.'

'How many?' asked Leonora, humouring her parent, wondering where the money was to come from. Dinner parties cost money. They could pawn the silver, she supposed with an inward chuckle; on the other hand she could make an enormous cottage pie and offer it to their guests...

'Oh, eight, I think, don't you? No, it would have to be seven or nine, wouldn't it? We can't have odd numbers.'

Lady Crosby sipped her tea. 'What shall you wear this evening?'

'Oh, the blue...'

'Very nice, dear, such a pretty colour; I have always liked that dress.'

So did I, reflected Leonora, when I first had it several years ago.

Getting into it later that evening, she decided that she hated it. Indeed, it was no longer the height of fashion, but it was well cut and fitted her splendid shape exactly where it should. She added the gold chain she had had for her twenty-first birthday, slipped Tony's ring on her finger and took a last dissatisfied look at her person, wrapped herself in a velvet coat she had worn to her twenty-first-birthday dance, and went downstairs to join her parents.

Sir William was impatiently stomping up and down the hall. 'Your mother has no idea of time,' he complained. 'Go and hurry her up, will you, Leonora? I'll get the car round.'

Lady Crosby was fluttering around her bedroom looking for things—her evening bag, the special hanky which went with it, her earrings...

Leonora found the bag and the hanky, assured her mother that she was wearing the earrings and urged her down to the hall and out into the cold dark evening, while Nanny went to open the car door.

The car, an elderly Daimler which Sir William had sworn that he would never part with despite the drain on his income, was at the entrance; Leonora bundled her mother into the front seat and got into the back, where she whiled away the brief journey thinking up suitable topics of conversation to get her through dinner. She would know everyone there, of course, but it was as well to be prepared....

The Willoughbys welcomed them warmly, for they had known each other for a long time. Leonora glanced round her as they went into the drawing room, seeing familiar faces, smiling and exchanging greetings; there was the vicar and his wife, old Colonel Howes and his daughter, the Merediths from the next village whose land adjoined her father's, Dr Fleming, looking ill, and his wife and, standing with them, the man in the car who had witnessed her undignified tumble.

'You haven't met our new doctor, have you, dear?' asked Mrs Willoughby, and saved Leonora the necessity of answering by adding, 'James Galbraith.' Mrs Willoughby smiled at him. 'This is Leonora Crosby—she lives at the Big House—you must come and meet her parents.'

Leonora offered a hand. Her 'How do you do?' was uttered with just the right amount of pleasant interest, but it had chilly undertones.

His hand was large and cool and firm and she felt compelled to look at him. Very handsome, she conceded— rather sleepy blue eyes and very fair hair, a splendid nose and a rather thin mouth. He was tall too, which was nice, she reflected; so often she found herself looking down on people from her five feet ten inches. Now she had to look up, quite a long way too!

'Six foot four?' she wondered out loud.

The Flemings had turned away to speak to someone else. Dr Galbraith's mouth quivered faintly. 'Five, actually. Are you feeling sore?'

She said austerely, 'I hardly think that is a question I need to answer, Dr Galbraith.'

She had gone rather pink and glanced around her, on the point of making an excuse to go and talk to the vicar. She was stopped by his saying, 'I speak in my professional capacity, Miss Crosby; presumably you will be one of my patients.'

'I am never ill,' said Leonora, unknowingly tempting fate.

Mrs Willoughby had joined them again. 'Getting to know each other?' she wanted to know. 'That's nice— take Leonora in to dinner, will you, James?' She tapped his sleeve. 'You don't mind if I call you James? Though if ever I need your skill I'll be sure to call you Doctor.'

Leonora had been sipping her sherry; now she put the

glass down. 'I really must circulate, and Nora Howes is dying to come and talk to you.'

He looked amused. 'Oh? How do you know that?'

'Woman's intuition.' She gave him a brief smile and crossed the room and he watched her go, thinking that a splendid creature such as she deserved a better dress.

She had been right about Nora Howes, who laid a hand on his sleeve, threw her head back and gave him an arch look. Older than Leonora, he supposed, as thin as a washboard and wearing a rather too elaborate dress for a dinner party in the country. But he could be charming when he liked and Nora relinquished him reluctantly as they went in to dinner, and he turned with relief to Leonora as the soup was served. Not a girl he could get interested in, he reflected—far too matter-of-fact and outspoken—but at least she didn't simper.

It was a round table so conversation, after a time, became more or less general. He had Mrs Fleming on his other side, a quiet, middle-aged woman, a good deal younger than her husband and anxious about him.

'I didn't want him to come,' she confided quietly, 'but he insisted. 'He's not well; he's going into hospital tomorrow.'

He said gently, 'You mustn't worry too much, Mrs Fleming. If he leads a quiet life for the next few months and keeps to his treatment he'll get a great deal better.'

She smiled at him. 'If anyone else had said that I should have supposed them to be pulling the wool over my eyes, but because it's you I believe what you've told me.'

'Thank you. I wish all patients were as trusting. Don't hesitate to call me if you're worried.'

'I won't. It's so nice that you're going to live at Buntings—such a lovely old house and it's been empty far too long.'

She turned to speak to her neighbour and presently everyone went back to the drawing room to drink coffee and gossip. It might be a small village but there was always something happening.

The party broke up shortly before eleven o'clock and since it was cold outside no one lingered to talk once they'd left the house. Sir William unlocked his car door and glanced at the Rolls-Royce parked beside him.

Who's the lucky owner? he wondered, and saw Dr Fleming getting in.

'Good Lord, Bill, have you come into a fortune?' he called.

'No, no, James owns it. Rather nice, isn't it?' He disappeared inside and Sir William got behind his wheel and backed the car. 'Lucky young devil,' he said to no one in particular. 'Come up on the pools, has he?'

Leonora made some vague reply. She was thinking about Tony. She hadn't seen him for a week or so; perhaps he would come at the weekend. She hoped so; she felt strangely unsettled and just seeing him would reassure her—she wasn't sure why she wanted to be reassured, but that didn't matter; Tony would set her world to rights again.

He did come, driving up on Saturday afternoon in his Porsche, and if his kiss and hug were lacking the fervour of a man in love she didn't notice because she was glad to see him.

He went indoors with her to meet her parents and make himself agreeable and then they went for a walk. He took her arm and talked and she listened happily to his plans. They would marry—he was a bit vague as to exactly when—and he would set about restoring her father's house. 'There's a chap I know who knows exactly what needs to be done. It'll be a showplace by the time it's finished. We can have friends down for the weekend…'

Leonora raised a puzzled face. 'But Tony, we shan't be living here; Mother and Father wouldn't much like a great many people coming to stay—even for a weekend.'

He said rather too quickly, 'Oh, I'm thinking of special occasions—Christmas and birthdays and so on; it's usual for families to get together at such times.' He smiled at her. 'Tell me, what's been happening since I was last here?'

'Nothing much. The Willoughbys' dinner party, and—I almost forgot—the new doctor to take over from Dr Fleming—he had a heart attack—not a severe one but he's got to retire.'

'Someone decent, I hope. Local chap?'

'Well, no, I don't think so. I don't know where he comes from. He's bought Buntings—that nice old house at the other end of the village.'

'Has he, indeed? Must have cost him a pretty penny. Married?'

'I've no idea. Very likely, I should think. Most GPs are, aren't they?'

Tony began to talk about himself then—the wheeling and dealing he had done, the money he had made, the important men of the business world he had met. Leonora listened and thought how lucky she was to be going to marry such a clever man.

They went to church the following morning and she stood beside Tony in the family pew, guiltily aware that she was glad the new doctor was there too and could see her handsome fiancé.

Dr Galbraith was handsome too, and his height and size added to that, but he was... She pondered for a moment. Perhaps it was the way he dressed, in elegant, beautifully tailored clothes, sober ties and, she had no doubt, handmade shoes—whereas Tony was very much the young man about town with his waistcoats and brightly coloured ties and striped shirts. She took a peep across the aisle and encountered the doctor's eyes, and blushed as though she had spoken her thoughts out loud and he had heard her.

She looked away hastily and listened to the Colonel reading the lesson, with a look of rapt attention, not hearing a word, and she took care not to look at the doctor again.

It was impossible to avoid him at the end of the service; he was standing in the church porch with the Flemings, talking to the vicar, and there was no help for it but to introduce Tony to him.

'The new GP,' observed Tony. 'I don't suppose there's much work for you around here. Wouldn't mind your job—peace and quiet in the country and all that. You fellows don't know when you're lucky. I'm in the City myself...'

The doctor said drily, 'Indeed? One of the unlucky ones? You must be glad to spend the weekend in this peaceful spot.'

Tony laughed. 'Not even a weekend—I must go back after lunch, try and catch up with the work, you know.'

'Ah, well, it's a pleasant run up to town. I dare say we shall meet again when next you're here.' The doctor smiled pleasantly and turned away to talk to the vicar's wife, who had joined them, and presently when he and the

Flemings left the little group he did no more than nod affably at Leonora, who gave him a decidedly chilly smile.

'A bit of a stiff neck, isn't he?' asked Tony as they walked back to the house. He gave his rather loud laugh. 'I don't need to have qualms about the two of you!'

'If that's a joke,' said Leonora, 'I don't think it's funny. And why do you have to go back after lunch?'

'Darling—' he was at his most cajoling '—I simply must. There's no let-up, you know, not in my world—the business world. Keeping one step ahead is vital…'

'Vital for what?'

'Making money, of course. Don't bother your pretty head; just leave it to me.'

'Will it always be like this? I mean, after we're married? Will you be dashing off at all hours of the day, and do we need a lot of money? Don't you earn enough for us to get married soon?'

He gave her a quick kiss. 'What a little worrier you are. I am that old-fashioned thing—comfortably off. We could marry tomorrow and live pleasantly, but I don't want to be just comfortably off; I want to be rich, darling—a flat in town, decently furnished, money to go abroad when we want to, all the clothes you want to buy, dinner parties, the theatre. I want you to have the best of everything.'

'Tony, I don't mind about any of that. I'm not a town girl; at least, I don't think I am. I like living in the country and I don't care if we haven't much money. After all, I'm used to that.' She added thoughtfully, 'Perhaps you've fallen in love with the wrong girl…'

He flung an arm around her. 'Darling, what nonsense. The moment I set eyes on you when we met at the Willoughbys I knew you were what I was looking for.'

Which was quite true—she was a very pretty girl, had

been ready to fall in love, and was an only child, with no large family to complicate matters. She lived in a lovely old house with plenty of land, which would be worth a fortune once he could get his hands on it.

He would have to go slowly, of course, and naturally he couldn't do anything to make Leonora unhappy. Her parents would be just as happy in a smaller house, somewhere close by, and he and Leonora could live in the big house. It would be a splendid focal point for meeting influential men and their wives—men who would give him a helping hand up the financial ladder.

Decently dressed, Leonora would prove an asset; she had lovely manners and a delightful voice. A bit outspoken at times and a good deal more intelligent than he had expected, but he was sure that he could persuade her to his way of thinking.

It was a couple of days later when Leonora met the doctor again. The icy weather had become quite mild and it rained from a dull sky. Sir William had caught cold and sat morosely by the fire, while his wife fussed around him and Nanny offered hot drinks and aspirin, which left Leonora looking after the household and doing the shopping, for, much as she loved her father, she could see that two females hovering over him was just about as much as he could stand. So she made the beds and hoovered and did most of the cooking and now they were running out of groceries.

In a mackintosh even older than the tweed coat, a hat, shapeless with age, rammed down onto her head, she picked up her basket, announced that she was going to the village and, accompanied by Wilkins, set out.

'At least we won't skid on ice,' she observed to

Wilkins, who was plodding along beside her. 'Though we are going to get very wet.'

Mrs Pike's shop was empty, which was a good thing for she allowed Wilkins to come in out of the rain, offering a sheet of newspaper which he was to sit on while Leonora took out her list.

A visit to Mrs Pike's was a leisurely affair unless she had a great many customers; she chatted while she collected bacon, cheese, the loaf the baker left each day, the marmalade Sir William preferred, tea and coffee, sugar and flour. Not that there was much to gossip about: Mrs Hick's new baby, the Kemp's youngest boy with a broken arm—'What do you expect from boys, anyway?' asked Mrs Pike—and Farmer Jenkins making a bit of trouble about his milk quota. 'Whatever that is, Miss Leonora; I'm sure I don't know what the world's coming to!'

This was one of Mrs Pike's frequent observations and the preliminary to a lengthy monologue of a gloomy nature, so it was a relief when two more customers came in together and Leonora was able to gather up her shopping and start for home.

It was still raining. Dr Galbraith, driving out of the village, saw Leonora's bedraggled figure ahead of him, marching along briskly, Wilkins beside her. He passed them and then pulled in to the side of the road, opened the door and said, 'Get in—I'm going past your place. Your dog can sit at the back.'

'Good morning, Doctor,' said Leonora pointedly. 'Please don't bother. We are both very wet; we shall spoil your car.'

He didn't answer but got out of the car and walked round to where she stood. 'Get in,' he said pleasantly, and opened the door for Wilkins, who was only too glad to get out of the rain.

'Oh, well, all right,' said Leonora ungraciously, and slid into the front of the car. 'I have warned you that we are both very wet.'

'Indeed you have, and now I'm wet as well.' He glanced at her. 'A waste of time, Leonora…'

'What's a waste of time?'

'Trying to get the better of me.' He was driving now and turned to smile at her. 'How are your mother and father?'

'They're very well—no, that's not quite true. Father's got a very bad cold; he's a shocking patient when he's not well and Mother gets worried.'

'In that case, perhaps it might be as well if I took a look at him. An antibiotic might get him back on his feet—colds can drag on at this time of year.'

'Yes, but aren't you on your rounds or something?'

'No.' He swept the car through the gates and up the neglected drive to the front door and got out to go round the bonnet and open her door and then free Wilkins.

'Do come in,' said Leonora, all at once minding her manners, 'and take off your coat. I'll fetch Mother.' She turned round as Nanny came down the staircase.

'Oh, good, here's Nanny. This is Dr Galbraith, our new doctor; he's kindly come to see Father.'

Nanny eyed the doctor. 'And that's a mercy. How do you do, Doctor? And a fine, well-set-up young man you are, to be sure. Give me the coat; I'll dry it out while Miss Leonora takes you to see the master.'

She turned her attention to Leonora then. 'And you too, Miss Leonora—off with that coat and that old hat and I'll give Wilkins a good rub down. There'll be coffee when you come down.'

Dismissed, the pair of them went upstairs to find her father sitting in a chair by a brisk fire with his wife bending over him. She looked up as they went in and gave a relieved sigh. 'Dr Galbraith, I was wondering if I should ask you to call. You met Leonora…'

'Yes, Lady Crosby, and it seemed sensible to take a look at Sir William, since I was passing.' He went to look at his patient and Leonora discovered that he was no longer a man who persisted in annoying her but an impersonal doctor with his head stuffed full of knowledge, and to be trusted. His quiet voice and his, 'Well, sir, may I take a look at you?' was reassuring.

Chapter 2

Sir William coughed, blew his nose, coughed again and spoke.

'Nothing much wrong—just this infernal cold—cough keeps me awake, makes me tired.'

Leonora helped him off with his dressing gown and followed her mother to the door. She paused to ask, 'Do you need me to stay?'

She was surprised when the doctor said, 'Please,' in an absent-minded voice as he bent over his patient.

She stood by the window and glanced out at the rain-sodden landscape, listening to the doctor's quiet voice and her father's querulous answers. He wasn't well; perhaps they should have called the doctor sooner, she thought worriedly.

She loved her parents and got on well with them; in-deed, she had been perfectly happy to stay home with them. Before her father had lost his money, there had been plans afoot to send her to friends in Italy, suggestions that she might train for a career, have a flat in town—the world had been her oyster.

She hadn't regretted the loss of any of these, although she sometimes longed for new clothes, a visit to the theatre, evenings out at some famous restaurant. The longings weren't deep enough to make her unhappy, and now that she and Tony were to marry it seemed to her that she would have the best of both worlds—living with Tony, sharing his social life, and coming home whenever she wanted to.

Dr Galbraith's voice disturbed her thoughts. 'If you would help your father with his dressing gown?'

He didn't look up as he wrote out a prescription. 'If you could get this made up? It's an antibiotic. And a couple of days in bed. Flu can hang around for a long time if it isn't treated promptly.'

He handed her the prescription and closed his bag. 'I'll call again in a day or so, but if you're bothered about anything don't hesitate to call me.'

'Hope I haven't given it to my wife,' observed Sir William.

'As I said, let me know if you are worried about anything.' He glanced at Leonora. 'Forewarned is forearmed.'

'Obliged to you for coming,' said Sir William. 'I'm sure there'll be coffee downstairs for you. Busy, are you?'

The doctor, who had been up all night with a premature baby, replied that no, he wasn't unduly so.

'Probably a good deal easier than a city practice,' said Sir William, blithely unaware that the doctor's practice extended for miles in every direction. Some of the outlying farms were well off the main roads, and the lanes leading to them were, as often as not, churned into muddy ruts.

Downstairs Lady Crosby was waiting for them in the drawing room, looking anxious.

'Fetch the coffee, Leonora; Nanny has it ready. Come and sit down, Doctor, and tell me if Sir William is ill or if it's just a bad cold.'

'Flu, Lady Crosby. He will need to keep to his bed for a few days and take the antibiotic I have prescribed. He should be perfectly all right within a week, provided he keeps warm and quiet; he isn't as young as he was.'

He smiled at her and she smiled back. 'Sixty-one— I'm a good deal younger.' Lady Crosby, who had been a very pretty girl, wasn't averse to a little admiration and her smile invited it.

She was disappointed and a little put out; she had been spoilt and pampered for most of her life, only during the last difficult years she had had to forgo the comforts and luxuries she had taken for granted. She loved her husband and daughter, but took their care and attention as her right. The expected compliment from the doctor wasn't forthcoming. All he said was, 'I'm going to Bath; perhaps your daughter might come with me and get the prescription I have written up for Sir William. I shall be returning within the hour and will give her a lift back.'

Leonora, coming in with the coffee, heard the last part of this and said, in her matter-of-fact way, 'Oh, there is no need for that. I can take the car—I might hold you up.'

'Nonsense, dear,' said her mother. 'Why take the car when you can get a lift? Dr Galbraith is coming back to the village. You'll probably have time to pop into that wool shop and see if you can match my embroidery silks...'

She poured the coffee. 'Have you taken a tray up to your father, dear? I dare say he would like a hot drink.' She smiled charmingly at the doctor. 'We shall take the greatest care of him, Doctor.'

He glanced from mother to daughter; Leonora had inherited her mother's good looks on a more generous scale; he fancied she had inherited her father's forthright and strong-willed nature. It was no life for a girl such as she—living with elderly parents and, he suspected, bearing the burden of the household management in the down-at-heel, still beautiful house. Still, he remembered, she was engaged; presumably she would marry shortly. Not that he had liked the man.

Leonora, wrapped up against the weather, got into the car presently. He was glad to see that she had found a decent hat and her gloves and handbag were beyond reproach. Not that he cared in the least about her appearance, but with her striking looks she deserved the right clothes.

Glancing at her profile, he set himself out to be pleasant and had the satisfaction of seeing her relax. Gradually he led the conversation round to more personal matters, putting a quiet question here and there so casually that she answered freely, unaware that she was talking about things that she had kept tucked away at the back of her head because neither her mother nor her father would want to hear about them, and nor would Tony: small niggling doubts, little worries, plans she had little hope of putting into effect.

They were on the outskirts of Bath when she said abruptly, 'I'm sorry, I must be boring you. I expect you get enough moaning from your patients.'

'No, no, talking never bores me, unless it is the kind

of chat you encounter at parties. I'm going to park at
the Royal National Hospital. There are several chemists
in Milsom Street; fetch the prescription and come back
to the car. There's a quiet restaurant by the abbey—I
hope you'll take pity on me and have lunch.' When she
opened her mouth to refuse he said, 'No, don't say that
you have to go home at once; you would be too late for
lunch anyway, and I promise you I'll get you home within
the next hour or so.' He smiled suddenly. 'I have an afternoon surgery…'

'Well, that would be nice; thank you. I don't like to
be away from home for very long because of Father…'

He had stopped the car by the hospital and got out to
open her door. 'I'll be fifteen minutes. If I'm longer than
that, go and wait in the entrance hall…'

He watched her walk away. She was just as nice to
look at from the back as from the front. He smiled a little
as he went into the hospital.

When she got back he was there, waiting for her.
'We'll leave the car here; it's only a few minutes' walk.
You know Bath well?'

The restaurant was small, quiet, and the food was
excellent. Leonora, savouring a perfectly grilled sole,
thought she must remember to tell Tony about it; it was
a long time since they had been out together for a meal—
he was happy to stay at home with her, he always told
her, and she spent hours in the kitchen conjuring up a
meal he would like from as little of the housekeeping
money as possible.

She wished that he were sitting opposite her now instead of Dr Galbraith and despised herself for the mean
thought. After all, he had no reason to give her lunch
and she had to admit he was a pleasant companion. All

the same, she had the sneaking feeling that behind that bland face there was a man she wouldn't care to cross swords with.

They talked as they ate, exchanging views on Bath, Pont Magna and its inhabitants, and the various houses in it.

'I used to go to Buntings when I was a little girl,' Leonora told him. 'It's a lovely old house. Are you happy there?'

'Yes. It is the kind of place where you feel instantly at home. I expect you feel that about your own home?'

'Oh, yes. It's badly in need of repairs, though. Some rich American wanted to buy it last year, but Father wouldn't hear of it. His family have lived in it for a very long time. It would break his heart to leave.'

'I can understand that. It is a delightful house. Rather large to look after, though.'

'Yes, but quite a few rooms are shut and Nanny and I can manage the rest.'

She frowned and he said smoothly, 'Nannies are marvellous, aren't they? Shall we go? I must get you back before someone wonders where you are.'

Less than an hour later he stopped the car at her home, got out to open her door and waited until she had gone inside. He had beautiful manners, she thought, and hoped that she had thanked him with sufficient warmth.

Her mother was in the drawing room. 'There you are, dear. Have you got those pills for your father? He's rather peevish so I came down here to have a little rest—I find looking after someone ill so very tiring. We'll have tea soon, shall we? Perhaps Nanny could make a few scones.'

Leonora said, 'Yes, Mother,' and went to look for Nanny.

In the kitchen Nanny asked, 'Have you had some lunch, Miss Leonora? There's plenty of that corned beef—'

'Dr Galbraith gave me lunch, Nanny—a rather splendid one too. Mother wants tea a bit earlier—and scones? I'll come and make them, but first I must go and see about Father.'

Sir William, back in his bed, was glad to see her.

'I've got your pills and you can start them straight away,' she told him cheerfully. 'And how about a cup of tea and some of that thin bread and butter Nanny cuts so beautifully?'

She sat down on the side of the bed. 'I don't suppose you feel like sausages for supper. How about scrambled eggs and creamed potato and jelly for pudding?'

'That sounds good.' Her father smiled at her. 'We shall be lost without you when you marry, my dear.' He paused to cough. 'You are quite sure, aren't you? Tony is a successful young man—he'll want to live in London.'

She shook her head. 'Not all the time—he was talking about coming down here whenever we could. He loves this house, you know.'

Her father said drily, 'It is a gold-mine for anyone with enough money to put it in order. As it is, it's mouldering away. At least it will be yours one day, Leonora.'

'Not for years, Father.' She got up and fetched a glass of water and watched him while he swallowed his pill. 'Every four hours,' she warned him. 'Now I'm going to get your tea.'

She dropped a kiss on his head and went down to the kitchen, where, since Nanny was making the scones, she got her father's tea-tray ready and presently bore it upstairs.

Back in the drawing room with her mother, she drew a chair closer to the fire. 'I must say that Dr Galbraith seems to be a very pleasant man. Charming manners, too. We must invite him to dinner one evening, Leonora— remind me to make a list of guests. We must think of something delicious to give them.'

Leonora said, 'Yes, Mother,' and bit into a scone. 'I dare say Father will enjoy that once he's feeling better.'

Her mother said vaguely, 'Oh, yes, of course, dear. What did you have for lunch? So kind of the doctor to give you a meal.'

When Leonora had told her she added, 'Ah, yes, I know the restaurant you mention. The food there is good but expensive. I dare say that, being a single man, he can afford such places. I'm surprised that he isn't married, but I expect he is merely waiting until he is settled in at Buntings. A doctor, especially one with a country prac- tice, needs a wife.'

Leonora murmured an agreement, and wondered why he should need one more than a GP with a town practice.

'He would have done very well for you,' went on Lady Crosby, 'but of course you've already got a fiancé in Tony. Most suitable and such a charming man.'

Leonora thought about Tony. He was charming and fun to be with. He teased her a good deal, told her that she was old-fashioned and strait-laced. 'I'll forgive you that,' he had told her, laughing. 'You'll change once I get you up to town.'

She had pointed out that she didn't want to change. 'I wouldn't be me,' she'd told him, aware that she had irri- tated him. The next moment, however, he had been laugh- ing again; perhaps she had mistaken the look on his face. They would be happy together, she felt sure; she looked at the diamond on her finger and told herself how happy she was at that very moment just thinking about him.

That night she dreamt of Dr Galbraith, and the dream persisted in staying in her head all next day. She did her best to dispel it by writing a long letter to Tony.

Her father was feeling a little better, although he was still coughing a good deal and looked tired. She wondered uneasily what would be done if the antibiotic didn't do its good work; Dr Galbraith hadn't said that he would call again...

He came the next morning and, since she was upstairs with the Hoover, it was her mother who opened the door to him.

'Dr Galbraith—how kind of you to call again. Just in time for coffee. I'll get Leonora or Nanny to bring it to the drawing room.' She smiled her charming smile. 'I do hate having it by myself...'

Any opinion the doctor might have had about this remark he kept to himself.

'I called to see Sir William and, much though I would enjoy a cup of coffee, I can't spare the time—I have quite a few visits to make this morning.' He smiled in his turn. 'If I might go up?'

'Oh, dear, we could have had a nice little chat. Do you want me to come up with you? Leonora is hoovering the bedrooms; I'm sure she'll see to anything you may want.'

The Hoover was making a good deal of noise; he had time to study Leonora's back view before she turned round. She was wearing a sensible pinny and had tied her hair in a bright scarf; the Hoover, being past its prime, tended to raise almost as much dust as it sucked up.

She switched it off when she saw him, wished him a

good morning and said, 'You want to see Father? He had quite a good night but he's chesty…'

She whipped off the pinny and also the scarf and led him into her father's room.

The doctor pronounced himself satisfied with his patient but added that he would need to remain in bed for several days yet. 'Get up for an hour or so, if you wish,' he said, 'but stay in this room. I'll come and see you again in a couple of days or so.'

Going downstairs with Leonora, he observed, 'Your father is by no means out of the woods. He has escaped pneumonia by a whisker and anything other than rest and a warm room, plenty to drink and plenty of sleep is liable to trigger off a more serious condition. He'll do well if he stays where he is—don't let him get out of bed for much more than an hour or so.'

He sounded just like the family doctor, thought Leonora waspishly, but then that was exactly what he was. Did he need to be quite so impersonal, though? After all, they had had lunch together…

Her mother came into the hall as they reached it and he bade her a pleasant goodbye, added a few reassuring words about Sir William's condition, smiled briefly at Leonora and drove away, leaving her feeling vaguely unsettled.

Tony came at the weekend, breezing into the house, explaining that he had torn himself away from his work to take them by surprise.

'You look as though you need a bit of cheering up,' he told Leonora, who certainly didn't look her best after four days of coping with her irascible parent. 'How is Sir William? Not too bad, I hope?'

'He is better, but he has a bad chest; he's getting up

today for a few hours but he mustn't go outside until his cough has cleared up.'

'Where is that delightful mother of yours?'

'She went to Colonel Howes's for coffee.' Leonora hesitated. 'Tony, would you mind awfully if I left you for a bit? I'll get some coffee for you and there are the morning papers in the drawing room. I haven't quite finished the bedrooms and I must make a bed for you. You are staying?'

'Well, of course, if it's too much bother...' He contrived to look hurt and she said quickly, 'No, no, of course it's not, and I shan't be long.'

'I'll go and have a chat with your father,' suggested Tony, getting out of the chair into which he had flung himself.

'No— Oh, dear, I keep saying no, don't I? He is shaving and getting dressed. We'll both be down presently. I'll just fetch the coffee. Did you have a good trip here?'

He said sulkily, 'Not bad. It's the deuce of a long way from town, though.'

I ought to be so pleased to see him, reflected Leonora, putting china on a tray and listening to Nanny's opinion of those who came for the weekend uninvited, but he might have phoned first. 'I'll have to go to the butcher's and get some chops.' She interrupted Nanny's indignant flow. 'Have we plenty of eggs?' she asked.

'No. We have not. Mr Beamish will have bacon for his breakfast and one or two of those mushrooms Mrs Fleming sent over. The cake's almost finished too.'

'Oh, I'll make another one, Nanny—there'll be time before lunch...'

'There's the doorbell,' said Nanny in a voice which suggested that she was much too busy to answer it. So

Leonora opened the door, to find Dr Galbraith towering over her. She stared up into his calm face and felt a ridiculous urge to burst into tears. She didn't say anything and presently he said placidly, 'I've come to see your father.'

'Yes, but—yes, of course. Do come in…'

'You were doing something urgent. If I'm interrupting do go and finish.' He looked her over slowly. 'You look put upon. What's the matter?'

As Tony came into the hall, the doctor said, 'Ah, yes, of course,' in a very quiet voice, and added a much louder, 'Good morning.'

'Ah, the local GP. Good morning to you. Come to check on the invalid, have you?'

'Yes.' Dr Galbraith turned towards Leonora. 'Shall we go up?'

'I'll come along too—the old chap's always glad to see me.'

The doctor was saved the necessity of answering as Nanny came into the hall with the coffee-tray.

'I'm putting your coffee in the drawing room, Mr Beamish; you'll need to drink it while it's hot.'

Tony, although he didn't like her, did as he was told, mentally promising himself that once he was married to Leonora one of the first of his acts would be to get rid of Nanny.

Going up the staircase, the doctor noted that Leonora looked less than her best; her hair was tied back and hung in something of a tangle down her back, and she was without make-up, not that that mattered for she had clear skin and a mouth which didn't need lipstick; moreover, she was wearing an elderly skirt and a sweater with the sleeves rolled up. But none of this really detracted from her undoubted good looks.

'Is Lady Crosby at home?' he asked casually.

'No, I'm sorry, but she's having coffee with the Howeses—you've met the Colonel and his daughter...'

He had dined with them on the previous evening but he didn't say so.

'Don't you care for visiting?' he wanted to know.

'Me? Oh, yes, it's nice meeting people. But today—well, the weekend, you know, and then I didn't know Tony was coming so there's a bit more to do.'

They had reached her father's door and the doctor didn't answer.

Her father was sitting in his dressing gown, looking out of the window. He turned as they went in, saying, 'Leonora? Is that my coffee? It's past ten o'clock.'

He saw the doctor then. 'Good morning. You see how much better I am. I shall get dressed presently and go downstairs for lunch.'

'Why not?' The doctor sat down beside him. 'Such a delightful view from this window even at this time of the year. How is the cough?'

'Better—much better—and I've taken those pills you left for me. Leonora sees to that, don't you, my dear?'

Leonora said, 'Yes, Father,' and admired the back of the doctor's head.

'A splendid nurse,' her father went on. 'We are indeed lucky to have a daughter who takes such good care of us both.'

'You will miss her when she marries,' observed the doctor, taking his patient's pulse.

'Yes, yes, of course, although Tony has a great liking for this house; I'm sure they will visit us as often as possible.'

The doctor didn't hurry but tapped Sir William's chest,

listened to his heart, asked a number of leisurely questions and finally pronounced himself satisfied. 'Stay indoors for another day or so,' he advised, 'and when you do go out wrap up warm.'

Tony came out of the drawing room as they reached the hall.

'Well, what's the verdict? I'm not surprised that Sir William has been ill—this house may look a thing of beauty but it's riddled with damp. Needs money spent on it. More sense if he found something smaller and modern.'

Leonora gave him a surprised look. 'Tony, you know as well as I do that Father and Mother will never move. Why should we? We're happy here—it's our home.'

He took her arm. 'Darling, of course it is. Come and have some coffee.' He nodded at Dr Galbraith. 'Nice to meet you,' he observed.

Leonora frowned. Tony was being rude. 'Thank you for coming, Doctor. I'll keep an eye on Father. You won't need to come again?'

'I think not, but do give me a ring if that cough doesn't clear up within the next week or ten days.' He shook hands, ignored Tony and went out to his car, got in and drove away.

'You were rude,' said Leonora, leading the way to the drawing room.

'Sorry, darling. I can't stand the fellow, looking down that long nose of his. Thinks he knows everything—I've met his sort before.'

'He's a good doctor,' said Leonora, 'and everyone likes him—except you.'

'Let's not argue about him. I've come to spend the

weekend with you, so let's enjoy ourselves. Heaven knows, it's hard enough to get away.'

Tony had sat down again. 'How about getting into something pretty and we'll go out to lunch?'

'Tony, I'd love to, but I can't. When you got here I was making beds—and when I've done that I must get lunch and see about making a cake and getting something made for this evening. Father has to have his coffee and his lunch, and Mother will be back presently. They like their tea at half past four and dinner has to be cooked...'

'For heaven's sake, Leonora...can't Nanny deal with all that?'

'No, she can't. The kitchen has to be cleaned, food has to be prepared, she has to answer the door and Father's bell if I'm busy and one of us will have to go to the village and do some extra shopping.'

'Well, I thought I would be welcome,' said Tony sulkily, 'but it seems I'd better leave as quickly as possible!'

'Don't be silly,' said Leonora briskly. 'You know how glad I am to see you, but what's the use of pretending that I can sit here, nicely dressed and made up, when it's simply not possible? We could go for a walk in the afternoon.'

She saw his irritable frown. 'I'm sorry, Tony...'

'Let's hope that next time I manage to get here you'll be looking more like my fiancée and not the home help.' He laughed as he spoke and she laughed with him, hiding her hurt. He was delightful and charming, she told herself, and she loved him, and she reminded herself that he worked very hard and had little time to enjoy his leisure.

All the same the beds had still to be made. It was fortunate that her mother returned, delighted at the sight of Tony, grumbling prettily at the awful coffee she had had to drink at Colonel Howes's. 'Darling,' she begged Leonora, 'do make me a cup—you make such good coffee.'

She settled down in her chair and turned to Tony. 'Now, tell me all the latest gossip...'

Her father wasn't best pleased to learn that Tony had come for the weekend. He loved his daughter dearly, was aware that she was missing the kind of life a girl of her age should be enjoying but was not sure what to do about it. When Tony had swept her off her feet and he had seen the happiness in her face, he had been glad for her sake, although he had had to bury the vague dislike he had for him. If Leonora loved him and he would make her happy, then that was more important than his own feelings. Tony, after all, was a successful young man, able to give Leonora the comforts and small luxuries which he, her father, had been unable to afford.

He expressed a pleasure he didn't feel and told her he would be down to lunch and she whisked herself away to finish the beds and tidy first the rooms and then herself. There wasn't time to change into something more eye-catching than the sweater and skirt but at least she could do something to her face and hair.

Going downstairs a little later, she could hear her mother and Tony laughing and talking in the drawing room, which gave her the chance to go to the kitchen and see what Nanny had found for lunch.

Cheese omelettes, they decided, and there was a tin of mushroom and garlic soup which they could eke out with some chicken stock. Melba toast and a salad.

'We'll worry about dinner presently,' promised Leonora. 'I'll do the table in a minute and after lunch I'll go down to the village. It had better be a joint, I suppose—five of us—roast this evening, cold tomorrow.'

That would make a hole in the housekeeping, she reflected, going to sit in the drawing room and listen to Tony being amusing about his life in London.

A good-looking man, she reflected lovingly, and such fun to be with. She hoped that once they were married she would make him happy—live his kind of life, like his friends, enjoy the dinner parties and theatres and social occasions which he had assured her were so very important to his work.

Presently she slipped away to see to lunch and give Nanny a hand, half hoping that he would go with her. But he merely smiled and waved a hand.

'Don't be too long, darling; I miss you.'

Perhaps it was as well that he had stayed talking to her mother and father, she decided, beating eggs, making a salad, laying the table...

After lunch she told him that she was going to the village. He frowned for a moment then smiled. 'A chance for us to talk,' he told her. 'Not paying visits, I hope.'

'No, no, just some shopping. It'll give you an appetite for tea.'

They met the vicar in the village street and she left them talking while she bought the meat. They were still talking when she joined them again.

Tony put an arm around her shoulders. 'Do we know when we want to get married, darling?' he asked. 'It all depends, actually, but it won't be long now. A June wedding, perhaps. That is, if the bride agrees to that.'

The vicar looked pleased. 'We haven't had a wedding for some time,' he observed, 'and June is a delightful month in which to be married.'

'A nice old man,' said Tony as they started back home. 'Very keen to see us married, isn't he?'

'Did you mean that—June—you said…?'

He took her free hand in his. 'Why not, darling? It will be a bit of a rush—but I suppose we could get the place tidied up by then.'

'What place?'

He stopped and turned to look at her. 'Leonora, surely you can see for yourself that that great house is too much for your father and mother? Suppose we move them out to something smaller? There's a nice little property a couple of miles away on the road to Bath. I'll have the house completely refurbished and it'll be a marvellous headquarters for me—us. Weekends for clients and friends. We'll have a flat in town, of course, but it's an easy run. I might even give you a car of your own so that you can go to and fro whenever you want.'

Leonora stared at him. 'You don't mean any of that, do you? I mean, turning Mother and Father out of their home? It's been in the family for almost two hundred years; Father would die; it's—it's his blood. Mother has all her friends here and she loves the house too—she came here when she married Father. It's a joke, isn't it?'

He put his arm round her shoulders. 'Darling, it's not a joke, it's common sense—can't you see that? Your father isn't exactly in the best of health, is he? Supposing he were to die—what would your mother do? Try and run this place on her own? She hasn't the faintest idea how to do it…'

'You forget me.' Leonora had twisted away from him. 'It's my home too and I won't leave it. And Father's almost well again—you heard what Dr Galbraith said—'

'A country GP?' Tony sounded derisive. 'He'll say whatever he thinks his patients want to hear.'

'That isn't true. What an abominable thing to say.'

She began to walk on and he caught up with her and took her arm.

'Darling, I'm sorry if I've made you cross. All right, I won't say another word about your parents leaving home, but you must know that your father is in financial difficulties, and what will happen if they foreclose the mortgage?'

That brought her up short. 'Mortgage? I didn't know...'

'How do you suppose he's been able to stay here for so long?'

'How did you know?'

'I make it my business to know these things. Besides, I am concerned for you, Leonora.'

'Oh.' She felt guilty then for suspecting him. Suspecting him of what? she wondered. 'I'm sorry, Tony. Don't let's talk about it any more. Father will get things sorted out once he is feeling quite well. Do please believe me when I say that nothing on earth will make Father or Mother move from the house, and that goes for me too!'

He caught her arm again. 'Darling, you're going to marry me, remember?' He laughed a gentle laugh which made her smile and then laugh with him.

They went on their way and just as they reached the open gates to the house Dr Galbraith drove past. He raised a hand in salute, wondering why the sight of Leonora apparently so happy in Tony's company should disturb him.

Probably because I don't like the fellow, he decided, and forgot about them.

The weekend went too quickly for Leonora. Of course, having Tony there made a lot of extra work; he had admitted soon after they'd met that he was quite useless around the house and since there was no need for him to do anything for himself at his flat—a service flat where he could get his meals and a cleaner came each day—he made no effort to help. Not that Leonora expected him to make his bed or wash up, but it would have been nice if he hadn't given Nanny his shoes to clean and expected his trousers pressed—or even if he'd carried a tray out to the kitchen…

It would be better when they were married, reflected Leonora; she was sure that he would be only too willing to help out when necessary once he realised that help was needed.

He went back very early on Monday morning, which meant that Leonora got up and cooked his breakfast first. It also meant that he used up almost all the hot water from the boiler and woke everyone up.

'I'll be down again just as soon as I can spare the time,' he told Leonora. 'And when I come do be ready for me, darling, and we'll have an evening out. Bath, perhaps? A decent meal and we could dance after.'

She agreed happily, ignoring the bit about the decent meal. Sunday lunch had been excellent, she had thought—roast beef, Yorkshire pudding, baked potatoes, vegetables from the garden and an apple tart for pudding. That was surely a decent meal? She kissed him goodbye and begged him to phone when he had time. 'Or write.'

'Write? My dear girl, when do I ever have time to write letters?' He squeezed her arm and gave her a charming smile. 'Be good.'

She gravely said, 'Yes, Tony,' and he laughed as he got into the car.

'Not much chance of being anything else, is there?' he shouted at her as he started the engine.

He would have to go carefully, he decided as he drove;

no more mention of moving her mother and father out of the house. Perhaps it might be a good idea to wait until they were married. He had no doubt at all that he could persuade her to do anything he asked of her once she was his wife.

A few weeks of comfortable living, new clothes, new faces, meals out—once she had a taste of all the things a girl wanted in the way of a carefree life she would come round to his way of thinking. The more he saw of the house, the more he intended to have it...

Leonora, happily unaware of his schemes, went indoors, placated her parents with very early morning tea, soothed a grumpy Nanny and went up to the attics to see if the rain had come in during the night. It had.

Chapter 3

At about the same time as Tony was getting into his car to drive back to London, Dr Galbraith was letting himself into his house. He had been called out in the very early hours to a farm some miles away from the village, where the farmer's elderly father had suffered a stroke and he'd waited with him until the ambulance had come to take him to Bath. He had followed it to the hospital, made sure that his patient was in good hands and then driven himself back home.

There was no question of going back to bed; he had morning surgery and a scattered round before mothers and babies' clinic in the early afternoon. He went quietly across the square hall and up the uncarpeted oak staircase to his room at the front of the old house. He had his hand on the door when another door at the far end of the passage opened and a tall, bony man emerged.

He was middle-aged, with a long, narrow face, dark hair streaked with grey, combed carefully over a bald patch, and an expression of gloom.

'Good morning, sir. You'll need a cup of coffee. I'll bring it up at once. Breakfast in an hour suit you?'

'Admirably, Cricket. I'm famished.'

Cricket went back to his room, shaking his head in a disapproving manner. He never failed to disapprove when the doctor was called out at night, but that didn't prevent him from making sure that there was a hot drink and a meal waiting for him. He had been with the doctor for a number of years now, running his house to perfection, cooking delicious meals, making sure that the cleaning lady did her work properly. In fact, he was a treasure.

The doctor drank his coffee, showered, dressed and went downstairs to his breakfast. It was light now, a chilly, breezy March morning, and he opened the door to the garden before going into the small sitting room at the back of the house, where Cricket had laid his breakfast.

It was a charming room, facing the rising sun, furnished comfortably with some nice old pieces and decidedly cosy, unlike the drawing room which was rather grand with its magnificent carpet, vast bow-fronted cabinets and the pair of sofas, one at each side of the marble fireplace. The drawing room also had comfortable chairs arranged here and there and a beautiful drum table in the bay window overlooking the front garden. It was a room the doctor used seldom, for dinner parties and on the occasions when his friends came to stay.

There was a dining room too, on the opposite side of the hall, with its Regency mahogany table and chairs and the splendid sideboard, and at the back of the hall his study, the room he used most of all.

It was a large house for an unmarried man but he was a big man and needed space around him. Besides, he loved the old place, having first seen it some years earlier when he had come to visit Dr Fleming, whom he had known for some time. It had seemed an act of Providence when he had agreed to take over Dr Fleming's practice and Buntings had been on the market.

He had his surgery in the village—a cottage which had been converted into a consulting room and a waiting room—although he saw patients at his home if necessary.

This morning there were more patients than usual: neglected colds which had settled on chests, elderly people with arthritis and rheumatism, a broken arm, a sprained ankle, septic fingers. Nothing dramatic, but they kept him busy for most of the morning; he was late starting his round.

He was barely a mile out of the village when his car phone rang. Mrs Crisp, his part-time receptionist and secretary, sounded urgent.

'There's a call from Willer's Farm. Mrs Willer—she's on her own except for a farm lad. The tractor driver has had an accident—a bad one, she says. Mr Willer's away—gone to a cattle market. She phoned Beckett's Farm but couldn't get an answer. There's no one else nearby.'

'Tell her I'm on my way. I should be there in twenty minutes.'

He put his large foot down and sent the car speeding along the road and then braked hard to avoid Leonora with Wilkins, coming round the curve in the middle of the road.

She nipped to one side, dragging Wilkins with her, and shouted sorry and would have gone on. He had come to a halt, though, and had the car door open, so that she felt compelled to repeat her apologies.

'Never mind that,' said the doctor impatiently. 'You're just what I need. You know Willer's Farm. There's been an accident there. I'm on my way and it seems there's no one there except Mrs Willer and a lad. I shall need help. Jump in, will you? I could use another pair of hands.'

'Wilkins?'

'In the car.' He leaned over and opened the door and Wilkins got in without being asked; a lazy dog by nature, he thought the chance of a ride wasn't to be missed.

Leonora got in beside the doctor, remarking calmly, 'I don't know anything about first aid, or at least not much, but I'm strong. I was going to the shop for Nanny; would you mind if I phoned her? She's waiting for some braising steak.'

The doctor handed her the phone without speaking and listened to her quiet voice telling Nanny that she might be home rather later than expected and perhaps someone else could go to the village. 'I've got Wilkins with me and we'll be back when you see us.'

She replaced the phone and sat quietly as he drove through the narrow, high-hedged lanes, wondering what they would find when they got to the farm.

Mrs Willer came running out to meet them as the doctor slowed the car across the farmyard, which was rutted and muddy and redolent of farmyard smells.

'He's on Lower Pike. The boy's with him; I came down to show you the way. He's real bad. It's 'is foot—got it caught in the tractor as 'e fell out.'

The doctor was bending over the car's boot, handing things to Leonora. He said merely, 'We'll take a look. How long has he been lying there? Is he conscious?'

'Now 'e is, Doctor… Not at first, 'e wasn't. Banged 'is 'ead.'

They were crossing the yard now, making for the open fields beyond, which sloped gently uphill to Higher Pike, and going at a good pace. Leonora, a splendid walker, found herself making an effort to keep up with the doctor's strides.

The next twenty minutes were like a very unpleasant dream. The tractor had reared up and toppled backwards and although Ben, the driver, had been flung free his foot had been trapped by the superstructure.

The doctor got down beside him and opened his bag. 'Pain bad?' he asked, and when Ben nodded he filled a syringe and plunged its contents into the arm he had bared. Presently, as the dope took effect, he examined his patient and then bent over his foot, trapped by a heavy iron crossbar.

'Open that bag,' He nodded towards the zippered bag he had been carrying. 'Hand me the things from it as I ask for them.' He looked over his shoulder. 'And you, boy, fetch me a spade, two spades, anything to dig with.'

He busied himself cleaning and covering the crushed foot, and Leonora, very much on her mettle, handed things from the bag when he asked for them. Most of them she had never seen before—forceps and probes and some nasty-looking scissors. Most of the time she managed not to look too closely…

All the while he worked, the doctor talked to Ben—a soothing flow of words uttered in a quiet, reassuring voice. 'We're going to dig the earth from under your foot to relieve the pressure on it,' he explained. 'I'm going to phone for an ambulance and help now; you'll soon be comfortable.'

Leonora listened to him talking into his phone; it seemed hours since they had arrived but when she glanced at her watch she saw that it was barely fifteen minutes.

The boy came back then with the spades. Dr Galbraith took one, handed him the other and told him what they were going to do, then he said to Leonora, 'Come here and kneel by Ben's foot. Don't touch it yet, but be ready to steady it.'

She knelt gingerly. The tractor loomed huge above her and she tried not to think what would happen should it shift. The foot was swathed in a protective covering, bloodstained but not frighteningly so. She crept nearer and held her hands ready.

They dug cautiously, inch by inch, so that presently there was a bit of space between Ben's foot and the cross-bar. It would need far more room than that to free the foot, she thought; the tractor would have to be righted.

The digging stopped then and the doctor took her place, his arm sheltering the foot as far as possible. If the tractor moves...thought Leonora, and didn't dare think further.

'Take Mrs Willer to the house and help her pack a bag for Ben,' said the doctor. 'Everything he'll need at the hospital. And then come back here.'

She led a shocked Mrs Willer back to the house, found a bag and together they packed it. They had done that when they heard the high-pitched wail of the ambulance and the louder, deeper note of the fire engine, and by the time they had got back to the tractor there were men everywhere.

It took time to right the tractor and more time to inspect Ben's foot thoroughly. Finally he was on a stretcher, being carried to the ambulance.

In answer to his, 'Come along, Leonora,' she followed the doctor to the car and got in. Wilkins, snoozing on the back seat, opened an eye in greeting and went back to sleep and she sat watching the doctor as he spoke to Mrs Willer.

Getting in beside her, he said, 'You have been a great help; thank you, Leonora. Ben is going to the Royal National at Bath; I must go there and speak to the casualty officer.' He picked up the phone. 'I'll explain to Nanny…' Which he did before handing the phone to her.

Nanny sounded anxious. 'Miss Leonora, are you all right? Am I to tell your ma and pa?'

'I'm fine, Nanny, really I am. I shan't be home for a little while. If you tell them that without any details…'

'Anyway, you're safe enough with Dr Galbraith and you've got the phone.'

At the hospital she got out with Wilkins and walked round with him while the doctor went inside. She was hungry and untidy and her skirt was covered with dried earth from the ploughed field but she felt happy; she had made herself useful even in a humble capacity and Dr Galbraith's brisk thanks had warmed her. Presently she saw him leave the hospital and went back to the car, into which Wilkins scrambled with evident relief. He had walked enough.

'Ben—that foot?' said Leonora, getting into the car. 'Will he be all right?'

'He's in Theatre now. If anyone can save it, it's the man who's operating.'

'Oh, good.' She added fiercely, 'He needs his feet—it's his livelihood…'

When he didn't answer, she said, 'What about your other patients? You had just started your round, hadn't you?'

'Mrs Crisp has sorted them out for me; there's nothing really urgent. I've a surgery this evening and I can do a round this afternoon. We'll go back now and clean up and have a meal.'

He picked up the phone again. 'Cricket? I'm bringing Miss Crosby back with me for lunch. We'll need to clean up first—say half an hour? Something quick.'

'Who's Cricket?' asked Leonora. 'And you don't have to ask me to lunch. Drop me off at the gate as you go past.'

'Cricket is my manservant; he runs my home. I should be totally lost without him. And will you lunch with me, Leonora? It is the least I can do to make amends for spoiling your quiet day.' He glanced at her. 'Besides, you're badly in need of a wash and brush-up.'

It was hardly a flattering reason for being asked to lunch. She had half a mind to refuse but curiosity to see his house and find out something about him got the better of her resentment, and then common sense came to the rescue and she laughed. He was offering practical help and she was hungry and, as he had pointed out, badly in need of a good wash.

'Thank you; that would be nice,' she told him sedately.

It was as he drew up before his door that Leonora spoke again.

'What about Wilkins? Do you have a dog?'

He came round the car to open her door. 'He's welcome to come in. I have a dog. My sister has borrowed him for a week or two while her husband is away. He'll be back next week. Cricket has two cats. I hardly think they will be in any danger from Wilkins; a remarkably mild animal, isn't he?'

'He's a darling,' said Leonora warmly, 'and he's partial to cats.'

Cricket opened the door, shook the hand she offered and instantly approved of her. Even with a smudge on her cheek and dirty hands she was a very pretty girl. Plenty of her, too; he liked a woman to look like a woman and here was one who, he decided, lived up to his strict ideals of what a young lady should be.

He ushered her indoors, tut-tutted gently at the state of her skirt and led her to the downstairs cloakroom. Halfway across the hall the doctor called after them.

'Get Miss Crosby a dressing gown, Cricket, and see if you can get some of that mud off her skirt, will you?'

'Certainly, sir. Is ten minutes too soon for lunch?'

'Just right. If I'm not down show Miss Crosby into the sitting room, will you? Thanks!'

Then he went up upstairs two at a time and Cricket ushered Leonora into the cloakroom, begged a moment's grace and came back within a minute with a bathrobe. 'If you would let me have your skirt, Miss Crosby, I'll have it as good as new before you leave.' He smiled at her. 'I will keep an eye on your dog, miss.'

She thanked him and, left alone, began on the task of getting clean again. Her skirt was horribly stained and it smelled, naturally enough, of the farm.

Presently, with a nicely washed face and her hair neatly pinned up, she got into the robe, opened the door cautiously and peered round it. Cricket had said that he would show her where to go...

Dr Galbraith was in the hall, lounging against the wall, Wilkins panting happily beside him.

'Come on out,' he invited. 'Cricket has lunch ready and I have to be at the surgery in less than an hour.'

He sounded, reflected Leonora, like someone's brother, and she did as she was told, following him, a little hampered by the robe, across the hall and into the sitting room overlooking the garden. Their lunch had been laid on a round table near the open fire and something smelled delicious. She pushed the over-long sleeves up her arms and sat down without further ado to sample Cricket's artichoke soup.

The doctor had made no comment about her appearance but he smiled a little at the sensible way she had tucked up the sleeves and wrapped the yards of extra material around her person, and he liked her lack of self-consciousness.

The soup was followed by a cheese pudding and a salad and they drank tonic water before Cricket brought in the coffee-tray. Since there wasn't much time and it was obvious to her that this wasn't a social occasion, Leonora made no attempt to make conversation.

The moment they had drunk their coffee she said, 'I'll go and put my own clothes on again. You'll want to be going.' She smiled at him. 'Thank you for lunch; it was delicious.'

He got up with her. 'I'll be in the garden with Wilkins,' he told her, and watched her gather up the trailing robe as she crossed the hall. A sensible girl, he thought; no non-sense about her. Beamish was a lucky man. He frowned. She was too good for the fellow.

Cricket had worked wonders with the stains on her skirt. Really, they had almost gone; he had pressed it too. How wonderful to have someone like that to look after you, Leonora mused. No wonder the doctor wasn't married; he must be very comfortable as he was. She hurried into her clothes, thanked Cricket for his help and got into the car once more.

'Drop us off in the village,' she told the doctor. 'Anywhere along the main street will do.'

'I shall drive you home.' His voice dared her to argue about it and she sat silent for a moment, trying to think of something to say. At length she said, 'You told me you had a dog; what do you call him?'

'Tod.'

'Unusual—is it a foreign name?'

She saw his slow smile. 'No, no. It isn't a name of my choosing but a young lady for whom I have an affection named him and Tod it is.'

Ha, thought Leonora, the girlfriend—there was bound to be someone. Her fertile imagination was already at work. Small and fragile and blue-eyed. Fair hair beautifully dressed, and wearing the very latest in fashion. She would have one of those sickening voices that made one squirm. Leonora, disliking this figment of her imagination, reflected that she would be the kind of girl to call a dog by such a silly name.

She said inadequately, 'How nice,' and waved to Mrs Pike standing outside her shop.

When he stopped before her home she said frostily, still influenced by her fancies, 'Thank you so much, Doctor. I do hope you won't be too busy for the rest of the day. And I hope that poor man will get better.'

He got out to open her door and stood beside her, looking at her thoughtfully. 'I'll let you know, and it is I who thank you for your help.'

He waited while she opened the door, and Wilkins rushed past her, intent on getting to the warmth of the

kitchen. 'Well, goodbye,' said Leonora awkwardly, and
went indoors.

Her mother and father were in the drawing room.

'Darling, where have you been? So awkward—I mean,
Nanny had to leave everything and go down to the village. Why ever should Dr Galbraith want you? An accident at Willer's Farm, Nanny says. Surely they could
have managed without you?'

Leonora opened her mouth to explain but her mother
went on, 'Your Tony phoned. He was quite annoyed because you weren't here. Perhaps you had better give him
a ring presently and explain.'

'Did he say why he had phoned?'

'No, dear. We were chatting for a while and I quite
forgot to ask.'

Leonora went to the kitchen and found Nanny preparing oxtail for supper.

'I'm sorry, Nanny, but Dr Galbraith didn't give me a
chance to refuse...'

'Quite right too. Bad accident, was it? He wouldn't
have asked for your help if he hadn't needed it. Tell me
about it. It's too early for tea but you could get the tray
ready while I finish this and get it into the oven.'

So Leonora recited her morning's activities, not leaving anything out, detailing her lunch and the perfections
of the doctor's house.

'Sounds nice,' said Nanny. 'And that man of his—
was he nice?'

'Yes, very. He took my skirt and cleaned it. You've no
idea how filthy it was—he pressed it too.'

'I'm sorry about Ben, but the doctor will see him right
and the Willers will keep an eye on him—give him light
work if he can't manage his usual jobs.'

Leonora ate a scone from the plate Nanny had just put on the table.

'You'll get fat,' said Nanny. 'Your young man rang up. Put out, he was.' She shot a quick glance at Leonora. 'Won't do no harm just for once...'

'What do you mean, Nanny?'

'Well, love, the men like to do a bit of chasing. It's not a bad idea to be difficult to get at times.'

'Nanny, you naughty old thing, where did you learn to play fast and loose with the gentlemen?' Leonora was laughing.

'Never you mind! It's sound common sense. No need to say you're sorry you weren't waiting here by the phone in the hopes he'd ring up.'

She picked up the plate of scones. 'They're for tea, Miss Leonora, and I'm not making another batch. You'd best go and tidy yourself. What the doctor thought of you I'll never know.'

The doctor was a man to keep his thoughts to himself so Nanny was never likely to find out. All the same she would have been pleased if she had found out; she had never taken a fancy to Tony Beamish—not good enough for her Miss Leonora, but clever enough to make her think she was in love with him.

'No good'll come of it!' said Nanny, buttering scones.

Leonora, feeling guilty but bearing Nanny's advice in mind, made no attempt to phone Tony, although once or twice during the rest of the afternoon and evening she very nearly did. She was on the point of going to bed when he rang up.

He was still annoyed. 'Where were you?' he wanted to know. 'What's all this about going to an accident and why didn't you phone me as soon as you got home?'

'Well, I am never quite sure where you are. It was a bad accident—one of the men on Willer's Farm—the tractor overturned—'

'Spare me the details,' begged Tony impatiently. 'And why you had to have anything to do with it I can't imagine.'

She told him, leaving out quite a bit because he was getting impatient again.

'Utterly ridiculous,' said Tony. 'That doctor must be thoroughly incompetent.'

'Don't be silly!' Leonora heard his indrawn breath. She had never called him silly before.

'I'm busy,' snapped Tony, 'and obviously you're over-wrought. I hope you will have the good sense to keep out of the man's way in future.' He rang off without saying goodbye, confident that he would get a letter from her in the morning begging forgiveness for being such a bad-tempered girl.

Leonora, however, had no intention of putting pen to paper. Love was blind but not as blind as all that; Tony hadn't sounded like Tony at all. Was there a side to him which she hadn't yet discovered? It wasn't as though she particularly liked Dr Galbraith. For that matter, he didn't particularly like her, ordering her around and telling her what to do and that she needed a wash.

Despite the horror of the accident, she had enjoyed herself. Being useful—really useful—had made her feel quite different. She would drive to Bath and visit Ben. Perhaps there was something that her father could do for him—not financial help, of course, that wasn't possible, but influence with authority, perhaps.

She drove over to Bath two days later with a box of

fruit and some flowers and found her way to the ward where Ben was lying.

He was in bed, propped up by pillows, his leg under a cradle, his weather-beaten face pale and lined, although he greeted her cheerfully.

She sat down beside his bed, offered the fruit and flowers and asked how he was getting on.

''Ad me foot put together again,' he told her. 'Take a bit of time, it will, but I'll be able to walk, so they tell me. Mustn't grumble.'

'How long will you be here?'

'A while yet. Got to learn to walk again, 'a'n't I?'

'Yes, of course. You'll go back to Willer's?'

'Mr Willer, 'e'll see me right…'

'I think you can claim compensation, Ben.'

'So 'tis said. Mr Willer, 'e'll attend to that.' He said awkwardly, 'I'm downright thankful for your help, Miss Crosby. Dr Galbraith told me as 'ow you gived a hand. 'E's been a trump too. Comes to see me regular; knows the surgeon who done me foot.'

'That's nice. Ben, is there anything that you want? Money? Books? Clothes?'

'I'm fine, thank you, miss. Proper good treatment I'm getting too. Pretty nurses and all.'

She stayed for an hour, dredging up bits of local gossip to interest him, but when the tea-trolley arrived she bade him goodbye. 'I'll be back,' she told him. 'The Willers are coming to see you in a day or two—I'll come again next week.'

She left the ward and was walking along the long corridor which led to the main staircase when she saw Dr Galbraith coming towards her. He wasn't alone; there were a couple of younger men in white jackets and a white-coated man with him, and although he wasn't wearing a white coat Leonora had the feeling that he was as remote as his companion, the possessor of knowledge she knew nothing of and therefore someone difficult to get to know, to be friends with.

Face to face, she wished him a good afternoon and made to walk on, but he put out an arm and caught her gently by the wrist.

'Leonora? You have been to see Ben? This is Mr Kirby who operated on his foot.'

He looked at his companion. 'This is Miss Crosby, who very kindly came to my aid at the farm.'

She shook hands and murmured that she mustn't keep them.

'How did you come? I'll give you a lift back…'

'I drove over, but thank you all the same.' She included everyone in her goodbye, aware that she wasn't behaving in her usual calm and collected manner. The look of amusement on Dr Galbraith's face sent the colour into her cheeks, which made things even worse.

It was two days later when her mother looked up from her letters over breakfast.

'Our little dinner party, Leonora. I thought twelve of us—just a nice number, don't you agree? We'll ask Colonel Howes and Nora, the Willoughbys, of course, the Merediths, the vicar—Dulcie Hunt is visiting her mother so he'll be glad of a little social life—and Dr Galbraith, and Tony simply must manage to come. We'll have it on a Saturday; that should make it easy for him.'

She counted on her fingers. 'With us that's twelve—'

'Mother,' said Leonora, 'I don't think it's a good idea to ask Dr Galbraith if Tony comes. They don't like each other…'

'Nonsense, darling, of course they do.' She made a great business of buttering her toast. 'Anyway, I've already invited them.' She gave Leonora a quick glance. 'Well, I hadn't much to do yesterday so I wrote the invitations and your father gave them to the postman in the afternoon.'

'When for?' asked Leonora. 'And have you any ideas about feeding them?'

'Darling, what a funny way of putting it... Saturday week. That gives Tony lots of time to arrange his work. I thought we might have artichoke soup. You did say there were a lot still in the garden. Willer sent over two brace of pheasants—a kind of thank-you for your help, he said; wasn't that nice? There must be some kind of vegetables still in the kitchen garden to go with them, and I'm sure Nanny will think of some delicious sweet. Thank heaven there are at least a couple of bottles of claret in the cellar.'

She smiled, well pleased with herself. 'So you see, darling, there's almost nothing to do and it'll cost hardly anything, and if we use the best silver and those lace table mats and you concoct one of your centrepieces it will all look much more than it is, if you see what I mean.'

'Yes, Mother,' said Leonora. Of course it would cost something—the best coffee beans, cream, cranberries for the sauce, more cream for the soup, after-dinner mints, sherry—two bottles at least—and a bottle of whisky for any of the men who wanted it. Her father wouldn't take kindly to her using his...

Then there would be bacon and baby sausages to go with the pheasant, and the 'delicious sweet' still to be decided upon. They couldn't afford it but it was too late to tell her mother that. Leonora cleared up the breakfast things and went to the kitchen to give a hand with the washing-up and confer with Nanny about a suitable pudding.

Tony phoned during the week. He had managed to squeeze out a weekend, he told her, and would be down at teatime on the Saturday, adding the rider that he hoped her father would be up to a dinner party. 'He's not as young as he was!' he cautioned. 'We must keep an eye on him.'

He was in such good humour that she thought it prudent not to mention that Dr Galbraith was to be one of the guests. After all, there would be twelve of them there and they didn't need to do more than bid each other a civil good evening. She must remember to make sure that they were as far apart at the table as possible.

She went once more to see Ben, anxious not to meet the doctor in the hospital but disappointed nonetheless when she didn't. Ben was doing well. He had been out of bed on crutches and was having physiotherapy. It would take a bit of time, he assured her, but he'd be as good as new by the time they'd finished with him.

She left him a bag of fruit and some magazines and drove home. When she saw Dr Galbraith again she must ask him just how fit Ben would be. The thought struck her that she might not have the chance to speak to him at the dinner party, not if Tony was there...

Saturday week came and with it a dozen or more things to see to. The floral arrangement she had already contrived from various bits of greenery, some daffodils and primroses and aconites from the neglected border at the front of the house. She polished the table, helped Nanny put in the extra leaf and arranged the lace mats.

The silver was old, kept in a baize bag in what had once been the butler's pantry, and she had polished it to a dazzling gleam; she had done the same with the crystal glasses and had washed the Coalport dinner service. They combined to make an elegant dinner table, and her mother, coming to see that things were just as she liked them, gave a satisfied sigh.

'We may be poor,' she observed, 'but we can still show the world a brave face. It looks very nice, dear.'

Leonora filled the Georgian salt cellars and went to the kitchen to start the syllabub. A dozen eggs was an extravagance; on the other hand the yolks could be made into *créme brûlée*, which if it wasn't all eaten at dinner could be used up on the following day...

She went upstairs after tea and looked through her wardrobe. Her clothes were good, for they had been bought when there had been enough money to have the best. They still looked good, too, but were sadly out of date. There was a silver-grey velvet somewhere at the back of the cupboard...

She hauled it out and tried it on and it didn't look too bad—very plain, with its modest, unfashionable neckline and long sleeves, but it fitted her nicely. She had a quick shower and got dressed; Tony had said that he would arrive in plenty of time for drinks and there were still one or two jobs to do in the kitchen, where Nanny was working miracles with the pheasants.

Downstairs she put on a pinny, tucked up her sleeves and began to whip the cream. The evening should be a success, she thought; her mother was pleased, her father was better, though somewhat irascible, Tony was coming...

He had come; he stood in the doorway looking at her. Frowning. She looked up, smiling as he came in and then puzzled.

'My dear girl, do you have to spend your time in the kitchen? The guests will be here in ten minutes or so and I expected to be met by an elegant fiancée sitting in the drawing room doing nothing.'

She made the mistake of thinking that he was joking. 'Tony, don't be so absurd. Of course I have to be here. Nanny can't possibly manage on her own; she's doing two people's work as it is. I'm almost ready. Go and pour yourself a drink; Father and Mother should be down at any minute.'

He turned away without another word, and since the cream had reached the peak of perfection she hardly noticed his going. The fleeting thought that he hadn't kissed her or even said how glad he was to see her passed through her head, but just at that moment she had a lot to think about if the dinner party was to be a success.

Ten minutes later she slipped into the drawing room to find that everyone had arrived, and she went from one to the other, exchanging greetings. They were all old friends—excepting Dr Galbraith, elegant in black tie, talking to Nora. He smiled down at her and she offered a hand, and since Tony had made no effort to speak to her, had barely glanced in her direction she let it lie in his firm grasp for longer than necessary and gave him a bewitching smile in return.

'I'm glad you could come. Have you got your dog— Tod—home yet?'

'Yesterday. He brought my sister with him. She had to return home at once, though—her youngest has the measles.'

'Oh, what bad luck, but nice to get it over with when you're young. We had it at about the same time, didn't we, Nora? We must have been seven or eight...'

The doctor stared down at her; she must have been an engaging small girl with those enormous eyes, he thought.

'Yes, well,' said Leonora, aware of the stare. 'I must just nip along to the kitchen—the soup, you know...'

They watched her go. 'She's such a dear,' said Nora. 'She practically runs this great place on her own. If it wasn't for Nanny she could never cope.'

Mrs Sims from the village, who occasionally obliged with the heavy cleaning, was waiting in the kitchen ready to carry in the soup tureen; the pheasants were done to a turn, everything was fine, declared Nanny.

Leonora went back to the drawing room, bent to whisper to her mother and everyone crossed the hall to the dining room. Leonora had had a fire burning in its elegant grate all day, sighing over every shovelful of coal and every log, but appearances had to be kept up and the room was nicely warm now. She took her seat beside Tony and watched Mrs Sims place the tureen in front of her mother. So far, so good...

Chapter 4

There was a good deal of lively conversation over the soup. Leonora, listening to Colonel Howes describing the delights of a genuine Indian curry, hardly noticed Tony's silence on her other side. When she was free to turn to him, he was talking to Nora beside him.

She glanced down the table; Dr Galbraith was sitting beside her mother, who was talking animatedly, and the vicar and her father were discussing the local fishing.

The soup plates were removed and her father began to carve the pheasants—quite a lengthy business, but the claret had loosened tongues and everyone was chatting, relaxed among friends...

'Will you stay until Monday?' she asked Tony. She smiled at him, no longer vexed; he was probably tired after a busy week and he hated to see her working around the house.

'There doesn't seem to be much point if you're going to be in the kitchen all day.'

She refused to get needled. 'Well, I shan't be. We might go for a good walk—blow the London cobwebs away.'

'London at this time of year is rather delightful. How is your father? I thought he looked very tired.'

'Did you?' She frowned. 'He's so much better—'

'I shall have a word with that doctor of his before I go—make sure he's getting proper treatment.'

Leonora helped herself to sprouts. 'Quite unnecessary, Tony; Father is in good hands.'

'It seems to me that that fellow has cast a spell over you all—he's probably quite incompetent!'

Leonora's eyes glittered with temper. 'That's an abominable thing to say. Would you have known how to get a man with a crushed foot free from a farm tractor?'

She turned back to Colonel Howes and began an animated conversation about the extension to be built to the village hall, and the doctor, watching her from under lowered lids and replying suitably to Lady Crosby's chatter, wondered what she and Tony were quarrelling about. They were being very discreet about it, but they were quarrelling.

In due course the pheasant was replaced by syllabub and the *crème brûlée,* and since Lady Crosby refused to accede to modern ideas the ladies were led away to the drawing room while the men remained to drink the port Sir William had brought up from the cellar.

Leonora slid away as the ladies went into the drawing room, to reappear presently with the tray of coffeepot, cream and sugar. The small table had already been placed by her mother's chair, bearing the Worcester cof-

fee-cups and the silver dishes of after-dinner mints. By
the time the men joined them, they were deep in comfortable talk—clothes, the price of food, their grandchildren,
and the difficulty of getting a gardener.

When the men came in there was a good deal of rear-
ranging of seats and Leonora was kept busy offering more
coffee and refilling cups, and by the time she had seen to
everyone Tony was sitting between Nora and Mrs Willoughby on one of the old-fashioned sofas. So she went
and sat by the vicar and listened to him talking about his
wife, to discover after a few minutes that Dr Galbraith
had joined them. A moment later her father walked over.

'Come along to my study,' he invited the vicar. 'I'll
show you that new trout fly I've just tied.' Which left
Leonora and the doctor together.

'A pleasant evening, Leonora.'

'Thank you.'

'Why were you and young Beamish quarrelling?' He
smiled. 'Still are?'

She was getting used to the way he eschewed the soft
approach. 'Well, you see, I was in the kitchen when he
got here—and he was disappointed because I wasn't in
the drawing room.'

'Quite.'

'I should have thought of that but I had the cream to
whip. I didn't think it mattered much. I mean, would you
have minded?'

'In the circumstances, and seeing that the success of
the dinner party largely rested on the cream being properly whipped, no!' He put down his coffee-cup. 'But there
was something else, wasn't there?'

'Well, yes. He thinks Father doesn't look well.' She
went pink. 'He—he wondered if...'

'Ah—he doubts my expertise.'

'I'm so sorry. I mean, no one else does; we all trust you and think you're a very good doctor.'

He hid a smile. 'Thank you. I won't let it worry me.'

'He said that he would talk to you.'

'Splendid. And since he is coming to join us now, what could be a better opportunity?' He glanced at her troubled face. 'Go and talk to someone else,' he suggested quietly, and turned a bland face to Tony.

He stood up as Leonora moved away and Tony frowned, put at a disadvantage by the doctor's height and size.

'You wanted to talk to me?' the doctor enquired pleasantly.

'Look here,' began Tony, 'I'm not at all happy about Sir William...'

Dr Galbraith said nothing.

'He isn't a young man.'

The doctor inclined his head; he looked so exactly like an eminent doctor listening with courteous patience to one of his patients that Tony's face darkened with annoyance.

'Isn't it ridiculous that Sir William should go on living in this great house? He needs to be in something smaller and modern where he would be properly looked after.' He caught the doctor's eye. 'Oh, Leonora looks after him very well, I know, but she's limited—no money. Now, if he were to sell the place or hand it over to her, I could restore it.'

'Yes?' queried the doctor gently. 'Would you live in it—with Leonora, of course?'

Tony said rudely, 'Oh, of course. We'd have a flat in town but we could come for weekends, bring guests.' He stopped, aware that he was talking too much. He essayed a smile. 'My dear chap, I'm sure you could persuade Sir William to settle in something more suitable to his age and lifestyle.'

The doctor said evenly, 'No, I couldn't do that. It isn't my business. Sir William lives here, it is his home, his ancestor's home, he loves it. Surely if you intend to restore the place there is no reason why he and Lady Crosby shouldn't live here? Why move? There is ample room for them, is there not?'

'I can't see that it is any concern of yours,' said Tony sulkily.

The vicar had joined them again and presently Tony went away. The talk hadn't been very successful, he reflected, and went in search of Leonora. He found her talking to Nora, who finally drifted away, so that he was able to give her his version of his talk with Dr Galbraith.

'Well,' said Leonora in a matter-of-fact way, 'he's quite right; there's no reason why Father should move from here. It's a silly idea. It would break his heart, besides being an enormous undertaking. You have no idea of the stuff that's stored in the attics.'

She saw his annoyance and said quickly, 'It's very good of you to bother, Tony—I'm sure Father appreciates your concern; we all do.' She added soberly, 'I suppose in due time I shall inherit the place, but not for a long while yet. If you want to restore it then, I won't mind...'

Tony said soberly, 'My dear girl, we shall probably be in our dotage. The place needs a complete overhaul now but it can't be done while your mother and father are still here.'

Leonora gave him a puzzled look and he saw that he had said too much. He took her arm and smiled at her.

'Darling, don't let's worry about it. As you say, your parents are very happy here. It is a lovely old place, just the right background for a dinner party. I must say it's a splendid evening and dinner was delicious. I can see that I am going to be very proud of my wife.'

They were words which dulled the faint feeling of unease Leonora had been trying to ignore. She told him about the pheasants and the artichoke soup. 'So, you see, it cost hardly anything...'

He squeezed her arm and laughed with her and Dr Galbraith, watching them from the other side of the room, thought it was a great pity that a sensible girl like Leonora should be taken in by young Beamish. She was too good for him and too honest, and once she had married him and found out about him, as she was bound to do eventually, she would keep her marriage vows and be a loyal wife and quietly break her heart. A pity that some decent man couldn't come along and marry her before Beamish had a chance to complete his plans.

It seemed strange to the doctor that Sir William hadn't seen what was happening, with all this talk about his health and the need to move away from his home. Could he not see that Beamish wanted to get his hands on the lovely old place and use it for his own ends? The doctor frowned; it seemed likely that the man was going to marry Leonora for that very reason.

He shrugged his enormous shoulders; it was none of his business.

Cricket, advancing to meet him as he let himself into his house later that evening, enquired as to whether he had had an enjoyable time. 'A very pleasant young lady, Miss Crosby,' said Cricket. 'I have had occasion to have a few words with Miss South—her old nanny, sir—and she told me that she is a most capable person and shortly to be married.'

'You old gossip,' said the doctor cheerfully. 'I had a very pleasant evening and now I am going to take Tod for a quick walk. I'll lock up when I get back.'

Presently he did just that, saw Tod into his basket in the kitchen and took himself off to bed. He had had a long and busy day and he slept the sleep of a tired man, never once thinking of Leonora.

However, Leonora, tired though she was, didn't sleep well. Tony had sewn the seeds of doubt in her mind; perhaps her father would be better off living in a smaller house where there was no need of buckets to catch the drips when it rained and the plumbing was up to date. What did Tony intend to do with her house after they were married? He had been enthusiastic about restoring it but for what reason? He had made it plain on several occasions that they would live in London because of his work.

She shook up her pillows and tried to settle down. They would have to have a talk about it, fix the date of the wedding and discuss their future. She closed her eyes and presently slept uneasily.

There was no chance to talk to Tony in the morning; when they got back from church he went with her father to the library and over lunch the talk was of nothing much. She suggested over their coffee that they might go for a walk but he told her that he would have to go back to London within the hour. 'You should see the pile of work on my desk,' he told her. 'But I was determined to come to your dinner party, darling. It was a great success. I'll be down again just as soon as I can manage it.'

She said soberly, 'Tony, I think we must have a talk—

about the wedding and where we're to live and—oh, a whole lot of things I'm not sure about.'

'Of course, darling. We will the very next time I come.' He bent to kiss her. 'You're my darling girl and we are going to be very happy.' He spoilt it for her by adding, 'And very rich...'

'I don't care about being rich, Tony.'

'You will. Lovely clothes, and theatres, and meeting all the right people.'

She said coolly, 'The right people live here too, Tony!'

He kissed her again. 'Yes, of course they do. I'll phone you this evening.'

It was later in the week, when she had walked down to the village to Mrs Pike's shop, that that lady leaned over the counter to say confidentially, 'Those gentlemen staying over at the Blue Man—they've not been bothering you, Miss Leonora?'

'Bothering me? I didn't know there was anyone staying in the village, Mrs Pike, and why should they bother me?'

'Well, they been asking questions about the house, wanting to know how many rooms there was and how much land there was with it. When Mr Bowles over at the Blue Man spoke up and asked them why they didn't go to the house and ask Sir William since they were so anxious to know, they shut up like clams, said as how they were just curious. All the same, they've been sitting in the bar of a night, dropping questions here and there. Your pa's not thinking of selling, like?'

'Absolutely not, Mrs Pike. What sort of men are they?'

'Oh, gents, miss, quite the city men, if you get my meaning; they wears ties and carries umbrellas. Nicely spoken too.'

'You don't know where they're from? I mean, has some house agent got it into his head that my father is going to sell the house? I can't understand it. Perhaps I'd better go across and tell them that they are mistaken.'

'Oh, I wouldn't do that, miss,' said Mrs Pike, 'seeing as how they'd know at once who you was. You leave it to me; I'll get my George to go over for a pint this evening. He's a sharp one; perhaps he can ferret something out.'

'Would he? That would be very kind. Mrs Pike, you won't talk about this to anyone, will you? I can assure you that my father has absolutely no intention of leaving the house.' She picked up her shopping. 'I'll come down in the morning…'

She went back home wishing there were someone she could talk to about it, but that wasn't possible; her parents would be upset and worried and Nanny would probably go down to the Blue Man and demand to see these men and give them a piece of her mind. A pity that she wasn't on better terms with Dr Galbraith, she reflected; he was someone one could confide in and get sensible advice from in return.

She worried about it all day and half the night and, making some excuse about fetching a particular brand of biscuits Mrs Pike was getting for her, went to the village directly after breakfast.

There were several people in the shop, and when it was empty at last Mrs Pike seemed very reluctant to talk.

'Mr Pike heard something?' she asked Mrs Pike. 'Something you don't like to tell me?'

'Well, yes, miss. Mind you, it's only gossip; you can't believe half you hear these days. I dare say there's a good reason…'

Leonora smiled and looked so calm that Mrs Pike decided to talk after all.

'Well, it's like this, miss—these gentlemen has come here to look over the house and see if it's worth doing up and if the land is good for selling to build on…'

At Leonora's quick breath she paused. 'The house is to be a kind of headquarters for visiting businessmen—them big nobs with millions.' She eyed Leonora carefully. 'I hates to say this, Miss Crosby, but the man who sent them is your Mr Beamish.'

Leonora had gone very pale but she said composedly, 'Mrs Pike, I can't thank you enough—or Mr Pike—for your help. I'm sure there's some misunderstanding but at least I know whom to see about it. I'm quite sure that my father knows nothing about this but I'll talk to Mr Beamish about it. There must be an explanation.'

'Yes, miss, that's what we thought. Mr Beamish seems such a nice gentleman…'

'Yes,' said Leonora, and added, 'I'll be off. I want to do some gardening.'

She made herself walk normally out of the shop, even turning to smile at Mrs Pike from the doorway, and somehow she had to go through the village looking the same as usual. If she could manage not to think about it until she got home… She gulped; when she got home she wouldn't be able to think about it either, let alone say anything.

She marched down the street, saying good morning and smiling as she went, with Wilkins close at her heels. She was going past the surgery when Dr Galbraith came out, shutting the door behind him. She would have gone past him with a brief greeting but he fell into step beside her.

'What is the matter?' he asked, and added, 'No, don't tell me for the moment. The car's across the street; we'll go back to Buntings.'

Because she would have burst into tears if she had attempted to speak just then, she went with him and got into the car and sat silently with Wilkins's elderly whiskers pressed into the back of her neck.

At the house the doctor got out, opened her door, let Wilkins out, and as Cricket came to the door said briskly, 'Could we have coffee, Cricket? In the sitting room, I think; Wilkins can go into the garden with Tod.'

Cricket cast a look at Leonora's face, murmured soothingly and went to the kitchen while the doctor led her across the hall and into the pleasant little room bright with sunshine.

The door to the garden was open and racing across the grass lawn came a dog, barking his pleasure at the sight of them. It was impossible to tell what kind of a dog he was, but there was a strong bias towards an Alsatian and more than a hint of retriever; he had a noble head and a curly coat and a feathery tail and liquid brown eyes.

'Tod,' said the doctor briefly. 'Sit down here; Wilkins can go into the garden too and make friends.' He said over one shoulder, 'Cry if you want to.'

'I have no intention of crying,' said Leonora stiffly, and burst into tears.

She hadn't wept like that for a long time, not since Bouncer, the family cat, had died of old age, lying in the sun at the back of the house. She sobbed and sniffed, hardly aware that she was making a fine mess of the doctor's jacket, her head buried against his shoulder while she muttered and mumbled and wept.

Presently she lifted a sodden face. 'I'm so sorry; I really am. I never cry—well, almost never.'

'A mistake; there's nothing like it for relieving the feelings.'

His voice was kind and his arms comforting. 'Now mop up and sit down and tell me all about it.'

He offered a large white handkerchief and nodded to Cricket to put the coffee-tray down on a side table, then he went to the door and stood watching the two dogs, who were still cautiously getting to know each other, not looking at her, giving her time to wipe away her tears and tuck back her hair. She gave a final sniff. 'I'll let you have your hanky back,' she told him. 'I'm quite all right now.'

He poured their coffee and gave her a cup and offered biscuits to the dogs.

'They seem to like each other,' said Leonora, anxious to get the conversation onto an impersonal footing again.

'Naturally. They are intelligent animals.' He sat down opposite her but not facing her directly. 'Begin at the beginning, Leonora.'

'It's all so silly; I mean, I don't believe a word of it. There must be some mistake.'

'If there is, we can, perhaps, discover it.' He was sitting back in his chair, quite at ease—a man, she reflected, who could solve the knottiest problem without fuss.

'Well,' she began, and poured it all out in rather a muddle, for, just for once, her common sense had forsaken her. 'I simply can't understand why Tony has sent these men. I'm quite sure he has said nothing to Father. Besides, Father wouldn't even listen to a plan like that—' she gulped '—to build houses on our land—and where are we supposed to live? It doesn't make sense.'

It made sense to the doctor although he didn't say so.

'Would you like to go to London and talk to Tony? Ask for an explanation? There may be a reason of which you know nothing. Perhaps he intends to surprise you in some way, but if you tell him that you are worried about the rumours he will tell you what he has in mind. Since he is to marry you, I imagine it is some scheme beneficial to you and your parents.'

He didn't imagine anything of the kind—Tony Beamish was capable of manipulating affairs to suit himself—but perhaps it wasn't as bad as Leonora thought it was. After all, the man loved her, presumably; he wouldn't want to hurt her in any way, even if it meant forgoing whatever ambitious plans he had.

Leonora said suddenly, 'I think you're right. I'll go up to town and see him. I'll not tell him I'm going. I've an aunt living in Chelsea—I can say I'm going to see her and go and see him after he gets back from work.'

'That sounds like a good idea. I have to go up to town myself tomorrow afternoon. I'll be there for a day or two. If you're ready to come back with me, well and good; otherwise you can get a train.'

'Thank you; I'd like that. I'll stay the night, perhaps two nights. I'm very grateful for your help.' She put down her coffee-cup. 'I'll go home…'

'I dare say you would like to wash your face first,' he observed in a matter-of-fact voice. 'Cricket will show you where to go.'

She was still pale when she rejoined him but quite composed. He doubted if her parents would notice anything amiss although Nanny probably would. She thanked Cricket for the coffee and waited while the doctor saw the dogs onto the back seat of the car.

As he drove the short distance to her home he told her, 'I'll be leaving around two o'clock—I'll call for you.'

At the house he got out to open her door and then allow a reluctant Wilkins to join her. 'You're quite sure that you want to go and see Beamish?'

She nodded. 'Oh, yes. Otherwise I'm going to fuss and fret, aren't I?'

He smiled down at her. 'You're a sensible woman, Leonora.'

After he had driven away she went slowly indoors, not sure that she liked being called 'a sensible woman' in that casual manner.

Her mother and father saw nothing unusual in her wish to visit Aunt Marion. 'A good idea, darling,' said her mother. 'It will make a nice change for you, and Aunt Marion loves company. Perhaps you'll see Tony. Don't stay too long, though; remember there's the village bazaar coming up and I've promised that we'll help—take a stall or something. Mrs Willoughby will tell you, I've no doubt. Lydia Dowling will be organising it so I expect you'll have to go to see her to talk about it.'

Nanny looked at Leonora sharply when she told her that she was going to visit her aunt for a day or two.

'A bit sudden, isn't it? Going to see that Mr Beamish, are you?'

'Well, yes, I expect so. Nanny, why don't you like him?'

Nanny bent over a saucepan, inspecting its contents. 'We all have our likes and dislikes,' she said reluctantly. 'I dare say I'll get around to liking him in a while.' She sniffed. 'Perhaps he'll improve with marriage.'

Leonora, packing an overnight bag later, hesitated as to what to take with her. She intended to see Tony on the following evening. There wouldn't be time to change when she reached her aunt's house but if she stayed for a second day she would need a dress, since Aunt Marion had old-fashioned notions about changing for dinner.

She crammed a stone-coloured jersey dress in with her night things and added a pair of high-heeled shoes. She would go in the tweed suit and easy shoes; both had seen better days but they had been good when new. Her handbag and gloves were beyond reproach. She had a very small income from a godmother's bequest—money she seldom touched, saving it for a rainy day. Well, that day had come; she would nip down to the village in the morning and get Mrs Pike to cash a cheque…

The doctor was punctual. He came into the house and spent five minutes talking to her mother and father before settling her in the car and getting in beside her. Beyond asking her if she was comfortable he had little to say as he drove along minor roads to reach the M4, and once on the motorway he shot smoothly ahead.

'Your aunt knows you are coming?'

'Yes, I phoned her last night. She's a very hospitable person and very sociable. She may not be there when I arrive but she has a marvellous housekeeper who's been with her for ages. I'm to stay for as long as I like.'

'Will you give me her phone number before I drop you off? I'll phone you when I'm ready to leave in case you would like a lift back.'

'That's very kind of you. I don't expect to be in London for more than a day or two. If Tony's free he might drive me home.' Before she could stop herself, she added, 'I'm sure it's a mistake—a misunderstanding. He'll explain…'

'There is always an explanation, Leonora, although sometimes we have to look for one. Will you see him this evening?'

'Yes, I'll go to his flat. I've never been there; it's in a street just off Curzon Street.'

The doctor raised his eyebrows. 'A very good address. He is a successful businessman, I should suppose.'

Somehow, talking about Tony made the whole puzzling business seem far-fetched. She said slowly, 'I wonder if I'm just being very silly…?'

'No. If the whole thing is, as you say, a misunderstanding, then the quicker it is put to rights the better. Five minutes' talk together and probably you will both be laughing over the matter.'

'Yes, I'm sure you're right. Are you going to be busy while you're in London?'

'A seminar and a couple of lectures I want to attend, friends to look up. A theatre, perhaps.'

He would have friends, she reflected, and since he was single, handsome and an asset to any dinner table he would be much in demand. Besides, perhaps he would see this girl who had called his dog by such a silly name. She switched her thoughts away from that; it was none of her business what he did in his private life.

Her aunt lived in a narrow street of small but elegant houses; the doctor, following Leonora's directions calmly, drew up before its pristine door, flanked by two bay trees in tubs, and got out to open Leonora's door.

She got out, waited while he fetched her overnight bag from the boot and then held out a hand. 'Thank you very much,' she told him. 'I hope I haven't brought you too much out of your way.'

'No, no. I'll wait until you are indoors…'

Her aunt's housekeeper answered her knock and she turned to smile at him as she went inside.

Mrs Fletcher, the housekeeper, greeted her placidly. 'The mistress is out, miss; I'm to show you to your room and give you tea. Mrs Thurston will be back around six o'clock.'

So Leonora tidied herself in the charming room overlooking the tiny back garden and had her tea in the elegant sitting room.

Aunt Marion, a childless widow, had been left comfortably off by a doting husband, so that she lived pleasantly in her little gem of a house, surrounded by charming furniture and leading the kind of life she enjoyed—shopping, bridge parties, theatres—at the same time retaining a warm heart and generous nature. Sir William was a good deal older than she and she saw very little of him, but years ago, when they were children, she had been his favourite sister, and still was.

She came home soon after Leonora had finished her tea, embraced her niece warmly and demanded to know why she had come on this unexpected visit.

'Not that I'm not delighted to have you, my dear—you know that—but it's not like you... Is there anything wrong at home?'

Leonora gave her reasons, carefully couched in neutral terms.

'Ah, yes, of course you must have a talk. The whole thing sounds preposterous to me, but I know what villages are—someone has got the wrong end of the stick.'

Leonora nodded, not at all certain about that; all the same, her aunt's bracing opinion put heart into her and when they had dined she declared her intention of going to Tony's flat.

'Now? Wouldn't you like to phone him first?'

'No, I don't think so. I mean, if I just walk in and ask him he'll tell me at once, if you see what I mean.'

Her aunt understood very well. She was another one who wasn't quite happy about Tony Beamish. Let the girl catch him on the hop, as it were!

'Take a taxi, dear,' she advised. 'Have you sufficient money?'

When the taxi stopped outside the block of flats where Tony lived, Leonora got out, paid the driver and stood a minute looking around her.

It was a dignified street, lined with large houses and sedate blocks of flats—the kind that had enormous porticos with a lot of glass and wrought iron and a uniformed man just inside the door. Tony had told her that he was on the first floor and she looked up as she reached the entrance, half expecting to see him at one of the windows.

The porter enquired whom she wished to visit and offered to phone Mr Beamish's flat and announce her.

She smiled at him. 'I'd rather you didn't; it's a surprise.' She declined the lift, walked up the wide stairs and knocked on the door bearing his name.

A sour-faced man opened it. She disliked him at once for no reason that she could think of and asked politely if she might see Mr Beamish.

'Tell him it is Miss Crosby,' she said, and went past him into a small hall, thickly carpeted, its walls hung with paintings and vases of flowers on the wall tables. A bit overdone, she thought, but probably Tony had a housekeeper as well as the sour-faced man. She sat down composedly on a small walnut hall chair and watched the door through which the man had gone.

Nothing happened for a few minutes, then the door was flung open and Tony came into the hall.

'What in heaven's name brings you here?' he demanded, and the happy excitement of seeing him again slowly shrivelled at the cold anger in his voice. He must have seen her face because he added quickly, 'Darling, what has happened? Is it your father—something dire?'

Leonora stayed on the chair. 'Hello, Tony. No, Father is very well. I want to talk to you.'

'My dear girl, why couldn't you have phoned?' He had controlled his annoyance now and bent to kiss her. 'I have guests—a dinner party. I simply can't leave them.' He glanced at the tweed suit and the sensible shoes. 'You aren't dressed...' he began.

Leonora got up. 'I'll come back tomorrow. Will you be here in the evening? About six o'clock? I won't keep you long and I shall be dining with Aunt Marion.'

'You do understand, Leonora? They're important people—colleagues in the business world.'

He kissed her again and she turned her cheek away and walked to the door. 'I'll see you tomorrow,' she told him in a rather small, polite voice, and went past the sour-faced man, who had appeared to open the door, and down the stairs.

At the entrance she asked the porter to get her a taxi, stood quietly until it arrived, then tipped the man and got in, outwardly serene while her thoughts were in chaos. Tony hadn't been pleased to see her; surely if he loved her he would have been only too glad to see her? She thought he had looked furiously angry; he had been, for a moment, a man she didn't know.

Her aunt was out when she got back, which meant that she could go to bed early, pleading tiredness after her

journey—something which the housekeeper found un-
derstandable. Not that Leonora slept, not until the small
hours. She pondered her few minutes with Tony, and
because she loved him—well, she was going to marry
him, wasn't she? So she must love him—she suppressed
the doubt at once and convinced herself that he had been
tired after his day's work. It had been her fault; she should
have warned him of her coming. She must learn to ac-
commodate her actions to suit his... She slept at last on
this high-minded resolve.

In the morning, yesterday evening's meeting faded
into something which had been regrettable and entirely
her fault, and hard on this thought there followed the one
that Tony would certainly have an explanation for the
goings-on in the village.

She spent the morning at Harrods with her aunt, pretending that she had all the clothes she wanted while her
aunt tried on hats, and in the afternoon she made a fourth
at bridge, a game at which she was only tolerably good.
However, since her aunt had been so kind as to have her
for a guest, she could do no other than express pleasure
at the prospect of several hours of anxious concentration.

They played for money too but, as Aunt Marion explained laughingly, the stakes would be very low, otherwise it wouldn't be fair to rob her niece.

Kindly fate allowed Leonora and her partner, a formidable dowager in a towering hat, to win as often as
they lost, so that she was a little better off by the time
they stopped for tea.

Then it was time for her to go and see Tony once more.

Chapter 5

The sour-faced man admitted Leonora when she reached Tony's flat. This time he led her through the hall and into a large room overlooking the street. It was splendidly furnished and its tall windows were elaborately curtained but she hardly noticed this. Tony was coming towards her, his arms outstretched.

'Darling, how lovely to see you. I am so sorry about yesterday evening. Sometimes the only chance I have to discuss things with colleagues is over a meal. Come and sit down and tell me why you wanted to see me so urgently!'

He went to a small table against one wall. 'What would you like to drink?' He glanced over his shoulder. 'I have to go out shortly—you said you were dining with your aunt so I saw no reason to cancel it.'

'No, of course not.' All the same she felt chilled by his

remark. It was as if he was fitting her in between more important engagements. She refused a drink and told herself not to be petty.

He came and sat down opposite her. 'This is delightful,' he told her, smiling. 'I have so often sat here and wished that you were here with me.' He sat back, at his ease. 'Now, what's all this about?'

She went straight to the point, already feeling confident that the whole business was a storm in a teacup.

'There are two men staying at the Blue Man; they have been asking questions—searching questions—about the house and our park. Two days ago I was told that they were there on behalf of someone who intends to buy the house and the land and build houses on it, as well as restoring the house. I was told that the someone was you, Tony.'

He was no longer smiling. His face was coldly angry and he didn't look at her.

'It's true,' said Leonora in a quiet voice. 'Why, Tony? Tell me why and perhaps I'll understand.'

He was smiling again, even laughing a little. 'Listen, darling. Your father's house needs to be restored; it's already half a ruin—no paintwork, faulty plumbing, doors broken, windows warped, floors uneven, brickwork crumbling. I intend to restore it and modernise it at the same time—new bathrooms, carpets, curtains, wallpapers, the lot.

'We will live on the top floor—a flat with its own entrance, of course—the rest will be used as a business centre. You have no idea of the number of clients I have who come here from Japan, the Middle East, the Continent. It's an ideal spot for them to come for conferences,

make decisions, arrange mergers. It'll be run at a profit—
I'll see to that.

'And yes, the park is useless as it is; the land will
bring in a splendid amount of money and the village will
benefit from an influx of new inhabitants. They will be
decent-sized places and the people who buy them will
bring money with them—the village will love that. Of
course I'll see that your father and mother have a suitable house—something that gorgon of a nanny can run
single-handed—and of course I'll see that your father is
financially comfortable.'

Leonora, listening to this rigmarole, couldn't believe
her ears. Rage had kept her silent—a rage strong enough
to make her forget that her world was tumbling round
her. Now she asked quietly, 'Is this why you wanted to
marry me? So that you could do all this?'

She showed no sign of her strong feelings. so Tony
said lightly, 'Well, I must admit that that was one of the
reasons...'

'There must be any number of girls like me,' said
Leonora, 'with elderly parents living in dilapidated old
houses; you shouldn't have much difficulty in finding
one.'

She stood up, took the ring off her finger and laid it
gently on the table by her chair. 'I'm not going to marry
you, Tony. I never want to see you again, and if you don't
recall those men and drop the whole idea I shall get our
solicitor to take the matter up.' She walked to the door.
'You're ruthless and wicked and greedy; I'm surprised
that I didn't see that. Luckily I do now.'

He crossed the room and caught her arm. 'Leonora,
darling, you can't go like this; I've taken you by surprise.

Go away and think about it. It's a splendid scheme and you'll benefit from it—everything you could ever want.'

She turned to look at him. 'All I ever want is to live at Pont Magna amongst friends and people I've known all my life.'

'But you love me—'

'I thought I did, but there's a difference.'

She gave him a little nod and went into the hall and through the door, which the sour-faced man had opened. She walked down the stairs, bade the porter a polite goodnight, asked him to get her a taxi and when it came got in.

When she got out at her aunt's house she was so white that the driver asked her if she felt ill and only drove away when she assured him that there was nothing wrong. She said the same to Mrs Fletcher and followed her obediently into the drawing room, feeling peculiar. I mustn't faint or cry, she thought.

Her aunt was there, sitting by the small, bright fire, and standing at the window was Dr Galbraith. They turned to look at her as she went in and she stood just inside the door, knowing that if she said anything she would burst into tears. But they had seen her face and understood.

'Come and sit down, Leonora,' said her aunt. 'Mrs Fletcher's bringing coffee. I'm sure you can do with a cup.'

So she sat down, still without speaking, until she asked in a tight voice, 'Why are you here, Doctor?'

He came and sat down, half turned away from her. 'I phoned to see if you wanted a lift home and Mrs Thurston suggested that I might come and wait for you here.'

'Oh—oh, I see. That's very kind of you...'

'Would you like to go home?' The casual friendliness of his voice was comforting.

She looked at her aunt.

'You would like it, wouldn't you, Leonora? Why not? You may be sure that I understand, my dear; you don't have to tell me anything.'

'Thank you, Aunt Marion. I'd like to go home very much if you don't mind. I—that is, Tony and I aren't getting married so I don't need to stay. It was very kind of you to have me… You don't think I'm rude? I don't mean to be!'

'Bless you, girl, of course I don't. I'd do the same in your shoes. Here's the coffee; drink it while it's hot, while Mrs Fletcher packs your bag for you. You'll be home by bedtime. So convenient that Dr Galbraith should be going back this evening.'

'Two days here is enough for me,' observed the doctor, which led to an exchange of views about London versus the country while Leonora drank her coffee, swallowing with it the tears she longed to shed.

Ten minutes later she wished her aunt goodbye and got into the car, her pretty face set in a rigid smile while she uttered her thanks once more.

'In a day or so, when you've had a good cry and found that life's worth living after all, you shall tell me all about it,' said Aunt Marion.

As he drove away the doctor observed casually, 'What a very sensible and delightful woman your aunt is. Do you want to phone your mother?'

'No, I don't think so; she might worry and wonder why I'm coming back…'

'We should be home well before bedtime. We'll stop on the way and have a meal.'

'I'm not hungry.'

He ignored that. 'There's rather a nice pub in a village just off the motorway once we've passed Reading. That should suit us nicely. There's plenty of time for you to have a good cry before we get there, and if I remember rightly the lighting is very dim there.'

She didn't know whether to laugh or cry. 'You think of everything,' she told him. 'I'd much rather go straight home.'

'Of course you would, but consider, Leonora. The moment you entered the door you would burst into tears, upset the household and make a complete muddle of explaining.'

She took an indignant breath. 'What a horrid thing to say. You seem to forget that I'm a grown woman and perfectly able to control myself.'

He said placidly, 'Well, it will take a little while to get to this pub; you can think about it and tell me what you want to do when we reach the turn-off.'

He had no more to say then, which meant that she had no way of ignoring her thoughts, so that presently her much vaunted self-control collapsed and she sat rigid while the tears rolled down her cheeks. It seemed that nothing would stop them; she looked sideways out of the window although it was already getting dark and there was nothing to see, swallowing the sobs.

They were bypassing Reading when the doctor handed her his handkerchief.

'Shall we go to the pub?' he asked with brisk friendliness.

She mopped her face, blew her pretty nose and said, 'Yes, please, only I must look a fright...'

'Does that matter? No one will know you there and

they will be locals chatting over their pints—and I don't mind what you look like.'

Despite her misery, Leonora took exception to that remark.

The village was four or five miles off the motorway, a handful of cottages, one or two handsome houses and the church, and opposite it the pub—a quite small place with a solid door and small windows.

The doctor had been quite right—it was indeed dimly lit and, although the bar was almost full, beyond a quick glance no one bothered to really look at them. Moreover, at one end of the bar there were tables, none of them occupied. He led her to a small table under the window.

'I'll fetch our drinks and see what we can have to eat. If you want the Ladies' it is in that far corner.'

He sounded exactly as she imagined a brother would sound—unfussed and casual. She nodded and took herself off and found the light in the cloakroom, unlike the one in the bar, was so powerful that it could show every wrinkle. No wrinkles in her case but certainly a rather tear-stained face, fortunately not beyond repair. She emerged presently, feeling a good deal better, and found the doctor sitting at the table reading the menu.

He got up as she reached him. 'I'd like you to drink what's in that glass,' he told her, 'and no arguing.'

'What is it?'

She took a sip since he didn't answer and said, 'Oh. Brandy, isn't it?'

He nodded. 'I am sure you would have liked a pot of tea—we'll have that later.'

She eyed his own glass. 'That looks like water...'

'Bottled water. I'm driving. Now, we have quite a choice.' He handed her the menu. 'Last time I was here

I had a jacket potato piled high with baked beans—it was delicious. Soup first? No? Then I'll order.'

He wandered over to the bar, gave his order, stopped to exchange a few cheerful comments with the men there and then wandered back again.

'Drink your brandy and then start at the beginning. Never mind if it's all a bit muddled; the thing is to get it off your chest so that you can think clearly about what you want to do next.'

She said tartly, 'You sound like an agony aunt in a women's magazine…'

'God forbid, but I do have five sisters. I grew up steeped, as it were, in the female sex. In a position to offer humble advice if asked for it.'

She said quickly, 'That was a horrid thing I said about being an agony aunt. I'm sorry. I'm sure you must be a very nice brother.'

'Thank you. And now, having established my suitability as confidant, tell me what has happened to bring about this unfortunate situation.'

The brandy had been a great help. She related the whole sorry business in a voice which only wobbled occasionally and while she talked she ate the potato and beans with an appetite she hadn't realised she had.

The doctor said nothing at all, not even when she stopped to subdue a particularly persistent wobble. It wasn't until they had finished and a pot of tea and cups and saucers had been set before them that he observed, 'There is a possibility that Beamish will come hotfoot after you, beg your forgiveness and scrap his plans. Have you considered that he might have had the best intentions?'

Leonora gave him a cold look. 'He said one of the reasons for marrying me was so that he could get his hands on the house and land.' She drew a furious breath, looking quite beautiful despite the slightly reddened nose.

'I'm not sure any more if he ever loved me. How can I be?'

The doctor sighed gently. It would be tragic if young Beamish could persuade her into thinking that the whole thing had been nothing but a misunderstanding—something he would be quite capable of doing—and it would be easy if he himself dropped sufficient hints as to the man's character to put her on her guard, but he had no right to interfere. In any case, he reminded himself, Leonora was no shy young girl; she must decide for herself what she wanted from life.

'I think that perhaps you will know that when you see him again.' At her look of doubt he added, 'Oh, you will, you know. You must follow your heart, Leonora.'

Back in the car, speeding along the motorway once more, sitting in a friendly silence, Leonora thought about the doctor's advice. It had been sound, unbiased and quite impersonal. She would take it, only she wished that he had been a little more sympathetic. There was no reason why he should be, she reminded herself; he had given her advice just as, doubtless, he gave advice to such of his patients who asked for it.

The lights were still on at the house when he drew up before it. He got out to open her door and said, 'I'll come in with you,' and she gave him a grateful look.

'I've my key,' she told him, and they went in together just as Nanny came into the hall from the kitchen end.

'Well, I must say that seeing you so sudden is a bit of a shock. You didn't phone.' She looked at the doctor as she spoke.

'Hello, Nanny,' said Leonora. 'I'm sorry if we made you jump. Dr Galbraith gave me a lift home. Are Mother and Father in the drawing room?'

Nanny nodded. 'You could do with a cup of coffee, the pair of you. I'll bring it presently.'

Lady Crosby was doing a jigsaw puzzle and Sir William was reading. It was Wilkins who came to meet them as they went in, delighted to see them.

'Leonora—we didn't expect you—you haven't phoned.' Her mother looked surprised. 'And Dr Galbraith.' She frowned. 'Tony isn't with you?' She glanced at her husband. 'Your father and I thought he might come back with you—you must have seen him.'

Her father had put down his book. 'Something's wrong?' he asked.

'I went to London to see Tony about something—something I had been told about him. We—that is, I decided that I don't want to marry him so we're not engaged any more.'

'There's more to it than that,' Sir William said sharply.

'Yes, but it can wait until tomorrow morning, Father. I had the chance to come back with Dr Galbraith. He most kindly gave me a lift.'

'Much obliged to you,' said her father. 'Come and sit down; I'm sure Nanny will have made us coffee.' He turned his head. 'Leonora, run and tell Nanny to bring it as soon as it's ready.'

When she had gone, relieved to be away from her mother's faint air of disapproval, he asked, 'All right, is she? More to it than she has said—'

'Yes, a good deal more, Sir William, but I am sure that Leonora will explain everything later. She has had a very trying time and she is tired.'

Sir William nodded. 'Then we won't pester her this evening. Good of you to bring her back. You know what happened, of course?'

The doctor looked grim. 'Yes, indeed I do.'

Leonora came in with the coffee-tray then, and after ten minutes or so of desultory talk the doctor got up to go.

Leonora went with him to the door. 'Thank you again,' she said, and offered a hand. 'And thank you for listening. You were quite right—it's much easier to think sensibly now I've talked about it. You didn't mind?'

He was still holding her hand. 'No, Leonora, I didn't mind. I hope that if you should need a shoulder to cry on at any time you'll use mine.'

He gave her a brotherly thump on the shoulder and went out to his car and drove away.

Once she was back in the drawing room her mother said with a little *moue* of discontent, 'Your father says we are to wait until tomorrow before you tell us exactly what has happened to bring you rushing back like this. You say you are no longer engaged to Tony... You must have a very good reason—'

Sir William said sharply, 'That is enough, my dear; Leonora is tired; no doubt she has had a long day with things to worry her. She should go to bed and in the morning, if she wishes, she will tell us what happened.'

So Leonora went thankfully to bed and rather to her surprise went to sleep at once, to wake the next morning feeling that she was able to cope with the situation and determined that if Tony should want to see her she would refuse.

That would be the only way, she reflected as she dressed and went downstairs to the kitchen, for if they were to meet again she wasn't sure if she could withstand his charm, despite knowing now that he had never really loved her-not with the kind of love she wanted. He had thought of her as someone who went with the house and the land, someone he would possibly treat with casual affection, load with jewellery and dress in lovely clothes and who would be expected to agree to all his plans.

'Well, I won't,' said Leonora, putting on the kettle, and she wished Nanny a good morning. She opened the door for Wilkins and stood taking great breaths of the early-morning air.

'And what's all this I hear from your ma?' asked Nanny.

Leonora fetched a teapot and spooned in the tea. 'I haven't explained yet,' she said, 'and I'll tell you all about it, Nanny, but first I have to tell Father and Mother.'

Which, over the breakfast table, proved a difficult task. Her father stared with disbelief.

'This house? My land? The park? I cannot believe it, Leonora…'

'No, I know it's difficult, Father, but it's true. Tony had it all planned—you and Mother were to be moved to a smaller house—'

'I could not possibly live in a small house,' observed her mother, 'and what about the Sheraton chairs and the William and Mary display cabinet? And the other furniture—it would never fit into a small house. I think it was most inconsiderate of him to even suggest such a thing. Why were we not told?'

Sir William asked, 'These men staying in the village—you say that Tony sent them? Leonora, I find this very difficult to believe.'

'So did I, Father, but it's true. I told Tony that he was

to recall the men and that there was no question of you selling the house and the land.'

'Quite right too, my dear.' Sir William, not the most sensitive of men, all the same added, 'I hope this hasn't upset you too much, Leonora.'

'I expect I'm as upset as any woman who expects to get married and then finds that she won't after all,' said Leonora.

Lady Crosby wiped away a tear. 'And I was planning the wedding. What will everyone think…?'

'I don't care what they think,' said Leonora with a snap, and took herself off to the kitchen before she lost her cool and burst into tears.

It was all right to cry against Nanny's elderly shoulder, pouring out her rage and disappointment and unhappiness in a jumble of words. She felt better then and sat down at the table with Wilkins pressed against her and drank the tea Nanny had made.

'He'll come after you,' said Nanny. 'If he wants the house and the land he'll not give them up without another try. And if you truly love him, dearie, it won't matter what he's done; you'll forgive him and he'll get his way. Even Sir William would give in eventually once you were wed and Tony could show him a good reason for parting with the house and giving it to you—and to him, of course.'

'I won't listen to him; I never want to see him again…'

'I dare say you'll have to, Miss Leonora; you can't run away if he comes here. Besides, you may have got over your rage by then and discovered that you love him enough to want to have him back.'

Leonora drank her tea. 'Nanny, have you ever been in love?'

'Bless the girl, of course I have. He was a deep-sea

fisherman—drowned, he was, years ago now. But we were in love and we loved each other. Being in love is one thing—it doesn't always last, but loving does.'

'Nanny, I didn't know. I'm so sorry. You never wanted to marry after that?'

'What for? I never met a man to touch my Ned.'

Nanny got to her feet. 'I'm going up to make the beds, if you'll tidy the drawing room. You'll be going to the village presently?'

'Yes, we want one or two things, don't we? I'm not sure what happens next.'

'Sir William will know what to do.'

Leonora hoovered and dusted and listened to her mother's gentle complaining. 'Of course,' she said, 'Tony is sure to come here and want to see you and no doubt explain everything.' Lady Crosby blew her nose daintily and glanced at Leonora. 'After all, he does love you.' She frowned at Leonora's wooden expression. 'Well, he does, doesn't he?'

'I think,' said Leonora carefully, 'that he loves this house and the land, and because he can only get them if I make up the package, as it were, he may be a little in love with me.'

'But you love him, darling?'

Leonora dusted a fragile porcelain figurine with great care. 'I'm not sure, Mother.'

Mrs Pike's shop was empty when Leonora went in, the faithful Wilkins at her heels. She gave her order and nibbled at the biscuit she was offered—a new line in slimming rusks—while Mrs Pike collected tea, sugar, rice and corned beef.

'They've gone,' she said, leaning over the counter and speaking in a loud whisper just as though they were surrounded by eavesdroppers. 'Them men at the Blue Man. Went first thing this morning. Had a phone call from London last night. Pike happened to be in the bar and couldn't help but hear. Very surprised they were too.'

Leonora finished the rusk. 'I'm not surprised; I saw Mr Beamish yesterday and—the matter has been settled.'

She took off a glove to tuck her hair back and Mrs Pike said sharply, 'Your ring, Miss Crosby—lost it, have you?'

Leonora went pink. 'No—no, Mr Beamish and I are not to be married after all.'

Mrs Pike wordlessly handed her another biscuit. 'Well, I never…and it were a whopping great diamond.'

'Yes, it was, wasn't it?' Leonora found to her surprise that she didn't mind not having it. On second thoughts she wasn't even sure that she liked diamonds.

She went back home presently and found her father in his study.

'They've gone, the two men.' She told him what Mrs Pike had said and then said, 'Father, do you suppose that Tony will want to see me or you and explain?'

'Yes, I do, my dear. You do not need to see him on your own unless you want to. I shall certainly want an explanation and an apology.'

There was no sign of Tony, however. No letter, no telephone call. After several days, Leonora stopped listening for the phone and looking through the post each morning, nor did she catch her breath each time a car went past the gates. She had phoned Aunt Marion to thank her for her visit and that lady had informed her that Tony had made no attempt to get in touch with her. 'Although why he should wish to do so I'm sure I don't know.'

The doctor, kept up to date with village gossip by Cricket, whose benevolent and discreet manner had quite won over the hearts and the confidences of the village ladies, knew better. Tony Beamish was no fool; he would bide his time, wait until Leonora had had the time to realise that her future was no longer the one she had been looking forward to. He was a conceited man and very sure of himself; he would bank on Leonora missing him and everything he stood for and at the right moment he would turn up to beg forgiveness and convince her that everything would be changed. If she loved him he would eventually get what he wanted.

He could do nothing about it, of course. Leonora wasn't some young, empty-headed girl; she could think for herself. All he could do was listen if she needed to talk.

It was a pity that he saw no sign of her for several days. He had a number of patients living on outlying farms and the surgery at that time of year was full with nasty chests, flu and a mild outbreak of chickenpox amongst the small fry. He drove to Bath to see Ben but, passing the gates to her home, he could see no sign of anyone.

Which was a shame, for Leonora needed to talk to someone. Her parents, outraged at Tony's behaviour, didn't wish to discuss the matter, and Nanny, friend and confidante though she was, had declared that she was in no position to give advice.

Tony arrived on Monday, ten days after Leonora had seen him in London. He drove up to the house, got out and looked it over before ringing the bell. Despite its shabby appearance, it was a lovely old place and he had no intention of giving it up lightly.

When Leonora opened the door he said eagerly, 'Hello, darling. Have you calmed down enough for us to have a talk? You didn't mean it, you know.' He smiled with charm. 'I've brought the ring with me...'

Leonora stood in the doorway, blocking his path.

'I've calmed down and I meant it,' she said, 'so you can go away again.'

He put a hand on her arm. 'You don't mean that, Leonora. Think of all the marvellous things you will miss—I'll be good to you—'

'No, you won't,' said Leonora. 'I don't want anything more to do with you, and if Father hears any more about your plans he intends to get our solicitor to deal with it.'

Tony laughed. 'I say—look here, old girl, you don't mean that. You can't have thought about it—the advantages...'

'To you, yes. Have you come to see Father?'

'No, no. At least, I thought if I saw you first then we might see him together and explain.'

'Explain what? That you deceived him as well as me? Go away, Tony.'

'I'm not going until we've had a talk, until I've been given the chance to explain.'

Leonora, not the nervous type, nevertheless didn't like the look on his face, and he had put his foot in the door so that shutting it in his face was no longer possible. I need help, she thought.

She got it. Dr Galbraith, on his way back from Bath, glanced as he always did at the house as he passed. He slowed, reversed and slid silently up the drive to the door. His good morning was uttered in a genial voice. 'As I was passing I thought I might just take a look at your father.'

He had, without apparent effort, got between Leonora and Tony and turned to smile at him now. 'Rather unexpected, isn't it?' he wanted to know cheerfully. 'You're not very popular around here, you know.' He shook his head in a disapproving fashion. 'You have got yourself a very bad name in the village.' He looked at Leonora. 'Is he bothering you, Leonora?'

At her eloquent look he added, 'If you've come to make your peace with Sir William I strongly advise against it. The best thing you can do, my dear chap, is to go back to wherever you came from and stay there!'

Tony found his voice. 'What business is it of yours? This is a private matter between Leonora and myself.'

The doctor shook his head. 'You're mistaken, Beamish; there's nothing private about it. The Crosbys have been here for a couple of hundred years, they're part of the village life, and, believe me, you haven't a single friend in Pont Magna.'

He smiled pleasantly but his eyes were blue ice and Tony was the first to look away. 'Don't think I am going to be intimidated by threats—' he began.

'Threats? No one is threatening you, Beamish—a friendly warning, perhaps.'

'There is no point in staying here,' said Tony. 'I shall come back when there is a chance to talk to you privately, darling.'

'Don't you "darling" me,' said Leonora frostily. 'I don't want to see you again and that is the last time I'll say it.'

'But you love me…' Tony infused a cajoling note into his voice.

'No, I don't. I thought I did, but I don't.'

A remark which the doctor found most satisfactory. Leonora was too good for that fellow, he reflected; some decent chap would come along and marry her sooner or later.

He watched Beamish go to his car and get in and drive away and then said briskly, 'Well, now that that's sorted out, shall I see your father?'

She had expected him to say something soothing, express satisfaction at the way she had dealt with Tony. She turned on her heel and led the way indoors, feeling hurt.

'I'm sure he'll be pleased to see you, Doctor,' she observed in a cool voice. 'I'll bring coffee; Father usually has a cup about now.'

She put her head round the study door. 'Father, here's Dr Galbraith to see you.'

Her father lowered *The Times*. 'Ask him to come in. I heard someone—I was wondering who it was.'

She stood aside to let the doctor pass then went into the kitchen and thumped cups and saucers down on a tray, knocked over the sugar bowl and used what Nanny called 'unsuitable language'.

'What's upset you, Miss Leonora?' asked her old friend. 'Who was that at the door? Leaving someone at the door is bad manners.'

'It was Tony Beamish and he did upset me and I had no intention of letting him come into the house,' said Leonora pettishly. 'Dr Galbraith's here; I'm taking coffee to the study. Where's Mother?'

'Up in her room, going through her wardrobe. A good thing too.'

Leonora found biscuits and put them on a plate and Nanny asked, 'That Tony of yours…?'

'He's not mine.'

'Good thing too. Making trouble, is he?'

'No—well, he wanted me to be engaged again.' She poured the coffee. 'Actually, he got a bit—well, awkward, but Dr Galbraith was passing and stopped.'

Nanny nodded in a satisfied way. 'And sent him right about.'

'Well, yes, but quite nicely, if you see what I mean.'

'Yes, I see,' said Nanny. 'Will you take a cup of coffee up to your mother when you come back?'

The two men were sitting chatting comfortably. The doctor got up and took the tray from Leonora as she went in but she didn't look at him as she went away again.

Her mother, occupied with her clothes, greeted her absent-mindedly.

'I do need new clothes,' she said plaintively. 'Did I hear someone talking in the hall?'

'Dr Galbraith is with Father. He called in as he was passing.'

'I'll come down and see him—perhaps he can give me something; I feel I need a change—a little holiday, perhaps, a few days in town with your aunt Marion. Breaking off your engagement to Tony has been a great disappointment to me, Leonora.'

'It was rather a disappointment to me, Mother.'

'Yes, dear, of course, and I suppose he has behaved very badly. Never mind, there are plenty more fish in the sea.'

'Perhaps I'm not a very good angler,' said Leonora, and went back to the kitchen.

She was still there, peeling potatoes with unnecessary ferocity, when the doctor came in.

'There you are. I've been talking to your mother; she feels rather under the weather, she tells me. I've written a prescription for her; may I leave it with you, Leonora?' He watched her face. 'Your father is very well. How about you?'

'I never need the doctor,' said Leonora, and began on another potato.

He smiled. 'Don't tempt fate,' he said, and went away as quietly as he had come.

Chapter 6

At lunch Lady Crosby said happily, 'Dr Galbraith has invited us to dine—rather short notice but he has friends coming down from London and he thought we might like to meet them. Next Saturday.'

Leonora remembered how she had sniffed and sobbed and made a fool of herself with the doctor. She said now, 'I'll have to refuse, Mother. I promised weeks ago that I'd babysit for Maggie—she and Gordon are going up to town to celebrate their anniversary. I said I'd spend the night.'

'For heaven's sake!' Her mother sounded impatient. 'They have a nursemaid, haven't they?'

'Yes, but she is very young and quite untrained. Did you accept for me as well as you and Father?'

'Yes, of course I did. Such a nice man, well connected too, and wealthy, I hear.'

'I'll write him a note,' said Leonora.

Which she did—a formal message of regret, couched in polite terms, which he read with some amusement and interest over his breakfast.

'Now why has she done that?' he enquired of the faithful Tod. 'Even if she had to refuse she could have phoned me or even called in at the surgery. We are, I suspect, to be Dr Galbraith and Miss Leonora Crosby again. A strange girl!'

He forgot about her then.

However, Leonora, who should by rights have been eating her heart out for the treacherous Tony, found herself thinking about the doctor. She liked him; he would be a splendid friend and she enjoyed his company and his matter-of-fact way of accepting events without fuss. But there was this vexed question of this young lady for whom he had a strong affection and, worse than that, her mother was making no secret of the fact that she would like it if Leonora and Dr Galbraith were to see more of each other. She would have to avoid him.

Luckily there would be a lot to do organising the fête, traditionally held in the park every year. Everyone had a hand in it, the practical making marmalade, cakes and sweets, embroidering small useless cushions and night-dress cases, knitting baby jackets, and the artistic painting local scenes.

Leonora, who drew and painted rather nicely, decided to shut herself in one of the attics and set to work. When she wasn't doing that she could go along to the Dowlings' and help with the writing of price tickets.

She took herself off to Maggie and Gordon's little house at the end of the village on Saturday afternoon and presently waved them goodbye as they drove off.

The house was charming, comfortably furnished and untidy. Leonora took her overnight bag up to the little guest room, had a chat with Sadie, the little nursery maid, and went about the business of making up feeds for three-month-old Tom. He was a placid baby, sleeping and feeding in a manner which would have delighted any writer of a childcare textbook.

The afternoon went by quickly, with a brisk walk in his pram, and feeding and bathing while Sadie got their tea and supper. And since Tom took his feed like a lamb at ten o'clock Leonora and Sadie went to bed and slept peacefully until the early morning.

It was a bright, chilly morning, and Leonora, sitting by the window in the little nursery, giving Tom his bottle, was content. It would be delightful to have a baby of her own, she reflected, small and cuddly like Tom—several babies in fact. If she had married Tony... She wondered then if he would have liked children. Certainly he wouldn't have had much time for them.

'I should like a husband,' she told Tom, 'who would get up in the night if the baby cried and who'd bring me a cup of tea without being asked and wouldn't mind babies dribbling onto his shoulder. He'd play cricket with the little boys and comfort the little girls when they cried...'

She tickled Tom under his chin to encourage him to finish his bottle. 'You don't have to listen to my nonsense,' she assured him. 'We'll go for a walk and blow away the cobwebs.'

She had enjoyed her day, she reflected as she walked home after Maggie and Gordon had returned. Sadie had had tea ready for them and she had sat listening to their account of their day, before bidding Tom a reluctant goodbye.

'He was so good,' she assured her friend. 'I'll babysit any time that you want me to.'

Her mother and father were in the drawing room, he

behind the Sunday papers and her mother sitting at a small table with a half-finished jigsaw puzzle.

'Enjoyed yourself?' asked her father, glancing up.

She bent to kiss his cheek. 'Yes, thank you, Father. Little Tom is a darling baby and so good.'

Her mother turned away impatiently from the puzzle. 'Darling, such a pity you couldn't come with us yesterday. I must say Dr Galbraith has a lovely house; I quite envy him some of his furniture—handed down in the family, I should think. There is a bow-fronted cabinet in the drawing room… And that man of his—Cricket— the kind of servant one dreams of and never finds! Dinner was excellent and these friends of his very pleasant. Ackroyd is the name—and funnily enough Mr Ackroyd knew your father's brother-in-law, Aunt Marion's husband, you know—when he was alive. She was quite nice too—rather quiet, but friendly enough. A good deal older than Dr Galbraith but I believe their daughter and he are on good terms. He should marry, of course.'

'I dare say he will, when he wants to,' said Leonora. 'I'm glad you enjoyed the evening.'

She wandered off to the kitchen and found Nanny cutting up vegetables for soup. Into her willing ears Leonora poured every small detail of little Tom's day. 'He's such a darling baby, Nanny, and so good.'

She ate a carrot and went out into the garden, having called Wilkins, and then beyond into the park, feeling restless. She had, she supposed, got used to the idea of marrying Tony in the not too distant future—a future she had taken for granted. Now the future stretched ahead of her empty, and just for the moment there seemed little purpose in it. She had been happily filling in time, helping to organise various village functions, accompanying her parents to friends' houses for dinner, summer picnics and winter bridge afternoons, but now these seemed a waste of time.

What else could she do? For a few years after she had left school she had travelled a little, visited friends, spent a week or two with Aunt Marion going to theatres, dancing, shopping. Since her father had lost his money, though, none of these things had been possible and she'd found herself more and more involved in coping with the running of the house since Nanny was the only other person to do that.

She couldn't blame her mother, who had never done the household chores and had very little idea of what they involved anyway. It looked as though she was destined to stay at home, getting longer and longer in the tooth, making do with too little money, doing the odd repairs, and painting in an amateurish way.

She jumped across the little stream which ran along the boundary of the park and wandered into the woods beyond while Wilkins padded to and fro. When he stood still and began to bark she paused too.

'What's up, Wilkins? Rabbits?'

It was very quiet under the trees but presently she heard footsteps—unhurried and deliberate—and Wilkins raced back the way they had come to meet them. Leonora stayed where she was; it was someone the dog knew and liked and for a moment she wondered if it was Tony but then dismissed the thought; Wilkins and Tony had never been more than guarded in their approach to each other.

Perhaps it was Dr Galbraith...

It was. He came towards her, still unhurried, Wilkins jumping up on his elderly legs and running in circles around him. His, 'Hello, Leonora,' was casual and friendly. 'I should have brought Tod with me...

'Nanny told me that you might be here.' He had reached her by now and strolled along beside her. 'There is something about which I wish to talk.'

'What?' asked Leonora baldly.

'Mrs Crisp has broken her arm. Would you consider taking over from her from the time being, a few weeks? Morning surgery is half past eight until eleven o'clock or thereabouts. Evening surgery five o'clock until seven—sometimes later. No surgery on Saturday evenings or Sunday.'

Leonora had listened with her mouth open. 'I can't type,' she managed. 'I don't know anything...'

'You know everyone in the village and for miles around. You know where people live, the jobs they have. You can answer the phone intelligently and not fly into hysterics if something crops up. It's an easy job for you. If I have to get someone from an agency they won't know their way around or where the patients live.'

Leonora closed her mouth at last. 'But I can't. I mean, I do most of the housekeeping at home and the shopping—and odd jobs around the place.'

'You would be paid like anyone else who works for a living. Surely there is someone in the village who could go to the house each day and give Nanny a hand?'

When she hesitated he added, 'You would be working—let me see—between twenty and thirty hours a week. There's a standard rate of pay.' He mentioned a sum which caused her mouth to drop open again.

'All that?' asked Leonora. She paused just long enough to do some most satisfying mental arithmetic. 'If you think I'll do I'll come and work for you.'

'Good. Now that's settled, how about coming back with me and I'll explain just what you have to do?'

'Well, yes, all right. I'd better take Wilkins back home first and tell Mother.'

He walked back with her, saying little, not mentioning the job again until they were in the house once more. As they went in through the garden door he asked, 'Do you want me to come with you?'

She considered this. 'Well, it might be a good idea.' She glanced at him. 'If you see what I mean?'

He nodded gravely. That the daughter of the house should have a job was something Lady Crosby wouldn't allow, but as a favour to the local doctor, an emergency, as it were—that would be a different matter.

So it proved to be. Leonora could not help but admire the way in which the doctor convinced her mother that working for him at the surgery wasn't so much a job as a vital service to the community and that Leonora, being known in the village, was exactly the right person to undertake it.

'Well, I do see that as a member of the family Leonora has a certain duty. I mean, we have lived here for very many years, as you must know. I am sure it is a worthwhile undertaking since Mrs Crisp is unable to work for you.'

Lady Crosby frowned suddenly. 'There is one drawback—Leonora has undertaken the running of this house. I am rather delicate myself, Dr Galbraith; my poor health does not allow me to exert myself.'

She sighed. 'Such a pity, but I do not see how we are to manage if Leonora is away for most of the day.'

'Perhaps that is a problem which can be solved. Leonora will, of course, receive a salary. There must be someone in the village who would come here and work with Nanny while Leonora is away.'

Lady Crosby brightened. 'Well, yes. You say she will receive a salary?' She turned to look at the silent Leonora. 'That will be nice, my dear. I'm sure if you can find someone suitable to replace you for the time being neither your father nor I will have any objection to you helping the doctor.'

She smiled at him. 'You will stay to dinner? We dine late on Sundays.'

He refused with easy good manners and added, 'Perhaps I might take Leonora with me for an hour or so? I can give her some idea of her duties and we might share supper at the same time. The sooner she is able to start work, the better for me and my patients.'

'Yes, yes, of course. I can quite see that the matter is an urgent one. Leonora, will you go to your father—he is in his study—and tell him what we have arranged?' She turned back to the doctor. 'Perhaps while she is doing that you will advise me about this nasty little pain I get in my chest… My heart, you know…'

'I can hardly advise without a full examination; I suggest that you come down to the surgery one afternoon. I'm usually free then and you can tell me what is troubling you.' He added with brisk reassurance, 'You look extremely well.'

'Ah, but my looks have never pitied me,' said Lady Crosby in a resigned voice, 'and I don't complain.'

Leonora came back then, promised to be back in an hour or two and went out to the car with the doctor.

The drive to the surgery was so short that there was no need to talk and once they were there he set about explaining her work to her in a businesslike way which precluded any light-hearted chit-chat. She listened cheerfully, poked her nose into cupboards and drawers and asked intelligent questions.

'Like to start in the morning?' he wanted to know.

'Tomorrow? Well, why not? But you won't get too annoyed if I do everything wrong?'

'No, no.' He was laughing at her. 'I'm quite sure you will be able to cope well enough, and Mrs Crisp has promised that she will pop in just in case you need to know more about things. Half past eight, then?'

'All right. I'll ask Nanny if she knows of anyone who will come up to the house and help her. I could ask Mrs Pike too…'

'Good, that's settled. Now let us go and have our supper.'

Leonora said thoughtfully, 'There's no need, you know. I mean, you've explained everything to me here…'

He swept her out to the car. 'There's bound to be something I've forgotten,' he told her. 'I'll probably think of it during supper. There will be no time in the morning.'

A sensible observation to which she agreed. With pleasure and relief. She was hungry.

Cricket, accompanied by a boisterous Tod, admitted them, allowing his usual gloomy expression to be lightened with a smile at the sight of Leonora.

'Miss Crosby is having supper with me, Cricket,' said Dr Galbraith, and he took Leonora's jacket and ushered her across the hall and into the drawing room.

'Fifteen minutes, sir,' said Cricket, and melted away to the kitchen, where he set about adding one or two extra items to the supper menu. He approved of Miss Crosby; it was a pity he hadn't been given more notice, for she was worthy of his culinary skill. He had already made baked pears, standing ready in their dish with the flavoured syrup poured over them, but he decided now to save them for tomorrow and prepare something else…

There was also time to prepare a dish of anchoïades. With commendable speed he assembled anchovies, garlic, olive oil and lemon juice, sliced bread and black pepper. Cricket fetched his pestle and mortar and set to work.

In the drawing room the doctor invited Leonora to sit down, opened the door to allow Tod to join them from the garden and offered her a drink. Then he began a rambling conversation about nothing much. Apparently her job wasn't to be discussed for the moment. Leonora sipped dry sherry and allowed herself to enjoy the moment. Since she was hungry, she allowed her thoughts to dwell on supper.

She was not to be disappointed. Presently, sated at the elegantly laid table, she enjoyed the anchovies followed by quiche Lorraine, embellished by a potato salad, green peas and mushrooms tossed in garlic and cream. She ate everything, rather surprised by the lavishness of what she had supposed would be a simple meal.

Dr Galbraith was surprised too, amused that Cricket had found the time to add to what would have been a well-cooked meal but without fancy trimmings. He wondered what they would be invited to eat for pudding and hid a smile when Cricket served them with ice cream, tastefully decorated with burnt almonds, glacé cherries and chocolate shavings, the whole topped with whipped cream—a dessert Cricket was well aware that the doctor would have spurned. As it was, he ate his portion with evident enjoyment, offered Leonora a second glass of wine and suggested that they should return to the drawing room.

'I should really go home,' said Leonora, not wishing to go.

'I'll drive you back presently, but you must have some coffee first. Cricket makes very good coffee.'

'There must be something else I should know,' suggested Leonora. Supper had been delicious and so had the wine. The lovely room was restful and Dr Galbraith was a soothing companion.

The doctor, sitting in his chair on the other side of the fireplace, with Tod pressed against his knee, replied easily, 'Oh, I'm sure you have got a good grasp of what has to be done. You know most of the patients, I would suppose, which should make things easy for you.'

He drove her home soon after and bade her a cheerful goodnight, refusing her offer to come in to see her parents, getting back into his car with a friendly wave and driving away.

Her mother and father were in the drawing room and Leonora couldn't help but contrast its shabbiness with the well cared for comfort of Buntings. Perhaps, she reflected, she could find another job when she was no longer needed at the surgery and save enough money to have something done to the house. That it needed thousands of pounds spent on it she chose to ignore; just to do the urgent repairs and paint over the worst bits would at least stave off the ravages of time.

As she went in her mother said, 'Ah, there you are, dear. Everything is settled, I hope? Your father agrees with me that you did quite rightly to offer to help Dr Galbraith; it behoves us all to give help when it is asked for.'

'Yes, Mother,' said Leonora, and caught her father's eye. Lady Crosby was quite sincere but they both knew that she was the last person anyone would ask for help. Indeed, she was more than likely the one who needed it.

She arrived in good time at the surgery in the morning after a quick breakfast in the kitchen with Nanny, to find the doctor's car outside and, when she went in, the waiting room almost full.

There was no sign of the doctor, though. She wished everyone a good morning, took off her jacket and set to work getting out patients' notes. She hadn't quite finished when the surgery bell pinged and she put her head round the door to answer it.

'I'm nearly ready,' she assured him. 'Shall I give you those I have?'

He said placidly, 'Good morning, Leonora. Yes, please do. Let me have the others later. There is no hurry. I spend about seven minutes with each patient, sometimes more.'

He held out his hand for the notes. 'Who is first? Mrs Dodge? Send her in, will you?'

Leonora withdrew her head and then poked it back again. 'I forgot to say good morning,' she said, and closed the door.

Once she got over her initial uncertainty, she began to enjoy herself. She knew everyone there, which made things easy, for they were eager to point out everything she didn't do correctly.

Mrs Crisp always put the patients' notes on the little shelf by the desk when they had been seen by the doctor, old Mr Trubshaw told her, and when a small girl became restless several voices advised her that the WC was down the passage, and as the last patient went in she paused to tell her to put the kettle on. 'For the doctor's coffee,' she pointed out kindly.

With the waiting room empty, Leonora found mugs and coffee and while the kettle boiled began to tidy the place.

She felt pleased with herself; she hadn't done so badly. True, there had been one or two hitches but she hoped that the doctor hadn't noticed them. As the surgery door opened she turned off the gas and looked round at him, hopefully expecting a few words of praise.

She was to be disappointed. He walked to the door with barely a glance in her direction. 'I may be delayed. Could you ring Mrs Crisp and ask her if she'll come here and take any calls? I'll do my best to get back by evening surgery.'

He gave her a brisk nod and closed the door behind him, so that she had no chance to say a word.

'Oh, well,' said Leonora, feeling deflated. 'Perhaps he's late on his rounds.' She made herself a cup of coffee and then phoned Mrs Crisp.

Mrs Crisp wasn't home. She had gone to Bath, her husband said, and probably wouldn't be back until the end of the week. Was there anything he could do?

Leonora said no, thank you and not to bother Mrs Crisp when she got back, and sat down to think what she should do. Obviously Dr Galbraith expected someone to be handy to take any calls or messages and he wasn't to know that Mrs Crisp, who had volunteered to come in in the afternoons, wasn't available.

'I can't leave here,' said Leonora, addressing the doctor's empty chair, and she picked up the phone again. Nanny answered it, which was a good thing for she only needed the barest explanation. 'I'll tell your ma. You've nothing to eat there?'

'No, but there's plenty of tea and coffee and a little milk.'

'Phone over to Mrs Pike and get her to make you a sandwich; the boy will bring it over for you.'

When Leonora said there was no need, Nanny replied, 'You do as I say, Miss Leonora. Otherwise you'll be flat on your back with hunger with the waiting room full of patients this evening.'

As usual, Nanny was right; as lunchtime approached Leonora's insides rumbled a reminder. She phoned Mrs Pike and ten minutes later sank her splendid teeth into the sandwiches that young Pike had brought over for her. She devoured the lot, made a pot of tea and planned her afternoon. If she had to sit there for several hours yet she might as well improve her mind and she had seen the books on the shelf in the surgery.

There had been several phone calls, none of them urgent, from patients wanting to make appointments, and it struck her suddenly that if the doctor was wanted urgently she had no idea where to find him.s

'He should have told me,' said Leonora, talking to herself since there was no one else to talk to, and she went to see if there was a phone number she could ring. There was, tucked into the blotter on his desk, where, she supposed, if she had been trained for the job, she would have looked the moment he went out of the door. She was studying it when the phone rang.

Shirley Bates—Leonora recognised the voice at once. A cheerfully sluttish young woman living in one of the houses behind the main street. She had a brood of small children, a careless, easygoing husband and was known for her laziness.

'It's Miss Leonora, isn't it? My Cecil's that poorly. Nasty cough and 'e's covered in pimples. Measles or the like. The others 'ave 'ad it, but 'e didn't. 'E's very 'ot, won't eat or drink.'

'The doctor's out,' said Leonora, 'but I'll ask him to

call and see Cecil as soon as he can. Could you put him to bed and give him plenty to drink and keep him warm?'

''E's in the kitchen watching telly, but I'll get 'im up to bed as soon as I've seen to the baby.' She sounded quite cheerful. 'Bye.'

Leonora wrote it all down and wondered if Cecil was someone the doctor would think urgent enough to be told about. Mrs Bates's children were a remarkably healthy brood despite their diet of potato crisps and fish and chips; on the other hand, Cecil, if she remembered rightly, was only five years old and measles could turn nasty if neglected.

She was weighing the pros and cons when the door opened and an old lady came in. Leonora knew her too. Old Mrs Squires, seventy-odd, widowed, and what her neighbours charitably called 'difficult'. She was comfortably off and lived alone in a small house in the main street and, having nothing better to do with her days, imagined herself to be suffering from various illnesses. She was also the local purveyor of gossip and Leonora greeted her warily.

'Mrs Squires—I'm afraid the doctor isn't here. Surgery is at five o'clock.'

'Well, of course I know that.' Mrs Squires seated herself in the waiting room. 'But I am feeling ill; he must be fetched here to see me. It's his duty.'

'He is out on a case,' said Leonora. 'I should go home and rest and come back at five o'clock.'

Mrs Squires shot her a cross look. 'I shall complain about your treatment, Miss Crosby—the Patient's Charter, you know.'

'But I haven't treated you, Mrs Squires. I really should

go home if I were you. I'll see that you are first in at five o'clock.'

'Very well.' But the old lady didn't budge. 'You're not wearing your ring. I did hear...well, never mind that. Broken it off, have you? Such a charming man too. Let's hope you get another chance.'

'Oh, I expect I shall,' said Leonora cheerfully, hiding her doubts and unhappiness. 'Now if you don't mind I must ask you to go. I have to turn out this room before the evening surgery.'

Mrs Squires tittered. 'Fancy you dusting and sweeping. The young lady from the house. I wonder what that Mr Beamish of yours would say to that?'

Leonora held her tongue and ignored a desire to shake Mrs Squires until her false teeth rattled in her head. Instead, she held the door open and smiled.

Mrs Squires, despite her rudeness a little in awe of the Crosby family, left, tottering dramatically on the step and hoping *sotto voce* that Leonora wouldn't regret her unkindness when she, a poor widow, was found dead in her bed.

Leonora shut the door and locked it and the phone rang.

It was Mrs Bates again. 'My Cecil, 'e's been sick all over the carpet; 'e's real poorly and 'e don't talk much. Gone all pale and limp.'

'I'll try and get the doctor at once, Shirley. Is Cecil in his bed?'

''E didn't want ter go. 'E's still in the kitchen.'

'Keep him warm and get him to drink a little. I'm sure the doctor won't be long. I'll phone him now.'

Leonora dialled the number on the desk and when someone answered she said with relief, 'Oh, it's you,

Mr Willis. Is Dr Galbraith there? May I speak to him? It's urgent.'

'I'll fetch him, Miss Leonora. He's on the point of leaving.'

'Well?' said the doctor in her ear.

'I'm glad I caught you,' said Leonora, relief making her voice sharp. 'Mrs Bates—the council houses—you know? Her Cecil's ill.'

She recited his symptoms in a voice which she strove to keep level. 'Will you go there? Thank heavens you aren't miles away…'

'Phone Mrs Bates and tell her I'm on my way. Why are you still at the surgery?'

'Because Mrs Crisp is in Bath, isn't she? Gone to see her mother.'

All she had in reply was a grunt before he hung up.

'Miserable man,' said Leonora, and put the kettle on and rang Mrs Bates once more. She would have a cup of tea; heaven knew, she deserved it after such a trying day. In an hour it would be surgery again and by the time she had tidied the place she would be just in time for dinner at home.

All the same, she reflected, putting a teabag in the pot, the day had gone quickly and she had had no time to think. A week or two like this, she thought ruefully, and Tony would seem like a dream—rather a bad one. But, good or bad, she had to get over it, hadn't she? And make a future for herself. While she'd been engaged to Tony, her head had been largely filled with plans for the future, the wedding, new clothes—she had expected to be happy ever after!

It was almost five o'clock and the waiting room was half-full when the doctor came in. Leonora had laid the case notes on his desk and, the moment he rang, ushered in Mrs Squires.

She was ushered out again within five minutes and Leonora wondered what he had told her to make her look so pleased with herself. Leonora sent in the next patient and wondered what the doctor had been doing all day. He hadn't said a word to her, had barely glanced at her as he'd gone to his surgery. He had told her that it was an easy job. Well, she thought rebelliously, let him find another slave to do his work. She had agreed to help out purely from kindness of heart; she didn't need the money…

A small voice reminded her that the money was going to be very useful. Provided she could persuade her father to accept it, it would allow the more urgent roof repairs to be made.

The last patient went away and she began tidying up magazines and setting chairs back in their places. She was on her knees collecting up the toys kept in one corner of the room for the benefit of the smaller patients when Dr Galbraith opened his door.

'Tell me what happened today…'

She recited the day's events in a rather cross voice. 'If you had taken the time to tell me what I was supposed to do,' she observed, 'or where you were going, or how long you would be away…'

She got up from the floor. 'Cecil? Is he very ill? Shirley Bates was so worried but I wasn't sure if you would consider him urgent.'

'I've sent him to Bristol. He has meningitis.'

She gulped in horror. 'Oh, heavens, should I have phoned you earlier? Or got an ambulance or something?'

'You acted exactly as you should have done.' His calm voice reassured her, 'I think that he has a very good chance of recovery. I am sorry that you have had such a hard time of it. You must be famished…'

'Well, yes, I am, but Mrs Pike sent over some sandwiches for me at lunchtime. Did you get something to eat?'

He looked faintly surprised. 'Er—Cricket will have something for me when I get home.'

'Is Mrs Willis ill? She's not been well since her daughter left home.'

The doctor sat astride a chair and leaned on its back. 'Her daughter is home. She had twins this morning.' He smiled. 'That is why I was in a hurry. I got there just in time.'

Leonora said slowly, 'Her parents love her very much… Is she all right? And the babies?'

'All very fit. Tell me, was Mrs Squires very trying?'

'Yes. She came in and sat down and said she was ill. I do hope she's not…' She gave him an anxious look. 'You see, I've known her for years and years and she has been ill with almost everything under the sun and no one believes her any more.' She frowned. 'I expect she's lonely but she's a gossip.'

'There is nothing wrong with Mrs Squires. And she is a gossip—a malicious one, I rather think. She told me that your callous treatment of her was on account of you being broken-hearted at the ending of your engagement.'

'She said that? The whole village will have heard it in twenty-four hours.'

'I think not. I appealed to her good nature.'

She said coldly, 'There was no need for you to do that.'

'To interfere? Have you heard from Beamish, Leonora?'

'No, of course not. And I don't want to talk about it.'

'Naturally not,' he agreed blandly. 'I hope that when you do you will address him in the icy tones you are using on me.'

He got up, ignoring her indignant breath. 'I'll take you home. Do you think you can face another day after this one?'

'Of course I can. I've enjoyed myself,' said Leonora, still frosty. 'Mrs Crisp will be away for a few days; I'll bring sandwiches with me tomorrow.'

'No need. I'll come for you when I've done the morning round and we can have lunch at Buntings. I'll have the phone with me and take any calls.'

'There is no need,' began Leonora. 'I don't mind in the least.' She added ingenuously, 'The day has gone so quickly there was no time to think.'

'Good. You are beginning to recover your pride and courage. Only I do beg of you that when you see Beamish you remember to hang onto both at all costs.'

'I have no intention of seeing Tony again.'

'One never knows what is around the corner,' said the doctor placidly. 'Now let me drive you home before they send a search party for you.'

He got out of the car to open her door when they reached the house.

'Thank you for holding the fort so sensibly, Leonora. Don't let your soft heart overrule your good sense when you see Beamish.'

'I'm not going to see him.'

He didn't answer her. Of course she would see him; he would even now be planning his visit, sure of its success. The doctor was very certain of that.

He was quite right.

Chapter 7

Leonora's second day at the surgery went smoothly.
True, she wasn't very quick at finding the patients' notes
in the filing cabinets but she was unfussed by the telephone and the appointments book.

The morning flashed by; she was surprised when the
last patient went away and Dr Galbraith put his head
round the door. 'How about coffee while I give you a
list of where I'll be? If you need me and can't reach me
from that, use the number on the desk—my own phone.
When is Mrs Crisp coming home?'

'Mr Crisp thought at the end of the week.'

'Good. She'll take over here for the afternoons.'

He drank his coffee and drove away and she set about
getting the notes out ready for the evening surgery. 'A
man of few words,' she said, as usual talking to herself, and then wondered what he was really like when

he wasn't being a doctor. She had had glimpses of that, but very briefly, and, for all she knew, his kindness and sympathy were all part of his being a doctor. Was he always calm and rather reserved? she wondered. Did he have a temper, get angry?

She washed the coffee-mugs and watered the potted plants on the waiting-room window-sill and after that there was a succession of phone calls—people wanting appointments, repeat prescriptions, a visit from the doctor—but there was nothing urgent and just before one o'clock he returned, popped her into the car and drove to Buntings.

Cricket was waiting for them, so was Tod, and they went briefly into the garden, going down to the end of it, throwing sticks for the dog and discussing bedding plants. It was a pretty garden, carefully tended but contriving to look as though everything growing in it had been there for ever and ever. Leonora stifled her envy. The garden at her house was twice as large and, despite her efforts, neglected.

Indoors again, they sat down to a cheese soufflé, salad, and a custard tart. They had their coffee at the table and Leonora, mindful of her duties, didn't linger over the meal.

'I must be getting back,' she said. 'Shall I ring you from the surgery so that you'll know I've taken the phone over again?'

'No—I'll drive you down. I want to see how Mrs Bates is coping. Cecil is going to be all right; she might like to visit him…'

'There isn't a bus until tomorrow.'

'I'm driving up to Bristol to see him. I'll take her with me.'

He's a kind man, reflected Leonora presently, watching him drive away from the surgery.

Another two days slipped by and Leonora now felt quite at home with the job. Indeed, she was vaguely regretful that Mrs Crisp would be home again tomorrow and would relieve her each afternoon, but despite the help Nanny had from Mrs Phelps from the village there was plenty to do when she was home, and her mother complained gently that while she was working the surgery took up so much time that it was impossible to have people to dinner; even an afternoon's bridge was difficult without Leonora being there to help with tea and make a fourth if needed.

'The bazaar, darling,' Lady Crosby had said with gentle reproach. 'Poor Lydia Dowling hasn't nearly enough helpers and you know what a great deal there is to do.'

Leonora had murmured a reply. Somehow, making pincushions and tray-cloths and sorting cast-off clothes for the jumble stall didn't seem important.

It was as the doctor was driving himself back from his morning rounds on Friday that he was passed on the road by a Porsche going too fast. Tony Beamish.

He glanced at his watch. Leonora would be back home by now; Mrs Crisp was always punctual and she had agreed to half past twelve as the time to take over for the afternoon. Any moment now Leonora would probably have to listen to Beamish's carefully planned explanations. Well, it was none of his business; she wasn't a child.

Later, as Cricket set his lunch before him, he gave a small, dry cough.

'Yes, Cricket?' Dr Galbraith was helping himself to ham but paused to look up.

'A message from Mrs Crisp, sir. She is unable to take over from Miss Crosby today. A migraine has laid her low.'

The doctor frowned. 'Miss Crosby is still at the surgery?'

'I presume so, sir. And Mrs Pike had occasion to telephone me a short time ago concerning your Bath Oliver biscuits which have arrived. Mr Pike was having a drink when Mr Beamish went to the pub. Very chirpy, she tells me, offered drinks all round and said he was on his way to see Miss Crosby. Unfortunately he was told that she was at the surgery.' Cricket paused to observe severely, 'It is regrettable how everyone knows everyone else's business in this village.' Then he resumed. 'Mr Beamish drank his whisky, asked if he could leave his car at the pub and was seen walking to the surgery.'

The doctor was about to sample the ham, but he put down his knife and fork, got to his feet and whistled to Tod.

'I'll be back presently, Cricket. You had better set another place.' He smiled at Cricket. 'I'll just take a look.'

Mrs Crisp's phone call, just as Leonora was getting ready to hand over to her, was tiresome but since there was nothing to be done about it she would have to stay at the surgery. Dr Galbraith should be home about one o'clock; she would ring him and ask what she was to do.

She made a pot of tea, sat down at her table in the waiting room and began to sort out the patients' notes for the evening surgery, and at the same time allowed her thoughts to dwell on the pay packet she expected the next day. She was to be paid by the hour and she had worked quite a few hours extra during the week. Even after paying for Mrs Phelps there would be a useful sum. Perhaps she could get her father to have Mr Sims, the local builder, round to take a look at the roof.

She looked up as the door opened and Tony walked in.

At the sight of him she gave a little gasp, put down her mug of tea and put her suddenly shaking hands in her lap out of sight.

'Darling, you didn't think I'd let you go, did you? You see, here I am ready to go on my knees. I've no excuses, only that I was overwhelmingly busy when you came to see me and hardly knew what I was saying. Forgive me?' His smile was charming. 'Shall we start again? Just give me the chance to explain and you'll see how right I am. A marvellous future for us both—your parents will see what a splendid plan it is; it just needs a little persuasion from you—they listen to you, don't they?'

He came a little nearer, still smiling.

'Go away,' said Leonora. 'I'm working. Besides, I have no wish to speak to you ever again and I'll never forgive you—'

'Oh, come now, darling, you know you still love me.' His voice was beguiling.

'No, I don't. I can't bear the sight of you.'

He laughed then. 'Oh, you know you don't mean that.'

'Oh, but I do, and if you come a step nearer I'll throw this mug of tea at you.'

Tony laughed again, lunged forward and took the mug from her—just as the doctor came quietly through the door, tapped his elbow and sent hot tea pouring down his shirt and fashionable city suit. A few drops splashed his face too and he wiped them away furiously.

'You clumsy...'

He saw who it was then; he saw Tod too, standing by his master, all gleaming teeth and rumbling growls.

'Am I interrupting something?' asked the doctor genially. 'Is Mr Beamish annoying you, Leonora?'

She said, 'Yes. Please make him go away. I don't seem able to make him understand that I don't want to see or hear from him again.'

'Quite right,' agreed the doctor. 'Perhaps I should

warn him that it might be as well if he did just that, for
I don't like to see my friends harassed.'

He smiled at Tony, his eyes cold. 'I am a mild man, but
if I get annoyed I can lose my temper. So be off with you,
Beamish, and don't show your face here again or there
might be trouble. You had better take that suit to the clean-
ers as soon as possible; tea stains are difficult to remove.'

He stood aside and added gently, 'If you go quietly
Tod won't bite you.'

Tony went without a word, casting an apprehensive
eye at Tod, who leered at him.

The doctor shut the door after Tony had gone and
turned to look at Leonora. She was still sitting at the
desk, looking at the notes on it, determined not to cry.
She had been overjoyed to see the doctor but now she felt
humiliated too. He seemed to be everlastingly helping her
out of awkward situations; he must consider her a fool...

'Well, now that's dealt with,' said the doctor, 'we'll go
back and have our lunch.'

She still wouldn't look at him. 'Thank you for coming when you did. It was lucky you did. Do you know
that Mrs Crisp can't come? I'll stay here—I've nothing
much to do at home this afternoon.'

'I'll take the calls on my phone; I'll drive you home
when we've eaten. I'm famished.'

'I'd rather not, if you don't mind.'

'I do mind. Where is your British phlegm, Leonora?'

'My phlegm? Oh...' She smiled then and looked at
him. 'Why do you always say the right thing, Dr Galbraith?' She got up and picked up the mug from the floor.
'I didn't know he was coming.' She gave the doctor a
questioning look. 'Did you?'

He smiled at her. 'Not until Cricket told me. Cricket always has his ear to the ground; he never misses a whisper of gossip or news and this is a small village. And Beamish passed me in his car as I drove back.' He saw her look. 'No, I didn't intend to interfere, Leonora. I supposed that you would be home and he would have to deal with your parents as well as you, and it is hardly any of my business. But Cricket's information rather changed my plans.'

'Well, thank you very much. I expect he would have gone but I—I was glad when you came in with Tod.'

'Oh, Tod can put the fear of God into anyone,' said the doctor easily.

'I think you can too,' said Leonora.

She went with him then, back through the village and into Buntings, to find Cricket waiting, his sombre countenance breaking into a wintry smile at the sight of her. While they had been gone he had whisked up a featherlight cheese omelette, made a jug of lemonade, since he had decided that Miss Crosby wasn't a young lady to drink the doctor's beer, and prepared a little dish of chocolates to go with the coffee.

All of which Leonora enjoyed, almost her normal, matter-of-fact self once more. Only as they drank their coffee did she ask, 'You don't think he'll come back again?'

'No, I'm quite sure he won't.' The doctor handed her the dish. 'Have another of these chocolates. I don't know where Cricket gets them but they are quite good.'

Presently he drove her home. 'I'll have a word with your father if I may,' he told her as they got out of the car.

'Yes, of course. Don't leave Tod there; he likes Wilkins; they can go into the garden.'

As Tod joined them she said, 'We could go in through the garden door. I dare say Wilkins is somewhere in the garden at the back.'

He came to meet them and after a moment's wariness he lumbered off with Tod.

The garden door needed a coat of paint and its framework was by no means solid, and inside the house, going down the stone-floored passage towards the kitchen, the doctor saw the woeful state of the walls. He said nothing, of course, but Leonora said over her shoulder, 'We don't use this part of the house very much. It will be a great deal drier once we've had the roof repaired.'

'Old houses are difficult to maintain,' observed the doctor mildly, 'but it is surprising how well they last. Well built in the first place, of course.'

'Great-Great-Grandfather had it built,' said Leonora, and opened the door into the kitchen.

Nanny was sitting in her own particular chair by the Aga, knitting, and made to get up.

'No, don't move, Nanny,' said Leonora. 'We came in this way because of the dogs. I'm just taking Dr Galbraith to see Father.'

'You'll stay for tea?' said Nanny.

He refused with regret. 'I must go back and do some work—letters and so on. They do pile up. Another time if I may.'

'You're always welcome in this house,' said Nanny, 'and I speak for everyone in it.'

Leonora took the doctor to her father's study and then left them and went in search of her mother.

'Darling—you're late home. Have you been busy? The Dowlings phoned; Mrs Dowling wants you to go over when you can spare a minute—something to do with the jumble stall. I didn't hear you come in.'

'I brought Dr Galbraith through the garden door; he wanted to see Father.'

'I wonder why?' Lady Crosby put down the book she was reading and looked at Leonora. 'Is your father ill? No one told me.'

'No, no, nothing like that. Tony Beamish came to the surgery earlier; I think Dr Galbraith thought it better if he talked to Father about him.'

'Oh, dear. Was he horrid? But you weren't alone with him?'

'Only for a short while before Dr Galbraith came back to the surgery.'

'And…?' said Lady Crosby. 'Did he send Tony packing?'

'Yes,' said Leonora. She would have liked to tell her mother all about it but, much as she loved her parent, she was aware that anything unpleasant or worrying was ignored by her. She would tell Nanny presently and they would have a good laugh over it.

The two men came into the room a little later and her father said, 'I'm sorry that you have been bothered by young Beamish, my dear. I understand from Dr Galbraith that we are unlikely to see or hear from him again.' Sir William blew out his moustache and looked fierce. 'The scoundrel, wanting to turn us out of our home, pretending to be in love with Leonora. It must have been pretence; no man would behave in such a manner towards the girl he intended to marry.'

The doctor, watching Leonora, saw her blush and reflected that she should do that more often; it turned her pretty face into a thing of beauty. Even in her rather dull country clothes she was lovely. He had a sudden wish to see her decked out in haute couture and jewels—sapphires and pearls, he thought, long, dangling earrings and rings on her fingers. She had pretty hands…

'You must come to dinner one evening.' Lady Crosby's voice cut into his thoughts. 'We don't entertain much these days, but we are always glad to see our friends and neighbours.' She smiled up at him. 'Is Leonora proving satisfactory at the surgery?'

'Indeed she is, Lady Crosby. I'm thinking of asking her to stay on permanently—part-time, perhaps, sharing with Mrs Crisp when she returns.'

'Really? Well, why not? It is quite proper for us to help in the village in any way we can.'

The doctor didn't bat an eyelid. 'You are quite right, Lady Crosby; I am glad you agree with me.' He shook hands then, said a few words to Sir William, and added casually to Leonora, 'I'll see you around five o'clock,' and followed her out into the hall. At the door he whistled for Tod and got into his car, aware that Leonora was glowering at him from the steps.

He didn't drive away but opened his door and got out, leaning on the car roof, watching her come towards him.

'What's all this, then?' she wanted to know. 'Have I been asked if I want to go on working for you?' She added coldly, 'It's usual to be asked before it's talked about.'

He considered this muddled speech. 'I apologise; I was attacking you from the rear, wasn't I? But when you've cooled down, Leonora, consider the offer, will you? And let me know when you've made up your mind.'

He got back into the car and she stuck her head through the window.

'Of course I'll come permanently,' she told him. She sniffed. 'Since I've been asked…'

'Splendid.' He raised a hand and drove away. 'Now what possessed me to do that?' he enquired of Tod sitting beside him.

Tod didn't answer. Eyes half-shut, he was comfortably drowsy after a good romp in the garden with Wilkins.

Leonora went back into the house and found her father in his study.

'You like the idea of working for Dr Galbraith?' he asked her as she went in. 'It curtails your freedom...'

'Father, if I had all day with nothing to do—' and that's a joke, she reflected, thinking of the bed-making and hoovering and cooking, about which he was apparently unaware '—I would have to fill it with doing the flowers and helping Mrs Dowling with her bazaars and visiting. I really enjoy it.'

She hesitated. 'And Father, I get well paid and I don't need the money.' A fib, that! 'Could we have the roof over the kitchen mended? If I lent you the money? I really have no use for it, and if I put it in the bank it's just there doing nothing, whereas the tiles are falling off all the time.' She saw his frown. 'Please, Father...'

'The money is yours, my dear; you must wish to spend it on some new clothes—something for your mother, perhaps.'

'There's enough for that as well. It's too soon to buy clothes for the summer anyway, but I'll take Mother up to town later on and we'll shop. The roof first, though!' She smiled at him. 'Just between us two.'

'I do not care to take money from my daughter,' said Sir William.

'You're not; I'm lending it. It makes sense, you know, for if one or two repairs aren't made the house will fall apart and won't be of much use to me when I eventually get it.'

'There's that, of course. Very well, my dear, provided that you promise to spend your money on yourself once the roof is seen to. I'll get Sims to come round and inspect it. He might deal with it while this weather holds.'

She went to him then and kissed the top of his head. 'Don't tell Mother.'

Sir William allowed himself to smile. 'No, no, I won't. In any case your mother has very little idea about repairs and so forth.'

Leonora went to the door. 'I'm going to make scones for tea…'

'Yes, yes, of course, Leonora. I'm sorry about Tony Beamish. Your whole future.'

Leonora said matter-of-factly, 'Father, it would have been a disastrous one. I much prefer the future Dr Galbraith has offered me and living here in the village. I would have been unhappy in London and I'm sure that is where Tony and I would have lived for most of the time.'

Nanny, told of Leonora's job probably turning out to be a permanent one, was pleased. 'You'll see a bit of life even if it's only the folk living around here. And you'll have a bit of money to call your own.' She glanced at Leonora. 'You like working for the doctor? You like him as a person?'

'Yes, I do. I didn't think I was going to at first but he kind of grows on one, Nanny, and he was rather splendid when Tony turned up.'

'So you'll go every morning and evening?'

'Yes, but for the moment I'll go all day; Mrs Crisp isn't coming back for a couple of days. She had a bad migraine so she's taking a few days off, but when she starts she'll relieve me at half past twelve and stay until I go back at half past four. Of course, I'll be free on Saturday afternoons and Sunday.'

'Well, that's nice,' said Nanny cosily, and thought how

well the pair of them were suited. Perhaps if they saw more of each other… 'I'll make the tea if those scones are ready; it's almost time for you to go to the surgery.'

Dr Galbraith had nothing to say about Tony when she saw him that evening. There weren't many patients and when he had seen the last one he bade her goodnight, reminded her to lock up carefully and drove away. She watched him go, feeling vaguely disgruntled, although she reminded herself that she had no reason to be.

The doctor would be away for the weekend; she had been given a phone number to contact his stand-in at Wells and the phone had been switched through to him. 'I'll be taking over again early on Monday morning. Enjoy your weekend.' He had gone before she could reply.

Well, she would enjoy her weekend, she supposed. A long-delayed visit to the Dowlings to discuss the bazaar, her turn to do the flowers in church, and her mother had some friends coming to tea in the afternoon. Leonora felt restless. She wondered where the doctor was going—to see whoever it was who had called his dog Tod? He had made no secret of his affection for her, had he? I hope she's nice, reflected Leonora; he deserves a good wife.

She thought about him a good deal during the weekend, imagining him in a variety of situations—at the theatre, dining out with the unknown girl, meeting friends. In fact she thought about him so much that she quite forgot to think about Tony. He had disappeared out of mind as well as out of sight.

Leonora's imaginings were very wide of the mark. The doctor spent his weekend with his sister, who lived with her farmer husband and three children in a lovely old house on the outskirts of Napton on the Hill, a small village in Warwickshire. Far from the theatre-going and

dining out that Leonora had envisaged, he walked and
rode and pottered around in old tweeds, ate huge meals
in the vast old-fashioned kitchen and kicked a football
around with his two small nephews. When he was tired
he sat down and his small niece climbed onto his lap and
demanded stories. She wanted to know about Tod too.

'He's very well,' her uncle assured her. 'Though that's
a funny sort of name you gave him. A young lady I know
doesn't much like it.'

'What young lady?' his sister, who had just joined
them, wanted to know.

'A quite beautiful young lady with a great deal of dark
hair and a sharp tongue. Very sensible too.'

'Lives in the village?'

'Yes. I imagine her ancestors owned it at one time.
She lives in a lovely house that's mouldering away for
lack of money, with her mother and father.'

'And does good works?'

'Oh, yes.'

'Well, go on,' said his sister. 'Is she married, engaged,
and do you like her?'

'She was going to be married but luckily no longer,
neither is she engaged—not at the moment. Yes, I like
her. A series of—er—happenings made it possible for
me to ask her to be my receptionist at the surgery. She's
quite good—needs the money to have the roof repaired.'

'But if she's the daughter of the manor...' began his
sister.

'I used cunning; I implied that she would be undertaking vital charitable work.'

'You've been to a lot of trouble.'

The doctor sat back with his eyes closed. 'Funnily

enough, until now I was unable to understand why.' He opened one eye. 'Is it time for tea?'

He was about to get into his car on Sunday evening when his brother-in-law said, 'Molly would like to come over and see you. Would that be all right?'

The doctor smiled. 'Jeffrey, Molly wants to get a look at my new receptionist. Of course you must all come— make it a Saturday if you can; on Sunday she is much taken up with church and Sunday lunch.'

He got into his car and Tod got in beside him. 'I'll do my best to arrange a meeting but it's quite likely that she will refuse to come. She isn't sure if she likes me. You see, I have been witness to some of her more delicate situations.' He laughed. 'Why, when we met for the first time she tripped up in the lane and sat down hard a few yards from the car. Very tart she was too, and then disarmed me completely by apologising for being rude. You'll like her.'

He thought about her as he drove back to Pont Magna. 'She is beginning to take up too many of my thoughts,' he told Tod, 'probably because I haven't met a girl like her before—and I'm not sure if I want that.'

He pulled one of Tod's silky ears gently. 'Ah, well, back to work in the morning and that will give me plenty to think about.'

So when Leonora arrived on Monday and poked her head round the surgery door to say good morning she was taken aback by his cool rejoinder and impersonal blandness.

He's quarrelled with her, she reflected, finding notes and marshalling the patients into seats. A full house too—nasty coughs, a black eye, a toddler with suspicious spots and the snuffles, and the verger, who had fallen down the last few steps of the narrow, winding stairs to the church tower and had got some nasty bruises as a result.

The doctor didn't wait for his coffee after surgery. 'You've got the phone number,' he reminded her. 'I'll call in when I get back. You had better come back to my place for lunch.'

'I've brought sandwiches, thank you.' She spoke in a cool voice; if he wanted to be frosty she would be too. 'There are a lot of patients for the evening clinic. If any more phone…?'

He took a quick look at the appointments book. 'I'll see two more—anyone else, unless it's urgent, must come in the morning. That's pretty full too—and young Beamish told me it was an easy job!'

He watched the colour creep into Leonora's cheeks. Did she still love the man? Surely not… His frown was so ferocious that she looked at him in astonishment but he had gone before she could say anything.

She spent the next hour or so tidying the place—cleaning bowls and the simple instruments he had used, cleaning up the magazines and toys—and finally put on the kettle for a cup of coffee to go with her sandwiches. There had been several phone calls for appointments and she had got out the notes for the evening surgery.

She made the coffee and bit into the first of Nanny's cheese sandwiches. The phone rang and she swallowed hastily and said, 'Hello, Dr Galbraith's surgery,' in a rather thick voice.

It was a call from Willis Farm. 'It's the baby—'e don't look well; the doctor must come 'fore 'e gets any worse.'

Leonora picked up the pen. 'It's Janice, isn't it? Which baby is it? You had a boy and a girl, didn't you?'

'Never you mind; just send the doctor.'

'He isn't here, but I can get him for you, only I must know what to tell him. Now, which baby?'

'The boy—we calls 'im Billy. Looks kind of poorly and keeps screaming.'

'The little girl's all right?'

'Yes, far as I can see. Where is 'e, then?'

'I can phone him at once. Isn't your mother there?'

'Ain't no one 'ere. Ma's gone ter Radstock Market and the men are down the ten-acre field.'

'Go back to the babies, Janice,' said Leonora. 'I'm going to phone the doctor now; he'll come just as soon as he can.'

She was putting the phone down when he walked in.

'That was Janice,' said Leonora. 'She says one of the twins is ill and she's alone—the men are at the other end of the farm, and her mother's in Radstock.'

'Did she tell you what was wrong?'

'Only that Billy looked poorly and screamed a lot.'

He went to his locked cupboard in the surgery and selected the items he wanted, put them in his bag and said, 'Right, then, we'd better go.'

We? She couldn't help casting a look at the sandwiches, but since he didn't respond she followed him out of the door, which he locked before opening the car door and urging her in.

He didn't appear to be hurrying but he hadn't wasted a moment. As they left the village street she asked, 'Why must I come with you? I don't know anything much about babies.'

He turned to look at her. 'No, no—you are coming as my chaperon.'

'Chap…' For a moment she was speechless. 'Whatever for?'

'Have you seen Janice since she came back from London?' he asked.

'No. She was a quiet girl—not very friendly with anyone else here, quite pretty, though—she had nice mousy hair…'

She gave him an enquiring look which he ignored, and he didn't speak again until he'd driven into the farmyard, got out, opened her door and fetched his bag from the back seat. A girl was standing at the open door watching them. If this was Janice, where was the mousy hair, the pretty face? This girl had shorn locks of a vibrant chestnut colour and so much make-up that it was hard to tell what she really looked like. She had a stud in one nostril, long, dangling earrings and the shortest skirt Leonora had ever seen.

'Where's this baby?' asked the doctor in a voice nicely compounded of professional reserve and kindness. 'Tell me exactly when he became ill. Is he feverish? Being sick?'

He went past her into the house, saying over his shoulder, 'Leonora, come with me, please.'

Janice led the way upstairs to where the babies were lying in their cots. The baby girl was sleeping but Billy was roaring his head off, red in the face, waving minute fists in rage. The doctor picked him up.

'He's sopping wet,' he observed mildly. 'Get some dry clothes for him—he needs changing for a start.'

Janice went to a chest of drawers and started rummaging in it and he handed the baby to Leonora, who rightly deduced that she was meant to undress the infant. She laid him gently in his cot again and took off his old-fash-

ioned gown and the wringing wet nappy and exposed a
small sore bottom.

'He needs a bath,' she said, and added, 'Sorry...'

'You haven't bathed the babies today,' stated the doctor. 'And when were they last changed? Billy isn't ill;
he's wet and very sore. Get a bath ready for them; let's
get both of them washed and then I'll examine them and
make sure there is nothing wrong. When did the district
nurse come?'

'Yesterday. Don't want 'er, old Nosy Parker; told 'er
she didn't need ter come any more.'

'Your mother knows this?'

'Ma don't know nothing.' She shrugged her shoulders
and went out and presently came back with a small bath
and then warm water.

The baby girl—Daisy—was awake now; Leonora,
without being asked, stripped the cots while the babies
were being bathed, made them up again with clean sheets
and then sat down with a towel on her lap so that Billy
could lie on it while his poor sore bottom was examined
by the doctor.

Leonora held him gently, stroking the fair hair on his
small head, telling him what a good boy he was, all the
while aware of the doctor's face within inches of her
own as he bent down, and aware too of a peculiar feeling somewhere under her ribs which resolved itself into
a flood of happiness. Not that she had the leisure to think
about it. Billy was wriggling like a very small eel and
crying again.

'When did they have their last feed?' asked the doctor.

'Oh, I dunno—this morning. Ma went early; she fed
'em.'

'Go and get their feed now. There is nothing wrong

with either of your babies. They were hungry, dirty and wet. Tell me, would you like them to go to the children's hospital for a few weeks while you decide what you intend to do?'

'Yeah, that's a good idea. What am I supposed to do with two kids anyway? Didn't want 'em, did I?'

'They could be adopted.'

'That suits me fine.' She flounced away to fetch the babies' bottles and the doctor got out his phone while Leonora tucked Daisy in her cot once more. Billy began to bawl again, so she picked him up and cuddled him, listening vaguely to the doctor's voice. He was on the phone for a long time.

She accepted a bottle from Janice and began to feed Billy; he gulped and choked in his haste and she wondered if he had been getting as much as he needed. The doctor must have had the same idea for he phoned again and then said, 'The district nurse is coming this afternoon; she will make up the babies' feeds for the rest of the day and make sure that they are all right. You will do exactly what she says, and as soon as it can be arranged Billy and Daisy will be taken to the hospital. I'll come and see your parents this evening.'

He glanced at Leonora. 'Ready to go? Nurse will be here within the next hour; she knows what to do.'

On the way back Leonora burst out, 'How could she? Such little babies and no one to love them—and that's all they want—food and warmth and love, isn't it?' She hadn't meant to weep but two tears escaped and ran down her cheeks.

The doctor, looking straight ahead, none the less saw them. He dropped a large hand on her arm for a moment. 'They will be adopted by people who will love them and care for them. I'll have to speak to her parents, of course, but I suspect that once she is free of the twins she will leave home again. In the meantime the district nurse will keep an eye on them and with luck we should get them transferred to hospital tomorrow or the next day.'

'It must be so satisfying to get things done,' said Leonora fiercely, 'to know what to do and to be able to get on with it.'

His reassuring grunt was comforting.

He glanced at his watch. 'It's three o'clock; at least no one has called on the phone. We'll get something to eat before we do anything else.'

'My sandwiches…' began Leonora.

'They'll be curling at the edges by now. Cricket will find us something.'

This was getting to be a habit, reflected Leonora— something which for some reason she found unsettling. 'If you don't mind I'll go straight to the surgery, Doctor.'

'I do mind—and call me James.' He didn't look at her but went on with casual friendliness, 'We are colleagues, are we not?'

'Well, yes, I suppose so,' she said doubtfully. 'You don't mind?'

His mouth twitched. 'Not at all. I should prefer it since we are to see a good deal of each other for the time being.'

Did that mean, she wondered worriedly, that he was already looking for another receptionist—a trained one who knew the difference between indigestion and a heart attack and who knew how to fend off those who came to the surgery apparently for the fun of it?

She said soberly, 'Very well, James.' After which it hardly seemed appropriate to mention the surgery again. Besides, she was hungry.

Chapter 8

Mrs Crisp came back in a day or two—and perhaps that was as well, thought Leonora. Working for the doctor in the surgery was one thing, but somehow lunching with him in his lovely house with Cricket beaming at her—and feeling so happy while she was there—was unsettling.

She was careful to work the hours he had suggested and made no effort to talk to him unless it was about a patient or phone call. He didn't seem to mind, she reflected forlornly. True, he had stopped one morning to tell her that Billy and Daisy were in hospital and thriving and their mother had packed her bag and left home again.

'How can you possibly leave two little babies?' Leonora had wanted to know.

He had smiled thinly and shaken his head and gone away again to see to his patients.

She was handing over to Mrs Crisp on her first after-

noon back when he came into the surgery, wished Mrs
Crisp a good day and then said, 'Leonora, my sister is
coming down on Saturday for the weekend. I'd like you
to come to tea.'

If they had been alone she would have made some
excuse—not that she didn't want to accept, but she had
decided, hadn't she, that she would take care not to get
too friendly. She wasn't very clear why this was necessary but that was beside the point. Mrs Crisp, standing
there smiling and nodding, made it difficult to refuse.
Besides, he didn't give her a chance to do so.

'Around three o'clock,' he said easily. 'We look forward to seeing you.'

When he'd gone Mrs Crisp observed chattily, 'I wonder who else will be there?'

Leonora felt a pang of relief and then disappointment;
there would be half the village there, no doubt. She reminded herself that that was exactly what she wanted.

Lady Crosby puckered her brows when Leonora told
her that she would be going to Buntings for tea. 'Strange
that Dr Galbraith didn't include your father and me. Will
there be many there, I wonder?'

'I've no idea. He mentioned his sister staying with
him—she has three small children, Mrs Crisp tells me.'

'In that case I would have refused. With children there
can be no conversation. I dare say there will be another
dinner party shortly. You haven't met any of his friends?'

'Mother, I'm at the surgery; even if he had friends
staying they wouldn't come there.' Was now the time to
mention the lunches she had had at Buntings? she wondered, and decided against saying anything. Her mother
would jump to the conclusion that Dr Galbraith—she
must remember to call him James—was interested in

her. Which he wasn't. Even when he had invited her to
tea he had sounded exactly like the family doctor talking to a patient.

On Saturday, uncertain as to who might be there, she
got into her jersey dress and a long cardigan, both in a
pleasant shade of turquoise-blue and both in a style guaranteed to be wearable five years hence, arranged her hair
in a chignon, made up nicely, thanking heaven that it was
a dry, quite warm day so that she could wear light shoes.
She had considered biking there but then she might arrive
a bit tousled. She bade her parents goodbye, told Nanny
she would be back around six o'clock, perhaps earlier,
and walked to Buntings.

Walking up the drive to the house, she gave a small
sigh of envy. It looked charming; the flowerbeds were
full of spring flowers now, and the shrubbery was newly
green. The door was open and as she reached it two small
boys darted out.

They came to a halt by her and offered grubby hands.
'You are Leonora,' said the taller of the two. 'I'm Paul;
he's George.'

Leonora shook hands. 'Hello, Paul; hello, George.
How did you know who I was?'

'Uncle James told us. Come inside.'

The doctor came to meet them as they entered the
hall. His greeting was casual and friendly. 'The house
is in an uproar; I hope you don't mind. Come and meet
Molly and my brother-in-law. There's another child somewhere—my niece.'

They all went into the drawing room and she shook
hands with Molly and Jeffrey and then stooped to take
the little girl's hand. 'I'm two,' she whispered, and bur-

ied her face in her mother's skirt. Presently she peeped
up at Leonora. 'Uncle James and me share Tod.'

'Now, that's nice,' said Leonora, bending down. 'I've
got a dog too. His name's Wilkins.'

A small hand was slipped into hers. 'I'll show you
Tod.'

They all went into the garden then, and the talk was
easy and pleasant and made her feel perfectly at home.
Tod was admired, stroked and offered a ball while they
strolled around, the children darting to and fro, the
grown-ups stopping to discuss some plant or other. Molly
tucked an arm into Leonora's, not asking questions, mentioning only casually Leonora's work at the surgery, but
telling her about the children and her life on the farm.

'I don't do any farm work—I wouldn't know how to
and Jeffrey has an agent—but it's a nice old house and
there's heaps of room for the children. We ride too—do
you?'

'I used to.' Something in Leonora's voice caused Molly
to start an animated conversation about her children.
'They're a handful even with Nanny's help. Of course,
they're as good as gold when they come down here. They
adore James; he makes a marvellous uncle and, heaven
knows, he has enough practice—we have four sisters,
did you know? Two of them are married with children.
They live a good way away, though—Scotland and the
depths of Cornwall. The other two are in Canada with
our father and mother—twins, waiting to go to univer-
sity; they're the youngest.'

'It must be lovely to have a brother and sisters…'

'Oh, it is. We all like each other too. Here's Cricket to
tell us tea is ready.'

It was a hilarious meal, sitting round the dining-room

table with the children, and Cricket had done them proud. Tiny sandwiches, a plate of bread and butter cut paper-thin, fairy cakes, gingerbread men and a magnificent chocolate cake.

There was even a high chair for the little girl and when Molly saw Leonora looking at it she said, 'James keeps one here; there's always a baby or a toddler; as fast as one is big enough to sit on a chair there's another one ready for the high chair!' She laughed. 'Mother and Father say they lose count of their grandchildren.'

It wasn't quite what Leonora had expected but she found herself wishing that she had a large family like the doctor's; their warmth and pleasure in each other's company was something she had never experienced and wasn't likely to. She didn't waste time repining, though. She ate a splendid tea, unaware of the doctor's eyes upon her, wholly taken up with the small boys sitting on either side of her.

After tea they played hide-and-seek round the house. As she raced round the passages, up and down the staircase, in and out of the rooms, Leonora's cheeks got flushed and her hair escaped in little curls; she was happy and a little excited, so that she looked prettier than ever.

Creeping up the back stairs, looking for a likely hiding place, she came face to face with the doctor.

They were at the end of a narrow passage leading to the back of the house, with doors on one side and a row of small windows overlooking the garden.

They stood looking at each other for a moment. 'Enjoying yourself, Leonora?' he asked, and smiled.

'Oh, yes—yes, I am. I'd forgotten what fun it was. We must hide...'

'We aren't really built for it, are we?' he observed. 'Rather on the big side.'

'Well, really!' began Leonora, suddenly aware of her magnificent proportions compared with Molly, who was a slender size eight. Her childish pleasure was pricked like a balloon. 'You're very rude,' she said tartly, and edged past him.

He put out a hand and stopped her very gently. 'I'm so sorry; would it make things better if I told you that I like my women big?'

He bent and kissed her quickly. 'Run along and hide. There's a large cupboard at the end of this passage.'

She wanted to run out of his house, get away from him, but she couldn't do that; she got into the cupboard and presently was discovered by a small boy shouting in triumph.

It was the children's bedtime then. Leonora was embraced in turn, shook hands with Molly and Jeffrey, thanked the doctor in a chilly voice for a pleasant afternoon, took her cardigan from Cricket and went to the door.

She found the doctor beside her. 'I'll walk with you,' he told her affably. 'The house will be bedlam until the children are in bed.'

Short of turning and running for it there was nothing she could do about it, not with Cricket watching. She said nothing at all in a rather marked manner, told Cricket what a delightful tea he had given them, and walked out of the door, stiff with dignity.

'Why are you cross?' asked the doctor blandly, strolling along beside her. 'Is it because I called you a big girl or because I kissed you?'

'Both,' snapped Leonora. 'And I would much prefer to walk home alone.'

He ignored this. 'But you are a big girl,' he pointed out in a reasonable voice. 'But, I must add, most splendidly shaped; to say otherwise would be an outrage.'

'You shouldn't talk to me like this,' said Leonora, marching along, very red in the face.

'Should I not have kissed you either? I enjoyed it.'

So did I, thought Leonora, although she wasn't going to say so. She kept a haughty silence and saw Mrs Pike peering at them from the closed door of her shop, which prompted her to say in a peevish voice, 'There is absolutely no need to walk home with me.'

He stopped and turned her round to face him. 'I do not know what has made you so contrary. We are colleagues, are we not? And I thought we were friends.' He grinned down at her. 'And I wonder what Mrs Pike thinks we are?'

'Is she still peeping? Oh, please, Dr Galbraith, may we walk on?'

'Call me James...'

'James,' she went on, 'you're impossible...'

She stopped. He wasn't impossible; he was James, who laughed at her because she was a big girl and was silly about being kissed, and she wished she had never met him. She wished too that she didn't love him. Why would she discover that in the middle of the village's main street with curtains twitching right and left of them?

They were walking on, side by side, not touching. She felt quite dizzy with the sudden discovery of her love. This was love, she realised; whatever she had felt for Tony hadn't been that—more of an infatuation, she supposed. She wanted to tell James, which was absurd;

instead, anxious to break the silence between them, she started to talk about the children.

He answered her with casual good nature and it amazed her that he couldn't know how she felt. But why should he?

At the house, he stayed for a short time, talking to her mother and father, then he bade her a brisk goodbye and strode off home, turning to wave at the open gate.

'Who else was there?' her mother wanted to know. 'He has many friends, I'm sure.'

'Well, there was his sister and brother-in-law and their three children.'

'No one else? How extraordinary. Was it boring, darling?'

'No. We played hide-and-seek all over the house—the children are charming.' Leonora smiled to herself. 'We had tea round the table in the dining room—with the children...'

'Surely there was a nanny?'

'Oh, yes. She was having the afternoon off.'

Lady Crosby picked up her book. 'Well, as long as you weren't bored, Leonora. It sounds to me like the waste of an afternoon—you would have enjoyed yourself more if you had gone to the Dowlings'. Their niece is staying—such a pretty girl; plenty of money, I hear; I'm surprised Dr Galbraith wasn't invited.'

Leonora felt an instant hatred for the niece. She said abruptly, 'I'll go and see if Nanny needs any help with dinner,' and took herself off to the kitchen, where she got in Nanny's way until she was told to take Wilkins for a walk. 'For I don't know what's got into you, Miss Leonora,' said Nanny. 'Proper crotchety you are and no mistake.'

So she took Wilkins out into the garden and then into the park, and since there was no one else to tell she told him all about James.

'I can quite see,' she told him, 'that it's being an only child. I mean I can't talk to Mother and Father, if you see what I mean—talk to them like they were all talking together at James's house, saying what they really meant and knowing that the others were listening…'

Wilkins pressed up against her, staring up into her face with soft brown eyes; he was her friend and offering sympathy, and Leonora, who almost never cried, cried a little now and felt better. 'I'll see him on Monday,' she said, and blew her pretty nose and went back indoors and laid the table for Nanny.

She woke several times during the night, thinking about James, longing to see him and at the same time dreading their meeting. She would have to behave as though nothing had changed and she wasn't sure if she would be able to manage that. To give up her job at the surgery would be the easiest way out of her dilemma; on the other hand, if she did that she wouldn't see him. Besides, Sims was going to start on the roof on Monday morning and would expect to be paid. She slept at length and woke with a heavy head.

Monday wasn't as bad as she had expected. For one thing the surgery was full and when the doctor came in there was no time for more than a brief good morning, and, for another, when he had dealt with his patients he went away at once, not waiting for his usual cup of coffee. He wasn't back when Mrs Crisp arrived and Leonora took herself off home.

If I can get through one day like that, I can get through the rest of them—until he finds a receptionist to suit him,

she thought. She had calculated that Mr Sims would take
three weeks to patch the roof; once that was done, if she
didn't want to go on working for James she could think up
some excuse and leave. After all, she had only gone to fill
a gap, hadn't she? She refused to think further than that;
a future without the doctor wasn't to be contemplated…

She managed very nicely during the next two weeks,
offering him chilly good mornings and good evenings,
making sure that there was never a chance for them to
be alone. It took all her ingenuity at times, and the doctor, puzzled and a little amused, wondered what she was
up to.

He played along with her; he was kind and friendly
and impassive. He knew by now that he loved her and
intended to marry her but he was content to await events.
Something was worrying his Leonora and, being a man
without conceit, he was quite unaware of the truth.

The roof repaired, Mr Sims took away his ladders and
Leonora's cheque, and since there was no further excuse
to make as to why she had to continue working Leonora
sought for a way of ending a situation which from her
point of view was becoming increasingly awkward. Only
the day before, James had suggested that she might like
to have lunch with him at Buntings so that she could admire the garden. Her refusal had been so instant that he
had lifted an eyebrow, watching her red face and listening to her trying to soften her sharp reply.

'That is, thank you very much, but I said I'd be home
as soon as possible; I've several things to see to.'

He had smiled then and said placidly, 'Of course—
another time.' Then he'd begun to talk about one of his
patients who wanted to alter his appointment.

It wouldn't do—she would have to think of something.

As it turned out, she had no need to do that.

It was the following day, when she got home in time for lunch, that she found Nanny sitting in the kitchen looking flushed, and coughing a nasty little dry cough.

'You've caught cold,' said Leonora, and bustled her off to bed with a hot-water bottle and a hot drink and some aspirin. 'You stay there, Nanny—I'll see to the lunch and tea, and get supper when I get back this evening. Don't you dare get out of bed.'

'I'll feel better presently,' said Nanny, and fell into an uneasy doze.

Lady Crosby, informed of Nanny's poorly state, made a little face.

'Oh, dear, poor Nanny. Do you suppose it's flu? I'd better not go near her; you know how easily I catch things. I expect you can manage, darling. We can have an easy meal this evening—something you can deal with when you get back from the surgery. I don't suppose we need to send for Dr Galbraith.'

'Well, if Nanny's not better tomorrow I think you had better, Mother.'

'Of course if Nanny's ill she must be looked after. You'll see him this evening, won't you? Or tomorrow morning? I dare say it's just a feverish cold. Nanny is never ill.'

Leonora got the lunch, tidied up, took a look at Nanny and found her sleeping, and went to get the tea-tray ready and then examine the contents of the fridge. It would have to be a corned beef pie, disguised in a handsome dish. There were vegetables enough and some prawns in the freezer—prawn cocktails, she decided, the pie with a variety of vegetables and an egg custard. She could make a sauce from strawberry jam when she got home that evening.

She made Nanny a jug of lemonade before she left, turned her pillows and bathed her hot face and asked her mother to take a look from time to time. 'You don't need to go into Nanny's room—if you'd just take a look to make sure she's all right.'

'Very well, dear, since there is no one else. Supposing Nanny wants something or feels worse?'

'I'm sure you can cope, Mother, and I'll be back in a couple of hours.'

Lady Crosby looked vexed. 'To think that you should have been marrying Tony and looking forward to a settled future…'

Leonora thought of several answers to that but none of them seemed suitable.

There was only a handful of patients at the surgery and Leonora glanced with relief at the clock as she started tidying up.

The doctor saw that. 'Going out this evening?' he asked casually.

'No. Oh, no. Nanny's got a bad cold so I said I'd get dinner this evening. She's keeping warm in bed.'

He was at his desk, locking the drawers, putting papers in his case.

'Not often ill, is she? A vigorous little lady.'

'She's a darling,' said Leonora warmly. 'I don't know how we would manage without her.'

'No—well, don't hang around. I'll lock up and see you in the morning. Let me know if you are worried about her and I'll take a look.'

'Yes, thank you, I will.'

She hurried home and found her mother playing patience in the drawing room while her father read.

'How's Nanny?' she asked.

Her mother looked up. 'Hello, darling. I peeped in once or twice; she seemed quite comfortable—coughing a bit, but what does one expect with a heavy cold?' She turned over a card. 'Are you going to be a clever girl and cook our dinner?' She smiled sweetly at Leonora. 'Something nice?' she added coaxingly.

'I'll surprise you,' said Leonora, and sped away, not to the kitchen but to Nanny's room.

Nanny was awake, hot and restless and thirsty. 'Your ma popped in but I didn't like to bother her,' she said when Leonora frowned at the empty jug.

'I'm going to wash your hands and face and put you into a fresh nightie and make your bed,' said Leonora. 'Then I'll bring you some soup and after that a cup of tea and some more aspirin.' She picked up the jug. 'Give me five minutes, Nanny.'

She whisked herself into the kitchen, popped the prepared pie in the oven, put the vegetables on the slow burner and set the soup to warm. There was still a lemon; she made a jug of lemonade, lavishly iced, and bore it back to Nanny's room before gently washing her, sitting her in a chair while she made the bed and fetched more pillows. Then she settled her against them, a shawl around her shoulders.

'That's better,' said Nanny. 'I do believe I'd like some of that soup.'

The dinner was cooking itself, thank heaven. Leonora took the soup upstairs and before Nanny started on it took her temperature. It was up—not frighteningly so, but none the less higher than it should be.

In the morning, she decided, she would ask James to come and see Nanny—perhaps an antibiotic...? At the moment Nanny seemed easier and when Leonora slipped up to look at her just before she dished up she was asleep.

She reassured her mother at dinner. 'Nanny's asleep at present; if she has a quiet night I dare say her temperature will be down in the morning.'

'We can't have Nanny ill,' observed her father. 'Perhaps we should get Dr Galbraith to look in tomorrow some-time.' He glanced at Leonora. 'You can manage, my dear. I dare say we can get extra help...'

He looked around vaguely as if to conjure domestic help out of the walls and Leonora said quickly, 'No need, Father, I can manage.'

And her mother said, 'Of course you can, darling, and I'll help.'

Leonora thanked her gravely, both she and her father aware that Lady Crosby had no intention of altering her gentle day's routine. She had always had a sheltered life, first as a girl with doting parents and then as a wife cherished by a husband who shrugged off her inability to cope with domestic problems.

At first that hadn't mattered, for there had been money enough to employ a housekeeper and help in the house, and now, since he had lost most of his money, it was too late to change her ways. Leonora knew that too and accepted it. All the same, if Nanny were to be ill for more than a day or two it would be difficult to manage even with the help she had from the village.

She was a sensible girl; she decided to worry about that if and when it happened, and after a last peep at Nanny went to bed.

It was just after three o'clock when she woke, and a

vague feeling of uneasiness got her out of bed, to creep out of her room and along the wide corridor leading to the passage where Nanny had her room.

Nanny was muttering and mumbling to herself, half choking on a nasty little cough, and she felt hotter than ever.

'Nanny,' said Leonora, 'how do you feel? Shall I get you a drink and bathe your face—cool you down a bit?'

Nanny didn't seem to hear, looking past her at the empty room, whispering to someone she couldn't see. Leonora turned the bedside lamp so that the light shone on Nanny. Her face was grey and somehow grown small and her breathing was harsh and quick.

Leonora flew through the house and down the staircase and picked up the phone. At the sound of the doctor's quiet voice she let out a great sigh of thankfulness.

'James, it's Nanny. She's ill—hot and restless and her breathing's funny—and she doesn't know me.'

'Unlock the front door and go back to her.' His matter-of-fact manner steadied her. 'I'll be with you in ten minutes.'

It was less than that when he came quietly into the room. He was wearing a thick sweater and trousers, his hair stood on end and there was a faint stubble on his chin, but his manner was as cool and self-assured as though he were in his surgery.

He took one look at Leonora. 'Go and put on a dressing gown before you catch cold; we may be here for a little while.'

His tone was impersonal but she flushed a little, until that moment forgetful of the fact that she had rushed to Nanny in a cotton nightie and bare feet. She nodded and disappeared silently, to reappear moments later, her dressing gown fastened tightly around her, slippers on her feet.

The doctor was bending over Nanny, going over her chest with his stethoscope. Presently he stood up. 'Pneumonia. I'll give her an injection—an antibiotic—and see if I can find her a bed. She needs hospital treatment.'

Leonora's eyes looked enormous in her pale face. 'She'll hate that…'

His voice was very gentle. 'At the moment she isn't very aware of where she is—she'll only need to stay for a few days until the antibiotics do their work, then we can have her back.'

He took his phone from his pocket and dialled and Leonora stood as quiet as a mouse, holding Nanny's hand, listening to his calm voice.

'There's a bed at Bath; I'll get an ambulance; the sooner she gets there the better.' He glanced at her. 'Get a bag and pack a few things, will you?'

'Yes. May I go with her? Please…'

'I'll take you in the car; I'll see her safely in bed and bring you back here—hopefully in time for morning surgery.'

She nodded. 'I'll go and dress and get Nanny's things together. Will you be all right here?'

He checked a smile and assured her gravely that he would be.

She tore into the first clothes she laid hands on, washed her face, dragged a comb through her hair and tied it back with a bit of ribbon, before going back to pack a bag for Nanny. An easy task. Nanny's drawers were immaculate, garments folded exactly, beautifully ironed, smelling of lavender bags. Leonora packed her old-fashioned nighties, her dressing gown and slippers and brush and comb and bag of toiletries, added her spectacles and the Bible she kept on her bedside table and closed the case.

The doctor was sitting on the edge of the bed, watching Nanny, completely relaxed. 'Shall I make a cup of tea?' she asked. 'I got you out of bed very early…'

'A splendid idea, and bring a pencil and paper with you. You must leave a note for your mother and father. You don't want to wake them?'

'They would worry. Perhaps I could phone them from the hospital.'

'A good idea. The ambulance should be here in fifteen minutes or so.'

She crept down to the kitchen and made tea. Wilkins, from his basket by the Aga, was pleased to see her, accepted a biscuit and went back to sleep, and she went back upstairs with two mugs and more biscuits on a tray.

While they ate and drank she composed a note and showed it to the doctor. 'Would that do? I don't want to upset them.'

He gave her a thoughtful look, read the note and handed it back. 'That's fine. If you've finished your tea, we'll get Nanny wrapped up ready for the ambulancemen. They may wake your parents…'

'Probably not; their room is at the back of the house and there's a door to the passage leading to it. Shall I creep in and leave the note? And then if they're awake I can tell them.'

He nodded without speaking and began to wrap Nanny carefully in a blanket. She was quieter now, unaware that she was coughing.

Leonora whispered, 'Is she very ill?' She added sharply, 'Tell me the truth.'

'Yes, but I hope that we have caught it in time. She's

a tough little lady.' He listened. 'There's the ambulance. Go and let them in; tell them to be quiet.'

When they came into the room, he told her to go to her parents' room with the note and then go down to the hall. 'And bring a jacket.'

Her parents didn't stir as she opened their door, put the note on a bedside table and crept out again, closing the door after her. The men were loading the stretcher into the ambulance as she reached the hall and as they shut its doors the doctor went to his car. 'Jump in—I'll close your front door.'

She got in and sat silently while he drove, keeping the ambulance in sight. It was beginning to get light now and she felt a strong urge to go to sleep but it was a comparatively short journey and she told herself that she wasn't really tired.

'Do you often do this—get up in the night?'

'Quite frequently. I don't need much sleep.' He didn't tell her that he had only been in bed for a couple of hours when she had phoned. 'How will you manage at home?'

'Oh, I'll manage,' she assured him. 'We've got help from the village now I'm at the surgery, and there's not much to do.'

Which, considering the size of her home and her mother's helplessness, wasn't true.

'You'll be able to manage the surgery as well as household chores? I dare say your mother will help out.'

Leonora's reply to that sounded so doubtful that he didn't say any more.

Trotting behind the trolley bearing Nanny to her ward, Leonora was wide awake again; the doctor was talking to a solemn-looking man in a long white coat and appeared to have forgotten her; it seemed best to keep close to Nanny.

Waiting by the bed, she saw him coming towards her, still with the same man and this time with a nurse, who told her to wait outside the ward. 'There's a rest room, dear. We'll talk to you presently.'

It seemed a long time before James came looking for her.

'Come and see Nanny and then we'll go back,' he told her briskly. 'She's in good hands and there is an excellent chance of her recovery. She won't know you but don't let that worry you. We'll come and see her this evening.'

Nanny looked comfortable propped up on pillows, very small against them. She was dozing and although she didn't respond to Leonora's kiss it seemed as though she was better.

The doctor's hand on her arm roused her to say goodbye to the nurse and go with him back to the car, and he popped her in, got in beside her and drove away.

'I'll take you home,' he told her presently. 'You can do your hair and so on and I'll collect you in half an hour. You'll breakfast with me and we'll open the surgery at the usual time.'

'Oh, but I can't—I mean, there's breakfast to get for Mother and Father.'

'I dare say your mother will manage that for once,' he observed. 'You've a day's work ahead of you, remember.'

'So have you.'

'Ah, but I have Cricket to cosset me. And he will enjoy cosseting you too.'

'Yes, that would be nice, but...'

'Dear girl, will you do as I say?' He sounded so kind

that she could have wept—just because she was tired and chilly and hungry.

She said, 'Yes, James,' in such a meek voice that he glanced at her in surprise.

At the house he went in with her, but there was no sound. He left her in the hall, reminding her that he would return in half an hour, and she went to her room, showered and dressed again, did her hair in its usual chignon and made up her tired face. There was just time to go to the kitchen, put the kettle on and lay a tray for early-morning tea. Wilkins, roused from sleep, went out into the garden, and she went upstairs to wake her parents.

There wasn't time to do more than give a quick explanation.

'I'll be back at lunchtime,' she told them. 'Wilkins has been out and you'll only have breakfast to get.'

Lady Crosby sat up in bed. 'My dear child, I'll do my best. You know I always do, however poorly I feel.'

'I dare say I can boil an egg,' said her father gruffly. 'Pity about Nanny.' He sipped his tea. 'I'll ring the hospital later. Is she very ill?'

'Yes, Father. I must go; I'll come home as soon as I can.'

She reached the door at the same time as the Rolls came to a silent halt before it. James got out and opened her door for her.

'You look as fresh as a daisy,' he observed. 'Parents awake?'

'Yes. Father said he'd phone the hospital later on.'

'I shall be going to see her this evening. Want to come with me?'

'Oh, yes.' He watched her tell-tale thoughts racing

across her face. 'What time? I mean, I'll have to get a meal.'

'Put something in the oven. We shan't be away long. We'll go directly after surgery.'

Cricket had the door open as they reached it and she was marched straight into the dining room, her nose twitching at the delicious smells coming from the open kitchen door. She was sat down, given a cup of coffee and then, urged by her host, fell to on bacon, eggs, mushrooms and fried bread, and then, again gently persuaded by the doctor, toast and marmalade and more coffee.

She could have curled up in a chair and slept then but she was whisked out into the garden and walked briskly round while Tod circled about them. It was a cool, bright morning and by the time they had to leave for the surgery she was wide awake again. Cricket, handing her her jacket with a fatherly air, actually smiled widely.

'That was the most delicious breakfast,' she told him, and gave him a smile to melt his elderly heart.

She thanked James too with an even sweeter smile and he, a man who prided himself on his self-control, nodded casually, so that her heart, which had been thumping happily in his company, plunged into her shoes. But what do I expect? she thought, getting into the car once again.

Chapter 9

There weren't many patients at the surgery; by eleven o'clock the place was empty and Leonora put the kettle on and got out two mugs and the coffee. Dr Galbraith's round was smaller than usual too—she had looked in the book to check that—so it was disappointing when he declined a drink and went away with a brisk, 'I'll see you at this evening's surgery.'

After he had gone, she had her coffee, got the patients' notes out ready for the evening, took a few phone calls and tidied the place, then sat down to wait for Mrs Crisp. She arrived punctually and Leonora explained hurriedly about Nanny.

'The poor dear,' said Mrs Crisp warmly. 'But there, she's not all that young, is she? And that great house to manage—just the two of you. I don't know how you do it; let me know if I can be of any help, Miss Leonora.'

Leonora thanked her and made for the door, to be stopped by Mrs Crisp's voice. 'I almost forgot—you've not had time to see the local paper, of course. The doctor's advertising for a receptionist—part-time, like you. I dare say you want to get back to your usual...' She paused and added awkwardly, 'What I mean is, I dare say Sir William isn't too keen on your working here in the village. The doctor did tell me you were just helping out until he could get someone to suit him. He asked me if I'd like the job full-time but of course I haven't the time for that, so he says, "Well, Mrs Crisp, you stay on part-time, and I'll find someone as soon as possible."' She smiled. 'He's a real gentlemen, isn't he?'

Leonora said brightly, 'I hope he finds someone—we're a bit out of the way, aren't we?' She smiled too. 'I must go; I'll be back on time.'

Perhaps it was a good thing she had no time to think once she got home. Her mother was in the kitchen, opening and shutting drawers and cupboards in an aimless way. 'Darling, here you are. I can't find anything, silly little me. Will you make a salad for lunch, and perhaps a cheese soufflé...?'

'Has Father phoned the hospital?' asked Leonora, dismissing the soufflé.'

'He thought it would be better to wait for an hour or so, darling. By then Nanny may be feeling better.'

Leonora went back into the hall and picked up the phone. Nanny was about the same, holding her own, she was told, and she could ring again that evening if she wished.

She went back to the kitchen. 'Where's Father, Mother?' she asked, and began opening drawers and cupboards, assembling lunch.

'In his study, dear. What shall we do about dinner this evening?' Lady Crosby sat down. 'Oh, dear, I am so upset…'

They had their lunch in the kitchen, which, Lady Crosby observed, took away every vestige of her appetite. 'I think I'd better go and lie down for a while; I've got one of my headaches coming on.'

Sir William helped to clear the table and Leonora said, 'I'm going to the hospital this evening with Dr Galbraith, Father. I'll get everything ready for supper and I'm sure Mother could manage if I'm not back. We're going directly after surgery.'

'Yes, yes, of course. I'll drive over in a day or so when Nanny feels more the thing!' He added uneasily, 'You're sure you can manage? I'm afraid your mother isn't up to doing much.'

'It isn't for long, Father, and I can manage.' She hoped she could; if and when Nanny came home, she would have her hands full. Perhaps the district nurse would help out. Time to worry about that later. There certainly wasn't time to worry now: beds to make, rooms to tidy, a tea-tray to set ready, a meal to prepare for the evening.

She arrived back at the surgery feeling tired and not looking her best.

The doctor, seeing this and saying nothing, wondered how best to help her; the wish to carry her off to Buntings and keep her there was hardly practical. Besides, he had had no indication that she would agree to that. It was a problem he had no time to solve at the moment.

Later, as he drove past her home, she cast a guilty look at the lighted windows. Her mother and father would be coping as best they could; she ought to be there looking after them.

James had seen her glance. 'They'll cope,' he told her easily. 'It will be only for a short time and both your mother and father are very fit for their age—and they are by no means old.'

'Old?' She sounded shocked. 'Mother's in her early fifties; she married very young.'

'There you are, then.' He began to talk about something else and when they reached the hospital took her straight to Nanny.

Nanny looked as though a puff of wind would blow her away, but at least she recognised them.

'Such a botheration,' she wheezed, 'me feeling poorly; your ma will never manage.' She peered up at Leonora's face. 'And you'll be worked to death.'

'No, no, Nanny, we're managing beautifully. You aren't to worry. It's only for a little while anyhow. You'll be back home in no time.'

The doctor, standing beside her, made no effort to contradict this statement. Presently he wandered away to speak to the house physician.

'He's a good man,' said Nanny between coughs. 'Tell your ma and pa not to come visiting me; there's no need. Getting the best of treatment—such nice girls the nurses are; nothing's too much trouble.' She glanced at the flowers Leonora had brought with her. 'They'll look a treat on my locker. Now don't you waste your time coming here, Miss Leonora; you've enough on your plate.'

'If Dr Galbraith gives me a lift, it's the easiest thing in the world,' said Leonora. 'Is there anything you want, Nanny—books or magazines?'

'Bless you, no.' Nanny stopped to cough; she was tired now and Leonora said quickly, 'I'm going now, but I'll be back. Take care!'

She bent to kiss her old friend and left the ward to stand about outside its doors wondering where the doctor had gone. He joined her presently.

'I've had a talk with the man in charge of Nanny. She's doing well, even after twelve hours. Not quite out of the woods yet… She was pleased to see you!'

Leonora nodded. 'Yes, she was bothered about looking after Mother and Father.' She added, 'She looks very ill…'

'She is ill but the tests which have been done are all satisfactory; give the antibiotics a chance and she'll be as good as new.'

He spoke in a manner which she couldn't help but believe; she went with him to the car feeling cheerful, ready to cope with the evening ahead.

At the house he got out of the car and helped her out, but when she asked him to go in with her he refused. 'I'm dining out,' he explained. 'I'll see you in the morning. Don't worry about Nanny; she will be all right.'

She went indoors then, after thanking him politely for the lift and saying that she hoped he would have a pleasant evening—something which she hardly expected to have herself. And nor did she; there was too much to do.

Back from his dinner party later that evening, the doctor went in search of Cricket.

'I need your help,' he told him. 'This is what I want you to do…'

So the following morning Cricket made his stately way to the Dowlings' residence and remained closeted with Jenks, their butler, for some time.

'On no account must Miss Crosby be told that these come from Dr Galbraith; tell Sir William that Mr Dowling sent them as a gift. They're quite ready to be put into the oven…'

Jenks nodded a bald head. 'I'll see that's done, but why the secrecy, or may I not ask?'

'I'm not at liberty to say more, but shall we just say that there may be wedding bells in the offing? Strictly between us, of course. Nothing said, I fancy—the doctor isn't a man to hurry and Miss Crosby needs a delicate hand. A charming young lady, I must add, but touchy about money matters; I gather there's not much of it up at the house. Any whiff of charity and she would retreat.'

When Leonora got home at lunchtime she was met by her mother.

'Darling, such luck—the Dowlings have sent over a brace of pheasants they can't use. Ready to pop into the oven too. Isn't that marvellous? Now you'll have almost no cooking to do this evening.'

Leonora, who had been cudgelling her brains as to how to present sausages disguised as something else, was relieved at the news.

Evening surgery wasn't busy, which was a good thing, for the doctor was called away as his last patient was preparing to leave—Mrs Squires, complaining of aches and pains, demanding a bottle of tonic. There was nothing like it, she assured the doctor. 'And I dare say you may be a very clever man, but there's a lot you could learn about tonics.'

He agreed placidly, wrote out a prescription and left her in Leonora's hands, bidding them goodbye as he went.

A mean trick, thought Leonora, longing to get home to deal with the pheasants and delayed by Mrs Squires, eager for a nice long chat. By the time she did get home she was tired and cross; the pheasants still had to be dealt with…but first of all she phoned the hospital. Nanny was doing well, responding to the antibiotics, eating a little, sleeping well. She told her father and he agreed to drive over to the hospital on the following day.

'In the afternoon, Father,' urged Leonora. 'If we go directly after lunch we can be back in time for surgery.'

At morning surgery the doctor told her that he had talked to the house physician at the hospital. 'Nanny's doing well; they'll be sending her home in five or six days; can you manage?'

'Oh, easily,' said Leonora instantly, and added mendaciously, 'I've help from the village, you know.'

'Splendid. I shall be driving to the hospital this evening; do you want a lift?'

'Father's going this afternoon and I said I'd go with him. Thank you for the offer.'

Determined to preserve a cool front, she succeeded in sounding frosty instead.

Later, sitting in his study with Tod sprawled over his feet, James pushed aside the work he was doing and applied his powerful brain to the subject of Leonora's sudden coolness. What had he done or not done? he wondered. Surely she hadn't found out about the pheasants? If she had he was sure that she would have taxed him with that in no uncertain terms. She was avoiding him and although she was tired and worried her distance was caused by even more than that—something was making her unhappy.

Surely she wasn't still in love with Beamish? With five sisters he was only too well aware of the vagaries to be encountered in the female. He wished very much to tell her of his love for her but if he spoke now he might ruin his chances…

As the days went by it was so obvious that Leonora was avoiding his company that he took care that they spent as little time together as possible. An outbreak of chickenpox kept him busy both in and out of the surgery, and though he drove her to see Nanny one evening he was careful to behave with detached friendliness. From Cricket he heard that the help from the village was quite inadequate, that Lady Crosby seemed unable to lift a finger round the house, that Sir William didn't seem to notice any shortcomings as long as he had his meals, and that there were lights showing at the house long after sensible people were in bed.

Nanny was to be sent home in two days' time; the pneumonia had been banished but she was still in need of rest, good food and attention. At the hospital Leonora greeted the news with a cheerful face, casting aside Nanny's anxious worries as to how they were to manage; indeed, to hear her, one would have thought that she had boundless help! The doctor said nothing until they were in the car going home.

'I will arrange for the nurse to come each day and get Nanny up and dressed, and again in the evening to settle her back in bed.'

'There's no need…'

He said levelly, 'I must remind you that I am Nanny's doctor, Leonora.'

'Oh, well, yes. Thank you.' She added in a stilted manner, 'We do appreciate your care and kindness. How long will it take Nanny to get quite well?'

'Ten days, two weeks. If she wishes to potter before then there is no reason why she shouldn't, but it would be best if she takes things very easily for another week.'

'I'll make sure of that.'

'I'll fetch her home on Sunday morning; perhaps you will come with me?'

'Yes, please.' She thanked him again as he dropped her off at the house.

She watched him drive away and then walked round the house to the garden door with Wilkins beside her. 'It's no good, Wilkins,' she observed. 'Everything's gone wrong, hasn't it? He's just the family doctor!'

He lived up to that for the next two days—always kind and friendly and at the same time aloof.

On Sunday she got into the car, delighted to be with James even if he was keeping her at a distance. But she need not have worried; he kept up a steady flow of cheerful talk and at the hospital went with her to the ward to fetch Nanny, who was dressed and ready and pale with the excitement of going back home again.

Leonora sat in the back of the car with her, exchanging places with Tod, who sat motionless beside his master, and listened to Nanny's observations about the nurses and doctors, the food and the treatments. 'They were all very kind,' said Nanny, 'but, of course, it's not like home, is it?'

The doctor carried her indoors and up the staircase to her room, taking no notice of her protests. 'I shall come to see you in a day or two; mind and do exactly what Leonora says—a week doing nothing much, Nanny. After that you can resume your reign in the kitchen.'

He spent a short time with Sir William and Lady Crosby while Leonora got Nanny back into her bed for a rest. 'Nurse will come morning and evening for the next week,' he told them. 'Leonora will need some help until Nanny is on her feet again; she has been quite ill and must do nothing much for a while.'

'Of course not,' agreed Lady Crosby. 'You may be sure we'll take good care of her. You'll stay for coffee? I'm sure Leonora will make some.'

'Thank you, I won't stop, but if I may I'll take a look at Nanny before I go.'

Nanny was sitting up in bed telling Leonora where to put her clothes. She turned a shrewd eye on him as he went in. 'This child will be worn out looking after me and this blessed great place; it's time I was on my feet.'

He sat down on the side of the bed. 'Just stay quiet for a little longer, Nanny. I won't allow Leonora to get worn out. Nurse is coming to help you each day and you may get up and sit here and walk about the room, but no more.'

He glanced about him. It was a cosy room and quite well furnished; someone had put flowers in a vase on the little table near the bed and the place was warm. He supposed that there was some kind of central heating, although keeping a house this size even comfortably warm must be a problem. Fortunately the weather was mild. He bade her goodbye, told Leonora not to see him out, and went away.

'Now that's the man for you,' said Nanny, twitching her elderly nose. She hadn't been blind, watching the pair of them behaving as though they'd only just met. She closed her eyes, ready for a nap. She need not worry; the doctor was a man to sort out his own problems, Leonora's with them too, of course.

The week went slowly by; Leonora went to and from the surgery, presenting a smiling face when anyone looked at her. After only four days she was tired already, but things would get easier, she told herself, and the nurse was a great help. Besides, Nanny was getting better each day; the doctor had been to see her that morning and pro-

nounced himself more than satisfied. As he'd left he had
asked Leonora if she was managing.

'Oh, yes. Thank you,' she had told him brightly, her
eyes daring him to ask any more questions.

The next evening, dining at Colonel Howes' house,
he was surprised to see Sir William and Lady Crosby
among the guests. He went to speak to them as soon as
he could. 'Is Leonora not with you?' he wanted to know.

'Well, Nanny can't be left and Leonora said she was
tired anyway; a nice quiet evening will do her good,'
Lady Crosby told him.

Dinner was barely finished when he told his host that
he had a night call to make. 'I'll slip away quietly,' he
said. 'Otherwise it might break up the evening.'

He went to his home first and found Cricket in the
kitchen.

'Food, Cricket,' said the doctor. 'Something nice and
quick to eat. I'll get a bottle from the cellar. What have
we got?'

'Cold chicken, Parma ham, some of my pâté if you
can make the toast. Egg custard. A salad, if I can have
five minutes.'

Ten minutes later the doctor, with Tod beside him,
was driving through the village. Turning into the gates,
he saw that most of the downstairs lights were on and,
bidding Tod be quiet, he got out of his car and walked
round the house to the garden door. It wasn't locked and
he went in, restraining Tod as Wilkins began to bark.
The old dog came running down the passage but stopped
barking when he saw who it was and the three of them
went on to the kitchen.

Leonora had her back to them. 'What's up, Wilkins?'
she asked, and turned round. The look on her face when

she saw James brought a gleam to his eyes although he remained unsmiling.

His expression showed nothing of his thoughts. That she offered no beautiful picture bothered him not at all. She was lovely—the most beautiful girl in the world—even dressed as she was in a worthy dressing gown and a pinny tied around her waist. Her hair hung in an untidy plait and her make-up had long ago passed its best. She was mopping the kitchen floor and the mop dripped unheeded as she stood looking at him.

He said in a soothing voice, 'Hello—I hope I didn't scare you. I thought we might have supper together.'

'Supper?' She stared at him and then smiled. 'Mother and Father have gone out to dinner...'

'Yes, I know; I was there.'

'You've had dinner—'

'I wasn't hungry but I am now.' He put his basket down on the kitchen table, took the mop from her, swabbed up the puddle it had made, and took it and the bucket over to the sink.

Leonora looked down at her person. 'I got ready for bed but it was a chance to get the housework done. I'll go and dress.'

'No need. Take off that pinny and wash your hands. I'm going to lock the garden door.'

When he came back he unpacked the basket, took the champagne from its cooler and poured two glasses.

'Champagne,' said Leonora faintly, and took a reviving sip. Somehow everything was all right; she looked a fright but James didn't seem to mind. They were friends again; if only they could stay like that. Only she would have to be careful not to betray her feelings. He found knives and forks and plates, and set out the food, refilling her glass.

Champagne on a very empty stomach did wonders for her ego; with a sigh of delight she demolished the delicacies Cricket had provided and had another glass of champagne.

'Stay there; I'll make coffee if you tell me which cupboard to get it from.'

They had their coffee, and she, in a delightful haze, had no idea what they talked about; all she knew was that she was happy.

James was happy too but to propose to his Leonora when she was so delightfully bemused with champagne wouldn't do at all. He cleared the supper things away, washed the dishes and put everything away tidily, and Leonora, watching him, said on a slightly boozy giggle, 'You'll make a good husband, James.'

He had his back to her. 'I value your opinion, Leonora,' he told her. Then in a quite different voice he added, 'I'm going to see Nanny; then when I am gone you are to go straight to bed—I want your promise about that.'

She gave the tiniest of hiccups and he smiled a little. 'I promise.'

He went away, going quietly through the house, and presently returned.

'Nanny is awake and perfectly all right. Come with me to the door and lock it after me.'

At the door she stooped to caress Tod. 'Thank you for a lovely supper, and please thank Cricket too.' She smiled up at him and he bent his head and kissed her—a hard, quick kiss which took her breath—and then walked swiftly away.

She locked the door then and went back to the kitchen

to settle Wilkins and put out the lights, all the while in a glow of happiness.

Upstairs she wandered into Nanny's room to say good-night.

Nanny gave her a thoughtful stare. 'Didn't I say that's the man for you?' she wanted to know. 'Go to bed, and sweet dreams, my pet.'

So Leonora did just that.

She went to work still in a glow of happiness the next morning, and the doctor gave a sigh of relief at the sight of her face as she wished him a good morning. His Leonora had at last allowed her feelings to show...

There were a lot of patients but none of them were seriously ill; they finished a little early and Leonora went to put the kettle on, turning to smile at James as he came into the waiting room.

'An easy morning,' he observed. 'Nanny is going on well?'

'Yes. She is longing to get into the kitchen; I do wonder what she is doing when I am not there.'

She had spoken jokingly but he answered seriously, 'Well, that's soon remedied. I have a receptionist coming on Monday so you will not need to come to the surgery any more.'

Leonora went pale. 'Not come? You mean you are giving me the sack?'

'Yes.'

'You don't want me here any more?'

'No. Oh, you have been entirely satisfactory—I'm not sure what I would have done without your help—but you did know that it was a temporary arrangement.' He smiled and her unhappy heart did a somersault. He went on, 'I hadn't meant to say anything—not here—but perhaps you'll come to Buntings and have lunch with me—there will be time to talk.'

'What about?' she asked, and before he could answer she said, 'No, I'm afraid I can't; I have to go home. Besides, there is nothing to talk about.' She went on rather wildly, 'And even if there was I wouldn't want to hear it.'

He turned off the gas under the kettle. 'Then you will have to hear it now...' He took the phone up as it rang and stood listening.

'Lacock's Farm? I'll be with you as quickly as possible. Get an ambulance and the fire brigade.'

He put the phone down. 'Where is Lacock's Farm exactly? Somewhere close to Norrington Common? How far?'

'Four miles. Off the road; there's a cart track to the farm.'

He was in the surgery, putting things into his bag. 'A barn roof has collapsed; there were a number of children inside. They've got three out, injured; there are several more inside.'

He came back into the waiting room, sweeping her along with him. 'You'll have to show me the way.'

He locked the surgery door, urged her into the car and drove off.

'Take the first turn on the left about half a mile away,' said Leonora, and moments later she added, 'Here, the road narrows. The track's about a mile on the right.'

The Rolls ate up the mile at a speed which boded ill for anything coming the other way; she let out a breath as James turned into the track. The pace was slower now. 'The farm is only a few hundred yards ahead,' she told him. 'You can't see it for the trees. It's on the left.'

The farmyard was large, with the farmhouse on its farther side and outbuildings on two sides, and beyond the house was the barn, its collapsed roof in a vast, sprawling pile, thatch and bricks and cob-walls still crumbling slowly.

The doctor drove up to the house, got out and opened Leonora's door, picked up his bag and strode to the barn. There were several people there: a woman standing in tears with a little girl in her arms, two men and a young boy climbing over the rubble searching.

The woman saw them first. 'Miss Crosby—Doctor. Tracey's hurt—her arm—and little Tim and Jilly are over there; there's no one to look after them.'

'See what you can do,' said the doctor to Leonora, and went over to the men.

'Into the house, I think,' said Leonora, hoping she would remember at least some of her first-aid lessons. 'I'll get the other two.'

She went to where they sat huddled on the ground, thanking heaven to find that they were more frightened than hurt. They had bumps and scratches but once in the house, where she could see them properly, she could find no bad injury. She sat them side by side on the old-fashioned sofa in the living room and turned her attention to Tracey.

The little girl was weeping copiously, which Leonora hoped was a good sign, but one small arm hung awkwardly, swollen and already showing bruises. Leonora opened drawers and cupboards, found a dinner napkin and made a sling. A warm drink, she remembered—sweet tea.

She sat a shocked Mrs Lacock beside the two children, settled Tracey on her lap and went in search of the teapot. She was in luck; the pot stood keeping warm beside the stove and if the tea was stewed she didn't think it would matter. She found mugs, milk and sugar and hurried back to the living room.

'Can you help the children to drink this and have some yourself? I'm going to see if I can do anything…'

The yard was slippery; they had been muck-spreading and she had to scramble carefully to where the men were clearing away rubble from the far end of the barn. As she reached them she saw the doctor stoop, draw a child out of the ruins and bend over her for a moment. She fetched up beside him and he handed the child to her. 'Take her indoors, lie her flat and cover her—a broken leg and concussion, I think; I'll come as soon as I can.'

The child was unconscious; Leonora laid her on a rug at Mrs Lacock's feet. 'Keep an eye on her,' she begged, and made her way back to the barn.

They were carefully edging a boy out of the medley of beams and thatch and stone and this time the doctor carried him back to the house and laid him down carefully beside the girl. 'Stay with him,' he told Leonora. 'There's still another child.'

She did what she could, thankful in a way that the two children were unconscious, keeping them covered warmly, wiping their small, dirty faces, gently cleaning the cuts she could reach without moving them. The sound of the ambulances, followed by the deeper note of the fire engine, didn't come a moment too soon, for the children needed expert care and despite her first aid there was little she could do.

There was activity now, men coming and going, taking over from the men and boy and James, who came into the house and began to examine the children. The paramedics came with him and Leonora, sitting with one of the children on her lap, watched him. For the moment she had forgotten that he had no interest in her, had made it clear that they were no more than acquaintances, living in the same village; he was the man she loved and always would love, unflappable in disaster, knowing what to do, never raising his voice, kind…

She watched for what seemed a very long time while he worked on the unconscious little boy and girl, who were taken away in the ambulance just as a shout heralded the rescue of the last child. Another boy. In a still worse state, she guessed, covered in dust and bits of thatch and blood. It was a long time before James was satisfied that he was well enough to be taken to the hospital. She could only guess at the emergency treatment he had been given.

It was the turn of the three children with Mrs Lacock, who between them were suffering from shock, a small broken arm and bruises and who after careful examination were got into the third ambulance and sent after the others.

The police were there now and James went away to talk to them, and a policewoman came into the house, asked Leonora if she was all right and went to make tea for everyone. Presently James came back, rolling down his shirtsleeves and putting on his jacket.

'You're all right?' he wanted to know. He spoke very gently. She looked like a scarecrow, covered in dust and earth and blood, her hair with half the pins missing. He thought she had never looked so beautiful.

'We'll go home,' he told her, 'and get clean and have a meal.'

Leonora got to her feet and followed him out to the car and sat quietly while he phoned Cricket. 'Let Lady Crosby know that Leonora is coming back with me, will you? We need to clean up and eat.'

'No,' said Leonora. 'I wish to go home.' Everything came rushing back then. 'And I do not wish to go to the surgery or to your house ever again!' She added as an afterthought, 'Thank you.'

James started the car. 'Ah, yes, I was interrupted, wasn't I? You will at least hear me out before you blight our lives for ever. Don't expect me to say any more at the moment; this infernal track takes all my patience.'

As he swept into the village she said once more, 'I want to go home.'

For answer he turned into his own gates. 'This is your home—or will be very shortly.'

She sat very still, not looking at him. 'You sacked me this morning...'

'Well, of course I did, you silly goose.'

He got out and ushered her into the house and Cricket came to meet them, tut-tutting at the sight of them.

'Show Miss Crosby to a room and a bathroom, Cricket, will you? And see if you can find a dressing gown or something similar while someone fetches some fresh clothes for her from the house.'

She was led away up the stairs to a pretty room with an adjoining bathroom. 'Just you have a nice hot bath, miss,' said Cricket, sounding very like Nanny. 'I'll arrange for someone to fetch your things and put a gown in the bedroom for you. And there's a tasty lunch ready when you are.'

Leonora stood in the middle of the room and looked at him. If only he knew how delightful it was to be taken care of. She blinked away tears and smiled. 'Thank you, Cricket; I won't be long.'

There were bath salts, bottles of fragrant oil, the very best of soaps, vast sponges and a shelf of lotions. There wasn't time to wash her dusty hair but she gave it a good brushing and got into a towelling bathrobe. It trailed on the ground and she had to roll up the sleeves and it shrouded her from neck to ankles. She went downstairs and found the doctor, very correctly dressed, in dark grey worsted and a dignified tie.

'We will eat first, then we will talk,' he said, resisting a strong desire to take her in his arms there and then; she was still wary of him and still cross…

Tod pranced to meet her and she bent to pat him before sitting down in the chair James was holding for her, surprised to find that she was hungry. Certainly the lunch Cricket served them would have tempted her even if she had had no appetite at all, and despite her unease the doctor's calm voice, rambling on in a soothing manner about nothing much, did a great deal to restore her usual good sense.

So she had got the sack, she reflected, spooning up a nice old-fashioned junket with clotted cream, but that was to be expected; she'd had no reason to expect otherwise, had she? And she had been warned: Mrs Crisp had told her about the advertisement. She wondered what the receptionist would be like. Young and clever, never keeping James waiting, highly efficient and pretty…

'You aren't listening,' said James. 'We will go into the drawing room, where you will clear your sadly muddled thoughts and listen to me.'

'I must go home,' said Leonora, striving for common sense.

'Have you forgotten what I told you just now?'

They had crossed into the drawing room and were standing by the door into the garden while Tod dashed in and out.

'No, no, of course not.' She looked up at him. 'Only I'm not sure what you meant.'

He took her in his arms. 'Then I will tell you, and I will repeat what I am about to say as often as necessary for the rest of our lives. I've fallen in love with you, my darling; I think I did that when we first met even if you weren't at your dignified best.' He smiled down at her. 'I love you, my dearest Leonora, and I want to marry you.'

She looked up at him with shining eyes. 'Oh, James— and I want to marry you too, only I thought that you didn't love me, or even like me very much, so I tried to stop loving you, only I couldn't…'

He kissed her then, gently. 'My dearest love. So you will marry me—and soon?'

'As soon as we can.' She paused to think. 'Well, I must have some clothes and Mother will want to arrange things, I expect. I wish we could just creep away and get married now.'

He kissed her again, this time in a manner to leave her breathless.

'Mother and Father and Nanny,' said Leonora presently. 'Who will look after them? And Mother will want me to have a big wedding and Father can't afford that… Oh, dear!'

James gathered her closer. He said with calm assurance, 'Will you leave everything to me, my darling?'

Leonora, looking up into his face and seeing the love in it and hearing his calm, assured voice, said at once, 'Yes, of course I will, James.'

She smiled at him, wanting him to kiss her again.

Which James duly did, to her entire satisfaction.

* * * * *

A GENTLE AWAKENING

Chapter 1

The hot June sunshine of a late afternoon bathed the narrow country road in warmth, and the only traveller on it dawdled along, pedalling slowly, partly from tiredness after a day's work, and partly from a reluctance to arrive at her home.

The village came in sight round the next curve: the bridge over the river, leading to the road which would eventually join the high road to Salisbury, and then the cottages on either side of the lane. They were charming, tiled or thatched, their red bricks glowing in the sunshine, their porches wreathed with clematis and roses. The cyclist came to a halt before one of these, and at the same time a silver-grey Bentley swam to a soundless halt beside her.

The girl got off her bike. She was small and thin, with gingery hair plaited into a thick rope over one shoulder, green eyes transforming an ordinary face into something which, while not pretty, certainly lifted it from the ordinary.

The car driver got out: a very large man, towering over her. Not so young, she decided, studying him calmly, but very good-looking, with dark hair sprinkled with grey, a formidable nose and heavy-lidded blue eyes. He smiled down at her, studying her in his turn, and then dismissing her from his thoughts. None the less, he smiled at her and his deep voice was pleasant.

'I wonder if you could help us? We wanted to stay the night in the village, but the Trout and Feathers can't put us up and we would rather not drive back to Wilton or Salisbury.' He glanced over his shoulder to where a small girl's face was thrust through the open window of the car. 'Just bed and breakfast—we can get a meal at the pub.'

He held out a hand. 'The name is Sedley—William Sedley.'

The girl offered a small brown hand and had it engulfed. 'Florina Payne, and yes, if you go on as far as the bridge, there is a farmhouse facing it; they haven't got a board up, but I'm sure they would put you up.' She wrinkled her ginger brows. 'There isn't anybody else in the village, I'm afraid. You would have to go back to Burford St Martin on the main road.'

She was thanked politely, and the child in the front seat waved to her as they drove off. She wheeled her bike along the brick path at the side of the cottage and went in through the kitchen door, thinking about the driver of the car, to have her thoughts rudely shattered by her father's voice.

'So there you are—took your time coming home, didn't you? And then wasted more of it talking to that fellow. What did he want, anyway?'

The speaker came into the kitchen, a middle-aged man with an ill-tempered face. 'You might at least get home punctually; you know I can't do anything much for myself, and here I am, alone all day and you crawling back when it suits you...'

He paused for breath and Florina said gently, 'Father, I came just as soon as I could get off. The hotel is very busy with the tourist season, you know, and that man only wanted to know where he could get a room for the night.'

Her father snorted. 'Pah, he could afford a hotel in Wilton, driving a Bentley!' He added spitefully, 'Wasting your time and his for that matter—who'd want to look twice at a ginger-headed plain Jane like you?'

Florina was laying the table and, although colour stole into her cheeks, she answered in a matter-of-fact voice. 'Well, it won't be a waste of time if he gets a room at the farm. Sit down, Father, tea won't be long.'

She would very much have liked to have sat down herself and had a cup of tea; it had been a busy day at the hotel. During the summer season, tourists expected meals at odd hours, and she and the other two cooks there had worked all day, whisking up omelettes, steaks, fish dishes, egg dishes and salads, just as fast as they could. They had taken it in turn to eat a sandwich and drink a mug of tea, but it had been a long day. She had worked there for three years now, hating the long cycle ride in the winter to and from her home, as well as the long hours and the lack of free time. But the pay, while not over-generous, was good; it supplemented her father's pension and brought him all the extra comforts he took as his right. That it might have given her the chance to buy pretty clothes had never entered his head; she was his daughter, twenty-seven years old, on the plain side, and it was her duty to look after him while he lived. Once or twice she had done her best to break free, and each time, when she had confronted him with a possible job away from home, he had clutched at his chest, gasped that he was dying and taken to his bed. A dutiful, but not loving daughter—for what was there to love?—she had accepted that after the one heart attack he had had several years ago, he could have another if he became upset or angry; so she had given in.

She was a sensible girl and didn't allow self-pity to overwhelm her. She was aware that she had no looks to speak of, and those that she had were hardly enhanced by the cheap clothes, bought with an eye to their hard-wearing quality rather than fashion.

Her father refused to cook for himself during the day. She left cold food ready for him before she left each morning, and tea was a substantial meal, which meant that she had to cook once more. Haddock and poached eggs, a plate of bread and butter, stewed fruit and custard, and tea afterwards. She had no appetite for it, but the suggestion that they might have salads and cold meat met with a stream of grumbles, and anything was better than that after a day's work.

They ate in silence. Her father had no interest in her day and, since he had done nothing himself, there was nothing to tell her. He got up from the table presently and went into the sitting-room to sit down before the TV. Florina started to clear the table, wash up and put everything ready for breakfast. By the time she had finished the evening was well advanced but still light; half an hour's walk would be pleasant, she decided. She cheerfully countered her father's objections to this and set off through the village, past the cottages, past the Trout and Feathers, past the lovely old house next the pub where old Admiral Riley lived, and along the tree-lined lane. It was still warm and very quiet, and if she stood still she could hear the river beyond the trees.

When she came to a gate she stopped to lean on it, well aware of the beauty of her surroundings, but too busy with her own thoughts to heed it. The need to escape was very strong; her mother had died five years previously and since then Florina had kept house for her father, pandering to his whims, because the doctor had warned her that a fit of temper or any major disturbance might bring on another heart attack. She had resigned herself to what was her plain duty, made the more irksome since her father had no affection for her. But things could be different now; her father had been for a check-up in Salisbury a week or so previously and, although he had told her that there was no improvement in his condition, she had quite by chance encountered the doctor, who had told her that her father was fit enough to resume a normal life.

'A part-time job, perhaps?' He smiled at Florina, whom he thought privately had had a raw deal. 'He was in a bank, wasn't he? Well, I dare say he could get taken on again. He's only in his mid-fifties, isn't he? And if he can't find something to do, I've suggested to him that he might take over the housework; a little activity would do him good. Give you a chance to have a holiday.'

She mulled over his news. Her father had flown into a rage when she had suggested that he might like to do a few chores around the house. He had clutched his chest and declared that she would be the death of him, and that she was the worst possible daughter that any man could have.

Florina, having heard it all before, received his remarks with equanimity and said no more, but now she turned over several schemes in her mind. A different job, if she could find one and, since her father no longer was in danger, preferably away from home. Something not too far away, so that she could return for the weekends… She was so deep in thought that she didn't hear anyone in the lane until they were almost level with her. The man and the little girl from the car, walking along hand in hand. When she turned to see who it was, the man inclined his head gravely and the little girl grinned and waved. Florina watched them walk on, back to the village. Presumably they had found their bed and breakfast, and tomorrow they would drive away in their lovely car and she would never see them again.

She waited until they were out of sight, and then started back to the house. She had to leave home just after seven each morning, and tomorrow it would be even earlier, for there was a wedding reception at the hotel.

She went back without haste, made their evening drinks, wished her father goodnight and went to her room, where she wasted five minutes examining her features in the looking-glass. There was, she considered, very little to be done about them: sandy hair, even though it gleamed and shone, was by no means considered beautiful, and a slightly tip-tilted nose and too wide a mouth held no charm. She got into bed and lay wondering about the man in the car. He had been very polite in a disinterested way; she could quite see that there was nothing in her person to attract a man, especially a man such as he, used, no doubt, to enchanting girls with golden hair and beautiful faces, wearing the latest fashions. Florina smiled at her silly thoughts and went off to sleep.

It was the beginning of the most gorgeous day when she left early the next morning. Sir William Sedley, standing at his bedroom window and drinking his early morning tea, watched her pedalling briskly along the lane. The sun shone on her sandy head, turning it to gold, and she was whistling. He wondered where she was going at that early hour. Then he forgot her, almost immediately.

It was a splendid morning and there was almost no traffic. Florina, going at a great rate on her elderly bike, wished that she could have been free to spend the day out of doors. The hotel kitchens, admirable though they were, were going to be uncomfortably warm. She slowed a little as she went through the small town, still quiet, and passed the nice old houses with the high walls of Wilton House behind them. The hotel was on the other side of the road, a pleasant building, surrounded by trees and with the river close by. She paused to take a look at the green peacefulness around her, then parked her bike and went in through the kitchen entrance.

She was punctual, as always, but the place was already a hive of activity; first breakfasts being cooked, waiters loading trays. Florina called 'good morning' and went over to her particular corner, intent on icing *petits fours*, filling vol-au-vents and decorating the salmon in aspic designed for the wedding reception.

She was a splendid cook, a talent she had inherited from her Dutch mother, together with a multitude of housewifely perfections which, sadly, her father had never appreciated. Florina sometimes wondered if her mother had been happy; she had been a quiet little woman, sensible and practical and cheerful, absorbing her father's ill-temper with apparent ease. Florina missed her still. Whether her father did so too, she didn't know, for he never talked of her. When, from time to time, she had tried to suggest a holiday with her mother's family, he had been so incensed that he had become alarmingly red in the face, and she had feared that he would have another heart attack.

Her thoughts, as busy as her fingers, darted to and fro, seeking an escape from a home which was no longer a home. Interlarded with them was the man in the car, although what business of his it was eluded her.

He wasn't thinking of her; he was strolling down the village street, his daughter beside him. His appointment was for ten o'clock and it wanted five minutes to the hour. The church clock struck the hour as they turned in through the open gates leading to the house where Admiral Riley lived.

It was a delightful place, L-shaped, its heavy wooden door half-way down one side. It stood open, and there was no need to thump the great knocker, for the old man came to meet them.

'Mrs Birch from the village, who looks after me while my wife is away, has gone to Wilton. So I'm alone, which is perhaps a good thing, for we can go round undisturbed.'

He led the way through the hall and into a very large room with a window at its end. There were more windows and an open door along one side. It was furnished with some handsome mahogany pieces, and a number of easy chairs, and there was a massive marble fireplace facing the windows. The admiral went across the room and bent down to roll back the carpet before the hearth.

'I don't know if the agent told you about this?' He chuckled and stood back so that his visitors could see what he had laid bare. A thick glass panel in the floor, and under it a steady flow of water. 'There used to be a mill wheel, but that's gone. The water runs under this room...' He led the way through the doors on to a wide patio and leaned over a stone balustrade. 'It comes out here and runs through the garden into the fields beyond.'

The little girl caught her father's hand. 'Swans, Daddy!' Her voice was a delighted squeak. 'Do they live here, in this garden?'

'Not quite in the garden,' said the Admiral. 'But they come for bread each day. You shall feed them presently, if you like.'

The kitchen wing was in the other side of the L-shape, a delightful mixture of old-fashioned pantries, with everything that any housewife could wish for. There were other rooms, too: a dining-room, a small sitting-room, a study lined with bookshelves. Upstairs, the rooms were light and airy; there were five of them and three bathrooms, as well as a great attic reached by a narrow little stair. 'My playroom,' whispered the little girl.

They went back to the drawing-room presently, and the Admiral fetched the coffee tray and bread for the swans. 'I've been here for more than twenty years,' he observed, 'and we hate to leave it, but my wife has to live in a warm climate. She's been in Italy for a couple of months and already she is greatly improved. May I ask where you come from, Sir William?'

'London—Knightsbridge. I'm a paediatrician, consultant at several hospitals. I want Pauline to grow up in the country and, provided I can get help to run the house, I can drive up and down to town and stay overnight when I must. There's a good school, I hear; Pauline can go by the day.'

'Too far for her to cycle.'

'Yes, whoever comes here to look after us will have to drive her in and fetch her each day. A problem I'll deal with later.' He smiled suddenly. 'I should like to buy your house, Admiral. May our solicitors get to work on it?'

He sat back in his chair, very relaxed, a calm man who had made up his mind without fuss. 'They'll take three weeks if we bully them,' he said. 'May I come again with someone to advise me about cooking stoves and so on?' He added, 'I'm a widower, but I have plans to re-marry.'

'Of course. I shall probably be ready to move out before the solicitors fix a date. Feel free to arrange for carpets and curtains and so forth. Wilton is small, but there are a couple of excellent furnishing firms.'

They finished their coffee in companionable silence; two men who arranged their lives without fuss.

Walking back through the village, presently, Sir William asked, 'You're pleased, darling? You'll be happy here? I'll get Nanny to come and live with us for a time...'

'Until you marry Miss Fortesque?' said Pauline in a sad voice, so that her father stopped to look down at her.

'Look, darling, I know it's a bit difficult for you to understand, but Wanda is very fond of you, and it'll be nice for you to have someone to come home to and talk to...'

'There's you, Daddy...'

'I shall be in town for several days in the week. Once Wanda's here she will be able to get to know everyone about, and you'll have lots of friends.'

Pauline's small, firm mouth closed into an obstinate line. 'I'd be quite happy with Nanny.'

'Yes, love, but Nanny retired last year, she won't want to start working all over again. If she comes for a few months…'

'Until you get married?'

'Until I get married,' repeated her father gently, and then, 'I thought you liked Wanda?'

Pauline shrugged her small shoulders. 'She's all right, but she's not like a mother, is she? She fusses about her clothes!'

'I imagine you'll fuss about yours when you're older. Now, what shall we do with the rest of our day?'

He drove her to Stourhead and they had lunch at the Spread Eagle pub. Then they wandered right round the lake, and on the way back in the afternoon they stopped in Shaftesbury and had a cream tea. It was well past six o'clock before they got back to the farm. It was a warm evening and the country was very beautiful; they wandered over the road to the bridge and leaned over to watch the river, waiting until their evening meal would be ready. The church clock struck seven as they left the bridge and strolled to the road. They had to wait a moment while a cyclist went by.

'That's the nice girl we saw yesterday,' said Pauline.

'Was she nice?' asked Sir William in an uninterested manner.

Pauline nodded her head vigorously. 'Oh, yes. When we live here I shall ask if I may be her friend.'

'A bit old for you, darling?' He had no idea of the girl's age, and he wasn't interested. 'You must go to bed directly after supper. We're going to make an early start in the morning.'

They were driving through Wilton when Pauline saw the small, ginger-haired figure getting off her bike as

they passed the hotel. 'Oh, there she is!' she cried excitedly. 'Daddy, do you suppose she works there?'

Sir William glanced sideways without slackening
speed. 'Very likely. I dare say you'll see more of her
when we come to live here.'

It was July when Admiral Riley left, and after that
there was a constant coming and going of delivery vans,
carpet layers, plumbers and painters. The village, via
the Trout and Feathers, knew all that was going on and,
naturally enough, Florina knew too. The new owner
would move in in two weeks' time, his small daughter
was going to school in Wilton, and there was a housekeeper coming. Also, Mrs Datchett from Rose Cottage,
and Mrs Deakin, whose husband was a farm worker,
were to go to work there four times a week.

'Disgraceful,' grumbled Florina's father. 'That great
house, with just a man and child in it…'

'But there's work for Mrs Datchett and Mrs Deakin,
close to their own homes, as well as for old Mr Meek,
who is seeing to the garden. And the tradespeople—
it's much better than leaving the house empty, Father.'

'Don't talk about things you don't understand,'
snapped Mr Payne. 'It's bad enough that you go gallivanting off to work each day, leaving me to manage
as best I can…'

Florina, laying the table for their meal, wasn't listening. She had heard it all before. It was wicked, she
supposed, not to love her father, but she had tried very
hard and been rebuffed so often that she had given up.
Once or twice she had questioned the amount of her
wages which he told her were necessary to supplement
his income, only to be told to mind her own business.
And she had done so, under the impression that his

health would suffer if she thwarted him. Now according to the doctor, there was no longer any fear of that.

She went into the kitchen to cook the liver and bacon. Moments later her father poked his head round the door and demanded to know if he was to get anything to eat. 'I dare say you'd like to see me dead,' he grumbled.

'No, Father, just a bit more cheerful,' said Florina. At the same time, she resolved to start looking for another job on the very next day.

As it happened, she had no need. She was getting on her bike the next morning when Mrs Datchett came out of Rose Cottage, just across the street, and accosted her.

'Eh, love, can you spare a minute? You've heard I'm to go up to the Wheel House to work? Well, the housekeeper who took me on asked me if I knew of a good cook, and I thought of you. Lovely kitchen it is, too, and a cushy job as you might say, with that Sir William away most of the time and only the little girl and that housekeeper there. I don't know what he'll pay, but you'd not have that bike ride every day. Why don't you have a go?'

Florina cycled to work, thinking hard. By the time she got there she had made her mind up to apply for the job; it could do no harm and it seemed to her that it was a direct sign from heaven that she should look for other work… To strengthen this argument, it was her half-day; usually spent in cleaning the house.

She got home about two o'clock and, instead of getting into an apron and getting out the vacuum cleaner, she went to her room, put on a clean blouse, brushed her blue skirt, did her hair in a severe style which did nothing for her looks, and went downstairs.

'Why are you going out?' enquired her father suspiciously.

'Don't worry, Father, I'll be back to get you your tea.' She skipped through the door before he could answer.

It was barely five minutes' walk to the Wheel House and Florina didn't give herself time to get nervous. She thumped the knocker, firmly, and then took several deep breaths. She had read somewhere that deep breathing helped if one felt nervous.

The door was opened and there was a tall, bony woman with grey hair and faded blue eyes. She looked stern and rather unwelcoming, so that Florina was glad of the deep breaths.

'Good afternoon. Mrs Datchett told me this morning that you were wanting a cook...'

'Sir William is wanting a cook. I'm the housekeeper. Do come in.'

She was led into a small sitting-room in the kitchen wing. 'Why do you want to come?'

'I work at a hotel in Wilton—I've been there for several years. I cycle there and back each day. I'd like to work on my own.' Florina added, anxiously, 'I'm a good cook, I can get references.'

'You live here?'

'Yes, just this side of the bridge.'

'You'd have to be here by eight o'clock each morning, make out the menus, keep the kitchen clean, cook lunch if Sir William is here, and dinner as well. You'd be free in the afternoons. You'd have help with the washing up and so on, but you might have to stay late some evenings. Do you want to live in?'

'I live very close by and I have to look after my father...'

The housekeeper nodded. 'Well, you're not quite what I had in mind, but I dare say you'll suit. You can come on a month's trial. There's Sir William at weekends, his daughter, Pauline, living here with me, and you must be prepared to cook for guests at the weekends. You do know that Sir William intends to marry?'

Florina shook her head. She hadn't realised until that moment that Sir William loomed so large in her life. The idea of him marrying left her with a feeling of disquiet, but she had no time to wonder about it, for the housekeeper said, 'Sir William will be moving in at the end of next week. Can you start then? A month's trial and, mind, he expects the best.'

She had to give a week's notice. She would go and see the hotel manager in the morning, for that would give him ten days in which to find someone to take her place.

'You haven't asked what your wages will be,' said the housekeeper, and mentioned a sum which sent Florina's ginger eyebrows up.

'That's a good deal more than I'm getting now,' she pointed out.

'Probably, but you'll have to work for it.'

'I'd like to work here,' said Florina. She would see Sir William sometimes, even if he never spoke to her.

'Very well, you'll get a letter in a day or two. My name is Frobisher, Miss Martha Frobisher. If you have any problems you'll bring them to me. Sir William is a busy man, he hasn't the time to bother with household matters.' She eyed Florina's small, neat person. 'What is your name?'

'Payne—Florina Payne.'

They wished each other goodbye with guarded politeness.

Mr Payne, apprised of his daughter's astonishing behaviour, called upon heaven to defend him from ungrateful daughters, painted a pathetic picture of his early death from neglect and starvation, since there would be no one to look after him. Finally he declared that he might as well be dead.

'Nonsense, Father,' said Florina kindly. 'You know that's not true. I'm likely to be at home more than I am now. You've had to boil your kettle for breakfast for years now, and I'll leave your lunch ready just as usual...'

'The housework—the whole place will go to rack and ruin.'

'I shall be home each afternoon, I can do the chores then. Besides, the doctor said it would do you good to be more active now you're better.'

'I shall never be better...'

Florina said cheerfully, 'I'll make a cup of tea. You'll feel better then.'

The manager was sorry that she wished to leave, but he understood that the chance of a job so close to her home wasn't to be missed. He wrote out a splendid reference which she slid through the letter-box at Wheel House, together with her letter accepting the job. If she didn't suit, of course, it would mean that she would be out of work at the end of a month; but she refused to entertain that idea, for she knew she was a good cook.

She went to the Wheel House the day before she was to start work, so that she might have a good look round her kitchen. It had everything, and the pantry and cupboards and fridge were bulging with food. She spent a satisfying afternoon arranging everything to her liking, and then went home to get her father's tea, a meal she sat through while he grumbled and complained at her lack of filial devotion. It was a relief, once she had tidied their meal away, to walk back to Wheel House and put the finishing touches to the kitchen. Miss Frobisher was upstairs somewhere, and the old house was quiet but for the gentle sound of running water from the mill. She had left the kitchen door open so the setting sun poured in, lighting the whole place as she made the last of her preparations for the morning. Sir William and Pauline would be arriving after lunch; she would bake a cake and scones in the morning and prepare everything for dinner that evening. She would have all day, so she wouldn't need to hurry.

She crossed to the door to close it and, with a final look round, went down the passage to the front hall. Sir William was standing there, his hands in his pockets, his head on one side, contemplating a large oil painting of a prissy-looking young lady in rose-coloured taffeta and ringlets, leaning over a gilded chair.

He glanced over his shoulder at her. 'Hello. She doesn't seem quite right there, does she? One of my more strait-laced forebears.' He smiled. 'I expect you're here for some reason?'

At the sight of him, Florina was experiencing a variety of sensations: a sudden rush of delight, peevishness at the thought of her untidy appearance, a deep sadness that he hadn't a clue as to who she was, which of course was ridiculous of her. And woven through this a variety of thoughts...suitable food which could be cooked quickly if he needed a meal.

He was watching her with faint amusement. 'Have we met?' He snapped a finger. 'Of course! You were so good as to tell us where we might stay when we first came here.'

'Yes,' said Florina breathlessly, 'that's me. I'm the cook. Miss Frobisher engaged me, but only if you approve.' She added to make it quite clear, 'I'm on a month's trial.'

'You don't look much like a cook.' He stared rather hard at the ginger plait hanging over one shoulder. 'But the proof of the pudding…as they say.'

He turned round as Miss Frobisher bustled in. 'Nanny, how nice to see you. I'm here a day too soon, aren't I? I've left Pauline with her aunt, but I'll drive back tomorrow and fetch her after lunch. I had a consultation in Salisbury and it seemed a good idea to come on here instead of driving back to town. Is everything just as it should be?'

'Aye, Sir William, it is. You'll be tired, no doubt. Cook will get you a light meal…'

'No need. I'll go to the Trout and Feathers. And I can't call you "cook", not with that pigtail. What is your name?'

'Florina Payne.' She caught Mrs Frobisher's stern eye, and added, 'Sir William.'

'Not an English name, but a pretty one.'

'My mother was Dutch, sir.'

'Indeed! I go to Holland from time to time.' He added kindly, 'Well, Florina, we'll see you in the morning— or do you live in?'

'In the village.'

'I'll need to leave early,' he observed, and strolled away towards the drawing-room.

Mrs Frobisher said, in a warning voice, 'So you had best be here at half-past seven, Florina, for he will want his breakfast at eight o'clock. You can have your own breakfast with me after he has gone.'

Florina glanced at the broad back disappearing through the open door of the drawing-room. She found the idea of cooking his breakfast positively exciting; an idea, she told herself sternly, which was both pointless and silly.

All the same, the thought of it sustained her through her father's diatribe when she got back home.

She made tea before she left in the morning, and took a cup up to her father, bade him a cheerful good morning, reminded him that everything was ready for his breakfast, just as usual, and walked quickly through the still quiet village. Wheel House was quiet, too. She went in through the kitchen door, using the key Mrs Frobisher had given her, and set to work. The kettle was boiling and the teapot warming when Sir William wandered in, wrapped in a rather splendid dressing-gown. She turned from cutting bread for toast and wished him a polite good morning. 'Where would you like your tea, sir?' she asked him. 'Breakfast will be in half an hour, sooner, if you wish.'

'Half an hour is fine. And I'll have my tea here.' He fetched a mug from the dresser, poured his tea and went to stand in the open doorway. 'What's for breakfast?'

'Bacon and eggs, with mushrooms, fried bread and tomato. Then, toast and marmalade, tea or coffee, sir.'

'Where did you learn to cook?' he asked idly.

'My mother taught me and I took a cookery course in Salisbury. I worked at the hotel in Wilton for several years.'

He nodded. 'I shall have guests sometimes. You could cope with that?'

She said seriously, 'Oh, yes.' She put a frying pan on the Aga. 'Would you like more tea, sir?'

He shook his head. 'Why not have a cup yourself?' He wandered to the door. 'Pauline will be glad to see you—she'll be here this afternoon.'

She set the table in the dining-room, and was making the toast when Miss Frobisher came into the kitchen. She eyed the laden tray with approval and her greeting held more warmth than usual. 'Sir William always likes a good breakfast; he's a big man and needs his strength for his work.' She shot a look at Florina. 'He's a doctor, did you know that? A very well known one. He was a dear little boy, I always knew he'd be successful. You'd better take that tray in, I can hear him coming downstairs.'

Florina laid the food on the table before him, casting a motherly glance at him hidden behind the morning paper. She had liked him on sight, she remembered, and that liking was growing by the minute. She would very much like to know all about him, of course, though she had the good sense to know that she never would.

Chapter 2

There was plenty to keep Florina busy that morning. After breakfast, shared with Mrs Frobisher, there was the menu to put together, the cake and scones to make and everything to prepare for the evening. That done, there was coffee to make for Mrs Frobisher, Mrs Deakin and Mrs Datchett, who came to sit around the kitchen table for a short break from their polishing and dusting. The latter two ladies were inclined to gossip, but received short shrift from the housekeeper, who didn't answer their questions about the new owner and silenced them with an intimidating eye.

'But he is going to marry?' persisted Mrs Deakin, not easily put off.

'It seems very likely,' conceded Mrs Frobisher, and Florina thought that there was a trace of disquiet in the housekeeper's voice.

Florina left an excellent light lunch ready for the

housekeeper, and took herself off home to get a meal for her father and herself. The breakfast dishes were still on the table and he was sitting in a chair, reading the paper.

He greeted her with a disgruntled, 'So there you are, and high time too!' Then he picked up his paper again, leaving her to clear the table, wash up and get a snack meal.

They ate in silence and Florina made short work of tidying everything away. Cleaning the house, dusting and carpet-sweeping took her another half an hour; there was an hour of leisure before she needed to return to Wheel House. She spent it in the big garden behind the cottage, weeding and tying back the clumps of old-fashioned flowers her mother had planted years ago, and which Florina tended still. She made tea for her father before she went, drank a cup herself, tidied her already neat person and returned to Wheel House. She had left everything ready for tea, and as she went round the back of the house to the kitchen wing she could hear the little girl's excited voice from the drawing-room, the door of which was open as she passed. Her hand was on the kitchen door when she was stopped.

The girl rushed at her from the room. 'I'm Pauline—oh, isn't this fun? Have you seen my room? It's pink and white! We've eaten almost all the scones and half the cake. Daddy says you must be a treasure in the kitchen.'

'Hello,' said Florina, and beamed at the pretty little face grinning at her. 'I'm so glad you enjoyed the cake. I'm going to get dinner ready now.'

'I'll help you.'

Pauline danced into the kitchen, examining the pots and saucepans, opening the cupboards and peering inside, peeping into the fridge. Florina, changing out of her dress into the striped cotton frock and large white

apron which was her uniform while she was working, called from the little cloakroom leading from the
kitchen, 'Put everything back where you found it, won't
you, Pauline?'

She reappeared to collect the ingredients for the watercress soup, *boeuf en croûte*, and the chocolate sauce
to go with the profiteroles.

Florina worked steadily, undeterred by Pauline's
stream of excited chatter. She was chopping mint and
Pauline was sitting on the table, running a finger round
the remnants of the chocolate sauce in the pan, when
Sir William wandered in.

'Something smells delightful. Is it a secret?'

'Watercress soup, *boeuf en croûte*, potatoes with
mint, courgettes, new carrots, spinach purée, profiteroles with chocolate sauce, cheese and biscuits and coffee,' recited Florina, finishing the last of the sauce.

'It sounds good. Are you cordon bleu trained, Florina?'

'Yes, but I think I learnt almost everything from my
mother—the cordon bleu just—just put the polish on.'

She had washed her hands, and was piling profiteroles into a pyramid on a china dish. It crossed her mind
that she felt completely at ease with Sir William, as
though she had known him for years… She really must
remember to call him Sir William. 'Dinner will be at
half-past seven unless you would like to change that,
Sir William?'

He said carelessly, 'Oh, no, why should I change it?
I'll take Pauline off your hands—we'll go for a stroll.'

Without Pauline's pleasant chatter and her father's
large presence, the kitchen seemed empty and quiet.
Florina went to and fro, putting the finishing touches
to the food. She was a little warm by now, but still very

neat. Mrs Frobisher, coming into the kitchen, nodded approvingly.

'You certainly know your work,' she allowed. 'Sir William is a very punctual man, so have the soup ready on the dot. I'll carry in the food.'

The meal over and the last of the dishes back in the kitchen, Florina put the coffee tray ready to be carried in, and started on the clearing up.

The china, glass and silver Mrs Deakin would see to in the morning, but she did her saucepans and cooking utensils. It had been a strict rule at the hotel and one she intended to continue. She had just finished burnishing the last pan when Mrs Frobisher came back with the coffee tray. 'Sir William is very satisfied with your cooking,' she told Florina, 'I'm to pass on his compliments. He wants to know if you can cook for a dinner party next weekend. Eight sitting down to table, and Miss Fortesque, his fiancée, will be staying for the weekend.'

'No problem. If there is anything special Sir William wants, I'll do my best.'

'I'll ask him. You're finished? Did you put everything to keep warm in the Aga? Good. I'll lay the table and you dish up. It's been a busy evening, but you've done very well. I've suggested to Sir William that we get a girl from the village to come in in the evenings and help you clear up and see to the vegetables and so on. Do you know of one?'

Florina thought. 'Yes, there is Jean Smith at Keeper's Cottage—she's left school, but she's got to wait a month or two before she can start work training as a nurse. She will be glad of the money.'

'I'll leave you to ask her to come along and see me. Now, let's have dinner. I've seen Pauline safely up to bed, and Sir William has got all he wants. Your father knows you won't be home until later?'

'Oh, yes. I left his supper ready for him.'

'You're kept busy,' observed Mrs Frobisher. 'Mind you, during the week it will be midday dinner and a light supper at seven o'clock. You'll have most of the evening free. It is a pity that you can't live in.'

'Oh, I don't mind working late or coming early in the morning,' said Florina, and tried not to sound anxious.

She did not quite succeed, though, for Mrs Frobisher said quickly, 'Oh, don't worry about that dinner, Sir William won't want to lose you on any account. I was only thinking that it would be much easier for you; there's a nice little room at the top of the back stairs with its own bathroom, and nicely furnished, too. Still, I dare say your father would miss you.'

Florina, serving them with the last of the profiteroles, agreed quietly.

She faced a long-drawn-out lecture when she got home. She listened with half an ear while she washed up his supper things and put everything ready for the morning. When her father paused at last, she surprised him and herself by saying, without heat, 'Father, the doctor said that it would be good for you to do a few things for yourself. There's no reason why you shouldn't clear away your meals and wash up. You could make your bed, too, and get your own tea. I'm really working hard for most of the day, and I give you almost all my money. You could even get a part-time job! Then you would have more money and I could have some money of my own.'

She waited patiently while he gobbled and snorted, and told her several times that she was a wicked and ungrateful girl.

'Why?' asked Florina. 'It's not wicked to get you to help a little, especially when the doctor says it would be good for you. And what do I have to be grateful for, Father?'

'A roof over your head, and food and a bed!' he shouted very angrily.

She could get those if she lived in at Wheel House… 'I'm thinking of leaving home,' she told him. 'I'll stay until you can get someone to come in and keep the house tidy and do the washing. You said a few days ago that a cousin of yours—Aunt Meg, was it? I don't remember her very well—had been widowed. She might be glad to come and live here with you…'

'You would leave your home? But you were born here, your mother lived here.'

'Yes, I know, Father, but now she isn't here any more it isn't home, not to me.' She added gently, 'You'll be happier if I'm not here, won't you?'

Her father's face turned alarmingly red. 'To think that a daughter of mine should say such a thing…'

'But it's true, isn't it, Father? And if Aunt Meg were here, she would be at home all day and be company for you. You wouldn't miss my money because she would pay her share, wouldn't she?'

He agreed in a grumbling voice. 'And, since you are determined to leave home and leave me to shift for myself, I'll write to her, I suppose. But don't you think you can come sneaking back here if you're ever out of a job.'

'There is always work for a good cook,' observed Florina.

Sunday was very much like Saturday, except that there was hot lunch and cold supper, which gave Florina a good deal more leisure. She left everything ready for tea and, intent on striking while the iron was hot, asked Mrs Frobisher if she had been serious when she had suggested that for her to live in would be more convenient for everyone.

'Yes, of course I was,' declared that lady. 'Why do you ask?'

Florina explained, leaving out the bits about her father's bad temper.

'A good idea. Come and see the room.'

It was a very nice room, its windows overlooking the river running through the garden. It was well furnished, too, with a small writing desk and an easy chair with a table beside it, and a divan bed along one wall with a fitted cover. There were pictures on the walls and a window-box cascading geraniums. There was a cupboard in one wall and a small bathroom, cunningly built into the roof. A minuscule kitchen contained a sink and a minature gas cooker, capable of turning out a meal for one, as well as an electric kettle.

'Why, it's perfect! Whoever thought of it?'

'Sir William. He enjoys comfort, and wants everyone around him to be comfortable, too. I believe that he will be pleased if you were to live here, Florina, but of course I'll say nothing until you've decided.'

She had a good deal more leisure for the rest of the week. Sir William left early on the Monday morning, but that leisure was very much encroached on by Pauline, who attached herself to Florina at every possible moment. Though Florina, who had perforce led a somewhat solitary life, enjoyed her company; it was fun to show the child where she could find mushrooms and wild strawberries, sit by the river and watch for water voles, and feed the swans. Pauline, who had spent almost all her life in London, loved every minute of it. But, if life was pleasant while she was at the Wheel

House, it was uncomfortable at home. Her father had indeed written to her aunt, and received a reply, full of enthusiasm for his scheme and suggesting that she would be ready to join him in a couple of weeks' time, news which apparently gave him no pleasure at all. Not that he wanted Florina to change her plans. Indeed, she had told him Mrs Frobisher knew that she was willing to live in, providing Sir William agreed. Cutting sandwiches for Pauline's tea, she had never felt so happy.

It had to be too good to last. On Friday morning she began her preparations for the weekend. She and Mrs Frobisher had decided on a menu, and the housekeeper had gone to Wilton and bought everything for Florina on her list, so it had only remained for her to assemble them ready for Saturday evening. Mrs Frobisher, who seemed to like her, in a guarded manner, had taken her upstairs in the afternoon to show her the guest room.

'Miss Fortesque is used to town ways,' she explained. 'She'll expect her breakfast in bed...' She sniffed. 'She'll not want me here when they're married.'

'But were you not Pauline's Nanny?'

'And Sir William's before her.' Miss Fortesque forgotten momentarily, Mrs Frobisher threw open the two doors close to the room they were viewing. 'Guest rooms,' she pointed out. 'Pauline's room is on the other side of the landing, as is Sir William's. You've noticed that there are more rooms above the kitchen. The housekeeper's—I sleep on this landing at present because otherwise Pauline would be alone... There is another bathroom and a third bedroom. I dare say Miss Fortesque will want someone else to live in. It's a large house and I doubt if she knows what a duster looks like.'

Certainly, dusters were the last things one would think of at the sight of Miss Fortesque, thought Flo-

rina, watching from the kitchen window as she stepped
from Sir William's car on Saturday morning. She was
the picture of elegance, the sort of elegance never seen
in the village: a sleeveless dress of what Florina was
sure was pure silk in palest blue, Italian sandals and
enormous hoop earrings matching the gold bracelets on
her arms. Florina sighed without knowing it, twitched
her apron so that it covered her small person correctly,
and went back to the preparation of *crêpes de volaille
Florentine*. She was making the cheese sauce when Sir
William wandered into the kitchen.

'Hello,' he said. 'Every time I see you, you're slav-
ing over a hot stove.'

She couldn't prevent her delight at seeing him showing on her face, although she didn't know that. 'I'm the
cook, sir,' she reminded him.

'Yes—I seem to have difficulty in remembering
that.' He smiled at her and called over his shoulder,
'Wanda, come and meet Florina.'

Miss Fortesque strolled in and linked an arm in his.
'Oh, hello. You're the cook?'

The air positively hummed with their mutual dislike, instantly recognized, even if silent. Sir William
watched them from half-shut lids.

'Florina is our treasure—she cooks like a dream, and
Pauline considers her to be her best friend.'

Wanda opened large blue eyes. 'Oh, the poor child,
has she no friends of her own sort?' She made a small
gesture. 'Is it wise to let her live here, William? At a
good boarding-school she would make friends with all
the right children.'

'Who are the right children?' he asked carelessly.
'Don't be a snob, Wanda. Pauline is happy; she'll be
going to day school in Wilton in September, and there's

plenty to occupy her here meantime.' He glanced at Florina. 'Does she bother you, Florina?'

'Not in the least, Sir William. She is learning to cook and she spends a great deal of time gardening. She and Mrs Frobisher go for long walks.'

Miss Fortesque turned on her heel. 'Oh, well, if you're quite content to leave her with the servants...' She smiled bewitchingly, 'I shall alter all that, of course. When are the others arriving?'

Florina was left to seethe over the Aga. The horrible girl was quite unsuitable to be Sir William's wife, and she would be a disastrous stepmother. If Sir William was as easy-going as he appeared to be, then Pauline would find herself at a boarding-school, and she and Nanny would be out of jobs. Not too bad for Nanny, for she had already officially retired, but it would mean finding work for herself, and away from home, too.

Despite her rage, she served up a lunch which was perfection itself, and shared a quick meal with Nanny. When Sir William, with his fiancée and Pauline, had driven off for a brief tour of the surrounding country, Florina arranged the tea tray and then got down to preparing dinner. The house was quiet: Mrs Frobisher had gone to put her feet up before tea, Mrs Deakin was doing the last of the washing up and Florina concentrated on her cooking. By the time she heard the car stop by the house, she was satisfied that there was nothing more to do for an hour or so.

Two other cars arrived then, and Mrs Frobisher, much refreshed by the nap, carried in the tea tray and the assortment of cakes and sandwiches Florina had got ready, before she came back to share a pot of tea with Florina.

The kitchen was warm; she opened the windows

wide and sat down gratefully, listening to Mrs Frobisher describing Sir William's guests. Rather nice, she was told, and had known him for years—doctors and their wives, rather older than he was.

'And, of course, Miss Fortesque,' added Nanny, and she sounded as though she had inadvertently sucked on a lemon. 'A well preserved woman, one might say, but of course she spends a great deal of time and money upon herself.'

Obviously Nanny didn't approve of Sir William's Wanda, but Florina didn't dare to say so; she murmured vaguely and her companion went on, 'Had her claws into him for months. I'm surprised at him—she'll be a bad wife for him and a worse stepmother for my little Pauline.' She passed her cup for more tea. 'He's so busy with all those sick children, he only sees her when she's dressed up and all charm and prettiness. Of course, that's very nice for the gentlemen when they've had a hard day's work, but when all's said and done they want a wife as well, someone who'll sit on the opposite side of the fireplace and knit while he reads the papers, listen when he wants to talk, and love his children.' Nanny snorted. 'All she likes to do is dance, and play bridge.'

'Perhaps she'll change,' suggested Florina gently, not quite sure if she should voice an opinion. Nanny was obviously labouring under strong feelings, and possibly she would regret her outburst later on.

'You're a good girl,' said Nanny, 'I've wanted to say all that to someone for weeks, and you're the only person I've felt I could talk to.'

To Florina's distress, Mrs Frobisher's eyes filled with tears. 'I had him as a baby,' she said.

'They're not married yet,' ventured Florina. She

added, very thoughtfully, 'It just needs someone to give fate a push and change things…'

Mrs Frobisher blew her nose, an awesome sound. 'You're a sensible girl as well as a good one, Florina.'

Florina dished up a splendid dinner: artichoke hearts with a sharp dressing of her own invention, lobster cardinal, medallions of beef with a wine sauce and truffles, and tiny pancakes filled with strawberries and smothered in thick cream.

When the coffee tray had gone in, she and Nanny sat down to eat what was left, before Nanny went away to see Pauline into bed. Mrs Deakin had come back to help with the clearing up, but all the same the evening was far gone, and Sir William seeing his guests on their way, by the time they were finished in the kitchen. Florina set everything ready for the morning, changed into her dress and, with Mrs Deakin for company, locked the kitchen door after her and started for home.

They were at the gate when Sir William loomed out from the shrubs alongside the short drive. 'A delightful meal, Florina! My compliments, and thank you, and Mrs Deakin, for working late.'

Mrs Deakin muttered happily; she was being paid overtime, and generously, for any work she did over and above her normal hours. Florina said quietly, 'Thank you, Sir William. Goodnight.'

He would go into his lovely house presently, she supposed, and Wanda would be waiting for him. Florina had caught a glimpse of her during the evening— a vision in scarlet chiffon. Enough to turn any man's head, even that of the placid, good-natured Sir William.

She was making a salad the next day when Miss Fortesque, in a startling blue jersey dress and a great many gold bangles, strolled into the kitchen.

'Hello, Cook, busy among your saucepans again? It's really surprising that even in the depths of the country it's possible to find someone who can turn out a decent meal.' She smiled sweetly. 'After town standards, you know, one hardly expects it.'

Florina shredded lettuce with hands which shook very slightly with temper, and said nothing.

'That sauce last night,' continued her visitor, 'I fancied that there was a touch too much garlic in it. Sir William didn't complain—he's really too easy-going…'

'When Sir William complains to me, Miss Fortesque, I shall listen to him,' said Florina very evenly.

Wanda's eyes opened wide. 'Don't you dare to speak to me like that, Cook! I'll have you dismissed…' She advanced, rather unwisely, too close to Florina, who had started to whip up a dressing for the salad. She increased her beating with a vigour which sent oily drops in all directions. The blue dress would never be the same again; a shower of little blobs had made a graceful pattern down its front.

Wanda's breath was a hiss of fury. 'You clumsy fool—look what you've done! It's ruined—I'll have to have a new dress, and I'll see that it's stopped out of your wages! I'll…'

Sir William's voice, very placid, cut her short. 'My dear Wanda, if you hadn't been standing so close, it wouldn't have happened. You can't blame Florina, you've only yourself to thank. Surely you know that cooks must be left in peace in their kitchens when they are cooking?'

Wanda shot him a furious glance. She said pettishly, 'I'll have to go and change. I hope you'll give the girl a good telling-off.'

She flounced out of the kitchen and Florina began

to slice tomatoes very thinly. Sir William spoke from the door. 'I found the sauce exactly right,' he said gently, and wandered away.

He took his fiancée back to town that evening, leaving behind a rather unhappy Pauline. He sought out Florina before he left, to tell her that for the next few weeks, while the child was on holiday, he would come down each weekend on Friday afternoons, and drive back early on Monday morning.

'Nanny tells me that you may decide to move in with us. Your father doesn't object to being alone?'

Her aunt had written to say that she would be arriving at the end of the week. She told him this, leaving out the details. He nodded pleasantly. 'I'm sure it will give you more leisure. I hope you'll be happy here. Pauline will be over the moon when you tell her.'

She thought wistfully that it would have been nice if he had expressed the same satisfaction, even if in a more modified form. She bade him a quiet goodnight, more or less drowned by Miss Fortesque's voice, pitched high, demanding that they should leave at once.

The week unfolded at a leisurely pace; Florina packed her things, got her room ready for her aunt and moved to the Wheel House. Her father bade her goodbye with no sign of regret, merely warning her again that she need not expect to go crying back to him when she found herself out of a job. She received this remark without rancour, aware that if he should fall ill again the first thing that he would do would be to demand that she should return home to look after him.

She enjoyed arranging her few possessions in her room at Wheel House, helped by a delighted Pauline. Once settled in, she found that she had a good deal more leisure. Cooking for the three of them took up only a part of her day; she helped Nanny with the ironing and the cleaning of the silver, took Pauline mushrooming in the early mornings, and, with Mrs Frobisher's consent, started to give her cooking lessons. By the time Sir William arrived on Friday afternoon, there was a dish of jam tarts and a fruit cake, a little soggy in the middle but still edible, both of which Pauline bore to the tea table with pride. Sir William, a kind and loving parent, ate quantities of both.

The weekend was one of the happiest Florina had spent for a long time. For one thing, there was a peaceful content over the old home. Sir William insisted that they all breakfast together in the kitchen, a meal which Florina cooked with an almost painful wish to serve up something to perfection, just to please him. She succeeded very well; he ate everything put before him, carrying on a cheerful conversation meanwhile, even making Nanny laugh, something she seldom did. They were at the toast and marmalade stage on Saturday morning, when Pauline said, 'I wish it could be like this always—just us, Daddy—you and me and Nanny and Florina. Must you marry Wanda? She wouldn't sit at the kitchen table, and she's always fussing about eating in case she gets fat.'

Florina saw the look on Sir William's face. There was a nasty temper hidden away behind that calm exterior, and to avert it she got to her feet, exclaiming loudly, 'Shall I make another pot of coffee? And how about more toast?' At the same time she cast a warning glance at Pauline.

The child had gone very red and tears weren't far off. She sighed and said, 'I'm sorry, Daddy.'

His face was placid again. 'That's all right, darling. What are we going to do today?'

The pair of them went off presently, and Florina prepared lunch, decided what to have for dinner, made the coffee and went to help Nanny with the beds. The rest of the weekend was peaceful, and Florina, taking along the coffee tray to the patio where Sir William had settled with the Sunday papers after church, while Pauline fed the swans, thought how delightful life was.

She gave him breakfast the next morning, happily aware that he would be back on Friday afternoon. Wanda Fortesque had gone to stay with friends in the south of France, and Florina allowed herself the childish hope that something, anything, would prevent her from ever coming back from there!

The weather changed suddenly during the day, by the evening it was chilly and grey, and Pauline seemed to have the beginnings of a cold.

Nanny came down to the kitchen after she had seen Pauline to bed. 'The child's feverish,' she declared. 'I think I'd better keep her in bed tomorrow; these summer colds can be heavy.'

But when morning came, Pauline was feeling worse; moreover, she had a pinky, blotchy rash.

'Measles,' said Nanny, and phoned for the doctor.

He came from Wilton that morning, confirmed Nanny's diagnosis, and observed that there was a lot of it about and that Pauline, having had an anti-measles injection when she was a little girl, would soon be on her feet again. 'Plenty to drink,' he advised, 'and keep her in bed until her temperature is down.' He patted Nanny reassuringly on the shoulder. 'Nothing to worry about.'

All the same, Nanny telephoned Sir William in London, only to be told that he was at the hospital and would be there all day. She put the phone down, undecided as to what to do, when it rang again.

Florina, making iced lemonade for the invalid, heard her talking at some length, and presently she came back to the kitchen.

'Sir William's not at home and won't be until the evening, but Miss Fortesque was there. She rang back when I told her I wanted him urgently, said she would tell him when he got back. I would rather have phoned the hospital, but that would be no use if he is in the theatre or the out-patients.'

By the time they were ready for bed, more than ready, for Florina had suggested that neither Mrs Deakin nor Mrs Datchett came to work until Pauline was better, for they both had children, there had been no word from Sir William. Nanny telephoned once more, only to be told by Miss Fortesque that he was still out.

Pauline was much better in the morning and Nanny, while still a tiny bit puzzled as to why Sir William hadn't telephoned, decided that there was no need to bother him, not until the evening at any rate. She and Florina spent another busy day, for the house was large and there was a certain amount of work to get through, as well as pandering to Pauline's increasing whims. Nanny had a headache by teatime, and Florina persuaded her to go to bed early.

'Only if you telephone Sir William,' declared Nanny.

Florina waited until she had taken up two supper trays, eaten a scratch meal of beans on toast herself, before dialling the number she had been given. Miss Fortesque answered. No, Sir William wasn't at home and wasn't likely to be for some time and was it urgent? He had had a busy day and needed his rest. She slammed down the receiver before Florina had got her mouth open.

Nanny had a rash in the morning, a high temperature, a terrible headache and a firmly rooted opinion that she was going to die.

'Nonsense, Mrs Frobisher,' said Florina robustly. 'You've got the measles. I'm going to get the doctor.'

He wasn't quite as cheerful about Nanny. It transpired that she had never had measles as a child, an illness, which he pointed out to Florina, that could be quite serious in anyone as elderly as Nanny. 'Keep her in bed,' he advised. 'Plenty of fluids, and don't let her read or use her eyes. Keep the blinds drawn and take her temperature every four hours. I'll be out to see her again tomorrow.' He added as an afterthought, 'Can you manage?'

Sir William would be home on the next day, so Florina assured the doctor that, of course, she could manage.

It was hard work. Pauline had made a quick recovery, although she still needed looking after and had to stay in bed for another day or so, but Nanny, suddenly an old, ill Nanny, needed constant attention. Not that she was a difficult patient, but she was feverish, her head ached and she fretted at lying in bed.

Florina, trotting up and down stairs with trays and cool drinks, was tempted to telephone Sir William again, but it hardly seemed worth it since he would be home in less than twenty-four hours. She settled her two patients for the night at last, and went to the kitchen to make out a menu for Sir William's dinner for the following evening. It would have to be something quick, and which could be left in the Aga to look after itself. She made a chocolate mousse and put it in the freezer, made a vegetable soup, and then decided that she would make a cheese soufflé—something which could be done at the last minute. She had picked some peas and beans earlier in the day, and there was plenty of fruit and cheese and biscuits. She went to take a last look at her two patients and then went to bed herself, to sleep the moment her head touched the pillow.

Doctor Stone came again the next morning, cautioned her that Pauline should stay in bed for another day or so, declared that Nanny was holding her own nicely, but that she would need careful nursing, accepted a cup of coffee and remarked that Florina was managing very well.

'No need to send you a nurse,' he told her, 'and, since there isn't one available at the moment, that's a good thing. Is Sir William coming down for the weekend?'

Florina said that, yes, he was, and thought tiredly of all the extra cooking there would be. She was, after all, the cook, and he had every right to expect well prepared meals to be set before him. Doctor Stone went, and she made a large quantity of lemonade, then made herself a sandwich and started to get a light lunch for Pauline. Nanny didn't want anything, but Florina made an egg nog and spent some precious time persuading her to drink it.

She spent more time settling Pauline for the afternoon. There was the radio, of course, and her cassette player, and since reading wasn't to be encouraged, a sketch-book had to be found with coloured crayons. Florina, finally free to go to the kitchen, put on a clean apron, tossed her plait over her shoulder and started to shell the peas.

She was very tired; she let the sound of the stream, racing under the house and on into the garden, soothe her. She was disturbed five minutes later by a leisurely tread in the hall, and a moment later Sir William said from the kitchen door, 'Hello! The house is very quiet.'

When she turned to look at him he saw her white, tired face.

'What's wrong, Florina?'

She heard the sudden briskness of his usually placid voice. 'Measles,' she said. 'Pauline started on Monday and now Nanny has it… Yesterday—I've had the doctor. Doctor Stone, from Wilton.'

'Why wasn't I told?'

'Nanny telephoned you on Monday night, and then again on Tuesday. I rang again on Thursday evening…'

Sir William didn't answer. He went to the telephone on the wall by the Aga, and dialled a number. Florina went back to shelling her peas and listened.

'Jolly? Get hold of our Shirley and bribe her to sleep in for a few nights with Mrs Jolly. Then pack a bag and drive down here as soon as you can. Take the Rover and make all speed. We have a problem on our hands. Measles, no less!'

'On your own?' he asked, as he put back the receiver.

'Well, yes. You see, Mrs Deakin and Mrs Datchett have children.'

'Very wise. I'm going to take a look. Is Pauline on the mend? She had her jab when she was small.'

'Yes, she's over the worst. Mrs Frobisher is really quite ill, though…'

She heard him going upstairs two at a time.

By the time he returned she had finished the peas, had the kettle boiling for tea and had laid a tray with the tea things and a plate of scones.

He sat down at the kitchen table and told her to get another cup. 'Very spotty, the pair of them. Nanny's going to take a little while to get over it, but Pauline's well out of the wood.' He shot the next question at her so fast that she answered it without once pausing to think.

'Who answered the telephone when you and Nanny telephoned?'

'Miss Fortesque...' She went red because he would think her sneaky. 'I'm sure it was a misunderstanding...'

He didn't answer that. 'You've had your hands full—up for a good deal of the night, too?'

'Well, yes. Nanny felt so hot and ill, but Pauline slept well.'

His rather sleepy gaze swept round the kitchen. 'You've been running the place, and cooking, as well as looking after Pauline and Nanny?'

She misunderstood him completely. 'Oh, but I had all day. Dinner will be ready at half-past seven, but I can put it forward half an hour if you wish. I don't settle them for the night until about nine o'clock. Pauline likes her supper about eight o'clock and Nanny doesn't want to eat at present—I've been giving her egg and milk and tea and lemonade.'

He smiled at her suddenly. 'My poor dear, you are tired to the bone, aren't you? You've got dinner fixed already?' When she nodded, he continued, 'We'll eat here together, then you can get supper for Pauline and I'll take it up; I'll see that Nanny takes her fluids, too, and then I'll wash up while you get Pauline ready for bed.'

She opened her mouth to protest, but he lifted a large hand to stop her. 'I'm going back to take another look at Nanny and then to phone Doctor Stone. Which room should Jolly have when he comes?'

'There is the small guest room at the end of the passage where Nanny is—I'll make up the bed...'

'Put the bed linen out; I'll see to the bed, you stay here and get on with dinner.'

Florina, whose father had always considered the making of a bed to be a woman's work, was surprised, but Sir William had spoken in a voice which, while quiet, obviously expected to be obeyed. She cleared away the tea tray and set the kitchen table for the two of them before getting the ingredients for the soufflé.

Sir William was as good as his word; she was ready soon after seven o'clock, and he fetched the sherry decanter from the dining-room and poured each of them a glass, and then sat down opposite her and ate dinner with a splendid appetite, talking about nothing much. When they had finished, he sent her upstairs to Pauline. 'I'll fetch the tray down; you tidy her up for the night and then come back here.'

It was pleasant to have someone there to arrange things; Florina did as she was told and half an hour later went back downstairs to find Sir William, one of Nanny's aprons strained around his person, making the coffee.

'Sit down and drink it,' he ordered her, 'then, if you'll see to Nanny, I'll finish up down here and say goodnight to Pauline.'

Nanny was quite willing to be settled for the night. Everything, she told Florina, would be quite all right now that Sir William was home. 'You cooked him a good dinner?' she demanded.

Florina said that yes, she had, but she didn't mention that she had shared it with him at the kitchen table. There was no sense in sending Nanny's temperature up! She wished her goodnight and went yawning down the staircase; bed would be delightful, but first she must make sure that the kitchen was ready for the morning. Sir William would want his breakfast, and there was early-morning tea, and what about Jolly—who was Jolly, anyway?

The kitchen door to the garden was still open and

Sir William was out on the patio, leaning over the balustrade, watching the stream below him.

'Come and have five minutes' peace,' he advised and she went to stand beside him, hot and dishevelled and very tired. He glanced sideways at her smiling faintly, surprised that it worried him to see her looking so weary. He didn't say anything and she was glad just to lean there, doing nothing until a car turning into the gates roused her.

'That will be Jolly,' said Sir William, and went round the side of the house to meet him.

Chapter 3

Florina was still standing on the patio when Sir William returned, with Jolly beside him. Jolly was the antithesis of his name. He had a long, narrow face, very solemn and pale, dark eyes, and hair greying at the temples, smoothed to a satin finish. He was dressed soberly in a black jacket and striped trousers, and wore an old-fashioned wing-collar and a black bow-tie.

Sir William halted in front of Florina. 'This is Jolly, who runs my home. Jolly, this is Florina, who cooks for me and has been coping on her own for the last couple of days. I think we'll send her to bed and we'll discuss what's best to be done. Off you go, Florina, sleep the clock round if you want to.'

She was quite shocked. 'Breakfast…'

'Ah, you don't really trust us with the frying-pan. I dare say you're right. Breakfast is at half-past eight. You do the cooking, we'll clear up. We'll work out a routine in the morning. Now, off with you.'

It was difficult to go against this casual friendliness. Besides, she had had a long day. She said goodnight to them both, and went upstairs to lie in the bath, half-asleep, and think about how nice Sir William was. But the cooling water brought her wide awake, and she tumbled into bed, to sleep soundly almost at once.

She was wakened by Sir William's voice, and shot up in bed, in an instant panic that she had overslept. He was wearing a rather grand dressing-gown, and stood by the bed with a mug from the kitchen in his hand.

He gave it to her and said cheerfully, 'Tea—you've slept well?' Then he sat himself down carefully on the side of the bed. He hadn't appeared to look at her, but he had taken in her face, rosy from sleep, her hair freed from its tidy plait, hanging in a mousy tangle round her shoulders. She looked a different girl from the pale, tired little creature he had found in the kitchen on the previous evening.

He went on easily, 'I've taken a look at our two invalids. Pauline is doing fine; Nanny's still feverish—she'll need a few days' nursing still, but luckily she's decided not to die this time, and is already giving orders about cleaning the bath and getting extra milk. A good sign!' He got off the bed. 'It's half-past seven. When you're ready, would you go along and make Nanny comfortable before breakfast? Jolly will see to the table for you and lay the trays and so forth. We'll eat in the kitchen; that will save dusting the dining-room.'

He smiled and nodded and wandered away, leaving her to drink her tea and then, as quickly as she could, to shower and dress, reflecting as she did so that she had never met anybody quite like him before. She couldn't remember her father ever bringing her a cup of tea in bed; he had always been at pains to point out to her, and her mother while she had been alive, that since a man spent his day working to keep a roof over their heads, it was only right that he should be properly looked after in his own home.

Her hair once more neatly plaited, wearing one of her striped cotton dresses, she went along to visit Pauline first, sitting up in bed and feeling so much better that she demanded to be allowed up.

'Not until your father says so,' said Florina briskly. 'I dare say he'll come to see you when he's had breakfast. What would you like? Are you hungry?'

They settled on scrambled eggs and, as Florina skimmed to the door, intent on dealing with Nanny, Pauline called after her, 'You are nice, Florina—the nicest friend I've ever had. Daddy likes you, too.'

A remark which sent a pleasant glow through Florina's person. It was delightful to be liked and needed. She beamed at Nanny's cross face, coaxed her to have her face and hands washed, smoothed her bed and suggested a pot of tea and some thin bread and butter.

'If you insist,' said Nanny peevishly, 'though I don't say I'll eat it.'

Jolly was in the kitchen, laying the table. He bade her a dignified good morning, expressed the hope that she had slept well, and started to cut bread for toast. Florina busied herself with the frying-pan, bacon, mushrooms and a bowl of eggs. 'Yes, thank you, Mr Jolly...'

'Jolly, miss. I am Sir William's manservant.'

She turned to look at him. 'Well, I'm his cook. I think that's what you should call me...'

His severe expression broke into a brief smile. 'If you don't object, I prefer to call you miss.'

'Well, if you want to, as long as Sir William doesn't mind.'

'What am I objecting to?' He was a large, rather heavily built man, but he moved with speed and silence.

'Mr—that is, Jolly wishes to call me miss, and I'm the cook...' She looked up briefly from scrambling eggs.

Sir William took a slice of bread and buttered it and began to eat.

'You're not Missus, are you?' he asked with interest.

'Certainly not!'

'Engaged or walking out, or whatever?'

'No, Sir William. Would you both like bacon and eggs and mushrooms and tomatoes?'

'Speaking for myself, yes, please, and I'm pretty sure Jolly would, too. Mrs Jolly always gives me fried bread and I dare say she gives it to Jolly, too.'

'Very well, Sir William. I'll just run up with Pauline's tray.'

'Give it to Jolly—what is Nanny having? Is this her tray? I'll take it up when you're ready.' He made the tea, whistling cheerfully, and presently they sat down to breakfast, a pleasant meal, with Sir William carrying on an easy conversation and Jolly, rather surprisingly, contributing his share of the talk. As for Florina, she had little to say. She was shy, for a start, and for another thing, meals with her father had been strictly for eating; no attempt had been made to enliven them with conversation.

Sir William got out the vacuum cleaner after breakfast and, while Jolly cleared the table and washed the dishes, he strode around his house, taking no notice of Florina's attempts to stop him, hoovering like a whirlwind.

'You have a poor opinion of my capabilities,' he observed. 'I think you should go away and shake up pillows and make beds. You can tell Pauline that if she stays quietly in bed, she may come down for tea this afternoon.'

She was half-way up the stairs when he asked, 'What are we eating for our lunch?' He switched off for a moment so that she could hear him. 'Ploughman's lunch? Then you won't need to cook. Is there any Stilton in the house?'

'Of course.' She spoke coldly, affronted that he should doubt her housekeeping.

He didn't notice. 'Good. Do you want any shopping done? I can run into Wilton with the car...' He was at the bottom of the staircase, looking up at her. 'Let me know when you come down.'

While she made the beds and attended to Pauline and Nanny, she reviewed the contents of the fridge and freezer. She would need eggs from the farm and a chicken as well as cream. There was a nice piece of beef in the freezer and vegetables in the garden. When she went back to the kitchen later, it was to find Jolly setting out mugs for coffee and bending in a dignified manner over the coffeepot on the Aga. Smiling widely at him, despite his forbidding appearance, she felt sure he was a very reliable man and, in his reserved way, she felt also that he was disposed to like her. As for Sir William, she didn't allow herself to think too much about him; he resembled a little too closely for her peace of mind the rather vague dreams she had of the man who would sweep her off her feet and marry her and live with her happily ever after. She reminded herself once again that day-dreaming got you nowhere. Indeed, it was downright silly when you had your living to earn.

She accepted a mug from Jolly, frowned fiercely when Sir William joined them, then she blushed, remembering how she had let her thoughts stray.

He gave her a quick glance and began to talk to Jolly. Presently, when he made some remark to her, she had regained her usual composed manner. The rest of the morning passed busily, and somehow the sight of Sir William standing at the sink scraping potatoes put her quite at her ease with him. The invalids attended to, the three of them sat down at the kitchen table again. She had made a bowl of salad, and Jolly had cut great hunks of bread and arranged the Stilton cheese on a dish flanked by pickles and chutney. Sir William had a tankard of beer beside him, Jolly had made himself a pot of tea and Florina had poured herself a glass of lemonade. Not at all the kind of meal Sir William was used to, reflected Florina, but he seemed happy enough, spreading his bread lavishly with butter and carving up the Stilton. They talked comfortably of small everyday matters and then fell to discussing how she should cook the chicken. *'Poulet au citron?'* suggested Florina, and caught Jolly's approving look.

'Nice,' observed Sir William, 'Mrs Jolly does a very nice *Poulet Normand.'*

This remark instantly put her on her mettle. 'If you prefer that, Sir William, I think I could manage it.'

He laughed. 'Don't be so modest, Florina. You could turn a stale loaf into a splendid meal with one hand tied behind your back!' He watched the colour wash over her cheeks; for a moment she looked quite pretty.

They were sitting at the table drinking their coffee, deciding which vegetables to have, when the front door was banged shut and high heels tapped across the hall's wooden floor. Wanda Fortesque pushed the kitchen door wide open and came to a halt just inside it, looking at them. It was evident that she was in a splendid rage and had no intention of hiding it, but Sir William didn't appear to have noticed that; he got up without haste.

'Wanda, my dear girl, what a delightful surprise!'

'Surprise?' she almost spat at him. 'I'd say it was a surprise! What's this? A *ménage à trois*?'

He said easily, 'Hardly, since there are five of us here. Come and sit down—have you lunched? Or would you like coffee?'

She stared at the table. 'I don't eat in the kitchen, William.' Her very beautiful lip curled. 'I thought you employed a cook.' Her peevish eye settled on Florina, sitting like a mouse, hardly daring to breathe. 'She can make me an omelette and salad and bring it to the dining-room. Oh, and some fruit. Why on earth is Jolly sitting here, doing nothing?'

Sir William put his hands in his pockets; he spoke pleasantly, but there was no expression on his face. 'Jolly is here because I asked him to come and, since you enquire, he has been working flat out since he arrived. You see, my dear, Nanny and Pauline have the measles—Nanny is quite ill. Florina had been managing on her own, deciding, quite rightly, that it was hardly fair to our usual help to expect them to come in from the village—measles is so very infectious…'

'Measles,' repeated Wanda, in a voice that had become a little shrill. She backed away. 'Why didn't you say so in the first place? I've not had them—the place must be full of germs.' She added wildly, 'It's spots, isn't it? Great red blotches, and puffy eyes and headaches.'

She turned on her heel and hurried back through the hall. Sir William went after her.

She turned to face him when they reached the door. 'Why didn't you tell me? You could have telephoned…' It was an accusation.

'I did,' he told her mildly. 'You weren't at home and you had left a message to say that I wasn't to ring you, you would ring me.' He added gently, 'I'm sorry you're upset, Wanda. Why not stay now you are here? You won't have to go near Pauline and Nanny.'

'You must be mad—supposing I caught them? There's the Springfields' party next week, and Mother is giving a dinner—and there is that dress show I simply mustn't miss…'

'Why not?' He was smiling now, but she didn't smile back.

'Don't be an idiot, William—I have to have clothes. I've hardly a rag to my back. I intend to be a wife you can be proud of. Besides, I know so many influential people; it's important to mix with the right people, especially when you're a doctor.'

He was still smiling but his eyes were chilly. 'I already mix with the right people, my dear. My patients.'

'You're impossible. I'll not listen to another word! You can come and apologise when you get back to town on Monday.'

He walked with her to her car. 'It doesn't seem likely that I'll be back on Monday,' he told her patiently, 'but I'll be in touch.'

Back in the kitchen he said calmly, 'Sorry about that—Miss Fortesque is rather—highly strung is the popular phrase, I believe. Some people are inordinately nervous of catching things.' He took the tea-towel from Florina and began to dry the dishes Jolly was washing.

'Will there be scones for tea?' he asked her. Then, as an afterthought, 'You've had measles?'

Florina said primly, 'No, but I don't in the least mind having them, though I'd rather not, as it would make things so awkward for everyone.'

He shouted with laughter and Jolly allowed himself a dry chuckle.

'Well, that's a bridge we'll cross when we come to it. What a boring job washing up is! Jolly, you should have told me...'

'It was mentioned a year or so ago, Sir William, if you remember, and a dishwasher was installed. A boon to Shirley, if I might say so.'

'Well, we'd better have one here, too. See to it, will you, Jolly?'

Florina, assembling the ingredients for the scones, marvelled at the way some people lived. Shouldn't he have consulted Miss Fortesque first? On second thoughts, no.

She put the scones in the Aga and went to see how the invalids were getting on. Pauline was happy enough, as good as gold in bed, knowing that presently she would be going downstairs for her tea. Nanny, however, badly needed a great deal of attention. She was hot, she was thirsty, she wanted her bed remade, and who had banged the front door and wakened her from a refreshing nap?

Florina soothed her, sped downstairs to take the scones from the oven, refill the jug of lemonade, and skip back again. Half an hour later, Nanny washed and in a fresh nightie, her bed remade, her hair combed, and sitting up against her pillows sipping lemonade, felt well enough to tell Florina that she was a good girl with a kind heart and she, for her part, was delighted to hear that Miss Fortesque had taken herself off again.

'I cannot think what Sir William sees in the creature,' she declared, and Florina silently agreed. Although perhaps a lovely face, and clothes in the height of fashion and an air of knowing that one was never wrong, could be irresistible to a man. She went down to the kitchen and got tea ready before starting on the chicken.

They played Monopoly after tea, still at the kitchen table, and Florina and Sir William took it in turns to visit Nanny. In between times she saw to dinner. There was a pause while everyone watched her pour the brandy into a skillet and hold a lighted match over it. The flames soared as she tipped the pan from side to side and, when they had died down, she poured the delicious liquid into the bowl of cream and covered the chicken before popping it into a pan and putting a lid on it. There was time for her to make her fortune at Monopoly, which she did while it simmered. Jolly laid the table, and Sir William went down to the cellar to fetch the wine while she made the sauce, cooked the rice and fried the triangles of bread to arrange around the chicken. Pauline had coaxed her father to let her stay up for dinner, and she sat watching Florina as she trotted to and fro between the table and the Aga, peering into the pans holding the baby carrots, the garden peas and the courgettes. Sir William, strolling in with the bottles under his arms, paused to watch her, her hair a little shaken loose from its plait, her small nose shining, intent on her work. A pleasant enough nonentity, he had decided when he had first seen her, but he had been wrong; small, unassuming and nothing much to look at, she still merited a second look. She would make a good nurse, too. He toyed with the idea and then discarded it. She was far too good a cook; besides, Pauline had developed a great liking for her.

'It smells delicious,' he observed, and put the bottles in the fridge. 'If I pour you a glass of sherry, will it upset the cooking?'

Everything was eaten, and Jolly pronounced the chicken every bit as good as that his wife could cook, adding rather severely, 'Although, of course, miss, it wouldn't do to go and tell her so.'

'It shall remain a secret, Jolly,' Sir William had promised. He smiled across the table at Florina. 'Did you conjure the crème caramel out of the air?'

She answered him quite seriously. 'No, Sir William. I baked them in the oven, with the milk pudding for Mrs Frobisher.'

'All of which she ate. Now take yourself off for an hour, while Jolly and I clear up.' When she would have protested he added, 'You need some fresh air, and heaven knows, you've earned some leisure.'

'I'll take a little walk then. Thank you both for washing up. First, I'll make sure that they are all right upstairs.'

She whisked herself out of the kitchen before he could say anything.

It was a light, warm evening for it was full summer. She strolled away from the village, past the outlying cottages, sniffing at the air, fragrant with meadowsweet, dog roses and valerian. She was tired, but she had enjoyed her day, all except the bit when Wanda Fortesque had walked in. Sir William, she reflected, must love her very much to put up with such peevishness. Florina sat on a gate and debated with herself as to whether she would like to go on working as the cook at Wheel House once Sir William had married. Or if, indeed, Wanda would want her to stay. It seemed unlikely; they shared a mutual dislike. On the other hand,

if she stayed, Pauline would have someone to talk to.
She was a nice child, and Sir William loved her, but
she didn't think Wanda would make a good stepmother.
From what Pauline had told her, her father had taken
her with him whenever he could, and made sure that
she had had all the usual treats a child of her age might
expect: the circus, the pantomime, museums, sailing,
swimming. Florina couldn't see Wanda taking part in
any of them.

She wandered back presently, and stopped just inside the gates to look at the house. It was beautiful in
the twilight, and the sound of the stream was soothing.
The drawing-room curtains hadn't been drawn, and she
could see Sir William sitting in an easy chair, smoking
his pipe and reading. Jolly came in while she stood there
and said something to him, then went away again, and
a moment later the kitchen light was switched on. She
thought guiltily that she had been away long enough,
and went round the side of the house through the patio,
past the open drawing-room doors.

'Had a pleasant walk?' asked Sir William from his
chair.

'Yes, thank you. Is there anything else you would
like, Sir William?' When he said no, nothing, she said,
'Then I'll say goodnight.'

Jolly was in the kitchen, laying the table for breakfast, and she thanked him for his help and added, 'I'll
take a look at Pauline and Mrs Frobisher. Can I do
anything for you before I go to bed?' She added shyly,
'You've done so much since you came, I'm so grateful...'

Jolly smiled. 'It's been a pleasure, miss. Goodnight.'

Sir William and Jolly didn't leave until Monday evening. Watching the car turn out of the drive, Florina felt

a pang of loneliness. Sunday had been a lovely day, with Pauline allowed up for a good deal of it, Nanny feeling better at last, and Sir William and Jolly dealing with the mundane jobs around the house, with a good deal of light-hearted talk on the part of Sir William and an indulgent chuckle or two from Jolly. She had expected them to leave on Sunday evening, but Sir William had gone into the study and spent a long time on the telephone; when he had come out, it was to announce that his registrar would deal with his cases at the hospital. So she had had another lovely day, with Pauline dressed and up, and Nanny sitting out of her bed for a short while, well enough to want to know what everyone was doing and scattering advice like confetti whenever she had the chance.

She was to telephone Sir William immediately if things should go wrong, or if she felt that everything was getting on top of her. Sir William had kissed Nanny's elderly cheek, hugged his daughter and dropped a casual kiss on Florina's cheek as she stood in the doorway to wave them goodbye. When the car had gone, she put a hand up to her cheek and touched it lightly. She was sure that kissing was quite usual among his kind of people and meant nothing other than a social custom; all the same, it had disturbed her.

The house seemed too large and very empty. Sir William and Jolly had left it in apple-pie order, and on Wednesday Mrs Deakin and Mrs Datchett were to return. So, since Pauline was up for most of the day, there would be very little to do. The week slipped by; Sir William telephoned each evening, talking at length to Pauline, after he had had a brief report from Florina. He would be down on Friday evening, he told her, and he would be coming alone.

With Nanny sitting comfortably beside the Aga and Pauline making a cake for tea, Florina bent her mind to food for the weekend. By the time the car came to a quiet halt before the house, she had a vegetable soup simmering on the Aga, *Boeuf flamand*, rich with beer and onions, in the oven and a strawberry pavlova in the fridge. Moreover, she had put on a clean apron, replaited her hair and done her face with the modest make-up at her disposal.

It was, therefore, disappointing when Sir William, his arm round Pauline's shoulders, wandered into the kitchen, and greeted Nanny warmly before glancing briefly at her with a casual, 'Hello, Florina. I hear that Pauline's made a cake for tea.'

She assented quietly; there was, after all, no need for him to ask how the week had gone; he had phoned each evening and she had given him a faithful account of the day. She made the tea and carried the tray out on to the patio while he went upstairs with Pauline. When they came down again she had shut the kitchen door, put a small tray beside Nanny's chair and gone back to her cooking, a mug of tea on the table beside her. She heard them on the patio presently and went to set the table in the dining-room. The cheerful meals in the kitchen had been all very well, but the circumstances had been unusual. She arranged the glass and silver just so on the starched linen cloth, set a bowl of roses in its centre and stood back to admire the effect.

'Very nice,' said Sir William from the door, 'very elegant. You have a talent for home-making, Florina— your husband will be a lucky man.'

He came into the room and sat on the edge of the table. 'I'm taking Pauline back with me on Sunday— she's going to spend a week with my sister's children at Eastdean, near Brighton. I'll drop her off on my way back to town. Nanny will stay here, but she is well enough to leave alone if you would like to take time off to shop or to go home. You don't mind being on your own with Nanny and Pauline? I've never asked you and I should have done.'

'I know everyone in the village,' she told him, 'and I'm not nervous. Will you be bringing Pauline back next weekend?' She added quickly, in case he thought it was none of her business, 'Just so that I can help her pack enough clothes...'

'We'll be back on Saturday morning; I won't be able to get away from hospital until Friday evening. I'll drive down to my sister's and spend the night. Oh, and I dare say Miss Fortesque will be joining us. She'll drive herself down some time on Saturday, but have lunch ready, will you?'

He wandered over to the door. 'You've had more than your share of hard work since you came here—and no free time, let alone days off. If and when you want a week's holiday, don't hesitate to ask, Florina.' He gave her a kind smile as he went.

In her room that night, getting ready for bed, she pondered a holiday. She couldn't remember when she had last had one—when her mother had been alive and the pair of them had gone to Holland once a year to see her mother's family, and she remembered that with wistful pleasure. After her mother's death, her father had said that there was no point in wasting money on visiting uncles and aunts and cousins whom he hardly knew. She wrote to them regularly in her perfect Dutch, for her mother had been firm about her speaking, writing and reading that language. 'For you are half-Dutch,' she had reminded Florina, 'and I don't want you to forget that.' It was so long now since she had visited her mother's family, but she had liked them and had felt at home in the old-fashioned house just outside Zierikzee. She would like to see them again, but it didn't seem very likely.

Sir William took Pauline for a short drive in the morning, and in the afternoon they sat on the patio, watching the swans below them. Florina, making a batch of congress tarts for tea, could hear them laughing and talking. After tea, before she needed to start cooking for the evening meal, she changed into one of her sensible cotton dresses and went home. Her father greeted her sourly and went back to reading his paper, but her aunt was glad to sit down and have half an hour's gossip. She had settled down nicely, she told Florina, and her father seemed happy enough. 'You've got yourself a nice job, love. That Sir William is spoken of very highly in the village. Had a busy time with the measles, though, didn't you?'

Her father didn't miss her, thought Florina regretfully, as she returned to the Wheel House, but at least she thought he seemed content, and Aunt Meg was happy. She went to the kitchen and started on dinner—avocado pears with a hot cheese sauce, trout caught locally, cooked with almonds, and a summer pudding.

After dinner, Sir William came into the kitchen and told her how much he had enjoyed his meal. He was kind but casual; there was none of the friendliness of the previous week.

He went after lunch the next day, taking Pauline with him; a Pauline who was flatteringly loath to leave Florina behind. The warmth of her goodbyes made up for the casual wave of the hand from her father as they drove off.

It was pleasant to have some leisure. Half-way

through the week, Florina left Mrs Datchett to keep Nanny company, and took herself off to Salisbury. She had her wages in her pocket and the summer sales were on. The shops were full of pretty summer dresses, but she went straight to Country Casuals where she found a jacket and skirt in a pleasing shade of peach pink and a matching blouse. She added low-heeled court shoes and a small handbag and left the shop, very well satisfied, even if a good deal lighter in her pocket. There was enough money left over to buy a cotton jersey dress, canvas sandals and some undies, even a new lipstick and a face cream guaranteed to erase wrinkles and bring a bloom to the cheeks of the users. Florina, who hadn't a wrinkle anyway, and owned a skin as clear as a child's, could have saved her money, but it smelled delicious and fulfilled her wish to improve her looks. She wasn't sure why.

She showed everything to Mrs Frobisher when she got back, and then hung her finery in the cupboard in her room, got into one of her sensible, unflattering cotton dresses and went to pick the raspberries. On Friday she would cycle into Wilton and get some melons; halved and filled with the raspberries and heaped with whipped cream and a dash of brandy, they would make a good dessert for Sir William and whoever came with him. He hadn't said that he was bringing guests but she must be prepared…

He arrived on Saturday morning, with Wanda beside him and a sulky Pauline on the back seat. Mrs Frobisher, on her feet once more, but not doing much as yet, opened the door to them, and Florina heard them talking and laughing in the hall; at least Wanda was laughing. A moment later, the kitchen door was flung open and Pauline danced in.

'Oh, Florina, I have missed you, it's lovely to be here again! Can I make cakes for tea? My aunt has a cook too, but she wouldn't let me go into the kitchen. My cousins are scared of her. I'm not scared of you.'

Florina was piping potato purée into elegant swirls. 'Oh, good! Of course you can make cakes. Any idea what you want to make?'

'Scones—like yours. Daddy says they melt in his mouth...'

'OK. Come back about three o'clock, Pauline. I'm going to pick the last of the raspberries after lunch; you can make the scones when I've done that.'

Pauline danced away, and she got on with her cooking, trying not to hear Wanda's voice on the patio, or her trilling laugh. With luck, she wouldn't have to see anything of her over the weekend; Mrs Deakin or Mrs Datchett would be early enough to take her breakfast tray up each morning.

Florina chopped parsley so viciously that Sir William, coming into the kitchen, said in mock alarm, 'Oh, dear, shall I come back later?'

Could she knock up some savoury bits and pieces? he wanted to know. He had asked a few local people in for drinks that evening, and could dinner be put back for half an hour?

On his way out of the kitchen he turned to look at her. 'Quite happy?' he wanted to know.

Her 'Yes, thank you, sir,' was offered without expression. There was no reason for her to be anything else. She had a good job, money in her pocket and a kind, considerate employer. Of course she was happy.

A dozen or so people came for drinks. She knew them by sight; people from the bigger country houses in the vicinity. Doctor Stone and his wife were there

too, and the Rector, and the dear old lady from Crow
Cottage at the other end of the village whose husband
had been the local vet. She lived alone now with several cats and an elderly dog. Florina had made cheese
straws, *petits fours* and tiny cheese puffs, while Pauline
made the scones. The first batch were a failure; Florina
put them into a bowl, observing that the swans would
soon dispose of them, and advised Pauline to try again.
'And this time they will be perfect,' she encouraged.

Edible, at any rate! Her father assured her that they
were delicious and ate four, and Pauline swelled with
pride, although the sight of Wanda taking a bite and
then refusing to finish hers took the edge off her pleasure. 'I expect I'm fussy,' said Wanda, laughing gently.
Then she shot a look of dislike at Pauline, who wanted
to know if she knew how to make scones.

'I have never needed to cook,' she said loftily. 'I have
other things with which to occupy my time.'

'It's a good thing that I have the means to employ
someone who can, my dear,' observed Sir William, and
cut himself a slice of Florina's apple cake. It was as light
as a feather and he felt that he deserved it after his small
daughter's offering. 'But it is reassuring to know that,
should I ever be without a cook, Pauline will at least
know an egg from a potato.'

He drove Wanda back to London on Sunday evening,
for she refused to get up early on Monday morning so
that he might be in the hospital in time for his mid-
morning clinic. She was, she declared, quite unable to
get up before nine o'clock each morning. Florina heard
her saying it and heartily despised her for it. Anyone
with any sense knew that one of the best parts of the
day was the hour just as the sun was rising. Besides,
Sir William was no lie-abed; hospitals, unless she was

very much mistaken, started their day early, and that would apply to most of the staff, including the most senior of the consultants.

Pauline came in from the front porch where she had been waving goodbye.

'It's super to be here again just with you and Nanny, only I wish Daddy were here, too.'

'Don't you like your home in London?' asked Florina. She was getting their supper and had made Nanny comfortable in a chair by the Aga.

'Oh, yes, that's super too, only Wanda is always there. She walks in and out as though it were her home, and it isn't, it's Daddy's and mine, and Jolly and Mrs Jolly's of course.' She added, 'Oh, and Shirley, she lives there too. Mrs Peek comes in each day to help, but she goes home after her dinner.'

'It sounds very pleasant,' said Florina a bit absent-mindedly: she was remembering that Wanda hadn't spoken to her at all during the weekend. Sir William hadn't said much, either, but he had thanked her for the bits and pieces she had made for the drinks party, and praised the roast beef she had served up for dinner on Saturday evening. He had also wished her goodbye until the following weekend.

'I'll be alone,' he had told her, 'perhaps we might have a picnic... Pauline has rather set her heart on one. You and Nanny, Pauline and I.'

The fine weather held; the three of them picked beans and peas and courgettes and tomatoes, and stocked up the freezer. And, with Pauline on a borrowed bike, Florina cycled with her to Wilton, and they shopped for the weekend and had ices at the little tea room in the High Street.

It was on the Thursday that she had a letter from her

Tante Minna in Holland. Florina's cousin Marijke was
going to be married, and would she go to the wedding
and, if possible, stay for a week or so? It was a long
time, wrote Tante Minna in her beautiful copperplate
Dutch, since Florina had been to see them, and, while
they were aware that her father had no wish to visit
them, her family in Holland felt that they should keep
in touch. The wedding was to be in a week and a half's
time and she hoped to hear…

A wedding, reflected Florina—a chance to wear her
new outfit and, since she could afford the fare, there
was no reason why she shouldn't accept. Sir William
had told her that if she wanted a holiday she had only
to ask. He would be back at home on the next day. She
spent the rest of the day and a good deal of the night
deciding exactly what she would say to him.

He looked tired when he came, but he still remembered to see her in the kitchen and to ask if everything
was all right. 'I see Nanny has quite recovered—I hope
Pauline hasn't been too much trouble?'

Florina gave a brief résumé of their week, and took
in the tea tray.

'Worn to the bone,' commented Nanny as they drank
their own tea in the kitchen. 'What he needs is peace
and quiet when he gets home of an evening, but that
Miss Fortesque is always on at him to go dining and
dancing.'

It wasn't the time to ask about holidays, and Florina
went to bed feeling frustrated. Perhaps she wouldn't
have the chance to ask him, and if she didn't this weekend it would be too late to make arrangements to go to
the wedding. She spent a poor night worrying about it,
which proved a waste of time for, as she was boiling

the kettle for early morning tea, he wandered into the kitchen in trousers and an open-necked shirt.

'Oh, you're up,' she said stupidly, and then, 'Good morning, Sir William.'

'Morning, Florina—too nice to stay in bed—I've been for a walk. Is that tea? Good.' He sat down on the side of the table and watched her, clean and starched and neat, getting mugs and sugar and milk. 'Have a cup with me, I want to talk.'

Her hand shook a little as she poured the milk. The sack? Wanda and he getting married? Something awful she had done?

'I'm wondering if you would like that week's holiday? In a week's time I have to go to Leiden to give a series of lectures, and I thought I would take Pauline with me. Nanny can stay here, and the Jollys can come down and keep her company. Our Shirley is quite happy to look after the house in town, and Mrs Peek will move in while we are away and keep her company...'

He broke off to look at her. Florina was gazing at him, her gentle mouth slightly open, wearing the bemused look of someone who had just received a smart tap on the head. 'In a week's time,' she repeated, a bit breathless. 'Oh, I'll be able to go to the wedding!'

'Yours?' asked Sir William.

She shook her head. 'No—my cousin—they live close to Zierikzee, and she's getting married, and I've been asked to go and it's just perfect! While you are in Leiden, I'll be able to stay with my aunt.'

She beamed at him and then asked soberly, 'That is, if you don't mind?'

He leaned over and poured the tea into two mugs. 'My dear girl, why should I mind? It's the hand of fate, of course you must go. How?'

'Oh, I'll fly, I did it with Mother several times, when she was alive we went each year, Basingstoke, you know, and then a bus to Gatwick…'

Sir William cut himself a slice of bread from the loaf she had put ready for toast. 'I know a better way. When is this wedding?' When she had told him, he said, 'It couldn't be better. We'll give you a lift in the car and drop you off…'

'It's out of your way,' she pointed out.

'A mile or so, besides I've always wanted to take a look at Zierikzee. Can you stay with your aunt until we pick you up on the way home?'

'Yes—oh, yes!' Her face glowed with delight and Sir William took a second look at her. Quite pretty in a quiet, unassuming way, and she had lovely eyes. He got off the table. 'That's settled, then. We'll work out the details later. Can you really be ready for this picnic by eleven o'clock? The New Forest, so Pauline tells me. She has it all planned.'

Florina nodded happily, in a delightful daze, quite unable to stop smiling. Sir William, on the way upstairs to his room, reflected that she was a funny little thing as well as being a marvellous cook. She didn't seem to have much fun, either, and this cousin's wedding would be a treat for her.

Chapter 4

The Bentley slid with deceptive speed around the southern outskirts of Salisbury, took the Ringwood road and at Downton turned off to Cadnam. Florina and Nanny, sitting in the back of the car, admired the scenery and listened to Pauline's happy chatter to her father. In Lyndhurst, a few miles further on from Cadnam, they stopped for coffee at an olde-worlde tea-shop, all dark oak and haughty waitresses dressed to match. The coffee was dreadful and Sir William muttered darkly over his, only cheered by Florina's recital of what she and Nanny had packed in the picnic basket.

Just outside the little town they entered the Forest, and presently turned off into a narrow lane which opened out into a rough circle of green grass surrounded by trees. It was pleasantly warm and Pauline pranced off, intent on exploring, taking her father with her. He had hesitated before they went, looking at Florina, but she had no intention of leaving Nanny alone.

'We'll get the lunch ready,' she said firmly, wishing with all her heart that she could go with them.

They were back after half an hour or so, and in the meantime she had spread their picnic on the ground near the car. They had brought a folding chair for Nanny, and she was sitting in it, telling Florina what to do, watching as she set out the little containers with sausage rolls, sandwiches, meat pies and cheese puffs. There was lemonade, too, and beer for Sir William as well as a thermos of hot coffee, and apples and pears. Sir William heaved a sigh of contentment as he made himself comfortable against a tree stump.

'The temptation to retire is very strong,' he observed and, at Florina's surprised look, 'No, I'm not sixty, Florina, although I feel all of that, sometimes.' He bit into a pie. 'This seems as good a time as any to plan out our week in Holland.' He glanced at Mrs Frobisher. 'Nanny, I'm taking Pauline over to Holland with me when I go in a week's time—we'll be gone for a week. The Jollys are coming down to keep you company. You'll like that, won't you? Florina is going to Holland too, to a cousin's wedding, and we'll bring her back with us. Now, how shall we go?' He looked at Florina who, having no idea at all, said nothing. 'Hovercraft, I think, and drive up from Calais.' He finished the pie and started on a sausage roll. 'Have you a passport, Florina? No— well go to the post office in Wilton and get a passport from there. There isn't time for you to get a new one through the normal channels; you'll need the old one for details, though. Pauline's on my passport. Let me see, if we leave Dover about ten o'clock, we should be in Zierikzee during the afternoon, and Amsterdam a couple of hours later. I start lectures on the Monday, so that will fit in very well.'

'Will Pauline be alone?' asked Florina.

'We're staying with friends. She'll have a marvellous time, they have four children.'

It was nice to know that Wanda wasn't to be of the party. Florina poured coffee and allowed her thoughts to dwell on the pleasures in store.

The weekend went too quickly. They all went to church on Sunday morning, and in the evening Sir William drove himself into Wilton to a friend's house for drinks. He had a lot of friends, reflected Florina, concentrating on the making of lemon sauce. In the morning he left early, while Nanny was still in bed. Pauline had come down to say goodbye, but she went back to bed again, leaving Florina to clear away Sir William's breakfast things and start the day's chores. He wouldn't be back until the next weekend, and it seemed a very long time.

Actually, the days passed quickly. Florina needed Pauline's help to gather together suitable clothes to take with her, there were beds to be made up and the house to be left in apple-pie order for the Jollys' arrival. There was her own wardrobe to decide upon; she would be able to wear her new clothes, but they would need to be augmented. Sir William phoned most evenings to talk to Pauline but, although he spoke to Nanny once or twice, he evinced no desire to speak to Florina.

He arrived rather late on Friday evening, and Jolly and his wife drove down at the same time in the other car. Pauline, already in bed, came bouncing down to fling her arms around his neck. 'We're all ready,' she assured him excitedly, 'and Florina is ready too, and she's filled the fridge with food that means Mrs Jolly won't have to bother too much. She washed her hair this afternoon and she did mine last night.'

She skipped away to greet the Jollys. 'There is supper for you and we put flowers in your bedroom.'

'Bed for you, Pauline,' said Nanny severely, appearing to greet Sir William and the Jollys. 'The child is excited,' she told Sir William.

'So am I, Nanny.' He went past her, into the kitchen where Florina was putting the finishing touches to the salad.

'Busy as usual?' he observed kindly. 'All ready for your holiday, Florina? I do wonder what on earth you'll do with yourself without your cooking stove?'

She smiled politely; she wasn't a girl to him, just the cook—it was a mortifying thought. She thrust it from her, and said soberly, 'Well, I haven't seen my family for some time, Sir William. I expect there will be a lot to talk about.'

That sounded dull enough, she thought crossly. If only he could see her, dressed in her new clothes, being chatted up by some handsome Dutch cousin—only all her cousins were either married or with no looks to speak of; and when would he see her anyway?

She wished that he would go away, not stand there looking at her in that faintly surprised fashion. It disturbed her, although she didn't know why.

They left very early on Sunday morning, driving through the still-sleeping village, past the pub, her home, the farm opposite the bridge and along the narrow country lane which would lead them to Wilton.

She had spent an afternoon with her father during the week, but he hadn't been particularly interested in her plans. She could do as she wished, he had observed grumpily, and he hadn't even expressed the hope that she would enjoy herself. Everyone else had; even Nanny, so sparing in her praise, had told her that she had earned a holiday. 'And I just hope you meet a nice young man,' she had added.

Florina, sitting in the back of the car, bubbling over with excitement, hoped that she would too. If she met a nice young man, then perhaps Sir William wouldn't seem quite so important in her life.

They had an uneventful, very comfortable journey. It made a great difference, she reflected, if you had money. You stopped when you wanted to at good hotels for coffee and lunch, with no need to look at the price list outside to see if you could afford it. Moreover you spoke French in France and when you reached Holland you switched to Dutch, which, while basic, got you what you wanted without any fuss. And you did all that with the calm assurance which was Sir William.

They were crossing the Zeeland Brug by mid-afternoon, glimpsing Zierikzee ahead of them. On dry land once more, Sir William said, over his shoulder, 'You must tell me where to go, Florina. It's outside the town, isn't it?'

She leaned forward, the better to speak to him. 'Yes, go straight on, don't turn into Zierikzee, go to the roundabout and take the road to Drieschor; Schudderbeurs is about two miles...'

The road was straight and narrow, snaking away into the distance. The sign to the village was small and anyone going too fast would miss it. Sir William slowed down when she warned him, and turned left down a narrow lane, joining a pleasant, leafy lane with a handful of cottages and villas on either side of it. There was an old-fashioned country house standing well back from the road with a wide sweep before it. As they went past it Sir William said, 'That looks pleasant; it's an hotel, too…'

'Yes. It's quite well known. I've never been there, it's expensive, but I believe it's quite super… My aunt lives just along that lane to the right.'

There were a handful of houses ringing the edge of wooded country, not large, but well maintained and with fair-sized gardens.

'It's this one.'

Sir William stopped, got out and opened her door. A door in the house opened at the same time and Tante Minna, looking not a day older than when Florina had seen her five years or more ago, came down the garden path. She had begun to talk the moment she had seen them; she was still talking when she opened the gate and hugged Florina, at the same time casting an eye over Sir William and Pauline. Florina disentangled herself gently. 'Tante Minna, how lovely to see you…' She had slipped into Dutch without a conscious effort. 'This is Sir William, I'm his cook, as I told you, and this is his daughter Pauline. They are on their way to Leiden and kindly gave me a lift.'

She had already told Aunt Minna all that in her letter, but she was wishful to bridge an awkward gap.

Tante Minna transferred her twinkling gaze to Sir William. Her English was adequate, about as adequate as his Dutch. They shook hands warmly and Tante Minna turned her attention to Pauline, and then took her by the arm and turned towards the house. 'You will take tea? It is ready. You will like to see my cat and her five kittens?'

They went into the house, light and airy and comfortably furnished. She said in Dutch to Florina, 'Will you explain that your uncle Constantine is in Goes?

Marijke and Jan and Pieter are here, though, and Felix Troost—his father is a partner in your uncle's firm. I believe you met him years ago...'

Florina translated, leaving out the bit about Felix Troost, and they went into the sitting-room where Florina was instantly enveloped in a round of hand-shaking and kissing, emerging to find Sir William talking easily to Felix, whose English was a good deal better than Sir William's Dutch. Pauline had disappeared with Florina's aunt, doubtless in search of the kittens. Indeed, she reappeared a few minutes later with a small fluffy creature tucked under one arm.

Her cousins hadn't changed much, Florina decided; Marijke, a year or two younger than herself, was plump and fair and pretty, good-natured and easy-going, Jan and Pieter, who had still been at school when she had last seen them, were young men now, towering over her, calling her little Rina and wanting to know why she wasn't married. But when the tea tray was brought in, the talk became general, while they drank the milkless tea in small porcelain cups and nibbled thin, crisp biscuits. Not very substantial for Sir William's vast frame, thought Florina, watching him, completely at his ease, discussing their journey with Pieter. He looked up, caught her eye and smiled, and she felt a pleasant glow spreading under her ribs.

He and Pauline left soon, for they still had rather more than an hour's drive ahead of them across the islands to Rotterdam, and then a further hour on the motorway to Amsterdam. But before they went Sir William sat himself down by Florina. 'We'll fetch you next Saturday,' he reminded her. 'I'd like to get to Wheel House in the fairly early evening, so we should leave here not later than two o'clock. Will you be ready then?'

'Yes, of course, Sir William. Would you like coffee here before we go?'

He shook his head. 'No time. We can have a quick stop on the way if we must.' He stood up. 'Have a good holiday, Florina. I envy you the peace and quiet here.'

She had forgotten that he was to give lectures for most of the week, and Amsterdam, delightful though it was, was also noisy. She said quietly, 'Perhaps you will be able to spare the time to spend a few days in the country—somewhere like Schudderbeurs, the *hostellerie* is quite famous, you know.'

'Yes, perhaps one day I'll do that.' He patted her shoulder and went out to his car with Pieter and Jan, leaving Pauline to say goodbye.

'I hope I shall like it,' she said uncertainly. 'Daddy won't be there for most of the day...'

'You'll have a gorgeous time,' said Florina cheerfully. 'We'll compare notes when we meet next Saturday, and think how nice it is for your father to have you for company.'

Pauline brightened. 'Yes, he likes me to be with him, that's why I don't see why he needs to marry Wanda. She hates quiet places, she likes to dance and go to the shops and theatre and have people to dinner.'

'Ah, well, perhaps she will change when your father marries her!' Florina kissed the pretty little face, and then walked out to the car and stood with her aunt and cousins, waving until it was out of sight.

'A very nice man,' commented Tante Minna. 'He is married?'

'No, but he is going to be—to a very lovely girl called Wanda.'

'And you do not like her, I think?' asked her aunt, sharp as a needle.

'Well, I don't think she's right for him. He works very hard and I believe he likes his work; it's a part of his life, if you know what I mean. She enjoys the bright lights and I think she's annoyed because he's just come to live at Wheel House—and you know how quiet the village is, Tante Minna! He has a house in London, too, though I don't know where it is, but he likes to spend his weekends at Wheel House, if he can.' She paused, 'And Pauline doesn't like her.'

'It seems that he needs to be rescued,' observed Tante Minna, and added briskly, 'Come indoors, child, and tell us all your news—it's so long…'

Florina made short work of that for, of course, what they really wanted to talk about was the wedding. Marijke took her upstairs to show her her wedding dress, and when they joined the family again she was regaled with the details of the ceremony, Christiaan's job, the flat they would live in and the furniture they had bought for it. Which reminded Florina to go upstairs to the small bedroom at the back of the house and fetch the present she had brought with her. Place mats, rather nice ones, depicting the English countryside, and received with delight by her cousin. Christiaan came then, and they had their evening meal with Oom Constantine, and when it was finished Felix Troost arrived again. He had been in Goes with Florina's uncle, he explained, but had had to call on someone on the way home. He was a good-looking young man, with blue eyes, set rather too close together, and a good deal of very fair hair. He was obviously at home there, and he greeted Florina with a slightly overdone charm. They shook hands and exchanged polite greetings, and she decided then and there that she didn't like him.

A feeling that she became uncertain of as the evening

progressed, for he was casually friendly, talking about
his work, wanting to know about her life in England.
She must have been mistaken in the sudden feeling of
dislike that she had had when they met, she reflected
as she got ready for bed. Anyway, she would be seeing
a good deal of him while she was staying with Tante
Minna, and he would be at the wedding and the reception afterwards at the hotel. She allowed her thoughts to
dwell on the peach-pink outfit with some satisfaction.
It was a pity that Sir William wouldn't see her in her
finery. She wondered what he was doing; dining and
dancing probably, with some elegant creature whose
dress would make the peach-pink look like something
run up by the local little dressmaker. She sighed sadly,
not knowing why she was sad.

Everyone was up early the next morning and, although the wedding wasn't until mid-afternoon, there
was a constant coming and going of family and friends.
Florina, nicely made up and wearing the peach-pink,
greeted aunts and uncles and cousins she hadn't seen
for years, exclaiming over engagements, new babies
and the various ailments of the more elderly. She blos-
somed out under observations that she had grown into
quite a presentable young woman, for, as one elderly
aunt observed in a ringing voice everyone could hear,
'A plain child you were, Florina. Your mother despaired
of you. Never thought you'd get yourself a husband…
engaged, are you?'

Black beady eyes studied her, and she blushed a little
and was eternally grateful to Felix, who flung an arm
round her shoulders and said, 'She's waiting for a good
honest Dutchman to ask her, aren't you, Florina?' And
he kissed her on one cheek. Everyone laughed then, and

she decided that she had been mistaken about Felix; he had sounded warmly friendly and he had been kind…

With the prospect of the wedding reception later on in the day, no one ate much of the lunch Aunt Minna provided. Guests were to go straight to the *Gemeentehuis*, but even the most distant relations who weren't seen from one year to the next came to the house, so that there was a good deal of good-natured confusion. Deciding who was to go in whose car took considerable time, and presently Florina found herself sitting beside Felix in his BMW with two elderly aunts on the back seat. It was the last to leave in the procession of cars, leaving Marijke, following the time-honoured custom, to wait for her bridegroom to fetch her from her home, bearing the bridal bouquet.

The *Gemeentehuis* was the centre of interest, and the congestion in the narrow street was making it worse than ever to drive through the little town. The guests trooped up the narrow steps into the ancient building and made their way to the Bride Chamber, a handsome apartment at the top of a broad staircase. Florina was urged into a seat in the front row of chairs, since she was a cousin of the bride, while Felix, being a family friend, found his way to a seat at the back, but not before giving her hand a squeeze and whispering that he would drive her to the church presently. She nodded, not really listening, for Marijke and Christiaan were taking their places in front of the *Burgermeester* and the short ceremony started.

Florina, watching closely, thought it seemed too businesslike. It certainly wouldn't do for her. She was glad that Marijke had wanted a church wedding as well, not that she herself was likely to marry, whether in Holland or in England. She didn't know any men, only Felix, and she didn't know him at all really, and Sir William, who didn't count, for he was going to marry Wanda. She fell to day-dreaming of some vague, faceless man who would meet her and fall in love with her at once and they would marry. These musings led, naturally enough, to what she would wear: cream satin, yards of it and a tulle veil. Marijke was wearing a picture hat trimmed with roses, and her dress was white lace. Florina had helped her to dress and had zipped the dress up, only after having urged her cousin to breathe in while she did so, for Marijke was a shade too plump for it. All the same, she looked delightful and her pinched waist had given her a most becoming colour. They were signing the register now, and a few minutes later the whole party followed the bride and groom out to the long line of cars.

The church was barely two minutes' drive, behind the Apple Market, bordering on the big market square, so that the entire wedding party could park in comfort before filing inside. It was a *Hervormdekerk*, and the service was sober and the short homily delivered sternly by the *Dominee*. Florina allowed her attention to wander, stealthily checking on the congregation, refreshing her memory as to who they were. She had forgotten over the years what a very large family her mother had; sitting there in the church she felt more Dutch than English. Her eye, roaming round the church, lighted upon Felix who smiled and nodded. He seemed like an old friend, and she smiled back, stifling the vague feeling of dislike she had for him.

The service ended and the bride and groom got into their flower-decked car and started on their slow tour of the town before driving back to Schudderbeurs, while everyone else went back to the *hostellerie*.

The wedding party was to be held in the large room built at the back of the hotel. It had been decorated with pot plants and flowers, and a buffet had been nicely arranged on a long table at one end. The afternoon was still warm and sunny, and the doors on to the garden had been opened so that the guests could spill outside. Florina, driven back by Felix, stood taking breaths of fresh air, listening idly to his rather conceited talk about himself and his work. He was doing his best to impress her, but she didn't feel impressed; indeed, she was shocked to find that she was bored. Suddenly she wanted to be back at Wheel House, busy at the stove while Sir William sat on the kitchen table, polishing off the scones she had made for tea.

She heard Felix say in a cocksure manner, 'And, of course, I shall be a partner in a year or so.' He gave a self-deprecating laugh. 'You can't keep a good man down, you know!'

She murmured politely and was glad that the bridal pair had arrived and everyone could sit down and eat the delicious food the hotel had provided. There was champagne, of course, and speeches. No wedding cake, for that wasn't the custom in Holland, but little dishes of chocolates and sweetmeats and more champagne. Presently, friends and acquaintances arrived, each with a present or flowers, to wish the bride and groom every happiness, and join in the dancing. It was great fun, reflected Florina, her ordinary face glowing with warmth and excitement, whirling around the floor with cousins and uncles and Felix; Felix more than anyone else, but what with the champagne and the cheerful, noisy party, she was content to dance the night away. She hadn't enjoyed herself so much for years.

Presently, the newly wedded pair disappeared in the

direction of the little white house in the hotel grounds, where they would spend the night before driving to their new flat in Goes on the following day. It was only in recent years that newly marrieds had abandoned the custom of going straight to their new home from the wedding reception. The little white house was much in demand among the young people, some of them coming from miles around.

The dancing went on for another hour or more before the guests finally left. Some of the more elderly were staying at the *hostellerie* for the night, the younger ones were either putting up with friends in the village or driving home through the night. Florina walked the short distance to her aunt's house, arm in arm with a bevy of cousins and Felix. He was to spend what remained of the night with friends in the village, and he parted from them on the doorstep, but not before he had asked her to spend the next day with him.

When she had hesitated, he had promised, 'We won't do anything strenuous, and I won't come round until eleven o'clock.'

And when she still hesitated, her cousins joined in. 'Oh, go on, Rina, none of us will want to do anything tomorrow, and you'll enjoy a day out.'

She wasn't too happy about it as she tumbled into bed, perhaps because she was tired. Besides, she could always change her mind in the morning.

She didn't; she was awake only a little later than usual and it was a glorious morning. There were only four days left of her holiday—she must make the most of them. She had a shower and dressed in the cotton jersey and went down to the roomy kitchen. Her aunt was already up; there was coffee on the stove and a basket of rolls and croissants on the table.

'Going out with Felix?' asked Tante Minna.

Florina nodded. 'You don't mind? He's not coming until eleven o'clock—I'll give you a hand around the house—you must be tired…'

'Yes, but it was a splendid wedding, wasn't it, *liefje*? When shall we see you marry, I wonder?'

Florina bit into a roll; Tante Minna was awfully like her mother. She felt her throat tighten at the thought but she answered lightly, 'I've no idea, but I promise that you shall dance at my wedding if every I have one…'

'Do they dance at English weddings?'

'Oh, rather, discotheques, the same as here.' But she wouldn't want that—only a quiet wedding in the church at home, and a handful of family and friends and, of course, the bridegroom—that vague but nebulous figure she could never put a face to. She finished her roll and tidied away her breakfast things and then, armed with a duster, set about bringing the sitting-room to that peak of pristine perfection which Tante Minna, wedding or no wedding, expected.

Presently her uncle appeared to drink his coffee and then go into the garden to inspect his roses, and after him, Felix, flamboyantly dressed, oozing charm and impatient of the coffee Tante Minna insisted on them having before they went. Florina got into the car beside him, told her aunt that they would be back in good time for the evening meal, eaten as was customary at six o'clock, and sat quietly while Felix roared through the tiny village and on to the road to Browershaven, away from Zierikzee.

The day wasn't a success. Felix talked about himself and, what was more, in a lofty fashion which Florina found tedious. He had no clear idea where they were going, but drove around the surrounding countryside in a haphazard fashion, and when she had suggested mildly that it would be nice to go to the coast he said, 'Oh, you don't want to walk on the beach, for heaven's sake.'

'Then what about Veere or Domburg?'

'Packed out. We'll go inland and find a place to eat, and park the car somewhere quiet and get to know each other.'

Florina wished that she hadn't come, but it was too late to do anything about it now. They stopped at a small roadside café, full of local men playing billiards and, unlike most Dutch cafés, not over-clean. She lingered over her *limonade* and kaas broodje, uneasy at the amount of beer Felix was drinking. With good reason, she was to discover, for, once more in the car, he stopped after a few miles and flung an arm around her shoulders.

Florina removed the arm and eyed him severely. 'Tante Minna expects me back before six o'clock, so be good enough to start back now. I'm sorry if I disappoint you, but I came with you for a pleasant day out and that's all.'

She was aware that she sounded priggish, even in Dutch, but she wasn't prepared for his snarling, 'Prudish little bitch—no wonder you haven't got a man. I wish you joy of your cooking. That's all you're fit for.'

Neither of them spoke again until they reached Tante Minna's house, and when Florina said goodbye in a cold voice Felix didn't answer.

'Had a nice day?' asked her aunt. Seeing her stony face, she added hastily, 'We are all going to Goes the day after tomorrow. You'll come won't you, *liefje*? Just the family—Marijke wants us all to see their flat.'

The last day of her holiday was pure pleasure. On Thursday, she joined a happy gathering of family at a proud Marijke's new home, which was smothered in flowers and pot plants from friends and such members of the family who hadn't been able to attend the wedding. Florina admired everything, drank a little too much wine, ate the *bitterballen* served with it, and agreed that the bridal bouquet, hung on the wall at the head of the bed, was the most beautiful she had ever seen. Presently, she sat down with everyone else to *nasi goreng* and an elaborate dessert of ice-cream. A day to remember, she assured her uncle when he wanted to know if she had enjoyed her holiday.

Sir William had said that he would pick her up after lunch on Saturday. She was up early to pack her small case, eat her roll and sliced cheese and drink her aunt's delicious coffee, before wheeling out her aunt's elderly bike from the garage and setting off for a last ride with Jan and Pieter. They went to Zierikzee to start with and had more coffee. Then they went on to Haamstede and cycled on to the lighthouse, where they sat in the sun and ate ice-creams. The morning had gone too quickly, as last mornings always do; they had to ride fast in order to get back to Tante Minna's in time for the midday lunch.

It was a leisurely meal, for there was time enough before Sir William would arrive. Presently, Florina did the last of her packing and closed her case. She did her face and hair too, anxious not to keep him waiting. She went to wait downstairs and found, to her annoyance, that Felix was there.

There was nothing in his manner to remind her of their last meeting; he greeted her as though they had parted the best of friends, and began as soon as he could to talk of the possibility of meeting her again. 'Mustn't lose sight of you,' he observed smugly, and flung an unwanted arm across her shoulders.

Florina edged away, and went into the garden on the pretext of saying goodbye to her uncle, but he followed her outside, seemingly intent on demonstrating that they were the best of friends, and more than that. He was standing with her when the Bentley slowed to a silent halt on the other side of the hedge. Florina, talking to her uncle, didn't see it at once, but Felix did; he put an arm round her waist and drew her close, and Sir William, getting out of his car, couldn't help but see it.

He turned away at once to say something to Pauline, so missing Florina's indignant shove as she pushed Felix away. At the same time, she saw the car, and a moment later Sir William, strolling towards her aunt's front door. The wealth of feeling which surged through her at the sight of him took her by surprise. He had been at the back of her thoughts all the while she had been at Tante Minna's but she hadn't understood why, but now she knew. *He* was the vague man of her day-dreams, the man she loved, had fallen in love with, not knowing it, weeks ago; ever since she had first set eyes on him, she realised with astonishment.

She hurried to meet him, thoughts tumbling about her head. It was bliss to see him again, but never, never must she show her feelings, although just at that moment she longed above all things to rush at him and fling her arms around his neck. This last thought was so horrifying that she went a bright pink, and looked so guilty that Sir William frowned at his own thoughts.

He glanced at Felix, decided that he didn't much like the look of him and countered Florina's breathless, 'Sir William…' with a pleasantly cool, 'Ah, Florina, we have arrived at the wrong moment. My apologies…'

This remark stopped her in her tracks. 'Wrong moment? I'm quite ready to leave, Sir William…'

'But not, perhaps, willing?'

She gaped at him, and when Felix sidled up to her and put an arm round her shoulders she barely noticed it. At that moment, Pauline came prancing over to fling her arms around her neck and declare that she was over the moon to see her darling Florina again.

There was a polite flurry of talk, then coffee was offered and refused, and goodbyes said. Presently, Florina found herself in the back of the car, listening to Pauline's chatter. Sir William was, for the most part, silent, but when he did make some casual remark it was in his usual placid manner. He asked no questions of Florina about her holiday and she, suddenly shy of him, sat tongue-tied. What should have been a happy end to her holiday was proving to be just the opposite. Her newly discovered love was bubbling away inside her. Although she knew that he had no interest in her, he had always treated her with what she had thought was friendship and she was willing to settle for that, but now she had the feeling that behind his placid manner there was a barrier.

To brood over her fancies was of no use, so she bestirred herself to listen to Pauline's plans: picnics and mushrooming and cycling with Florina and cookery lessons…

'Wanda will be staying with us for at least a week,' said her father. 'You'll be able to go out with her if I am not at home.'

Pauline made a face over her shoulder to Florina, who smiled in a neutral fashion. The smile froze when Sir William added pleasantly, 'Florina has a job to do, Pauline. You mustn't monopolise her free time.'

That remark, thought Florina, puts me nicely in my place.

Chapter 5

They arrived back at Wheel House to a most satisfyingly warm welcome. The journey had gone smoothly, although Florina, knowing Sir William, would have been surprised if it had been otherwise. She had spent the greater part of the journey alternately day-dreaming and worrying as to why his manner towards her had become so cool—still friendly, but she had to admit it was the friendliness of an employer towards an employee.

They all sat down to supper round the kitchen table, talking cheerfully with Sir William asking questions of Jolly and being given a résumé of the week's happenings. Presently, an excited Pauline was escorted off to bed by Nanny, and Sir William turned to Jolly.

'I'll need to be away by seven o'clock at the latest. I'd like you and Mrs Jolly to drive back at the same time. I've a list for ten o'clock, so I'll offload my bag at the house and go straight on to the hospital. I'll not be back for lunch, and I'm taking Miss Fortesque out to dinner—if there is anything you want me for, I'll be home round about tea time.'

Florina said, in a colourless voice, 'Would you like breakfast at half-past six, Sir William?'

'We shan't need you, Florina. Mrs Jolly will see to that.' He added, in a kind, impersonal voice, '*You* must be tired, why don't you go to bed?'

So she went, exchanging polite goodnights. There had been no chance to thank him for taking her to Holland, and he had evinced no wish to know if she had enjoyed herself, but then, why should he? She was the cook and she had better remember that. Besides, she had no part in his life; Wanda had that. She cried herself to sleep and woke early to listen to the Jollys quietly leaving the room on the other side of the landing. Presently she smelled the bacon frying and the fragrance of toast, and heard the murmur of voices. Her window gave her a view of the road running through the village, providing she craned her neck, and soon she saw the two cars disappearing on their way to London.

Sir William had given her no instructions, but when she went downstairs later and started to clear the table and lay it again for their breakfast, Nanny joined her.

'You didn't have much to say for yourself at supper,' she observed, her sharp eyes studying Florina's swollen eyelids. 'Wasn't your holiday all you'd hoped for?' She added, 'Did you want to stay in Holland?'

'No. Oh, no! And I had a super time. It was a lovely wedding, and it was so nice to see everyone again. It is lovely to be back, though...'

Nanny grunted. 'Well, I missed you, for what it's worth.' She accepted the cup of tea that Florina offered, and sat down by the open door. 'Sir William won't be back until Friday evening, and Miss Fortesque's coming with him. He intends to give a small dinner party on Saturday—six, I think he said, and if the weather is fine he wants to take a picnic up on to Bulbarrow Down. He's asked the Meggisons from Butt House—they've three children, haven't they? Company for Pauline. He said he would telephone during the week about the food.' She passed her cup and Florina refilled it. 'He said to have a quiet week and to see that Pauline got out of doors. If she wants to go to Salisbury she may, he says, provided that one of us goes with her. She will be starting school soon.' Nanny looked round the pleasant kitchen. 'I shall miss this…'

Florina, slicing bread for toast, looked up, startled. 'Mrs Frobisher—you're not going away?'

'Just as soon as that Miss Fortesque can persuade Sir William that I'm not needed.' There was a pause and the stern, elderly voice wavered slightly. 'With Pauline at school, she'll say that there's nothing for me to do…'

'But that's rubbish!' cried Florina. 'You see to the silver and the mending, and keep the accounts and look after everything.'

'I do my best, but it's my opinion that once they're married she'll pack Pauline off to a boarding-school and come down here as little as possible.'

'But Sir William loves this house. I dare say he has a beautiful home in London, too, but you can love two houses… Besides, he works so hard, and he can do what he likes here.'

If Nanny found Florina's outburst surprising, she gave no sign. She said, 'Well he's old enough and wise enough to know what he wants, but he deserves better. His first marriage wasn't happy—he married too young. I told him so at the time, and I'll make no bones about saying that it was a relief when she was killed in a car accident, gallivanting off with one of her men friends while he worked. A bad wife, and a worse mother, poor young woman.' She gave Florina a quick look. 'I can't think why I'm telling you all this, but you're fond of Pauline, aren't you, and you like Sir William?'

'Oh, yes,' said Florina, putting so much feeling into the two words that Nanny nodded gently, well aware why she had unburdened herself. One never knew, she thought, and there was no harm in spying out the land, as it were. Florina had come back from Holland sad and too quiet, and Sir William had been holding down some problem or other behind that placid face of his—no one was going to tell her different. She had known him all his life, hadn't she? And she wouldn't let anyone tell her not to interfere if she saw the chance.

'Well, have you any plans for today?' she asked briskly.

'Well, I'll go through the cupboards, then go up to the farm shop if we are short of anything. Perhaps Pauline…'

She was interrupted by the little girl dancing into the kitchen to hug first Nanny and then her.

'It's marvellous to be back!' she declared. 'I want to go cycling—Florina, do say you will, and we can go into Wilton and buy Daddy a birthday present.'

She inspected the table. 'Oh, good, it's scrambled eggs—I'm famished. Daddy woke me to say goodbye. Did he say goodbye to you, Florina?'

'No, dear, but I'm sure he won't mind us going into Wilton. When do you want to go?'

The week passed too quickly. There was so much to do: the swans to feed, the Meggison children to visit for tea, long rambling walks to take and the promised visit to Wilton. Sir William telephoned each evening, but it wasn't until Thursday that he asked to speak to Florina.

He began without preamble. 'Florina, Miss Fortesque and I will be down on Friday evening, so lay on a good dinner, will you? There will be six of us for dinner on Saturday. Any ideas?'

She had been listening to his calm voice, but not his words. With a great effort, she tore her thoughts away from him and mentally thumbed through her cookery books. 'Watercress soup? Grilled trout with pepper sauce? Fillets of lamb with rosemary and thyme and *pommes lyonnaises* and a fresh tomato purée…' She thought for a moment. 'I've got pears in wine or peaches in brandy…'

'My dear girl—my mouth is watering. It sounds splendid. About the picnic on Sunday—shall I leave that to you?'

She said sedately, 'Very well, Sir William. Just lunch?'

'Yes—we'll be back for one of your splendid teas.' He rang off, leaving her quiet, and quite certain that she was going to be so busy at the weekend that she would barely glimpse him, let alone speak to him. Although what did that matter? she reflected sadly. She was the cook and let her never forget it.

With female perversity, she dragged her hair back into a severe plait on Saturday, didn't bother with make-up and, once the serious business of preparing dinner was finished, went to her room and got into a freshly starched dress and white apron. Pauline, prancing into the kitchen to see what there was for tea, stopped short at the sight of her.

'Florina, how severe you look! And you've forgotten your lipstick.'

'No time,' said Florina briskly, taking a fruitcake from the Aga. 'There are some fairy cakes on the table, and I've made strawberry jam sandwiches. Don't eat too much or you won't want your dinner.'

Pauline gave her a look of affection. 'You sound just like a mum,' she observed. 'Do you suppose Wanda will be a nice mum?'

'Oh, I expect so,' lied Florina briskly. She would be awful, she thought, no sticky fingers, no quick cuddles with grubby toddlers. There would be a nursemaid, young and not in the least cosy, and the children would be on show for half an hour after tea. She wondered if Sir William would stand for that; that's if there *were* any more children.

'You look so sad,' said Pauline, 'ever since you left Holland.'

Nanny had said the same thing, reflected Florina. She would have to mend her ways or leave. Unthinkable! 'Well, I'm not.' She made her voice sound cheerful. 'Sit down for a minute and tell me what you would like to have to eat on this picnic.'

Sir William arrived soon after six o'clock, with Wanda exquisite in an outfit in cyclamen and hunter's green; not in the least suitable for a weekend in a small country village, but guaranteed to give its inhabitants something to talk about for a few days.

She got out of the car and went into the house ahead of him, calling in a petulant voice, 'Where's everyone? I want my bags taken up to my room; I'm not fit to be seen!'

She paused by the passage leading to the kitchen and addressed Florina's back, busy at the Aga.

'Cook, leave that, and get my things from the car.'

Florina took no notice; she was at the precise point when the sauce she was making would either be a triumph of culinary art or an inedible failure.

She didn't turn round when she heard Sir William say,

'Florina has her work, Wanda. You can't expect her to leave it to carry your cases. I'll bring them up in a moment.'

Florina heard his laughing greeting to Pauline, their voices fading as they went out to the car. He had always come to the kitchen to ask her how she was, but this evening he didn't, perhaps because he had gone upstairs with Wanda's cases. She knew soon enough that that wasn't so, for she heard him talking to Nanny in the hall. She went about the business of dinner: mushrooms cooked in wine and cream for starters, minute steaks with duchesse potatoes and braised celery, lemon sorbet and Bavarian creams with lashings of cream. She had baked rolls, too, and curled the farm butter and arranged a cheeseboard. To please Wanda, she had made a dish of carrot straws, shreds of celery, slivers of cabbage and apple. She had made home-made chocolates, too, to go with the coffee, something she knew Pauline would like.

There was half an hour before she needed to dish up, so she slipped up to her room and tidied her hair. Then, since there was no one about, she went out to the patio. It was a lovely evening, turning to dusk, and the white swans were gliding away to settle for the night. A bat or two skimmed past, and somewhere in the distance an owl hooted. From the nearby pub there were muted sounds of cheerful talk and laughter. A peaceful rural scene; no wonder Sir William liked to spend his weekends in his lovely country home. Florina fell to wondering about his house in London; in its way it was probably as charming as Wheel House. Well, she would never see it, nor would she know more of his life than she did now, and that was precious little.

She gave a great sigh and then spun round as Sir William said from the drawing-room door, 'Hello, Florina, you look sad. Did you leave your heart in Holland?'

She stammered a little. 'Oh, good evening, Sir William. No no, of course not...' She retreated to the kitchen door. 'I was just waiting here before I dish up—I hope you don't mind?'

He said testily, 'Mind? Why should I mind? You have as much right to be here as I. Has Pauline been plaguing you?'

'Heavens, no, she's a dear child! We've had such fun, biking and walking and she likes to cook.' She hesitated. 'I suppose she couldn't have a dog or a cat? She loves animals—the swans come when she calls, and we were at the farm the other day when the Jersey cow calved—you don't mind?'

'I entirely approve, Florina, and of course we'll have a dog—*and* a cat. She will have to look after them while I'm in London. Of course when she's at school, you will have to do the looking after.'

'I'll enjoy that—she'll be so happy.'

He said thoughtfully, 'I should have thought of it for myself.'

'I think that you have a great deal to think of, Sir William?' She forgot everything for a moment and gave him a sweet, loving look, and he stared back at her without speaking.

'It's time to dish up.' She was suddenly shy, anxious to get back to the kitchen. But presently, through the open door, she heard Pauline come on to the patio and her squeals of delight when she was told about the dog and cat.

Her delight wasn't echoed by Wanda, who had wandered into the drawing-room unsuitably dressed in flame-coloured taffeta. 'I loathe cats, and I detest dogs with their filthy paws. There'll be neither, Pauline, so you can forget it.'

Florina, in the dining-room, setting the soup tureen on the serving-table, stopped to listen.

'I'm afraid you'll have to overcome your dislike, Wanda.' Sir William sounded at his most placid. 'I have promised Pauline that she shall have them.'

'Well, don't expect me to come here...'

His quiet, 'Very well, my dear,' made her pause.

'Oh, darling, don't be unkind—after all, I bury myself down here in this God-forsaken hole just to please you.'

He sounded interested. 'Is that how it seems to you?'

Wanda pouted prettily. 'No decent restaurants within miles, nowhere to go dancing, no shops. You've no idea what sacrifices I'm making for you, my angel.'

'You would like us to live in town permanently?'

Wanda gave a little crow of delight. 'There! I knew you would see it my way.'

'You're mistaken, Wanda. We'll have to talk about it later on.' He put an arm round his daughter's shoulders. 'Next weekend, we'll have a look for a cat and a dog.'

Florina glanced at the clock, and skipped to the hall to tap on the door and sound the dinner gong. It wasn't quite time, but she considered that intervention of some sort would be a good idea. That wasn't the last of it, however. Long after dinner was finished and Pauline was in bed, as Florina and Nanny were clearing away their own meal, Wanda came into the kitchen.

'I suppose it was you who put Pauline up to badgering her father for cats and dogs? Well, Cook, you can take it from me, once Sir William and I are married I'll get rid of them, and you'll go at the same time.'

Nanny drew in a hissing breath, ready to do battle, but Florina forestalled her. 'I should think Sir William will wish to be consulted before you do anything so unwise, Miss Fortesque. And in any case, I've no intention of listening to your threats.'

Wanda glared back at her, her eyes, narrow slits of dislike. 'Wormed your way in, haven't you?' she observed spitefully. 'Just because you can cook—you're only a servant...'

She stopped when she heard Sir William's footsteps crossing the hall.

'I was just telling Cook how delicious dinner was.'

She turned her back on the kitchen and hooked an arm through his. 'How about a stroll before bed, darling?'

'The hussy!' Nanny's rather dry voice was full of indignation. 'If he only knew what was going on...'

'Well, there is nothing we can do about it, Mrs Frobisher.' Florina began to set the table for breakfast and found that she was shaking with rage.

'Huh!' Nanny put a great deal of feeling into the sound. 'But Sir William is no fool and he has got eyes in his head—I'm not despairing.'

But Florina was; she might love him with her whole heart, but she was powerless to do anything about it. Especially now that he had somehow contrived to put a barrier between them. And what could she have done? If she had been as attractive as Wanda and as beautifully dressed and, moreover, living in Sir William's world, she would have made no bones about competing with Wanda. But famous paediatricians didn't fall in love with their cooks, not in real life, anyway. She laid the last plate tidily in its place and offered to make Nanny a cup of tea before she went to bed.

Pauline spent a good deal of the following morning in the kitchen. She had refused to go to Salisbury with her father and Wanda, who declared that she had to do some urgent shopping. Florina suggested that she should make cakes for tea, and went on with her own preparations for dinner. Lunch was to be cold and there was a raised pie she had made on the previous day, and a salad. She would have an hour to spare in the afternoon, and she planned to go and see her father.

With the exception of Wanda, they had shared breakfast round the kitchen table, and Sir William had gone off with Pauline directly afterwards, to reappear a few minutes before Wanda, who trailed downstairs, declaring that she hadn't slept a wink and demanding to be taken to the shops without delay.

'I'm glad she's gone,' declared Pauline sorrowfully, and burst into tears.

'Hush now, love,' said Florina, 'things are never as bad as they seem.' Then she offered the making of cakes, so that the child cheered up, and presently was laughing with Florina.

Lunch dealt with, Florina changed into a dress and went through the village to see her father. She had paid him a hurried visit soon after they had got back from Holland but, despite her gifts of tobacco and whisky, he had been morose. When she went up the familiar path and opened the door, she saw that today's visit wasn't going to be a success, either. It was with relief that she went back to Wheel House, got back into her overall and apron, and went to work on the dinner.

She knew everyone who came that evening. They glimpsed her as they passed the short passage to the kitchen, and called her a good evening, and after the meal they came to the patio door to tell her what a splendid meal it had been, and ask her how she did it. It didn't seem quite the right thing but, since Sir William was with them and evinced no sign of annoyance, she supposed that he didn't mind. Presently Nanny took coffee

into the drawing-room, and then went upstairs to see if
Pauline was asleep, while Florina got their own meal.

They didn't linger over it. It was Sunday the next day,
and there would be no help from the village and there
was the picnic to prepare in the morning. They did their
chores, turned out the lights and went to their beds.

Sir William had said that he would drive Wanda back
after tea. Florina did her chores and then sat for a while
on the patio with Nanny, drinking their coffee in the sun
and watching the swans. They had an early lunch and,
with Nanny comfortably resting on her bed, Florina got
tea ready. Sir William had suggested that they might have
it on the patio, since the Meggisons and their three children would return with them. She set out cakes and sandwiches, scones, jam and cream on the kitchen table, then
covered the lot with damp cloths, and went to her room to
do her hair and tidy. There would still be time to sit in the
garden for an hour and leaf through the Sunday papers.

As things were to turn out, there wasn't. The picnic
party returned early, making over-bright conversation,
while the children looked mutinous. Florina's heart sank
when she saw Sir William's face, smoothed of all expression and covering, she had no doubt, a well-bottled-up
rage. She had known the Meggisons for years; she greeted
them now and led the children away to wash their hands,
while Wanda, looking sulky, led Mrs Meggison upstairs.

Back again, with the children milling round her, Florina took another look at Sir William. He was talking
to Ralph Meggison, but he turned to her as she went
out on the patio.

'Wanda had a headache,' he told her, in a voice which
gave nothing away. 'I'm afraid we've cut your afternoon short.'

Florina gave her head a small shake. 'Tea is quite ready—would you like it now?'

'As soon as we are all here...'

'If Miss Fortesque's headache is bad, would the children like to have tea in the kitchen?'

'That's a very good idea. Could you bear the noise?'

'I shall like it,' she said, and meant it.

The children helped to take some of the food out to the patio, and Pauline took a tea tray up to Nanny before they gathered round the kitchen table to fall upon the food, making a great noise and laughing immoderately.

Florina laughed with them, and saw that they minded their manners and had a good tea. Finally, when they were finished, the eldest Meggison child said, 'Gosh, this is fun! We'd have hated being out there with her.'

'And who is her?' asked Florina. 'The cat's mother?'

They fell about laughing. It was Pauline who whispered, 'Wanda, of course. She grumbled all the while— it was too hot and there were wasps and the grass was damp and the food was all wrong...'

Florina bristled. 'Wrong? What was wrong? I put in everything I thought would make a picnic lunch.'

'It was super,' they hastened to reassure her. 'We ate everything. Only she was cross all the time.'

The youngest Meggison added, in a piping voice, 'She's not a country lady, not like you, Florina. You know where the mushrooms are and the blackberries and nuts. Pauline says you're going to have a dog and a cat...'

They were all shouting out suitable names to each other when Sir William joined them.

He pulled up a chair, stretched out a hand for a cake and observed, 'You *are* having fun! I've been thinking, Pauline. You had better come up to London next weekend. There's an animal sanctuary I know of—we should be able to find something suitable.' He added, as an afterthought, 'Florina, you had better come, too. I'll come down on Friday evening and we can drive back early on Saturday morning. I'll bring you and the animals back here on Sunday.'

Pauline flung herself at him, shrieking with joy. Florina, sitting sedately in her chair, would have liked to do the same. She would have the chance to see his home in London, get a glimpse of his other life, too! She looked up and caught his eye. 'Nanny will be all alone,' she pointed out.

'Mrs Deakin will sleep here. You'll need an overnight bag, that's all.' He took another cake, munched slowly and said, 'I must leave in half an hour.'

He got up, hugged Pauline, nodded to the other children, then smiled a sudden, tender smile at Florina and wandered back to the patio, leaving Florina with a red face, which was viewed with interest by her companions.

'You're very red,' said the youngest Meggison. 'Why?'

Pauline rushed to her rescue. 'It's all the cooking she does. She had to make all the food for the picnic and our tea…'

'Why didn't you come with us on our picnic?' persisted the tiresome child.

Florina had recovered her calm. 'Well, if I had, you wouldn't have had any tea. Now, if you've all finished, do you want to feed the swans? I expect you will have to go home soon.'

They all scampered away, and presently the entire Meggison family put their heads round the door to say goodbye. The youngest Meggison's parting protest that Florina should have gone to the picnic, too, left her feeling awkward, since it was uttered in piercing tones which Sir William and Wanda must have heard.

Before he left, Sir William came into the kitchen. Nanny was sitting at the table stringing beans, and Florina was at the sink peeling potatoes. He kissed Nanny on a cheek and looked across at Florina.

'Thank you for making the weekend pleasant. I'll be down on Friday as soon as I can manage.'

Her sedate, 'Very well, Sir William,' was at variance with her flushed cheeks, and he stared at her for a long moment before turning on his heel and going out to the car.

Wanda was already in it. Florina could hear her complaining voice and his mild reply as he drove away, pursued by Pauline's shrieking goodbyes.

Friday seemed an age away, but, in fact, the days went quickly. Pauline changed her mind a dozen times as to what she would wear in London, a problem Florina didn't have. If it stayed fine, she would be able to wear her pink outfit that she had bought for the trip to Holland, if it turned wet and chilly it would have to be the rather worthy suit she had had for several years.

When she got up on Friday morning the first thing she did was to hang out of the window and study the sky. It showed all the signs of a splendid day and she heaved a great sigh, for she would be able to wear the pink suit. But, to be on the safe side, she would take the jersey dress and a mac.

Sir William arrived soon after tea, and when Florina offered to make a fresh pot she was rewarded, as he sat down at the kitchen table with Pauline beside him, listening to her excited chatter and eating the buns left over from their own tea. He had given her a casual greeting, kissed Nanny who had come bustling to meet him, and presently declared that he needed some exercise and would take Pauline off for a walk. This was a good thing for Florina's peace of mind; just the sight of him had sent all thoughts of cooking out of her head. She applied herself to that now and, punctual to the minute, dished up an elegant dinner which Pauline shared along with him.

In the evening, after Pauline had gone to bed, he went along to his study, and only emerged just as she was about to go to bed, in order to remind her that they would be leaving at nine o'clock, and could they have breakfast an hour before that? His goodnight was casual, rather as though he had forgotten her. It was like looking at someone through a glass window; you could see them but you couldn't get at them, as it were.

There was a good deal of traffic on the road in the morning, but most of it was leaving London, not going into it. The Bentley sped silently up the motorway with Pauline talking non-stop and Florina sitting in the back in a contented haze of happiness, for was she not to spend the next two days in Sir William's house? Probably she wouldn't see much of him, but it was his home... She had worried at first, in case Wanda would be there too, but Pauline had asked her father and he had observed that she was spending the weekend with friends, which meant that Florina could sit back and dream about the weekend. She came awake when they stopped for coffee, joined in the talk without hearing more than half of it, and then climbed back into the car to continue her dreams, hardly noticing when Sir William slowed as they reached the outskirts of London. But gradually she became aware that he had turned away from the main streets and was threading his way through a quieter part of the city, its streets lined with tall Regency houses facing narrow railinged gardens in their centres.

The traffic here was sparse, and mostly private cars. She wasn't sure where they were, but it looked very pleasant. If one could live in such streets, she reflected, then life in London might be quite bearable.

Sir William had turned out of one street into another very similar, and stopped the car half-way along a row of narrow houses, their bow windows glistening in the sun, their front doors pristine with new paint. He got out, as Pauline skipped out on her side and ran up the short flight of steps to the door of the house before them. He opened Florina's door and ushered her out, too.

By the time they had joined Pauline at the door, Jolly had opened it, received Sir William's greeting with dignity, Pauline's delighted outburst with scarcely concealed pleasure and Florina's composed good morning with an almost avuncular mien, before standing aside to admit them.

The lobby opened out into a semicircular hall, with a graceful staircase at one side and several doors leading out of it. Sir William flung one open now and urged Florina to enter. The room was at the back of the house overlooking a small, but delightfully planned garden.

'I use this room when I'm here alone,' he explained. 'The drawing-room is upstairs, and a bit too grand unless I have guests.'

Florina, taking in the elegant furnishings, the portraits on the walls and the generously draped brocade curtains, found the room delightful but grand enough. She wondered what the drawing-room would be like. This room had a pleasant air of homeliness about it. She sat down at his request, drank the coffee Mrs Jolly brought in and, having done so, got to her feet when

Pauline suggested that she should show her her room before they had lunch.

They mounted the stairs behind Mrs Jolly, and Florina was shown into a room at the head of the stairs: a beautiful room, all pink and white, with its own bathroom and a view of the street below.

'I'm next door,' Pauline explained. 'Come and see my room when you're ready.'

Warned by Mrs Jolly that lunch would be in fifteen minutes, Florina wasted five of them inspecting her room. It was really a dream, the kind of room any girl would wish for. She wondered who had furnished it right down to the last tablet of soap and matching bath oil. There was even shampoo and hand lotion, all matching. She did her face and tidied her hair, and then knocked on Pauline's door.

Her room was as pretty as Florina's, but here the furnishings were in a pale apricot, and the bed and dressing-table were painted white.

'Do you like your room?' asked Pauline eagerly. 'Daddy let me help him furnish some of the bedrooms. Of course, Wanda doesn't like them. She told Daddy that she was going to do the whole house over.'

'A pity,' observed Florina in a neutral voice. 'I find them delightful, but people have different tastes.'

They went back to the sitting-room and Florina was given a sherry before they crossed the hall to the dining-room. Its walls were papered in a rich red, the mahogany gleaming with polish. Florina, good cook that she was, could find nothing wrong with the shrimp patties, the lamb cooked with rosemary and the fresh fruit salad and cream which followed them.

They had their coffee at the table and, as they were finishing it, Sir William said, 'We will go tomorrow

morning and choose a dog and cat. This afternoon I
thought perhaps we might go to a matinée: I've tickets
for *Cats* which starts at three o'clock. I have some telephone calls to make, then we'll take Florina round the
house, shall we, Pauline?'

Florina went to bed that night in a haze of happiness;
the day had been perfect, never to be forgotten. They
had explored the house at a leisurely pace, allowing
her plenty of time to admire everything. It was perfect,
she thought, and she said so, forgetting that Wanda was
going to change the lovely old furniture and the chintzes
and velvets. Afterwards, they had gone to the theatre,
and then to tea at the Ritz and finally back home, to sit
by the window overlooking the garden, arguing happily about names for the animals.

They would leave at half-past nine the next morning,
Sir William had said at dinner. 'For I have to go to the
hospital and check on a couple of patients.'

After dinner, when Pauline had gone to bed, Florina sat opposite him, listening to him talking about
his work. He had paused briefly to ask, 'Am I boring
you? Wanda dislikes hearing about illness, but I think
that you are interested.'

She had told him fervently that she was and, being
a sensible girl, never hesitated to stop him so that he
might explain something she hadn't understood.

She could have stayed there all night listening to him
talking, but remembered in time that she was the cook,
however pleasant he was being. So she made rather a
muddled retreat in a flurry of goodnights and thanks,
and Sir William's eyes had gleamed with amusement.
He had made the muddle worse by bending to kiss her
as she reached the door, so that just for a moment she
forgot that she was the cook.

Chapter 6

They spent almost two hours in the animal sanctuary. Finally, they left with an ecstatic Pauline sitting on the back seat with a large woolly dog beside her, and a mother cat and her kitten in a basket on her lap. The dog was half-grown, his ancestry so numerous that it was impossible to classify him, but he had an honest face and eyes which shone with gratitude and anxious affection. His coat was curly, and once he had recovered his full health and strength its brown colour would be glossy. He had been found by a hiker tied to a tree and left to starve. The cat and kitten had been picked up on a motorway, tied in a plastic bag. They were black and white, the pair of them, and still timid, not believing their luck.

Florina, sitting beside Sir William, listened to the child talking to her new pets and spoke her thoughts aloud. 'Isn't it nice to hear Pauline happy?'

Sir William threw her a quick sideways look. 'Is she not always happy?'

'Almost always.'

'But she is sometimes unhappy. Will you tell me why?'

'No, I can't tell you that—at least I can, but I don't choose to do so.' She added hastily, 'I don't mean to be rude, Sir William.'

His grunt could have meant anything. Presently he broke his silence. 'I shall be away for the whole of next week, and I think it likely that I shall remain in town over the weekend. Nanny will be with you, of course, but you can always phone if you need anything—Jolly will know where I am.'

She said meekly, 'Yes, Sir William,' and wondered where he would be going. To stay with Wanda? Very likely. She sat silent, brooding about it.

Back at the house, Pauline ran off to the kitchen to show Mrs Jolly her pets, and Sir William excused himself on the grounds of telephone calls to make and departed to his study, which left Florina standing in the hall, not sure what to do. It was Jolly who entered the hall just then and told her that lunch would be in half an hour, and if she cared to go into the drawing-room she would find drinks on the table under the window.

So she went in there and sat down in one of the smaller of the easy chairs. She didn't pour herself a drink, and she was surprised at Jolly mentioning it. After all, she should really be in the kitchen...

The house was quiet. But from the closed door leading to the kitchen came the sound of Pauline's excited voice. The study door was shut, so Florina nipped smartly out of the room, and crossed the hall silently. The dining-room door was half-open; she peeped round it—the table was set for three persons. She took a soft step forward and was brought to a startled halt by Sir William, speaking within inches of her ear. 'Set your mind at rest, Florina, you are lunching with us.'

She had whizzed round to gape up at his amused face. 'How did you know? I mean, I expected to eat with the Jollys,' she added fiercely. 'You forget that I work for you, Sir William.'

'Yes, I do,' he agreed, 'but for quite different reasons than those you are supposing.' He turned her smartly around. 'Shall we have a drink? We shall have to leave soon after lunch—I've a date for this evening. I'll not be down at the weekend, as I've told you already. I've a long-standing invitation I most particularly wish to keep.'

She said nothing to this. It would be with Wanda, of course; even when she wasn't there she made her presence felt, tearing Florina's futile day-dreams to shreds. She sat down in the chair she had just vacated, and sipped her sherry while Sir William began a rather one-sided conversation. It was a relief when Pauline came to join them.

'The pets are having their dinner,' she explained. 'Daddy, what shall we call them?'

Names were discussed at some length during lunch. Presently, they all got into the Bentley to drive back to Wheel House, Pauline in the back with the animals and Florina beside Sir William. It would be polite to talk a little, she reflected, so she ventured a few remarks about the pleasures of the weekend and was answered in such a vague fashion that she soon gave up. Perhaps he didn't like chatter as he drove, although Pauline never stopped talking when she sat with him and he hadn't seemed to mind.

She was taken by surprise when he said, 'Don't stop talking. You have a gentle voice, very soothing. It helps me to think.'

She glanced at his profile. He was looking severe but, when he looked at her, suddenly his smile wasn't in the least severe. She began to talk about the garden and the swans and the delight of the mill stream running under the house, rambling on, speaking her thoughts aloud.

When they reached Wheel House she slipped away to the kitchen after Nanny's brief greeting, and carried in the tray set ready. Then she went to her room and put her things away. By the time she went downstairs tea was almost over, and Sir William was preparing to leave. She bade him a quiet goodbye and he nodded casually. 'Think up some of your super menus, will you? I'll be back with Wanda the weekend after next.'

'I'll look forward to that,' she told herself silently.

The two weeks went quickly, what with walking the dog, and initiating the cat and her kitten into the life of comfort they were undoubtedly going to lead. Pauline had chosen their names—Mother and Child—for, as she pointed out to Florina, that's what they were. The dog she called Bobby, because she found he answered to that name. Florina taught her to whistle, and the dog, while not looking particularly intelligent, was obedient and devoted to her. The days were placid, and even her father's ill humour couldn't spoil Florina's content. True, her thoughts dwelt overlong upon Sir William, and any titbit of news about him when he telephoned Pauline she listened to, and stored away to mull over when she had gone to bed. It was a good thing that towards the end of the fortnight she had to begin in earnest on the weekend's food. She helped around the house too, and made sure that Pauline's school uniform was ready for the autumn term was almost upon them.

Nanny, usually so brisk, looked dejected. 'They'll be married, mark my words,' she observed to Florina, as they sat together after Pauline had gone up to bed. 'The child will be at school, and next term she'll find herself a boarder there, with that woman persuading Sir William that it is just what Pauline longs for. Then it will be me, packed off, away from here. And take it from me, Florina, you won't be long following me! She won't risk having you in the house. You're young—and a nice girl—not pretty, but there is more to a girl than a handsome face...'

Florina murmured a reassurance she didn't feel. Being young and nice was no help at all against Wanda's cherished good looks.

Sir William arrived in time for a late tea. Florina heard the car draw up and shut the door upon the sound of Wanda's voice, strident with ill temper, raised in complaint as she came into the house.

She heard her say to Nanny, who had gone into the hall, 'Still here, Nanny? There can't be anything for you to do—according to Sir William that cook of his is quite capable of running the place. You must be longing to retire again.'

It augured ill for the weekend and Florina, warming the teapot, wished it over. The less she saw of Sir William, the better for her peace of mind. Even so, she longed to see him. She made the tea, put the tea cosy over the pot and began to butter scones.

'Well, well!' Sir William's quiet voice took her by surprise. 'My own kitchen door shut against me! Pauline has been commandeered to help Wanda unpack.'

He took a scone and ate it with relish. 'And how are you, Florina?'

He studied her face carefully, and she reddened under his gaze. 'Very well, thank you, Sir William.'

He began on another scone. 'Jolly is with us. Will you or Nanny see that he is comfortable? He has driven down in a Mini—you can drive? You'll be able to take Pauline to school and fetch her.'

She said faintly, 'Oh, will I?' and passed the plate of scones, since he seemed bent on eating the lot.

'There aren't all that number of people I would trust to drive her. Could you escape from the stove tomorrow morning—before breakfast? We'll go for a run?'

All her resolutions about keeping out of his way disappeared like smoke. 'It's breakfast at half-past eight...'

'Couldn't be better. Seven o'clock be OK?' He didn't wait for her answer, but took another scone and wandered out of the kitchen, leaving her door open.

Which meant that after a few moments she heard Wanda's voice as she came downstairs. She was still complaining and Nanny, coming for the tea tray, had a face like a thunder cloud. 'In a fine temper, she is—wanted to stop at some posh hotel for tea, but Sir William wanted to come straight home.'

She stalked off with the tray and Florina set the table for their own tea, helped by Jolly, who had just come into the house.

It was a pleasant meal, with Jolly and Nanny keeping the conversation carefully to generalities. This was a disappointment to Florina, who had hoped to glean news about Sir William and Wanda. After tea, there was no time to talk. There was dinner to see to which kept her in the kitchen for several hours, aware that Pauline's voice, raised and tearful, interlarded by Bobby's bark and Wanda's regrettably shrill tones, were hardly contributing to a happy evening.

Mother and Child were curled up cosily before the Aga, presently to be joined by a furious Pauline and Bobby, who, being good-natured himself, expected everyone else to be the same.

'I hate her!' declared Pauline. 'If Daddy marries her, me and Bobby will run away. She said he smelled nasty.' She sniffed, 'Daddy said it was time for his supper, and then him and me—I—will take him for his walk.'

Daddy seemed good at pouring oil on troubled waters. Florina watched Pauline feeding the animals. The child was entirely engrossed in this, and happy, but how soon would her happiness be shattered once Wanda had become her stepmother? Sir William, much as she loved him, had been remarkably mistaken in his choice of a second wife. Men, thought Florina, however clever, could be remarkably dim at times.

She was in the kitchen all the evening, so that she saw neither Sir William nor Wanda. It was bedtime by the time they had eaten their own supper and cleared it away. Since Jolly had undertaken to remain up until Sir William retired himself, she and Nanny said goodnight and went to their respective rooms.

It was one o'clock in the morning when Florina woke on the thought that she had forgotten to put the porridge oats to soak. Nanny was a firm believer in porridge, but it had to be said that she insisted it was made according to her recipe—old-fashioned and time-consuming. She got out of bed, without stopping to put on a dressing-gown and slippers, and nipped down to the kitchen. There would be no one around at that hour. She put the exact amount of oats into water in a double saucepan, added the pinch of salt Nanny insisted upon, and stirred it smoothly before filling the steamer with hot water and setting the whole upon the Aga. Having done which, she stepped back and glanced at the clock, and then let out a startled yelp as Sir William, speaking from the door where he had been lounging watching her, observed, 'Such devotion to duty! It's one o'clock in the morning, Florina.'

She curled her toes into the rug before the stove and longed for her dressing-gown. 'Yes—well, you see I forgot the porridge. Nanny likes it made in a certain way, and I forgot to soak it. I'm very sorry if I disturbed you...'

He said gravely, 'Oh, you disturb me, but you have no need to be sorry about it.' He stood looking at her for a long moment, and when he spoke his voice was very gentle. 'Go to bed, my dear.'

She flew away without a word, intent on escape, wishing with all her heart that she *was* his dear. Sleep escaped her for the next hour or so, so that the night was short, but she got up and dressed and plaited her hair neatly at the usual time. Then she went down to the kitchen, intent on making tea before they set out, thankful that it would give her something to do, for, remembering their early-morning meeting, she was stiff with shyness.

Sir William was already there, with the tea made and poured into mugs. His good morning was casually friendly, and he scarcely looked at her, so she calmed down and, by the time they reached the garage, she was almost her usual calm self.

Sir William was hardly the build for a Mini. Florina, despite the smallness of her person, found it a tight fit with the pair of them. To make more room he had flung an arm along the back of the seat and she was very aware of it; nevertheless, she made herself concentrate on her driving, going along the narrow country road to Wilton and then back on the main Salisbury road, and taking the turning to the village, over the bridge opposite the farm.

'Quite happy about ferrying Pauline to and fro?' he asked as she ran the little car into the garage. He got out, strolling beside her towards the kitchen door. 'If Pauline's up we'll take Bobby for a walk.' He turned on his heel and then stopped and turned around to face her. 'You have such beautiful hair—a shining mouse curtain. You should wear it loose always.'

'It would get in the soup,' said Florina.

Wanda came downstairs mid-morning, beautifully dressed and made-up, ready to be entertained. It was a pity that everyone should be in the kitchen with the door to the patio open, milling around, drinking coffee, feeding the swans from the patio, playing with the cats and brushing Bobby. In the middle of this cheerful hubbub, Florina stood at the table making a batch of rolls, quite undisturbed by it all. Nobody else noticed Wanda's entrance, and Florina paused long enough to say politely, 'Good morning, Miss Fortesque. Would you like coffee?'

Sir William looked up briefly from Bobby's grooming. 'Hello, Wanda, Pauline and I are going to her school to see her headmistress—like to come with us?'

Wanda shuddered delicately. 'Certainly not. I can't sleep in this house. I'll rest on the patio, if someone takes that dog away. Cook, you can bring me some coffee once I'm settled.'

Sir William said quietly, 'Jolly will do that. Come on, Pauline, we'll be off.' He whistled to Bobby, remarked that they would be back for lunch, and disappeared in the direction of the garage.

Wanda needed a lot of settling: fresh coffee, more cushions, a light rug, the novel she had left in her bedroom. Nanny, looking more and more po-faced, handed these over wordlessly and then disappeared, and so presently did Jolly, leaving Florina to take the rolls from the oven and then start on lunch.

She was arranging cold salmon artistically on a bed of cress and cucumber, when Wanda called her. It would have given Florina great satisfaction to have ignored her, but Wanda was a guest and, what was more, a cherished one. And Florina, in a mixed-up, miserable way, would have done anything to make Sir William happy, even if it meant being nice to Wanda. She washed her hands well and went on to the patio, prepared to offer cool drinks, more cushions or anything else the girl demanded.

She was completely taken aback when Wanda said, 'Don't think I haven't eyes in my head. I've watched you toadying to Sir William—God knows what crazy ideas you've got in that silly head. I dare say you fancy you are in love with him. Well, you can forget it. The day we marry, and that shall not be too far away, you'll get your notice, so you had better start looking for another job.'

Florina, usually so mild, seethed with a splendid rage. She said in a very quiet voice, 'You have no right to talk to me like this. When Sir William tells me to leave, then I shall go, but not one minute before. I think that you are a rude, spoiled young woman, who has no love or thought for anyone. You don't deserve to be happy, but then, you never will…' She put her neat head on one side and studied the other girl, who was staring speechlessly at her. 'You may report all that I've said to Sir William, but I wish to be there just in case you forget what you said to me, too.'

'If it's the last thing I do,' breathed Wanda, 'I'll see you pay for this.' She sat up and caught Florina a smart slap.

'Cool off, Miss Fortesque.' Florina, who hadn't realised that she could feel so royally angry, picked up the jug of lemonade on the table by Wanda's chair, and poured it slowly over the top of her head. The rather syrupy stuff caused havoc to Wanda's artlessly arranged hair, and did even more damage to her complexion. She jumped to her feet, shrieking threats as she raced away to her room, and Florina put down the jug and went back to the salmon. She had cooked her goose, but just for a moment she didn't care.

Jolly was in the kitchen. He eyed her with a benign smile and a good deal of respect. 'I saw and heard everything, Miss Florina. If necessary I will substantiate anything you may need to say to Sir William. I was prepared to come to your assistance, but it proved unnecessary.'

The enormity of what she had done was permeating through her like an unexpected heavy fall of rain. 'Oh, Mr Jolly, thank you. You're very kind. It was very wrong of me and I forgot that I was just the cook. She'll have me sacked.'

'I believe that you may set your mind at rest on that score,' observed Jolly, who had had several interesting chats with Nanny and was totally in agreement with her. Florina would be a splendid wife for Sir William—and she was in love with him—although she was unaware of how much that showed. As for Sir William, he was old enough and wise enough to get himself out of the mess he had so carelessly let himself get into. Jolly had no doubt that he would do it in his own good time, and when it suited him, and with such skill that Miss Fortesque would believe that she had been the one to call their marriage off. In the meantime, Jolly made a mental note to call Florina 'Miss Florina'—it would be a step in the right direction.

There was no sign of Wanda until lunch time, a meal she ate in a haughty silence which Sir William didn't appear to notice. When they had finished she said in an unnaturally quiet voice, 'William, I must talk to you—now.'

Jolly conveyed this news to the kitchen and Florina, hearing it, lost her appetite completely. Indeed, she was feeling quite sick by the time they had finished, and when Sir William strolled in, she went so white that the freckles sprinkling her nose stood out darkly.

He crossed to the Aga, stooped so as to stroke Mother and Child curled together in a neat ball, and said in his placid way, 'I'd like a word with Florina, if you wouldn't mind…'

Florina watched Jolly and Nanny go through the door, put her hands on the back of the chair she was standing behind and met Sir William's gaze.

'Miss Fortesque has told me a most extraordinary tale—have you anything to add, Florina?' His voice was kind.

'No.'

'There are always two sides to a disagreement. I should like to hear yours.'

'No.'

He smiled a little. He studied the nails of one hand. 'Pauline was listening at the study door, and indeed Miss Fortesque was speaking so loudly, I was forced to send her to her room so that she could indulge her mirth.'

'Please don't ask me to apologise. I'm not the least sorry for what I did. I expect you're going to give me notice.'

He looked surprised. 'Why should I do that? I had hoped that you knew me well enough to tell me your version, but it seems that it is not so.'

Florina burst out, 'How can I tell you? You are going to marry Miss Fortesque.'

He smiled again. 'That is your reason?' And, when she nodded, 'I think that it might be better to say no more about the matter.' He started for the door and paused to look back at her. 'It seems that lemonade plays havoc with tinted hair.'

Jolly was in the hall, so obviously waiting for him that Sir William said, 'Come into the study, Jolly. I take it that you wish to speak to me?'

Jolly closed the door behind him. 'I was in the kitchen, Sir William, and, begging your pardon, Miss Fortesque was that nasty—Miss Florina was so polite too, in the face of all the nasty rubbish...'

'Rubbish, Jolly?'

Jolly, who had an excellent memory, repeated what had been said. He noticed with satisfaction that Sir William's face had no expression upon it, which meant that he was concealing strong feelings. He wisely added nothing more.

Sir William was silent for several moments. 'Thank you, Jolly. You did right to tell me. I have told Florina that the matter is to be forgotten.'

'Very good, Sir William. Miss Florina is a nice young lady and easily hurt.'

'Quite so.' He smiled suddenly, and looked young

and faintly wicked. 'Will you go to Pauline's room and ask her if she wants to take Bobby and me for a walk? Miss Fortesque is resting in her room, but I dare say she'll be down for tea.'

The rest of the weekend passed off peacefully. Florina kept to her kitchen and tried to expunge her bad behaviour by cooking mouth-watering meals and keeping out of the way of Sir William and Wanda. Pauline, when she wasn't with her father, spent her time in the kitchen, with Bobby in close attendance, curled up before the Aga with the cats.

'Wanda is so cross, I'd rather be here with you,' she explained. 'Daddy said I wasn't to talk about it, but I laughed and laughed. But she is horrid—I shall run away...'

'Now, love, don't talk like that. It would break your father's heart if you were to leave him. He loves you so much.'

'So why is he going to marry Wanda? He doesn't love her.'

'You mustn't say that, she is a a very lovely lady.'

'With a black heart,' declared Pauline, so fiercely that they both laughed.

The house seemed very empty when the Bentley had gone the next day. Sir William had bade Florina a casual goodbye, kissed Pauline and Nanny, swept Wanda into the front seat before there was time for her to say anything, ushered Jolly into the back of the car and driven off. He hadn't said anything about the following weekend. Perhaps he would stay in town to placate Wanda, take her dining and dancing, so that she could wear her lovely clothes and show off the enormous ring she wore on her engagement finger.

Florina retired to the kitchen and got supper, with a good deal of unnecessary clashing of saucepans.

There was plenty to keep her busy during the next few days: tomato chutney to make, vegetables from the garden to blanch and pack into the freezer, and she had Pauline to keep her company when she wasn't having her sewing and knitting lessons with Nanny, something the old lady insisted upon. It was quite late on Thursday evening when Florina heard a car turn into the drive and a moment later the front door shutting. She went down the passage into the hall and Sir William was there. He was standing in the centre of the lovely old Persian carpet, staring at the wall, but he turned to look at her. He was tired; his face had lines in it she hadn't seen before.

She said at once, 'You'd like something to eat—I'll have it ready in ten minutes. Shall I pour you a drink?' She shook her head in a motherly fashion. 'You've had a very busy day.'

He gave a short sigh and then smiled at her. 'Pour me a whisky, will you? Will Pauline be awake?'

She glanced at the clock. 'Probably not, but she would love you to wake her up.'

She watched him going upstairs two at a time, and then went into the drawing-room to switch on a lamp or two and pour out his whisky. The room looked lovely in the soft light, and the gentle flow of the mill stream under the floor was soothing. She hurried back to the kitchen, to warm up soup. An omelette would be quick, and there were mushrooms she could use. She was laying a tray when he came in, the glass in his hand. 'I'll have it here—anything will do…' He sat down at the table and watched her whisking the eggs. 'I should have telephoned you. I'm examining students at Bristol tomorrow, and on Monday and Tuesday. I'll drive up each day—I don't need to be there until ten o'clock and I can be back here in the early evening.'

Florina poured the soup into a pitkin and set it before him. Her heart sang with delight at the prospect of him being at Wheel House. She said happily, 'Oh, now nice—to have you here...' She paused and then went on quickly, 'Nice for all of us.'

Since he was staring at her rather hard, the spoon in his hand, she added, 'Do eat your soup, Sir William, and I'll make your omelette. There's bread and butter on the table. Would you like coffee now or later?'

'Now, if you will have it with me.'

She got two mugs and filled them from the pot on the Aga, put one before him and then went back to the frying-pan, where the mushrooms were sizzling gently. He began to talk, going over his week and, although for half the time she had very little idea of what he was talking about, she listened with interest, dishing up the omelette and then watching him eat it while she drank her coffee. This was how it should be, she reflected: someone waiting for him each evening to share his day's work with him and see that he ate a proper meal and could talk without interruption...

'Of course, you won't understand half of what I'm saying,' observed Sir William and passed his mug for more coffee.

'Well, no—I wish I did! I can understand why you love your work. I think that I would have liked to have been a nurse and to have known a bit more about all the things that you have been talking about. I'm too old to start training now, though.'

'Old?'

'I'm twenty-seven, Sir William.'

'I'm thirty-nine, Florina.' He leaned back in his chair. 'Is there any of that jam you made last week?'

She fetched it, put the loaf and a dish of butter on the table and watched him demolish a slice. When he had finished, she said matter-of-factly, 'You should go to bed, Sir William. When will you be leaving in the morning?'

'Eight o'clock.'

'Will breakfast at half-past seven suit you, or would you like it earlier?'

'That will do very well. I'll help you with these things. You should be in bed yourself.'

He ignored her refusal of help, but found a tea-cloth and dried the dishes as she washed them. He waited as she saw to the animals and climbed the stairs to her room, and then went back to the hall. But he didn't go at once to his bed, he went into the drawing-room and sat down in his great chair, deep in thought. Presently he got to his feet, stretched hugely, turned off the lights and went upstairs. His thoughts must have been pleasant ones, for he was chuckling as he went.

Florina was dishing up the breakfast when he came into the kitchen with Pauline, dressing-gowned and bare-footed, so she did a second lot of bacon and eggs and, much as she would have liked to have stayed, took herself off on the plea of giving Bobby a quick run in the garden. She didn't go back until she judged Sir William would be ready to leave, but he was still sitting at the table. There was a faint frown on his face, and Pauline's lower lip was thrust out in an ominous fashion. He got up as Florina came in, kissed his daughter, whispered in her ear—something which made her small face brighten—observed that he would be back around six o'clock and went to the patio door, fending off Bobby's efforts to go with him, and passing Florina as he went. His swift kiss took her by surprise, and he had gone before she could do more than gasp.

'Why did Daddy kiss you?' Pauline wanted to know. 'Perhaps it was because Wanda wasn't here—though she doesn't like being kissed. She says it spoils her make-up.'

The child stared at Florina. 'You haven't got anything on your face, have you, Florina? You are awfully red…'

The days went too quickly. The brief glimpses she had of Sir William in the morning coloured her whole day, and in the evenings once he was home, even though he saw little of her, she could hear him talking to Pauline, calling the dog, chattering with Nanny. Once dinner was over and the house was quiet, she listened to his quiet footfall crossing the hall to the study and gently closing the door. She pictured him sitting at his desk, making notes or correcting papers. He might just as easily be writing to Wanda or talking to her on the telephone, but she tried not to think of that.

Tuesday came too soon. He left after breakfast and didn't intend to come back until the weekend, for he would drive straight back to London from Bristol. He mentioned casually, as he went, that probably he would be bringing Miss Fortesque with him at the weekend.

Pauline cried when he had gone, climbing on to Florina's lap and sobbing into her shoulder. 'Do you suppose they'll be married?' she asked.

'Most unlikely,' said Florina bracingly. 'Your father would never do that without telling you, love. So cheer up and wash your face. We'll take Bobby for a nice walk, and when we get back you can go into the garden for a bit and keep an eye on Mother and Child, in case they stray off.'

She had reassured the child, but not herself. She had long ago discovered that Sir William was not a man to display his feelings, or, for that matter, disclose his plans. He was quite capable of doing exactly what he wished, without disclosing either the one or the other, and Wanda was a very attractive girl. Florina went and had a look at herself in the small looking-glass in the downstairs cloakroom and derived no comfort from that. The quicker she erased Sir William from her thoughts, the better. It would help, of course, if she could find a substitute for him, but she had known all the young men in the village since she was a small girl, and they had either got engaged or married or had left home. She didn't know anyone… She did, though. Felix, the only young man to show any interest in her, and one she had no wish ever to meet again.

She went to get Nanny's breakfast tray ready, re-flecting that the chances of seeing Felix again were so remote that she need not give him another thought.

Chapter 7

Florina took Pauline and Bobby for short trips in the car during the next few days, and even Nanny consented to be driven into Wilton for an afternoon's shopping. Summer was giving way slowly to the first breath of autumn, and there weren't many days left before Pauline would be going to school. The three of them made the most of it, and it wasn't until Friday morning, when Sir William telephoned, that they remembered that Wanda would be with him that weekend. Reluctantly, Nanny prepared the rooms while Florina bent her mind to the menus for the next few days. She was rolling pastry for the vol-au-vents when she heard a car stop in the drive. Her heart gave a great leap—perhaps Sir William had come early, and, better still, Wanda might not be with him. She heard Nanny go to the door and the murmur of voices, and then Nanny came into the kitchen.

'Someone for you—a young man—says he is an old

friend.' She looked at Florina's floury hands. 'I'll put him in the small sitting-room.'

Florina frowned. 'But I haven't any old friends—not young men...' She remembered Felix, then raised a worried face to Nanny. 'Oh, if it's Felix—I don't want to see him, Nanny.' She added by way of explanation, 'He's from Holland. I met him when I went over there for the wedding.'

'Well, if he's come all this way, you can't refuse to see him. It's only good manners,' declared Nanny, a stickler for doing the right thing.

She went away before Florina could think of any more excuses. Florina finished rolling her pastry, put it in the fridge to keep cool and washed her hands. She didn't bother to look in the looking-glass; her face was flushed from her cooking and her hair, still in its plait, could have done with a comb. But if it *was* Felix, and something told her that it was, then she had no wish to improve her looks for him. She would give him short shrift, she decided crossly as she opened the sitting-room door.

It *was* Felix, debonair and very sure of himself. He came across the room to meet her, just as though they were good friends with a fondness for each other. But she ignored his outstretched hands and said crisply, 'Hello, Felix. I'm afraid I have no time to talk, I've too much to do. Are you on your way somewhere? Tante Minna didn't mention you in her letter.'

'I didn't tell her. I'm putting up at the Trout and Feathers; I thought you could do with a bit of livening up. I've got the car, we can drive around, go dancing, hit a few of the night-spots.'

'You must be out of your mind! I work here, it's a full-time job, and when I'm free I don't want to go dancing or anything else, especially with you, Felix. I can't think why you came.'

'Let's say I don't like being thwarted.' He smiled widely, and she thought that his eyes seemed closer together than she had remembered.

'I don't know what you mean...' They had been speaking Dutch, but now she switched to English. 'You are wasting your time here, Felix. I have neither the time nor the inclination to go out with you, even if it were possible.'

He shrugged his shoulders. 'I've taken the room for a week. There's no reason why I shouldn't spend it here if I wish.'

'None at all, but please don't come bothering me. Now, you will have to excuse me, I'm busy.'

'No coffee? Where's your Dutch hospitality?'

'I'm not in a position to offer that, Felix. I'm cook here.'

She led the way through the hall and opened the door. On the threshold, he paused. 'Just a minute. Doesn't your father live here?'

'Yes, he does, but he has no interest in Mother's side of the family—not since she died.'

'Ah, well, they will know where he lives if I ask at the pub.'

He gave her a mocking salute and got into his car.

She shut the door slowly and found Nanny in the hall beside her. The old lady's stern features were relaxed into a look of concern, so that Florina found herself pouring out a rather muddled account of her meeting with Felix at Tante Minna's house, and her dislike of him. 'I thought I'd been unfair to him,' she explained, 'for he was very nice at the wedding. It was afterwards...'

Nanny nodded. 'A conceited young man, and not a very pleasant one,' she commented. 'Did Sir William meet him?'

'Yes.' Florina went pink, for undoubtedly he thought that she and Felix were rather more than firm friends, even though she had denied it. What was he going to think if Felix came to see her? And he was quite capable of it…

She went back to the kitchen and finished the pastry. She was so worried that she curdled the *béarnaise* sauce, which meant that she had to add iced water, a teaspoon at a time, and beat like mad until it was smooth again.

Preparations for the evening's dinner dealt with, she and Pauline took Bobby for his walk. She expected to meet Felix at every corner, but there was no sign of him. Perhaps he had realised that there was no chance of seeing much of her, and had driven off somewhere where there was more entertainment. She was able to wish Sir William a rather colourless good evening when he arrived, and was relieved to hear Wanda go straight upstairs without bothering to say anything to anyone.

'And how is the village?' enquired Sir William. 'Anything exciting happened since I was last here?'

'Nothing—nothing at all,' said Florina, so quickly that he took a long look at her. Guilt was written all over her nice little face, but he forebore from pursuing the matter. Instead, he sighed inwardly; she was holding something back, and until she had learned to trust him utterly there was little he could do about it. He made some casual remark about Mother and Child sitting as usual before the Aga, then strolled away. He could, of course, question Nanny, but he dismissed the idea at once. Florina would have to tell him herself. Until she trusted him he couldn't be sure…

It was after breakfast the next morning that Felix walked up the drive, rang the bell, and demanded of Nanny, who had answered to door, to see Sir William. He was charming about it, but very determined, and she had no choice but to put him in the small sitting-room and tell Sir William.

So this was Florina's secret, he reflected, shaking hands with Felix, good manners masking his dislike.

'This is a surprise,' he observed. 'You are on holiday?'

Felix gave him a look of well simulated surprise. 'Oh, hasn't Florina told you? I'm staying in the village for a week—so that we can see something of each other. I thought that she would be free for part of each day so that we could be together…'

Sir William said mildly, 'I'm afraid that she doesn't get a great deal of time to herself, especially at the weekends. If you had warned her before you came, something could have been arranged. Perhaps she can manage a half-day after the weekend.'

He got to his feet and Felix, perforce, got to his. 'So sorry,' Sir William said. 'You'll forgive me, I'm sure. I have a guest and have the morning planned.'

He bade Felix goodbye at the door and remained there until he was out of sight, then he shut the door quietly and went along to the kitchen.

Florina was peeling potatoes at the sink, lulled into a sense of false security, so that the enquiring face she turned towards him was serene. But it took only a few seconds for her to realise that something was wrong.

Sir William wandered over to the table and sat on it.

'Your friend Felix has just called to see me. Why didn't you tell me he was in the village, Florina?'

She plunged at once into a muddled speech. 'I don't want to—that is he came yesterday—I didn't think—' She made matters worse by adding, 'I didn't have time to talk to him…'

'But you had time to tell me. Remember? I asked you if there was any news and you said—I quote, "Nothing— nothing at all." Why so secretive, Florina? Did you think that I might not allow my cook to have followers?'

'He's not a follower,' she mumbled.

'He followed you here. I think I'm entitled to…' He fell silent as the door opened and Pauline came in, Bobby in her arms.

'Daddy, Wanda is still in bed. Could we go for a walk until she gets up? There's a darling little calf at the farm. Florina and I went to look at it and we can go any time we like, so I don't suppose they'll mind you, instead.'

She looked at Florina's pale, strained face and then at her father.

'Are you quarrelling?' she wanted to know.

Sir William put a hand on her small shoulders and went to the door.

'When you are old and wise enough, darling, you will understand that one never quarrels with one's cook.' He sounded savage.

Florina finished the potatoes and started scraping carrots. She felt numb and her head was quite empty of thought. Presently, the whole of the little scene came flooding back, and her eyes filled with tears so that she could hardly see what she was doing. Finally, indignation swallowed up every other feeling. He hadn't given her a chance to explain, he had taken it for granted that the wretched Felix actually meant something to her, and he had been unkind, more than that, utterly beastly. It would serve him right if she were to spend an evening with Felix…

She finished the carrots and started on the salsify, and when Nanny came into the kitchen presently, she left the sink and poured coffee for them both.

Nanny sipped appreciatively. 'You make very good coffee, child.' She glanced at Florina's pink nose. 'What's upset Sir William, I wonder? In a nasty old temper when he left the house. Not that any that didn't know him well would even guess at it, but I've known him since he was a baby!'

She took another quick peep at Florina. 'Had all his plans laid, I dare say, and someone's messed them up. Did I see that young man coming up the drive an hour or so ago? I wonder what he wanted? A trouble-maker if ever I saw one.'

Florina said, 'He came to see if I could go out with him. I imagine that he let Sir William think that I knew he was coming to stay.' She poured more coffee. 'Nanny, I'd rather not talk about it, if you don't mind.'

Nanny nodded. 'Least said…' She didn't finish because Wanda came into the kitchen. 'Oh, there you are—this is the worst run household I've ever had to endure. I want coffee in the drawing-room. I won't wait for Sir William.' She turned on her heel and then paused. 'Who was that young man who called earlier this morning? Rather good-looking, I thought. Why haven't I met him before? Does he come from the village—he looked a cut above that.'

Nanny was silent, so was Florina.

'Well, who was he?' She laughed suddenly. 'Never your boyfriend, Cook? I find that hard to believe.' Her laugh became a snigger. 'It was!' She watched Florina's face glow. 'What a joke! Are you the best he can manage? Does Sir William know?' And, when no one answered, 'Yes, he does. I wonder what he thought of it? His marvellous cook with a boyfriend up her sleeve. Well you'll be free to marry him, if that is what he wants, won't you? For you won't be here much longer, I promise you that.'

She swept out of the kitchen, leaving the two of them silent. Presently Nanny said, 'You did quite right not to say anything.' Her sharp eyes searched Florina's pale face. 'She will use this to her advantage—urge Sir William to let you go, so that you can get married…'

Florina nodded miserably. 'But Nanny, I don't want to marry him—even if he were the last man left on earth.'

'I know that. Is he serious about you?'

Florina shook her head. 'I didn't respond and he expected me to. He got very angry…'

'A nasty type. You had better tell Sir William. He'll see that he doesn't bother you again.'

Florina said quite violently, 'No—no, I don't want to talk about it to him. Please don't say anything to him, Nanny. Promise?'

Nanny said briefly, 'I'll promise, if it will make you happy, though you're making a big mistake.' She wouldn't break her promise, but if she could see a way round that she would take it. If there was a misunderstanding at this stage it would be a great pity. Here was Florina, bless the girl, head over heels in love with Sir William and making no effort to do anything about it because cooks didn't marry their employers, especially when they were wealthy and at the top of their profession. And Sir William already engaged to that awful Miss Fortesque…and he as uncertain as a young man in the throes of his first love affair. Nanny, incurably romantic under her severe exterior, sighed deeply, refused more coffee and went away to tidy the chaos in Wanda's bedroom, bearing a tray of coffee for that lady as she went.

Florina stayed in the kitchen, bent on keeping out of sight. She was putting the finished touches to a trifle when Pauline and Bobby joined her. 'Daddy wants his coffee. I said I'd take it. We had a lovely walk and Bobby ran for miles.'

She peered into Florina's face. 'Darling Florina, you look so sad. Was Daddy angry with you?'

Florina arranged the tray and put a plate of little almond biscuits beside the coffeepot. 'Good gracious, no, love! I'm not a bit sad, only rather headachy. Go carefully with the tray. Shall I put another cup on it, for you?'

'May I have my milk here with you? Wanda told Daddy that she wanted to speak to him seriously. She's being all charming and smiling—I bet she's up to no good...'

Florina agreed silently, although she said firmly, 'Pauline, you mustn't say things like that about your father's guests. It would hurt his feelings.'

Pauline picked up the tray. She said, with the frankness of children, 'But he hasn't any feelings for her, I can tell; he's always so polite to her. I can't think why he's going to marry her.'

'People marry because they love each other.'

Pauline kissed her cheek. 'Dear Florina, you're such a darling, but not always quite with it.' She took a biscuit and munched it. 'If Daddy was poor and just Mr Sedley, she wouldn't want to marry him. She worked on him—you know—all sweet interest and how clever he is and all that rubbish. I suppose he thought she'd make quite a good stepmother for me, and he just let himself be conned.' She kissed Florina again, picked up the tray and skipped off before Florina's shocked rebuke could reach her ears.

She was back quickly. 'Daddy's angry! His face is all calm and his eyes are almost shut. I couldn't hear what Wanda was saying but her voice sounded as though she was in church. You know, all hushed and very solemn.'

Florina muttered something neither hushed nor solemn, and said rather loudly, 'I expect they are discussing their wedding.'

Pauline drank some of her milk and, since Florina wasn't looking, poured some of it into Mother's saucer. 'No, they weren't, because I listened a teeny bit as I was closing the door and she said, "Let's have him for drinks, darling."'

Florina dropped the wooden spoon she was holding and took a long time to pick it up.

'Someone from the village, I expect,' she said, knowing in her heart that it was Felix. Well, if it was, she would keep out of sight. She would be busy with dinner, anyway.

It wasn't until after tea that Nanny came to tell her that someone was coming for drinks. 'Sir William didn't say who it was.' She caught sight of Florina's face. 'That young man…this is Wanda's doing. She can be very persuasive when she wants; probably painted a pathetic picture of you pining for his company. Did you see very much of him in Holland? And did Sir William see you together?'

Florina nodded dumbly. 'I wish I could run away!'

'Run away? Unthinkable! Besides you're not the girl I think you are if you do. Must I still keep my promise?'

Florina lifted a stubborn chin. 'Yes, please.' She added hopefully, 'Probably he won't come in here. He'll be a guest, after all, and only a casual caller...'

It was worse than anything she could have imagined. She was piping creamed potatoes on to a baking tray when the door opened and Sir William, Wanda and Felix came into the kitchen.

It was Wanda who spoke. 'Oh, Cook—here is Felix.' She paused to give him a conspiratorial look. 'You don't mind if I call you that?' She smiled at Florina with eyes like flints. 'He can't wait to talk to you. You are such a marvellous cook that I'm sure it won't bother you if he stays while you work for a while?'

Florina looked at her and then at Felix, grinning at seeing her cornered. Lastly, she looked at Sir William. He was leaning against the door, apparently only mildly interested. She said in a high voice which she managed to keep steady, 'I'm sorry, I can't work in this kitchen unless I'm alone.'

'In that case,' said Sir William, 'let us leave you alone, in peace. I don't want my dinner spoilt.'

Wanda didn't give up easily. 'Pauline is always here...'

He said mildly, 'Certainly she is, but she helps Florina, fetching and carrying, washing up and generally making herself quite useful. And I entirely approve, I should like her to be as good a cook as Florina. I doubt if—er—Felix wishes to wash the dishes.' He turned politely to him. 'You must have another drink before you go. I'm sure we shall be able to arrange something at a more propitious time.'

The party left the kitchen, leaving her shaking with temper. She attacked the food she was preparing quite savagely, curdling a sauce and burning the *croûtons*. With the kitchen full of blue smoke and the pungent smell of the charred remains at the foot of the pan, she clashed lids, dropped spoons and spilt some clarifying butter on to the floor.

It was to this scene of chaos that Sir William returned.

'Something is burning,' he observed.

'I know that!' she snapped. 'Dinner is ruined.' An exaggeration, but excusable in the circumstances.

His fine mouth twitched. 'I'm sorry that we upset you by coming into the kitchen. Wanda was sure that you would be delighted, and certainly there was no need for you to be so reluctant to mention it to me…'

'Reluctant? Reluctant?' said Florina shrilly. 'And pray why should I be that? In any case, it's my business, Sir William.' Rage sat strangely upon her, her eyes blazed in her usually tranquil face, her soft mouth shook. Sir William eyed her very thoughtfully.

'This Felix,' he said at last. 'Are you in love with him?' When she remained silent, he went on, 'No, don't tell me again that it's not my business. After all, it's my dinner which is ruined. But you're not going to tell me, are you, Florina? I wonder why that is?'

She spoke in a small whispering voice. 'You made up your mind that I was being deceitful about him, you—you said he was my follower—that was to remind me that I was your cook, so if you don't mind I will not tell you anything, Sir William. I will make sure that he doesn't come here again. I'm sorry if it has embarrassed you.'

'Good God, girl, why should it do that? On the contrary, it enlightened me.' He was going to say more, but the door was pushed open with an impatient hand, and Wanda came in. She was wearing a white crêpe dress and her hair was carefully arranged in careless curls; she looked sweet and feminine and most appealing.

'William, I'm so glad you are here, now you can hear me say how sorry I am to Cook. I embarrassed her, but I truly thought she would be pleased.' Her blue eyes swam with tears, as she turned to Florina. 'You must think I'm quite horrid. Don't bear a grudge against me, will you? I told Felix that I was sure that you would have time to see something of him while he is here. After all, you won't have anything much to do once we are gone.'

She tucked a hand under Sir William's arm, and smiled at him prettily. 'Don't be cross with me, darling, for giving orders in your house. After all, it's soon to be mine as well, isn't it?'

Sir William said nothing to that, only stared at Florina. 'We'll go,' he said briskly. 'Florina has had enough interruptions.'

Alone once more, Florina set about rescuing the dinner from disaster. 'Not that I care if everything is burnt to a cinder,' she said to Mother. 'Anyway, you and Child can have the egg custard—it's not fit to put on the table.'

Sir William made no attempt to seek her out. Indeed, it seemed to her that he was avoiding her. Usually he came into the kitchen with Pauline in the morning while she fed Bobby and the cats, sitting astride a chair, talking to Florina about the village and telling her his plans for the garden, but not any more. Nor, to her relief, did she see anything of Felix. Sunday came and went, there were friends for drinks, and very soon after lunch he drove back to London with Wanda, smiling a small, triumphant smile, sitting beside him. He had bidden Florina goodbye in a pleasant manner, but the easy friendship between them had gone.

She got through the rest of the day somehow, presenting a bright face to Pauline and Nanny, and presently retiring to bed to weep silently for the impossible dreams which would never return. At least she had derived a spurious happiness from them.

It was several days later when Pauline came dancing into the kitchen to tell her that her father wanted to speak to her. Florina lifted the receiver with the air of one expecting it to bite her and said a cautious 'hello'.

Sir William's firm voice was crisp. 'Florina? Jolly will drive Mrs Jolly down tomorrow. They will arrive some time after lunch and he will return here after having tea with you. Mrs Jolly will take over from you for two days so that you may be completely free, so make any arrangements you like with Felix; he told me that he wouldn't be returning until Saturday morning.' He added, in a strangely expressionless voice, 'I hope you will have a pleasant time together.'

He had rung off before she could do more than let out a gasp of surprise. Florina toyed with the idea of ringing him back and denying all wish to see Felix again, but that might make matters worse. She detected Wanda's hand in the business and flounced off in search of Nanny.

That lady heard her out. 'Dear, dear, here's a pretty kettle of fish. Does Felix know about this?'

'I don't know, I shouldn't think so—I'm sure Sir William wouldn't phone him deliberately, just to tell him.'

'Miss Fortesque might,' suggested Nanny. 'You must think of something, so that if he comes round here you are ready for him.' Her stern face broke into a smile. 'I have it! Isn't Pauline to spend the next day or so with the Meggisons? You know them, don't you? Could you not go with her? Heaven knows, they have more than enough room for you in that house of theirs.'

'Yes, but what would I say? I can't just invite myself.'

'You can tell them the truth, the bare bones of it, at any rate. If that man comes, don't say anything about it, but get hold of Mrs Meggison and go there with Pauline—she's to get there early after breakfast, isn't she? He is not likely to call as early as that. Don't worry about him, I'll deal with the gentleman.'

'Won't Jolly tell Sir William?'

'Bless you, child, he'll not breathe a word…'

'I'm deceiving Sir William…'

'He's been deceiving himself for months,' observed Nanny cryptically. 'You can tell him when he comes at the weekend.'

Felix arrived later that day and Florina, bolstered by the knowledge that Nanny was on the landing, listening, admitted him into the hall, but no further.

'So, Miss Fortesque kept her promise. She said she would persuade Sir William to give you a couple of days off. I'll be round for you tomorrow about eleven o'clock, and don't try any tricks. Everyone knows in the village that we are going to be married.' He chuckled at her look of outrage. 'Don't worry, darling, I'll be off and away at the end of the week, but I don't like being snubbed by a plain-faced girl who can't say boo to a goose. I'm just getting my own back.' He made her a mock salute. 'Be seeing you! I've planned a very interesting day for us both.'

She shut the door on him and then locked it. They had spoken in Dutch and Nanny, descending the stairs, had to have it all translated.

'Conceited jackanapes!' she declared. 'Who does he think he is? Why, he's nothing but a great lout under all that charm. Now, off you go and ring Mrs Meggison, and make sure you'll be collected well before ten o'clock.'

'Yes, but what about Pauline? Won't she think it's strange?'

'Why should she? She knows that the Meggisons are old friends of yours, and she loves being with you.'

Mrs Meggison raised no objections, in fact, she was delighted. 'I have to go to the dentist in the morning and I was wondering what to do about the children—now you will be here to keep an eye on them. It couldn't be better, my dear. Can you stay until Saturday? We'll send you both back directly after breakfast if Sir William doesn't mind.'

'He won't mind at all,' said Florina mendaciously, and put down the receiver with a great sigh of relief.

The Meggisons were genuinely pleased to see her. 'You can't think how glad I am that you came,' declared Mrs Meggison. 'There's a new au pair girl coming next week—Danish—and the boys go back to school then, but with all four of them at home I've been run off my feet. Cook and Meg have enough to do; I can't ask them to keep an eye on the children as well. They are all in the garden. Perhaps Pauline would like to trot out and be with them while I show you your rooms.'

It was a nice old house; a little shabby, but the furniture was old and cared for and the rooms held all the warmth of a happy family life. Florina, safely away from Felix's unwanted attentions, enjoyed every minute of their two days, even though she had almost no time to herself. There was so much to do. The school holidays were almost over and they wanted to extract the last ounce of pleasure from them. They worked wonders for Pauline, too, tearing around, climbing trees, riding the elderly donkey the Meggisons kept in the orchard, eating out-of-doors in the untidy garden at the back of the house. The pair of them, much refreshed, climbed into Mr Meggison's Land Rover with mixed feelings. Pauline sorry to be leaving her friends, but anxious to see Bobby and Mother and Child again. Florina was relieved that Felix would be gone, but panicky about meeting Sir William. She hadn't told Pauline to say nothing about her stay with the Meggisons; she had been deceitful, but she didn't intend that the little girl should be involved, too. For deceit it was, whichever way she looked at it. She got out of the Land Rover when they reached Wheel House, mentally braced against meeting Sir William.

Jolly opened the door, beaming a welcome, and invited Mr Meggison to make himself at home in the drawing-room while he sent for Sir William.

'In the kitchen garden, sir, and if Pauline would go and fetch him...'

Pauline went, dancing away, shrieking with delight as Jolly went on smoothly, 'Mrs Jolly is in the kitchen, Miss Florina—there'll be coffee there and I have no doubt she will wish to have a chat with you. We return to London later this morning, but Sir William and Miss Fortesque are here for the weekend.'

Florina had her coffee and a comfortable chat with Mrs Jolly, and then went to her room to change her clothes; there had been no sign of Sir William, and Miss Fortesque had been driven into Salisbury by Jolly directly after breakfast to have her hair done. Mrs Jolly had cleared the kitchen, but since Jolly and she were driving back to London before lunch, Florina would prepare it.

It was almost two hours later, while she was mixing a salad with one eye on the clock, anxious not to be late with the meal, when Sir William strolled into the kitchen.

'I believe we should have a talk,' he observed, at his most placid.

'Oh, yes, of course, Sir William, but lunch will be late...'

She had gone pale, but she didn't avoid his eyes.

'Never mind lunch! You had two days free so that

you might spend them with Felix, instead of which, you chose to go to the Meggisons. Why?'

He had taken one of the Windsor chairs by the Aga, and Mother and Child had lost no time in clambering on to his knee. He stroked them with a large, gentle hand and waited for her to answer.

She said coldly, 'I don't know why you should suppose that I should want to spend my leisure with Felix. I didn't ask him to come here in the first place and, as far as I know, I gave you no reason to suppose that I did.'

She sliced tomatoes briskly, ruining most of them because her hand wasn't steady on the knife.

'You didn't make that clear, and I still wonder why. Am I not to know, Florina?'

She was making a hash of a cucumber. The salad wouldn't be fit to eat.

'No, Sir William. I'm sorry I didn't tell you that I was going to the Meggisons, but I didn't think it would matter…'

'On the contrary, it matters very much, but that's something we need not go into for the moment. So I take it that you have no plans to marry?'

'No.'

He set the cats back in their basket, got to his feet and wandered to the door. 'Good, Pauline will be so pleased. You should be more careful in the future, Florina. I've been quite concerned about you.'

He went away, closing the door quietly behind him, leaving her to start on another salad, which would be fit to put on the table.

She was feeding the swans after lunch was finished, when Wanda came on to the patio. Sir William and Pauline had taken Bobby for a walk, and the house was quiet, Mrs Deakin had gone and Nanny was in her room resting.

'I don't know what game you're playing, Cook,' Wanda's voice was soft and angry. 'Whatever it is, it won't do you any good. By next weekend we shall announce the date of the wedding, and don't think it will be months ahead. Sir William will get a special licence and we can marry within days. You had better start looking for another job.' She sniggered. 'You are a fool! You and your silly day-dreams, did you suppose that a man like Sir William would look at you twice? When he does look at you he is looking at his cook, my dear, not you. You had better go back to your Dutch family and find yourself a husband there—you haven't much chance here, even with the village men.' She turned away. 'Don't say that I haven't warned you. You will not stay a day longer than is necessary once I have married Sir William.'

Florina stood where she was, staring down at the water below and the family of swans gobbling up the bread she was throwing to them still. It was something to do while she tried to collect her thoughts.

That Wanda was going to get rid of her was a certainty, and to go to Holland was surely a way out of a situation which was fast becoming unbearable. On the other hand, she would be running away and, as Nanny said, she wasn't a girl to do that. Would there by any point in remaining in England? It wasn't as if she would see Sir William again.

She threw the last crust and watched the swans demolish it. She couldn't see them very clearly for the tears she was struggling to hold back.

'Why are you crying?' asked Sir William and, since she didn't answer, threw an arm round her shoulders and stared down at the swans, too.

Chapter 8

The urge to put her head on Sir William's vast chest and tell him everything, even that she loved him, was something Florina only prevented herself from doing by the greatest effort. Instead, she sniffed, blew her small red nose and stayed obstinately silent.

Sir William sounded calmly friendly. 'Your father—he lives close by, does he not? Would you like to spend a day or two with him? He could probably dispel the rumours Felix has spread.'

'It's kind of you to suggest it, Sir William, but Father and I...he wanted a son, and he has no interest in the Dutch side of me. He tried to turn Mother into an Englishwoman, but he never succeeded—he didn't succeed with me, either.' Her voice was small and thin.

Sir William, who had heard that before from various sources in the village, said comfortably, 'Well, what would you like to do, Florina? You haven't been happy since we came back from Holland, have you? Did something happen then to upset you—and I don't mean Felix?' He added, 'Would it help if you went back there for a week or two? Not to your aunt, for Felix goes there, does he not? I have some good friends in the Hague and Amsterdam; and in Friesland, too—a temporary job, perhaps?'

She was very conscious of his arm on her shoulders. Did he want to be rid of her, in order to placate Wanda and at the same time to spare her from the ignominy of getting the sack? She didn't know, and did it really matter? she reflected.

'I hope you will stay with us.' He had answered her unspoken thoughts so promptly that for a moment she wondered if she had voiced them out loud. 'At least until Pauline is settled in her new school. Will you think about it for a week or so?'

He gave her a comforting pat on the arm, remarking that he had to work in his study, and he left her there.

They exchanged barely a dozen words before he left for London, and as for Wanda, she behaved as though Florina wasn't there; she ignored Nanny, too, and avoided Pauline, but hung on to Sir William's arm on every possible occasion, the very picture of a compliant, adoring wife-to-be.

They wouldn't be down on the following weekend, Sir William told his daughter; he had a consultation on Saturday in Suffolk and he might possibly need to spend the night there. 'I'll phone you each evening,' he promised, 'and you can tell me all about school.'

The week went quickly but now there was another routine, no longer the easy-going times of the holidays, but up early, school uniform to get into, breakfast and then the drive to Wilton, with Bobby on the back seat of the car. It was Florina who took him off for his walks now during the day, although when Pauline got home each afternoon the three of them went into the fields around the village while Pauline recited the happenings of her day to Florina. She was at least happy at school; she knew some of the girls there and the teachers were nice. She had homework to do, of course, and Florina sat at the kitchen table with her and helped when she was asked, while Nanny sat by the Aga, knitting. It was pleasant and peaceful, but Florina worried that it wasn't the life Pauline should have. She needed a mother; her father loved her but he had his work and she suspected that without Wanda he would have more time to spend with his daughter. When Wanda was his wife, that didn't mean that she was going to be Pauline's mother; indeed, with herself and Nanny out of the way, the child would be packed off to boarding-school. Wanda wasn't the kind of woman to share her husband, even with his own child.

The weekend came and since the weather was still fine, the Meggisons came over for tea on Saturday and played croquet on the velvet-smooth lawn behind the house, until Florina called them in for supper and presently drove them back home in the Mini, very squashed with Bobby insisting on coming, too.

When Florina went to say goodnight to Pauline, the child flung her arms round her neck. 'Such a lovely day,' she said sleepily. 'If only Daddy could have been here too.'

'That would have been nice,' agreed Florina sedately, and her heart danced against her ribs at the thought. 'But he said he'd be home here on Friday.'

It was, however, sooner than Friday when she saw him again.

It was on Tuesday morning, while they were driving along the country road to Wilton, that a car, driven much too fast, overtook them on a bend to crash head on into a Land Rover coming towards it.

Florina pulled into the ditch by the roadside; the two cars were a hundred yards ahead of her, askew across the road, the drivers already climbing out, shouting at each other. Pauline had clutched her arm when the cars had collided and then covered her ears from the thumps and bangs of the impact.

Florina opened her door a few inches. 'I'll go and see if they can move out of the way; if they can't we'll have to go round along the main road.' She glanced at Bobby, barking his head off and shivering. 'Don't get out, darling, and don't let Bobby out; he's very frightened and he'll run away.'

She nipped out of the car smartly and shut the door against the terrified dog, and ran up the road.

No one was hurt, only furiously angry. The two men were hurling abuse at each other until she took advantage of a pause in their vituperation.

'Am I able to get past you?' She had to shout to make them listen. 'I'm taking Pauline to school...' She had recognised one of the farm hands from the village, standing by the Land Rover. 'Will you be able to move soon?'

'Now, luv, that I can't say—this lunatic was coming too fast—you must have seen him—we'll have to get the police and take numbers and the rest. You'd best go round, and back over the bridge.'

There seemed nothing else to do, and Florina turned to go back to the Mini in time to see the door open and Pauline get out. Bobby scrambled out after her, and then, yelping madly, raced away through a gap in the hedge, into the fields beyond. Within seconds Pauline had gone after him, climbing the five-barred gate in the hedge. She took no notice of Florina's shout, just as Bobby took no notice of the child's cries.

Florina reached the car, snatched up the dog's lead, slammed the door shut and climbed the gate in her turn. The men were still arguing, she could hear them even at that distance, much too taken up with their own problems to bother about hers. Bobby was well away by now, running erratically across a further field, newly ploughed, and Pauline wasn't too far behind him. Florina saved her breath and ran as she had never run before. She knew the country around her well; beyond the ploughed field was a small wood, its heavy undergrowth overgrown with rough scrub and brambles, and beyond that was the river winding its way into Wilton, not isolated but unproductive so that not even gypsies went near it.

Bobby had reached the wood, but Pauline was finding the ploughed field heavy-going. However, she didn't stop when Florina shouted, so she had reached the wood before Florina was half-way there.

The wood was quiet when she reached it, save for the birds and the frenzied distant barking of Bobby. There was neither sight nor sound of Pauline; she was probably on the far side by now, making for the river.

The brambles made speed impossible if she weren't to be scratched to pieces, but scratches were the least of her worries. The wood ran down steeply to the river, which, while not wide or deep, was swift-running and, at this time of the year, cluttered with weeds and reeds; Pauline might rush along without looking and fall into it. Bobby was still yelping and barking and she was sure that she heard Pauline's voice; it spurred her on through the brambles, quite regardless of the thorns.

The wood was narrow at that point, and she emerged finally, oozing blood from the scratches which covered her hands and arms and legs. Her dress was torn, as were her tights, and her hair hopelessly tangled, hung in an untidy curtain down her back. She swept it out of her eyes and paused to look around her. Bobby was whining now, but there was no sign of Pauline. She shouted at the top of her voice and started down the steep slope to the river. There were willows and bushes along its banks; she found the child within inches of the water, lying white and silent with Bobby beside her. He greeted her with a joyful bark, bent to lick the little girl's face, and made no effort to run away as she fastened his lead before kneeling beside Pauline.

There was a bruise on Pauline's forehead and a few beads of blood. Florina, her heart thumping with fear, picked up a flaccid hand and felt for a pulse. It was steady and quite strong, so she put the hand down and began to search for other injuries. There were plenty of scratches but, as far as she could tell, no broken bones. She made Pauline as comfortable as she could, tied Bobby's lead to a nearby tree-stump, and tried to decide what to do. She glanced at her watch; it was barely half an hour since they had started their mad race across the fields. She thought it unlikely that either man would have noticed it, for they had been far too occupied with their argument. Pauline was concussed, she thought, but even if she regained consciousness, she didn't dare to let the child walk back to the car; it must be the best part of a mile away. She could only hope that the farm worker would tell someone when he got back to the village, better still, he might go to the police station. This hope was instantly squashed; there was no room to turn on that particular stretch of the road, and they would have to manhandle the car to one side so that the Land Rover could squeeze past. In the village the police could be informed and someone sent to take the car away; it had received by far the most damage.

She sat down by Pauline and lifted the child's head very gently on to her lap. They might be there for hours; even if the men noticed that the Mini was standing there and no one was in it, they might have thought that they had walked back to the village.

Which was exactly what they had thought; it was almost half an hour before they had got the car on to the side of the road and the Land Rover proceeded on its way, and it was pure chance that the driver saw Nanny walking down the road to get some eggs from the farm. 'They'll be back now,' he observed. 'I didn't pass them on the road.'

'But they aren't here. Did you see them get out of the car? They weren't hurt?'

'No, luv, but that little old dog was kicking up a fine row, ran off, he did, though lord knows where.' He started the engine. 'They'll turn up, safe and sound, but I'll tell the police—we'll have to go to the station in Wilton, and they'll come out here, I've no doubt of that.'

Nanny went on her way to the farm, collected the eggs, and marched back to Wheel House. There was no sign of Florina or Pauline, so she phoned the school; there was always the chance that they had walked the rest of the way...

They hadn't, and when she phoned the police at Wilton they had no news of them. They would ring back, they told her, the moment they knew anything; they couldn't have gone far...

It was a pity that an elderly woman living half a mile along the road from the accident should declare that she had heard a dog barking behind her cottage, on the opposite side of the road to where Bobby had escaped; she thought, too, that she had seen someone running. She was vague and uncertain as to exactly when she had seen them and the excitement of being the centre of interest for the moment led her to embroider her talk, so that the two policemen who had been detailed to search for Florina and Pauline set off in the opposite direction to the wood and the river.

Sir William wasn't in when Nanny telephoned his house, but Jolly undertook to track him down and tell him. 'He'll be at the hospital,' he told her, 'but he's not operating, he mentioned that at breakfast and he said that he had a quiet morning—just ward rounds. He will be with you in a couple of hours.'

It was less than that; Sir William spent ten precious minutes ringing the police, aware that if he warned them he would be allowed to travel at maximum speed provided they had his car number and he gave his reasons.

The Bentley made short work of the ninety miles, and he walked into his house to find Nanny on the telephone. She said 'Thank you,' and put the receiver down as he reached her. 'Thank God you've come, Sir William, I'm that worried!' She studied his face. He looked much as usual, but he was pale and there was a muscle twitching in his cheek. 'You'll have a cup of coffee,' and when he held up a hand, 'You can drink it while I tell you all that I know.'

She was upset, but very sensible too—time enough to give way to tears when they were safe and sound. Sir William listened and drank his coffee and observed, 'The police have drawn a blank so far in Wilton and the direction of Broad Chalke; I'll try the other side, it's open country, isn't it? Where exactly did the accident happen?'

'The Land Rover driver said on the sharp bend about two miles along the road, almost parallel with that road you can see on the left...'

Florina, with Pauline's head heavy on her lap, glanced at the sky; the clouds were piling up and although it was barely one o'clock, there was a faint chill heralding the still distant evening. Pauline had stirred a little, but she hadn't dared to move. Bobby, quite quiet now, sat beside her, aware that something was wrong, fidgeting a little. She had shouted for a time, but there had been no answer and the trees in the wood deadened the sound of any traffic on the distant road. She had racked her brains to find a way to get them out of the fix, but she could think of nothing. It was unlikely that anyone would come that way, for there was no reason to do so, and who would take a country walk through brambles, anyway, but it surprised her a little that no one had searched for them; they weren't all that far away from the scene of the accident.

Pauline stirred again and this time she opened her eyes. 'Florina?' she stared up in a puzzled way. 'I've got such a fearful headache.'

'Yes, darling, I expect you have. You fell over and you bumped your head. Don't move or it will hurt still more. As soon as someone comes, we'll have you home and tucked up in bed.'

'Bobby—where is Bobby?'

'Right here, beside me. Now close your eyes, my love, and have a nap; I'll wake you when someone comes...'

'Daddy will find us.'

Florina said stoutly, 'Of course he will,' and blinked away a tear. She was thoroughly scared by now, as much by her inability to think of a way of getting back through the wood, as by the fact that no one had come within shouting distance.

It was at that precise moment that someone did shout, and for a few seconds she was too surprised to answer. But Bobby set up a joyful barking and began to tug at his lead. Florina shouted, then set him free and watched him tear up the bank and into the wood, to emerge a few moments later with Sir William hard on his heels.

She was beyond words, she could only stare at him as he came to a halt beside her and squatted down on his heels. He let out a great sigh and said, 'Oh, my dears...' and his arm drew her close for a moment before he bent to examine Pauline.

She stirred under his gentle hand and opened her eyes. 'Daddy—oh, I knew you'd come, Florina said you would. Can we go home now?'

'Yes, darling, but just me take a look and see where you're hurt.'

Florina found her voice. 'She was unconscious when I found her, that was half-past nine. I didn't move her, she came round about eleven o'clock.'

He nodded without looking at her. 'There doesn't seem to be much wrong except concussion. We'll get you both home and put her to bed—she had better be X-rayed, but I think it's safe to leave that until the morning.' He looked at her then. 'And you, Florina, are you hurt?'

'Only a few scratches. Will you carry her through the wood?'

'The pub landlord and Dick from the farm came with

me—they are searching at either end of the wood.' He put his fingers between his teeth and whistled and presently she heard their answering whistles.

'Shall I wait for them here? I'll bring Bobby with me, then you can go ahead with Pauline.'

For the first time he smiled. 'Having found you, Florina, I have no intention of leaving you again.' He watched the look of puzzlement on her face, and added, 'They will be here very soon.'

Going back was easier. The two men went ahead, beating back the brambles with their sticks, with Sir William carrying Pauline behind them and, behind him, protected by his vast size, came Florina, leading a sober Bobby on his lead.

At the roadside she made to get into the Mini, but Sir William said no. 'You will come with us, Florina. Dick had a lift here; he can drive the Mini back, if he will.' He grinned at the two men. 'We'll have a pint together later.'

He laid Pauline on the back seat, swept Florina on to the seat beside him and drove back to Wheel House.

Nanny was waiting. 'Bed for Pauline, Nanny. I'll leave her to you for a moment; she's been concussed so you know what to do. Florina, get out of those clothes, have a hot bath and come downstairs to me. I must phone the police and Pauline's school.'

He went on up the stairs with Pauline, and Florina went to her own room, undressed slowly and sank thankfully into a steaming bath. The sight of herself in the wardrobe mirror had made her gasp in horror; her hair was full of twigs and leaves, her dress was ruined and her tights were streaked with blood from scratches. She gave a slightly hysterical giggle and then fell to weeping. But the bath was soothing, and then, once more in her cotton dress and apron, her hair brushed and plaited as usual, a dusting of powder on her scratched face, she went back to the kitchen.

Sir William was there, pouring tea. 'I don't know about you,' he remarked cheerfully, 'but when I've been scared I've found that a cup of tea works wonders at restoring my nerve.'

'You've never been scared…' She gasped at him in amazement.

'Just lately, I have, on occasion, been scared to death. Come and sit down and tell me just what happened. I've told the police, and Mrs Deakin kindly called at your father's house and told him all was well.'

'I'm sorry we've been such a nuisance.' She glanced at Bobby, lying with the cats, fast asleep. 'It wasn't anyone's fault, at least, it was the man who overtook us—he was going too fast, the Land Rover couldn't do anything about it. I shouldn't have got out of the car, only both men were shouting at each other and I had to find out if anyone was hurt and if we had a chance of getting by…'

'Pauline got out with you…?'

'Oh, no, of course not, but I'm sure she was afraid, and Bobby was beside himself; he'd gone in a flash and she left after him. I'm sure she thought that she would be able to catch him easily, but the poor beast was terrified.'

Sir William picked up one of her hands from the table; it was covered in scratches and he examined them, his head bent so that she couldn't see his face. 'My poor dear…' His hand tightened on hers and it was as though an electric current had flooded her whole person. She sought to pull her hand away, but he merely tightened his grip as he lifted his head and looked at her, half smiling, his eyes half hidden beneath their heavy lids. She stared back at him, her eyes wide. It was a magic moment for her, shattered almost before she had realised it by Nanny's entrance. Sir William let her hand go without haste and asked, 'Everything all right, Nanny?' in his calm voice.

Nanny had looked at them and away again. 'The child wants to sit up and she says she's hungry.'

He got up. 'I'll go and take a good look; I don't think there's much damage done, and there's no reason why she shouldn't have a light meal, but wait until I've looked at her.'

He went away and Nanny went to the Aga to see if the kettle was boiling.

'We could all do with something,' she observed briskly. 'Do you feel up to getting a meal ready, Florina?'

Florina gave her a sweet bemused look. 'Of course, Nanny. Soup and scrambled eggs with toast and mushrooms and coffee.'

She went to get the eggs, still in a dream, unwilling to give it up for reality. For his hand on hers and his look, tender and urgent, must have been a dream: a conclusion substantiated by his return presently with the prosaic suggestion that Pauline could have both the soup and the scrambled eggs, and wouldn't it be a good idea if she and Nanny had a meal as well? As for himself, he went on, he would go to the Trout and Feathers and have a drink with the landlord and some bread and cheese.

So she shook the dreams from her head and set about getting lunch. They had finished and tidied the kitchen and Nanny had gone to sit with Pauline when Sir William returned. He came straight into the kitchen and sat down on the table. 'I'll feel easier in my mind if I take Pauline back with me; she can be X-rayed at my hospital and if there is anything amiss it can be put right. I'm almost certain that there's nothing to worry about, but I must be sure. We'll leave after breakfast; you will come with us, Florina?'

Her heart gave a great leap, so that she caught her breath.

'Very well, Sir William. Are we to stay overnight?'

'Yes, pack for two or three days, to be on the safe side. I'm going to Pauline's school now. When does Mrs Deakin come?'

'Not until tomorrow morning.'

'Then will you go and see her and ask if she will sleep here with Nanny? If she can't, perhaps Mrs Datchett would oblige us. They'll be paid, of course.'

He went to the door; stopped there to turn and look at her. 'You're all right? I'll give you something for those scratches; you've had ATS injections?'

She nodded, striving to be matter of fact. 'Oh, yes, I had a booster done about six months ago. I'll go along to Mrs Deakin now. Does Pauline know that she is going back with you?'

'No. I'll tell her when I get back. I'll have dinner here with you and Nanny—shall we say eight o'clock? That gives Nanny a chance to settle Pauline first. I'll go up and see her now before I go out.'

He nodded casually and left her there.

Mrs Deakin would be delighted to oblige; she was saving up for a new washing machine and Sir William was a generous employer. Florina skimmed back quickly, not liking to leave Nanny alone, but Nanny was sitting in the rocking chair in Pauline's room, knitting while Pauline slept. Florina made a cup of tea and took it upstairs to her, whispered about plans for the evening and took herself off back to the kitchen. There was plenty to do; a good thing, for she had to forget about Sir William. She bustled about assembling a suitable meal for him: spinach soup, lamb chops, courgettes in red wine, calabrese and devilled potatoes, with an apricot tart and cream to follow. She would have time to make the little dry biscuits he liked with his cheese; she rolled up her sleeves and started her preparations.

She took up Pauline's supper tray and sat with her while Nanny had an hour to herself. The little girl was apparently none the worse for their adventure; she ate her supper without demur and now that she was safely home and in her bed was inclined to giggle a good deal about their adventure. She submitted to Florina's sponging of her face and hands, declared herself ready to go to sleep and, when her father came quietly in, did no more than murmur sleepily at him.

He felt her head, took her pulse and pronounced himself satisfied, kissed the child and picked up the supper tray and beckoned Florina to go with him.

'I've phoned the hospital,' he told her. 'We'll leave just before eight o'clock. She can travel as she is, wrapped up in a blanket. Pack her some clothes, though.'

He was matter-of-fact—more than that, casual—and she strove to match him. They ate their dinner carrying on a guarded conversation about nothing much, and Nanny, sitting between them, watched their faces and thought hopefully of the next day or two in London, praying that Wanda wouldn't be there, and that they would have time together; that was all they needed. Sir William, she was sure now, had realised that he was in love with Florina, and as for Florina, there was no doubt in Nanny's mind where her heart lay. Things would sort themselves out, she reflected comfortably.

The journey to London was uneventful. Pauline lay on the back seat with Florina beside her, and she was content to be quiet, and Florina had her own thoughts, her eyes on the back of Sir William's handsome head.

There were people waiting for them when they reached the hospital: porters with a stretcher, Sir William's registrar, one of his housemen and the children's ward sister, young, pretty and cheerful. She said a friendly 'Hi,' to Florina, standing a little apart, not sure what was expected of her, before she accompanied the stretcher into the hospital.

It was Sir William who paused long enough to say, 'My registrar, Jack Collins, and my houseman, Colin Weekes.' He caught her by the arm. 'You might as well come along, too.'

She sat when bidden, in the X-ray Department waiting-room, for what seemed a very long time. People came and went: nurses, porters, a variety of persons bustling along as though the very existence of the hospital depended upon them, and presently Sir William strolled in, looking, she had to admit, exactly like a senior consultant should look. He was trailed by a number of people, who stood back politely as he came to a halt beside her.

'No problems,' he told her. 'A few days taking things quietly and Pauline will be quite well. I'll drive you both home now, but I must come back here for the rest of the day. The Jollys will look after you. Get Pauline to bed, will you? Don't let her read or watch television, but she can sit up a little.' He nodded. 'Ready?'

Jolly was waiting for them. Sir William carried his small daughter up the stairs to her room with Mrs Jolly and Florina hard on his heels, while Jolly fetched their bags. In no time at all, Pauline had been settled in her bed, her few clothes unpacked, and Sir William, with a murmured word to Jolly, had departed again.

Florina found herself in the same room that she had had previously, bidden by Mrs Jolly to make haste and tidy herself, and, since Pauline was a little peevish and excited, would it be a good idea if she had her lunch in the child's room? There was a small table there and perhaps Pauline would settle down and have a nice nap if someone was with her.

Which presently, was exactly what happened. Florina sat quietly where she was for a time, thinking about Sir William. She had been foolish to fall in love with him, although she could quite see that one couldn't always pick and choose whom one loved, but their worlds were so far apart, her visit to the hospital had emphasised that…

She picked up her tray, carried it downstairs and stayed for a few minutes in the kitchen talking to Mrs Jolly. 'You'll need a breath of air,' declared that lady. 'I'll bring you both up a nice tea presently and sit with Pauline while you have a quick walk. Sir William won't be home before six o'clock.'

'That's kind of you, Mrs Jolly; perhaps I'll do that. Pauline mustn't read or watch television. I thought I'd read aloud to her before her supper.'

She went back through the baize door into the hall just as Jolly went to answer the front door. It was Wanda, who pushed past him and then stopped dead in her tracks as she caught sight of Florina.

'What are you doing here?' she demanded. Her blue eyes narrowed. 'Up to your tricks again, are you? What a sly creature you are—the moment my back is turned.'

She had crossed the hall and was standing at the foot of the stairs so that Florina couldn't get past her without pushing.

Florina, conscious that Jolly was hovering by the baize door, kept her temper. 'Pauline had an accident; Sir William has brought her here so that she could go to the hospital for an X-ray—somebody had to come with her. She is upstairs asleep.'

Wanda didn't answer, and Florina said politely, 'I'm going upstairs to sit with her—if you wouldn't mind moving...'

Wanda didn't budge. She turned her head and said very rudely: 'You can go back to the kitchen, Jolly.' But he didn't move, only glanced at Florina. She smiled and nodded to reassure him, and he went reluctantly away.

'How long are you staying here?' demanded Wanda.

'Until Pauline is well enough to go back to Wheel House. Sir William will decide...'

'Oh, Sir William, Sir William!' gibed Wanda. 'He's the top and bottom of your existence, isn't he? You're such a fool too, just because he treats you decently and appears to take an interest in you—don't you know that that is part of his work? Being kind and sympathetic—turning on the charm for hysterical mothers, listening to their silly whining about their kids.'

Florina interrupted her then. 'That is not true and it's a wicked thing to say! Sir William is kind and good and he loves his work. You can say what you like about me, but you are not going to say a word against him.'

Wanda burst out laughing. 'Oh, lord, you're so funny—if only you could see that plain face of yours.' She said suddenly, seriously, 'Do you know that we are to be married next week? Your precious Sir William didn't tell you that, did he? But why should he? You are only his cook, and not for much longer, either.'

She turned away and sauntered towards the drawing-room. 'You'd better get back upstairs and keep an eye on that child before she does something stupid.'

Florina went up the stairs without a word, shaking with rage and misery and, under those feelings, prey to first doubts. Wanda had sounded so sure of herself, and indeed, there was no reason at all why Sir William should tell her his plans. She went into Pauline's room and sat down to think, thankful that Pauline was dozing. Her head remained obstinately empty of thoughts; it was a relief when the little girl wakened and demanded to be read to. So Florina read *The Wind in the Willows*, until Pauline declared that she would like her tea.

'I'll pop down and get us a tray, love,' promised Florina. The house was quiet when she went downstairs. There was still some time before Sir William would return, perhaps she would be able to think a few sensible thoughts by then.

She was in the hall when the drawing-room door opened and Wanda came out.

'Had time to think?' she wanted to know. 'Not that it will make any difference; only a fool like you would be so stupid…'

The street door opened and Sir William asked quietly, 'Who is stupid?'

Florina had a cowardly impulse to turn and run back upstairs but quelled it; even Wanda had been taken by surprise. 'Wanda, I didn't expect to find you here…'

She shrugged that aside. 'I'll tell you who's stupid,' she said spitefully. 'Your cook.' She laughed. 'She's in love with you, William.'

He didn't look at Florina. 'Yes, I know.' He spoke

gently. 'You haven't told me why you are here. Shall we go into my study while you tell me?'

He still hadn't looked at Florina, standing like a small statue, her face as stony as her person.

It was only when the door had been closed gently behind them that she moved. She went to the kitchen and fetched the tea tray, oblivious of the Jollys' concerned faces, and only when Mrs Jolly offered to sit with Pauline so that she might have an hour or two to herself did she say in a wispy voice, 'I'd rather stay with her, thank you so much, Mrs Jolly.'

She carried the tray back upstairs, saw to Pauline's wants and poured herself a cup of tea. Mrs Jolly had gone to a lot of trouble with their tea; little scones, feather-light, mouth-watering sandwiches, small iced cakes—Florina, pleading a headache in answer to Pauline's anxious enquiries as to why she didn't eat anything, plunged into talk. There was plenty to say about Bobby and the cats, and school, and whether would Nanny remember to feed the swans. Once tea was over Florina got out *The Wind in the Willows* again and began to read in her quiet voice.

She was interrupted by Sir William, who sauntered in, embraced his daughter and said in a perfectly normal voice, 'I'll sit with Pauline for a while, Florina. I dare say you would like a breath of air. I have to go out this evening, but I shall be back after dinner—I should like to talk to you then.'

She kept her eyes on his waistcoat. Her 'Very well, Sir William,' was uttered in what she hoped was a voice which showed no trace of a wobble.

She went out because she could think of nothing else to do. A nice quiet cry in her bedroom would have eased

her, but if she cried her nose remained regrettably pink
for hours afterwards and so did her eyelids.

She marched briskly, unheeding of her surroundings for half an hour, and then she turned round and
marched back again. The exercise had brought some
colour into her white face, but her insides were in tur-
moil. She would have given a great deal not to have to
see Sir William later that evening; she could, of course,
retire to bed with a migraine, only if she did he would
undoubtedly feel it his duty to prescribe for her. 'Don't
be a coward,' she muttered as she rang the doorbell to
be admitted by a silently sympathetic Jolly. 'Sir William has just gone out, Miss Florina; he hopes to be
back by nine o'clock. Dinner will be at half-past seven
in the small sitting-room. Mrs Jolly would like to know
if she can help in any way with Pauline.'

'We've given her a great deal of extra work as it
is. I'll go up to her and settle her down before dinner.
Wouldn't it be less trouble if I were to join you and
Mrs Jolly?'

'Sir William's orders, Miss Florina—I dare say he
thinks that after the exciting time that you've had you
could do with some peace and quiet.'

Pauline was tired at any rate; she ate her supper,
submitted to being washed and having a fresh nightie,
and declared sleepily that she was quite ready to go to
sleep. Florina kissed her goodnight, left a small table
lamp burning and went away to tidy herself. She had
no appetite, indeed she was feeling slightly sick at the
thought of the coming interview, but she would have
to wear a brave face…

She managed to swallow at least some of the delicious food Jolly put before her, and, since there was
still some time before Sir William would return, she

sat over her coffee, still at the table, so lost in a hotch-potch of muddled thoughts that she didn't hear Sir William's return.

When she looked up he was standing in the open doorway, watching her. She was so startled that her cup clattered into the saucer and she got clumsily to her feet, her head suddenly clear. She loved him; it didn't matter that he knew, for what difference would that make? She had felt a burning shame in the hall listening to Wanda's spite tearing her secret to shreds, but now she merely felt cold and detached, as though she was watching herself, a self who wasn't her at all.

Sir William's eyes hadn't left her face. He said, 'If you've finished your coffee, will you come to the study?'

She walked past him without a word, for really she had nothing to say. He opened the door and she went past him and sat, very straight-backed and composed in the chair he offered her.

Chapter 9

Sir William sat down in his chair behind the desk and rather disconcertingly remained silent. He sat back, un-smiling, apparently deep in thought, which gave Florina time to admire his stylish appearance. He was wearing a dinner-jacket, beautifully tailored, and a plain dress-shirt of dazzling whiteness. Dinner with Wanda, thought Florina; somewhere wildly fashionable where all the best people went. Wanda would have been tricked out in the forefront of fashion—taffeta was in fashion, preferably in a vivid colour like petunia. She frowned—definitely not a colour for Wanda—ice blue, perhaps, or black…

She became aware that Sir William had said something and she murmured, 'I'm sorry… I was thinking.'

Because he had nothing to say to that she gushed on, in terror of a silence between them. 'Wanda—Miss

Fortesque, you know—she looks her best in black or that very pale blue…'

Behind the gravity of his face she suspected that he was laughing, but all he said was, 'Just for the moment, shall we leave her out of it?' He leaned forward and put his elbows on the desk.

'I think that you should go away for a time, Florina. You have had a tiresome few weeks.' His eyes searched her face and he went on deliberately, 'That is something which we don't need to discuss. I have a colleague at the hospital, a Dutchman over here for a seminar. He will be returning home in a couple of days' time and it so happens that the English girl who helps to look after his children is anxious to go off on holiday. It might suit you very well to take over from her for a few weeks?'

'You don't want me to be your cook?' said Florina baldly.

He smiled faintly. 'That is a difficult question to answer at the moment. The situation is such that I believe the best thing for you is to accept Doctor van Thurssen's offer.'

Florina was feeling reckless; it didn't matter any more what she said, in a day or two she would be gone and probably he hoped that once back in Holland she would find work and stay there.

'You would like me out of the way?' She spoke with deliberate flippancy.

'Exactly, Florina.' He sat back in his chair, staring at her. 'You have no objection to going?'

'I think it is a marvellous idea.' She met his eyes, her own wide, holding back tears.

'I'll get Jolly to drive you back to Wheel House tomorrow so that you can pack your things; he will fetch you back in two days time so that you can travel with

Doctor van Thurssen. Can you be ready to drive to the hospital with me in the morning—just before eight o'clock—so that you can meet him?'

'Certainly, Sir William. Would you be kind enough to write me a reference?'

He looked surprised, so she added woodenly, 'So that I can get another job.' She got up. 'If there is nothing else to discuss I should like to go to bed, Sir William.'

He got up at once and opened the door, bidding her goodnight in a calm fashion, they might have been discussing the menu for a dinner party. She went up to her room and sat down on the bed, a prey to a thousand and one thoughts, none of them at all pleasant. She had been so intent on preserving a cool front that she had forgotten to ask exactly what she would be expected to do— and was she to be paid or was this doctor merely doing Sir William a good turn? And for how long? Until this other girl came back? And then what? She could always go and stay with Tante Minna, but if she did that she would have to see Felix. Supposing she had refused Sir William's offer, would he have given her notice? There was Pauline to consider too; she was so fond of the child and she thought that Pauline was fond of her. Sir William was behaving strangely; not at all what she would have expected of him. Suddenly the realisation that she wasn't going to see him again once she had left the house was too much for her; there was no point in keeping a stiff upper lip with no one to see it; so she buried her face in the pillows and had a good cry.

She was up early after a night which had been far too long and wakeful, but Sir William was up even earlier, going soft-footed to his small daughter's room. She was awake; he drew the curtains back and sat down on the bed.

'Can you keep a secret?' He wanted to know and when she nodded, he continued, 'Florina is going away, and when I've explained why I think you'll be very pleased...'

It didn't take long and when he had finished, 'Not so much as a breath or a hint,' he warned her and submitted to her delighted hug before taking himself off down to his study, where he spent ten minutes or so on the telephone to Nanny. It was breakfast time by then; he was sitting at the table when Florina joined him, to carry on a polite conversation while she pushed food around her plate. He made no mention of their talk of the previous evening, for which she was thankful; she couldn't have borne that.

'I'll drop you off at the main entrance,' he told her as he drove to the hospital, and she nodded silently. In a few minutes now she would bid him goodbye; she had been to Pauline's room before they had left the house but she had said nothing about leaving. She would have to do that presently, after she had seen Doctor van Thurssen, and since she was to leave with Jolly by ten o'clock it would have to be a hurried explanation. Just as well, perhaps.

Sir William drew up at the main doors and got out. 'There's no need... I can find my way...' She was gabbling while she tried to think of something cool and dignified to say by way of goodbye.

Sir William took no notice, he took her arm and ushered her into the entrance hall and over to the porter's lodge. Here he relinquished his grasp. 'Benson will take you to Doctor van Thurssen.' He nodded to the elderly porter, who came out of his lodge to join them. At least it would make her goodbye more easily said. She put out a hand and had it engulfed in Sir William's firm grasp.

Conscious of Benson's sharp eyes, she said gruffly, 'Goodbye, Sir William. Thank you for arranging everything.' It was a great effort to add, 'I hope you will be very happy.'

She even managed a smile, rather shaky at the corners.

'I'm quite certain that I shall be, Florina.'

He looked at Benson, who said at once, 'This way, miss,' and marched away towards a long passage at the back of the hall, so that she was forced to follow him. It took her every ounce of will-power not to turn round for a last glimpse of Sir William. He hadn't said goodbye, she reflected on a spurt of anger; loving him had been a great waste of time and what a good thing that she was going away—right away, where there would be nothing to remind her of him and perhaps in time she would be able to forget what a fool she had made of herself over him. She went pink with shame just thinking about it, so that when Benson opened a door and ushered her into a large gloomy room he paused to say, 'You're out of breath, miss—I hurried too much, quite red in the face you are.'

Doctor van Thurssen was looking out of one of the windows, although there was nothing to see, only the bare brick walls of a wing of the hospital. He turned round as she went in, a man in his late thirties with sandy hair and a pleasant, rugged face. He was tall and stoutly built and his eyes were a clear light blue. He would be from the north, she guessed, and remembered that she still knew no details of this job which had been thrust upon her.

He shook her briskly by the hand and spoke in Dutch. 'This is very good of you, Miss Payne. I hope you don't feel that you've been rushed into this; my wife really needs someone to help out with the children until our Nanny comes back.'

'I'll be glad to help, but I don't know very much. Where do you live?'

'Do you know Friesland? I have a practice in Hindeloopen, I'm also consultant at the children's hospital in Leeuwarden. We have six children; the youngest is almost two years old, the eldest fourteen. Ellie, who looks after them, will be away for two weeks. I shall be driving back tomorrow, taking the car ferry from Harwich, if you could manage to be ready by then? You will, of course be given your air ticket to return, as to salary...' He mentioned a generous sum and looked at her hopefully.

She liked him; six children seemed a lot, but the older ones wouldn't need much done for them, and presumably there was other help in the house. She agreed at once, glad to have something solid to hold on to in a nebulous future.

She took a taxi back, for time was running out. Back at the house she hurried to Pauline's room, rehearsing suitable things to say, but there was no need; Pauline said cheerfully, 'Daddy told me you were to have a holiday and you are going to Holland. Will you bring me back some of those little almond biscuits—your aunt gave me some?' She flung her arms tightly round Florina's neck. 'I shall miss you but Daddy says you must have some time to yourself because you've had too much on your mind. Were you very lost when Bobby ran away? Daddy said you couldn't see the wood for the trees—it was a nasty wood, wasn't it? All those brambles...'

'Yes, darling. You'll look after Nanny and the ani-

mals, won't you?' Florina got up off the bed and bent
to kiss Pauline. 'Jolly is waiting for me, I must go…'

'Did you say goodbye to Daddy?'

It was difficult to speak. 'Yes.' She managed to smile
as she went.

Jolly hadn't much to say during the drive to Wheel
House, and the fact that she was leaving wasn't mentioned. He was a loyal old servant and she would have
been surprised if he had referred to it. But he was kind
and helpful and she believed him when he said that both
he and Mrs Jolly would miss her, but that wasn't until
the next morning, after she had packed her things, arranged for most of them to be sent to her father's house,
and bidden Nanny goodbye. Nanny had had very little
to say and Florina had been rather hurt over her lack
of concern for her future. She had been kind and had
fussed around Florina, and she and Jolly did everything
to help her, but they hadn't expressed any interest in
her future. She thought sadly that even Pauline hadn't
minded overmuch. She had got up early and stripped her
bed and left the room tidy, reflecting that she wouldn't
be missed and would certainly be quickly forgotten in
the bustle of the forthcoming wedding.

Her father, when she had walked through the village
to see him, had said in a satisfied voice, 'I told you so,
didn't I? But you knew best, and look where it's landed
you. You'd better find yourself work in Holland, for I
can't afford to keep you.'

They were to drive to the hospital where she was to
meet Doctor van Thurssen, and as Jolly helped her out
of the car and carried her case into the entrance hall
she looked around, longing to see Sir William just once
more, but no one was there. She said goodbye to Jolly
and sat down to wait.

Doctor van Thurssen came presently and they went out to his car. It was parked in the consultants' car park and the Bentley was beside it; there was no one in it, of course. If she had turned her head and looked up at the windows of the children's ward she would have seen Sir William standing at one of them, watching her. It was only when Doctor van Thurssen had driven away that he turned back to resume his round of his little patients.

If Florina had been happier, she would have enjoyed the journey to Hindeloopen. They had caught the mid-day ferry, arriving at the Hoek in the evening, and then driving north, to arrive some four hours later at his home. It was dark by then and she was hungry, for they had stopped only long enough to eat a sandwich and drink coffee, and the sight of the brightly lit house on the edge of the little town was very welcome. A welcome echoed by Mevrouw van Thurssen, who greeted her warmly, took her to her room, bade her take off her outdoor things and return downstairs for her supper.

The room was pleasant, nicely furnished and large and the bed looked inviting. She was very tired, but she was hungry too. She went back downstairs and was ushered into a lofty dining-room, furnished with a massive square table and solid chairs, given a glass of sherry and told kindly to sit herself down at the table. Supper was all that a hungry girl could have wished for, and while they ate Mevrouw van Thurssen outlined her duties.

'Of course, the older children go to school, but Lisa, the youngest, is at home. Saska—she's five— goes to *Kleuterschool* in the mornings, and Jan and Welmer go to the *Opleidingschool* here—they are seven and ten— and then Olda and Sebo both go to Bolsward each day. Either the doctor or I drive them there and back—' she hesitated. 'I don't suppose you drive? Of course, Ellie has a licence, so she was able to take them sometimes…'

'Yes, I've an international licence and I brought it with me. I drove quite a bit when I came to Holland with my mother, although that is some years ago.'

They beamed at her. 'How fortunate we are in having you, Florina—may I call you that? Now, I am sure that you are tired. In the morning you shall meet the children, and perhaps if you come with me to Bolsward you can see where the schools are? Lutsje can take Saska to school and look after Lisa while we are away. Perhaps we could do as Ellie and I do? One of us goes to Bolsward and the other takes Saska to her school and takes Lisa at the same time in the pushchair.'

In bed, Florina closed her eyes resolutely. She had plenty to think about until she went to sleep, and in the morning she would feel quite different; she had turned a page in her life and she wasn't going to look back at it. After all, she was quite at home in Holland; Friesland was a little different perhaps, but she had slipped back into Dutch again without any effort, it should be easy enough to get a job and it didn't matter where… Here her good resolutions were forgotten; she went back over her day and wished herself back in England, at Wheel House, cooking something delicious for Sir William who would come into the kitchen and say hello in his calm fashion. She wondered if he had missed her—just as a cook, of course—but probably by now Wanda had already engaged a French chef…

He had seemed almost relieved to see her go. 'Oh, William,' she mumbled into the pillow. She cried a little then, until at last she slept.

There was little time to think in the morning; the entire family breakfasted together before Doctor van

Thurssen went to his surgery, and then, with Lisa left in the care of Lutsje, who would take Saska to school, Florina got into the family estate car with the two elder children and was driven to Bolsward. Olda and Sebo were at different schools; their mother dropped them off and turned for home. 'If you take them tomorrow,' she suggested, 'I could to go to Sneek in the morning. And perhaps you would fetch Saska at midday?'

After that the day flew past. The household was well run; Mevrouw van Thurssen had plenty of help, but there was always something or someone in need of attention, and the day had a certain routine which had to be kept. The family was a happy one and close-knit, and she was kept busy until she had helped put Lisa and Saska to bed. After supper, she helped Welmer with his English lessons. When the children were in bed, she sat for a while with the doctor and his wife, drinking a last cup of coffee before going to her own bed. She was tired by then, too tired to think clearly about her own affairs. In a day or two, she promised herself, she would decide what she was going to do. She slept on the thought.

A week went by and she was no nearer a decision; by now she had become involved in the life of the Thurssen family; the children liked her; she worked hard, cooked when there was no one else to do it, sewed, bathed the smaller children, ferried the older ones to and from school and helped out with their homework in the evenings. But it wasn't all work; at the weekend they had all crammed into the estate car and spent the day on board the doctor's yacht which he kept moored at Sneek—the weather had been fine, if a little chilly, and Florina had enjoyed every minute of it.

On the way back, Olda, sitting beside her, said, 'We like our Ellie, but I wish you could stay with us too.'

It brought Florina up with a jolt. Ellie was due back in a week and she had done nothing about her future. It was a question of whether she should stay in Holland, get a work permit and find a job, or go back to England. She had a little money saved, enough to live on for a week or two while she found work. London, she supposed, where there were hotels and big private houses where cooks were employed; it seemed sensible to go there. At the very back of her mind was the thought that if she went there to work, she might, just might, see Sir William; not to speak to, of course. She was aware that this was a terribly stupid wish on her part; the quicker she forgot him the better. If she went to see her father she would have to take care to do so during the week when Sir William wouldn't be at Wheel House.

It was all very well to make good resolutions, but she was never free from his image beneath her eyelids and, however busy she was, he popped up in the back of her head, ready to fill her thoughts. All day and every day she was wondering what he was doing, and that evening, pleading tiredness after their outing, she went to bed as soon as the last of the children had settled down for the night. But she didn't sleep, she lay picturing him at Wheel House, sitting in his lovely drawing-room with the mill stream murmuring and Wanda with him, looking gorgeous and dressed to kill.

She was quite wrong; he was indeed in his drawing-room and Wanda was with him, not sitting but storming up and down the room, stuttering with bad temper. He had, for his own purposes, taken her for a walk that afternoon; a long walk along bridle paths and over fields of rough grass, circumventing ploughed fields and climbing any number of gates. All the while he had talked cheerfully about the pleasures of the country. 'We'll come every weekend,' he assured her, 'and spend any free days that I have here. I must get you a bike, it's marvellous exercise. You'll feel years younger.'

Wanda, her tights laddered, stung by nettles and unsuitably shod in high heels, almost spat at him; she would have argued with him but she had needed all her breath to keep up with his easy stride.

'Just wait until we get back,' she told him furiously. And she had had to wait until they had dined—rather sketchily because Nanny and Mrs Deakin were good plain cooks with small repertoires. Wanda had suggested getting a cordon bleu cook, but Sir William had said easily that there was no hurry, and when she had pointed out that there was no reason why they shouldn't marry within the next week or so, he hadn't been in a hurry about that either; he had a backlog of theatre cases and an overflowing outpatients' clinic. An unsettling remark, since she had spread it around that they were marrying shortly.

Wanda glared at his broad back now and wondered if it was worth it—he was successful and rich and handsome, everything a girl such as herself expected of a husband; he was also proving tiresomely stubborn. She allowed herself to reflect upon the American millionaire William had introduced her to only that very week. Now, there was a man eminently suitable; possessed of oil wells that never required his presence, able to live wherever fancy took him; a real lover of bright lights. He had sent her flowers and she had half promised to see him again; after all, William was so seldom free and, if he was, he liked to have a quiet evening at home.

In the drawing-room, drinking Mrs Deakin's instant

coffee, she allowed bad temper to get the better of her good sense. 'This is the worst weekend I've ever had to spend,' she raged. 'This coffee is unspeakable and I'll tell you now, William, I will not live here, not even for weekends. You can sell the place, I hate it.'

Sir William swallowed some more coffee and thought of Florina. 'No, I don't wish to see it sold, Wanda. In fact I'm thinking of taking on less work and spending more time here.'

She came to a halt in front of him. 'You mean that? You really mean it?'

'Oh, yes, I would like to enjoy my wife and children, and I would need to have more time for that.'

'But you're at the top of your profession—you're well known, you know everyone who matters.'

'I begin to think that the people who matter to you aren't those who matter to me, Wanda.'

She stamped her foot. 'I want some fun, I want to go out dancing and have parties and buy pretty clothes.'

He said thoughtfully, 'When we first met, you told me that you wanted to have a home of your own—you even mentioned children...'

'Well, I found you attractive and I wanted to impress you, I suppose. I must say, William, you have changed. If I marry you, will you send Pauline to boarding-school and get rid of that awful old Nanny and give up this dump? We could have such fun in London; you would have much more time to go out if you didn't have to come racing down here all the time.'

He looked at her from under half closed lids and said mildly, 'No, Wanda, I won't do any of those things.'

'Then don't expect me to!' she shouted at him, as she tugged the diamond ring off her finger and threw it at him. 'I'm going to bed and you can drive me back in the morning. I never want to see you again! All these months wasted…'

She flung out of the room and Sir William went to the side table poured himself a whisky and sat down again. He was smiling to himself—quite a wicked smile. Presently he went into his study and picked up the telephone.

It was Florina's last day; Ellie would be back in the morning. She had packed her case, telephoned a surprised Tante Minna, done the daily chores she had come to enjoy so much and now she was sitting on the side of Lisa's cot reading her a bedtime story. It was when the child gave a sudden chortle that she paused to look up from the book. Doctor van Thurssen had walked into the night nursery and with him was Sir William.

Florina's voice faltered and died. She made no answer to the doctor's 'Good evening' as he picked his small daughter up from her cot and sat her on his lap. She had no breath for that. She could only stare at Sir William and gulp her heart back where it belonged.

'Is it not convenient?' observed Doctor van Thurssen cheerfully. 'Here is Sir William come to fetch you home.'

She was on her feet, wild ideas of escape mixed with delight at seeing him again. She must be firm, she told herself, and cool and matter-of-fact. She said, in a voice she strove to keep just that, 'I have arranged to go to my aunt.'

Sir William crossed the room towards her and she retreated a few steps, which she realised, too late, was silly; the door was further away than ever. Moreover, there was only the wall behind her and he had fetched up so close to her that she had only to stretch out her hands to touch him. She clasped them prudently and kept her eyes on his waistcoat.

He said in his placid voice, but this time edged with steel, 'I shall take you home, Florina, where you belong.' And Doctor van Thurssen, who had been tucking his small daughter back into her cot, capped this with a brisk, 'Most satisfactory—it could not be better for you, Florina.' And while she was still trying to frame a watertight argument against it, he swept them both downstairs.

Somehow, for the rest of the evening, Florina was thwarted from her purpose to be alone with Sir William; she had to tell him that nothing on earth would make her go back to Wheel House with him, but there was no chance, even when, in desperation, as she and Mevrouw van Thurssen were on their way to bed, she tried to interrupt the men's learned discussion about the treatment of childish illnesses; they barely paused to listen to her request for five minutes of Sir William's time. He simply smiled kindly at her and pointed out that they would have plenty of time to talk as they drove back the next day. She had bidden them a stony goodnight and gone upstairs with Mevrouw van Thurssen, fuming silently.

Everyone was at breakfast and everyone talked; there was not the slightest chance of being heard above the cheerful din. She glowered at Sir William, who apparently didn't notice, although his eyes gleamed with amusement behind their lids. It wasn't until goodbyes had been said and she was sitting beside him in the Bentley that she had her chance at last. She had rehearsed what she was going to say for a good deal of the night. Clear, pithy remarks which would leave him no doubt as to her intention to remain in Holland. Unfortunately not one single word came to mind. She blurted out instead, 'I wish to go to Tante Minna...'

'A bit out of our way, but I think we could squeeze in an hour or so—I'd like to get home latish this evening.'

'I'm not going back with you, Sir William,' her voice was waspish and she was horrified to know that she was near to tears.

'For what reason?' He sounded mildly curious.

'You know perfectly well what the reason is.' She felt quite reckless, what did it matter what she said now? He already knew that she loved him. She pursued her train of thought out loud. 'Wanda told you...'

'Why yes, she did, but she told me something I already knew, Florina.'

Florina sniffed. 'Well, then, why do you persist... She won't have me in the house.' She stamped a foot in temper and he laughed softly.

'And you can stop laughing, you know quite well I wanted to get you alone yesterday...'

'Oh, yes, it needed a lot of will-power on my part to prevent it, too.'

'What do you mean?' He skimmed past a huge articulated lorry. 'You are driving very fast.'

'The better to get home, my dear.'

'I'm not your dear.' Really, the conversation was getting her nowhere. 'Sir William, please understand this, I will not come back to Wheel House—Wanda...'

'Let us leave Wanda out of it, shall we? She is not at Wheel House and I think it enormously unlikely that we shall ever meet again—she is enamoured of a wealthy American and they are probably already married!'

Florina digested this in silence. 'You sent me away—' she began.

'My darling girl, consider—it was obvious to everyone—the likelihood of my not marrying Wanda once I had met you became a foregone conclusion. To everyone but you—if I had not sent you away you would probably have spent your time in earnest endeavours to get us to the altar.'

'You mean Wanda doesn't want to marry you? She jilted you?'

'Yes, with a little help from circumstances.'

She cast a quick look at him; he looked smug. 'What did you do?'

'Oh, nothing really—a long country walk, rather a muddy one, I'm afraid—and the nettles at this time of year. Nanny and Mrs Deakin cooked dinner, and I refused to sell Wheel House and live for ever and ever in London.'

They drove for some miles in silence while Florina sorted out her thoughts. There was no reason why she shouldn't go back to Wheel House now. Just once or twice she had felt a rush of pure excitement wondering what he would say next, only he hadn't said anything, and by that she meant he hadn't said that he loved her. But for what other reason would he take all the trouble to fetch her back? Because she was a good cook?

She frowned, staring ahead of her as the car tore along the motorway. Perhaps it would be wiser if she were to stay in Holland. Perhaps he thought that she was suffering from an infatuation which would pass once she was back in her kitchen. She became aware that he was slowing the car into the slow lane and she looked at him.

'If I tell you that I love you—am in love with you, and have been since the moment I saw you, my darling, will you be content to leave it at that until we are home? I can't kiss you adequately in the fast lane, and nothing else will do!' He smiled at her with a tenderness which made her gulp. All she could do was nod, and he reached out and caught her hand for a moment. 'We will marry as soon as it can be arranged. Now sit quiet and think about the wedding cake while I drive.'

She said, 'Yes, William,' in a meek voice, and then, 'I'm sure Tante Minna would understand if we don't go to see her.' Then, because her heart was bursting with happiness, 'I do love you very much, William.'

He was steering back into the fast lane, but he put out a hand and caught one of hers and kissed it.

She was caught up in a lovely dream. They stopped for coffee and a quick lunch and Sir William maintained a gentle flow of talk, although afterwards she was unable to remember a word which had been spoken. When at last he drew up before the door of Wheel House and she saw the lighted windows, she heaved a great sigh of joy. It wasn't a dream, it was all true; she turned a face alight with love and happiness to him as he opened the car door for her. There was such a lot that she wanted to say but all she managed was 'Oh, William!'

He bent and kissed her and then glanced at the house. 'They will be waiting for us,' he observed, 'but first...' He kissed her again, this time at length and lingeringly. 'You'll marry me, my dearest? I can't imagine being without you—you'll have no peace, for I'll want you with me all the time—we'll live in London during the week and come here each weekend...'

'Pauline?'

'I've talked to her; she likes the idea of being a weekly boarder and she can't wait to be your stepdaughter. Nanny will stay here.' He kissed her once more. 'You know, I thought just for a while that you had fallen for Felix. I could have killed him with my bare hands...'

She reached up to kiss him in her turn. 'I dislike him intensely,' she assured him vigorously, 'and always did—only it was rather difficult to talk about.' She smiled up at him and his arms tightened around her.

'You're the one I've been waiting for,' he said softly, 'all my life—and now I don't need to wait any longer.' He put up a gentle finger and stroked her face. 'Such a beautiful girl...'

She had thought that she would never be happier, but she saw that she had been mistaken; she was bursting with happiness. William had called her beautiful and, what was more, he meant it.

He opened the door and they went into the house together.

* * * * *

*When Jed Dalloway started over, ranching a
mountain plot for his recluse boss is what saved him.
So when hometown girl April Reed offers a deal
to develop the land, Jed tells her no sale.
But his heart doesn't get the message...*

*Read on for a sneak preview of
the next book in* New York Times *bestselling author
Allison Leigh's Return to the Double C miniseries,*
A Promise to Keep.

"Don't look at me like that, April."

She raised her gaze to his. "Like what?"

His fingers tightened in her hair and her mouth ran dry.
She swallowed. Moistened her lips.

She wasn't sure if she moved first. Or if it was him.

But then his mouth was on hers and like everything
else about him, she felt engulfed by an inferno. Or maybe
the burning was coming from inside her.

There was no way to know.

No reason to care.

Her hands slid up the granite chest, behind his neck,
where his skin felt even hotter beneath her fingertips, and
slipped through his thick hair, which was not hot, but
instead felt cool and unexpectedly silky.

His arm around her tightened, his hand pressing her
closer while his kiss deepened. Consuming. Exhilarating.

Her head was whirling, sounds roaring.

It was only a kiss.

But she was melting.

She was flying.

And then she realized the sounds weren't just inside her head.

Someone was laying on a horn.

She jerked back, her gaze skittering over Jed's as they both turned to peer through the curtain of white light shining over them.

"Mind getting at least one of these vehicles out of the way?" The shout was male and obviously amused.

"Oh for cryin'—" She exhaled. "That's my uncle Matthew," she told Jed, pushing him away. "And I'm sorry to say, but we are probably never going to live this down."

Don't miss
A Promise to Keep *by Allison Leigh,*
available March 2020 wherever
Harlequin Special Edition books and ebooks are sold.

Harlequin.com

HSEEXP0220

HARLEQUIN

*Heartfelt or suspenseful,
inspiring or passionate, Harlequin
has your happily-ever-after.*

With new books published
every month, you are sure to find the
satisfying escape you know you deserve.

SIGN UP FOR THE HARLEQUIN NEWSLETTER

Be the first to hear about great new
reads and exciting offers!

Harlequin.com/newsletters

IF YOU ENJOYED THIS BOOK
WE THINK YOU WILL ALSO LOVE

LOVE INSPIRED
INSPIRATIONAL ROMANCE

Uplifting stories of faith, forgiveness and hope.

Fall in love with stories where faith helps
guide you through life's challenges, and discover
the promise of a new beginning.

6 NEW BOOKS AVAILABLE EVERY MONTH!